Laurie Kingery

and

USA TODAY Bestselling Author

Lyn Cote

Hill Country Christmas
&
Her Captain's Heart

HARLEQUIN® LOVE INSPIRED®CLASSICS

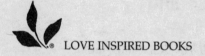 LOVE INSPIRED BOOKS

ISBN-13: 978-1-335-65277-5

Hill Country Christmas & Her Captain's Heart

Copyright © 2018 by Harlequin Books S.A.

The publisher acknowledges the copyright holders of the individual works as follows:

Hill Country Christmas
Copyright © 2008 by Laurie A. Kingery

Her Captain's Heart
Copyright © 2008 by Lyn Cote

Recycling programs for this product may not exist in your area.

www.Harlequin.com

Printed in U.S.A.

CONTENTS

Laurie Kingery is a Texas-transplant-to-Ohio who writes romance set in post–Civil War Texas. She was nominated for a Carol Award for her second Love Inspired Historical novel, *The Outlaw's Lady*, and is currently writing a series about mail-order grooms in a small town in the Texas Hill Country.

Books by Laurie Kingery

Love Inspired Historical

Hill Country Christmas
The Outlaw's Lady

Bridegroom Brothers

The Preacher's Bride Claim

Brides of Simpson Creek

Mail Order Cowboy
The Doctor Takes a Wife
The Sheriff's Sweetheart
The Rancher's Courtship
The Preacher's Bride
Hill Country Cattleman
A Hero in the Making
Hill Country Courtship
Lawman in Disguise

Visit the Author Profile page at Harlequin.com for more titles.

HILL COUNTRY CHRISTMAS

Laurie Kingery

Delight thyself also in the Lord; and
he shall give thee the desires of thine heart.
—*Psalms 37:4*

To the beautiful Hill Country of Texas,
the place my soul feels most at home this side
of Heaven, and to all my relatives in Texas,
especially Aunt Joann.

Chapter One

"He was a good man, Miss Delia. He's certainly in the arms of Jesus now."

"God rest his soul."

"God bless you in your time of sorrow, Miss Delia."

The hillside that had been covered in the golden glory of a Texas spring when Reverend McKinney had begun to fade—primroses and coreopsis, gaillardia and red-centered Indian blanket, punctuated here and there by bluebonnets lingering from the month before—was now, after the summer sun had done its work, sere and brown. It seemed a fitting backdrop for the unrelieved black garments of the figures in the valley who stood around the deep rectangular hole into which a coffin had just been lowered.

Sorrow didn't begin to name the endless depth of Delia's grief. Her grandpa had been the only element of stability she had experienced in her eighteen years of life, and now he was gone.

Another voice intruded on her thoughts. "I'm sorry for your loss, Miss Delia. If you need anything, you have but to let me or any of my family know. Reverend McKinney was a pillar of this community, and we would not want his granddaughter to be in need."

Under the black brim of her bonnet, Delia Keller raised her eyes to the speaker. "Thank you, Charles. I appreciate it." If she had hoped for more from the mayor's son, she made sure her face did not give her away. She didn't want Charles Ladley's pity, if that was all she could have from him.

The tight starched neckline of her borrowed bombazine mourning dress threatened to choke her.

Oh, Heavenly Father, what am I to do now?

A few of the ladies began to drift away from the gravestones toward the makeshift tables laden with covered baskets that were spread out under the live oak trees between the small church and the cemetery. Soon, Delia knew, they would have a hearty dinner spread out for those who had attended the funeral—ham and fried chicken, black-eyed peas, freshly baked biscuits, chocolate cake and pecan pralines. There would be pitchers of lemonade and cold tea. As the chief mourner, Delia would be expected to partake, sample and praise each lady's culinary offering.

The thought of putting so much as a crumb in her mouth made nausea roil in her stomach. The noon heat beat down on her head through her bonnet. She couldn't do it.

She'd thought everyone had left her side and she was alone at the grave site, but now Delia felt a gentle touch on her wrist. "Miss Keller, are you all right?"

It was Reverend Calhoun from Mason, who had kindly come to conduct the funeral, since Llano Crossing was now preacherless.

She looked away from the concern in his old eyes, afraid she would dissolve into tears but knowing it was safe to confide in him.

"What am I going to do, Reverend Calhoun? My whole life was taking care of my grandpa."

He gave her an understanding smile. "You needn't decide that today, my dear," he reminded her. "You've suffered a loss, a grievous loss, and it'll take a while to find your feet. But the Lord will show you a way."

Delia blinked, wiping away a tear that managed to escape from her eyes. She had no patience with platitudes this morning. "The town will be finding a new preacher, and he'll need to live in the parsonage—where am I to go? I have no money, no employment…" *No beau,* she added to herself. She wouldn't be going to live in the beautiful white house Charles Ladley would build someday for his bride, and the worst thing was, she didn't even know why not.

"The Lord will reveal all that to you, Miss Keller," the preacher assured her, confidence mingled with compassion in his deep, resonant voice, "in the fullness of time. He takes care of the birds in the air and the lilies of the field, you know. Now come—it looks as if the good ladies of Llano Crossing have prepared a nice meal for you." Nodding toward the tables under the trees, he said, "Why don't we—"

"I… I don't think I can stay for it," she said quickly, keeping her gaze on the toes of her high-button boots, but away from the grave. "I just… I just want to go back to the parsonage and lie down." *While I still can lie down there—and try to imagine what I'm going to do.*

"Nonsense, child, you need to put some food in your stomach, and take heart from the others who loved Reverend McKinney," urged his wife, a comfortable-looking gray-haired woman who had returned to her husband's side. "You'll feel better after you've eaten a bite, I'm sure."

Delia did not want to argue with her, and fortunately the visiting preacher made it unnecessary.

"Mrs. Calhoun, can't you see the girl is pale as a wilted primrose? I'm sure she knows what's best for her. There's bound to be plenty of food left, and we can bring her a plateful to tempt her appetite after she's had a nap. Miss Delia, we'll see you later," Reverend Calhoun said with finality. A look passed between husband and wife.

"All right, Mr. Calhoun, I'll walk with her," Mrs. Calhoun said, to Delia's dismay. "You go say the blessing so everyone can start eating. I'll be back in just a few minutes."

Placing an arm around Delia's waist, as if she feared the girl might swoon without it, Mrs. Calhoun started forward.

The parsonage sat some fifty yards down the road from the church. If she wasn't allowed to walk home by herself, Delia figured that at least, once there, she would insist she could find her way to her bedroom without any help. She would be alone in minutes.

They had nearly reached the gate that let out onto the dusty road when they spotted the horse and rider trotting toward them from the west, trailed by a swirl of dust.

"If he's coming for the funeral, he's a little late," Mrs. Calhoun said with a sniff.

"Oh, I don't imagine he is," Delia said. She thought everyone who had ever attended the Llano Crossing Church had been present for the funeral service. The church had been filled to bursting, with folks overflowing out onto the steps. "Probably just another cowboy coming into town to enjoy Saturday night."

Mrs. Calhoun pursed her mouth. "And tomorrow all he'll have is an aching head to show for his month's wages."

As the rider drew nearer, however, Delia began to doubt he'd come from any of the many nearby ranches. In back of the saddle were bulging saddlebags, a blanket roll and a rifle. The silver buckskin he rode was wet to his hocks, as if he'd just crossed the Llano at one of its deeper points upstream, rather than waiting to cross at the town that bore the name of the bridge that spanned the river.

He reined the horse to a walk a few yards away; then,

as he reached them, he halted the horse with a soft *whoa*. He laid a finger on the broad brim of his hat in an automatic gesture.

"Ladies, is Llano Crossing up ahead?"

His voice was gravelly and rough, as if it had been unused for a long while. His eyes, which were studying her with a frankness she had never been subjected to, were the glacial gray-blue color of a wolf's. She felt herself shiver as if the sudden chill breeze of a norther had blown upon her spine.

Out of the corner of her eye, Delia saw Mrs. Calhoun give a rigid nod. "Just around the bend in the road."

"And would a traveler find a hotel there where he could pass the night?" he asked, without taking those wolfish eyes off Delia.

She saw Mrs. Calhoun stiffen even more before she replied, "He would, if he were a law-abiding, respectable sort."

Delia saw the threat of a smile cross the stranger's face like slow heat lightning. He looked as if he would ask something more of Delia, then apparently thought better of it. "Much obliged, ma'am," he said, touching his hat brim yet again, his gaze drifting over to Mrs. Calhoun just long enough to be polite.

The corner of his mouth twitched as if it wanted to turn upward; then, as if noticing the somber hue of Delia's black dress, it resumed its previous thin line as he nodded and touched the buckskin with his boot heel. "Ladies," he murmured, and once he and the horse were a few yards from them, he nudged the horse into an easy lope.

Mrs. Calhoun sniffed again. "Well! He might have shown some respect."

Delia glanced at her, surprised at the indignation in the woman's voice. "He touched his hat."

"I mean to our mourning, my dear! Why, he was staring at you like a wolf set loose in a sheep pen!"

Since a wolf was the very creature she had been reminded of also, Delia blinked in surprise. Mrs. Calhoun was probably expecting too much of the man, though, if she thought that the stranger would give a long, involved condolence speech merely because the two of them were dressed in black.

"A saddle tramp, I shouldn't wonder," Mrs. Calhoun muttered disapprovingly. "There are so many of them drifting through ever since the war. Like tumbleweeds."

Delia was sure Mrs. Calhoun was right, but she didn't want to encourage the woman to linger, so she remained silent as they reached the low, crumbling rock wall that separated the parsonage yard from the road.

"Thank you for your kindness, Mrs. Calhoun. I'll be fine," Delia said as she stepped onto the flower-bordered pathway that led up to the white frame house. "I'll see you later."

The preacher's wife took the hint after giving Delia one last look of concern.

"All right, if you're certain you don't want someone to sit with you," Mrs. Calhoun said uncertainly, but then she started walking briskly back in the direction they had come, as if afraid the other mourners would devour everything on the tables before she got back to them. She paused only long enough to call back over her shoulder, "Pastor Calhoun and I will be quiet as mice when we return, in case you're still napping. Get some rest, dear."

Delia was sure she wouldn't so much as close her eyes, but at least she had freed herself from the suffocating, if well-meant, sympathy.

She was awakened sometime during the night by Reverend Calhoun's sonorous snoring coming from her grandpa's former room down the hall. Padding quietly to the kitchen at the back of the one-story frame house, she found that her visitors had been as good as their word and had left her a delicious supper of fried chicken, biscuits and pralines from the funeral dinner. She ate, and then waited for dawn, praying some answers about her future would arrive with the sun.

"I don't feel right about leaving so soon," Mrs. Calhoun fretted two days later, after they had breakfasted on eggs Delia had collected from her grandpa's—she still thought of them as her grandpa's—hens. "Why, this girl is a bereaved orphan! It isn't decent to leave her like this, Mr. Calhoun!"

"I'm not *actually* an orphan, Mrs. Calhoun," Delia informed her. "My father is traveling in the west. I'm sure he'll be home one of these days soon." She'd said these words so many times before. "If he'd known about Grandpa's illness, he'd have been home already, I'm sure," she added, hoping it sounded like she believed what she was saying.

Mrs. Calhoun, who'd been in the act of levering her bulk up from the chair, turned to her. "Now dear, I know that must be a comforting thought, but your neighbor, Mrs. Purvis, told me you and your grandpa had heard nothing from your father since he left! I'll pray he returns home, but don't you think he would have done so already if he was going to?" Her voice was so pityingly compassionate that Delia wanted to grind her teeth.

"Papa *will* be home someday," she said. "I know he will. After Mama died, he got itchy feet, as Grandpa called it."

"He could've gone to fight alongside our boys in gray," Mrs. Calhoun said, disapproval plain on her face.

Delia didn't bother to tell her that if her father had been inclined to be a soldier at all, he probably would've worn blue. Feelings about the War Between the States still ran high in these parts.

"He said he'd gotten married so young that he'd never had the chance to see the West. He promised he was going to be home just as soon as he struck it rich."

She hated the way her voice quavered as she remembered the hurt she had felt as she watched him ride off seven years ago. *Why was I not enough for you, Papa?*

Mrs. Calhoun tsk-tsked. "'For the love of money is the root of all evil,'" she quoted sententiously. She looked as if she was going to say something more.

"If I have not charity, love profiteth me nothing," the old preacher paraphrased, giving his wife a quelling look before turning to Delia. "I pray your faith will soon be rewarded, child."

Delia tried to assume a carefree expression. "I'll be fine, Mr. and Mrs. Calhoun. Really, I will. If I need anything, the Purvises said just to ask."

She wished the preacher and his wife had gone yesterday, but since yesterday was Sunday, Pastor Calhoun felt an obligation to conduct the regular worship service at the Llano Crossing Church. Who knew how long it would be before the town would have another preacher?

It had seemed so strange—*wrong*, even—for someone else to be standing in the pulpit in her grandpa's place, speaking about God. Reverend Calhoun wasn't a bad preacher, and he certainly knew his Bible, but he didn't have Delia's grandfather's dry humor. Nor did he place his pocket watch on the pulpit as Reverend McKinney had done so he'd know when it was time to close. It had taken several pointed looks from a deacon before Reverend Calhoun had ceased his flow of oratory and said the benediction.

Afterward, of course, Mrs. Calhoun hadn't felt right about traveling on the Sabbath, so Delia had been obliged to endure the woman's well-meant but stifling clucking over her and insistence that she knew best what Delia ought to be doing at every moment for the rest of that endless day.

"Mrs. Calhoun, if we leave now we'll be home before supper," Preacher Calhoun said now, laying his napkin aside and rising from the table. "Miss Delia has assured us she will write if she needs anything, or better yet, have someone ride with her up the road to Mason for a long visit, won't you, my dear?"

Delia assured them she would.

"Perhaps I should just help Delia with these dishes." Mrs. Calhoun fretted, waving a plump hand over the crumbs of toast and yellow flecks of egg that adorned the plates. "It's not Christian to eat and dash off like that, Mr. Calhoun."

The preacher raised eyes Heavenward as if asking for patience. "And then you'll say it's too close to dinnertime. No, Mrs. Calhoun, we are leaving this very minute. Delia won't mind. Goodbye, Delia, and thank you for your hospitality in this trying time. Please know I'll be praying for you every day."

"Thank you, Reverend Calhoun," Delia said, keeping her eyes downcast lest his wife discern just how relieved she was that they were leaving. Having guests could be exhausting in the best of times. Now she was eager to be alone with her thoughts and not have the constant duty of being pleasant and hospitable.

She picked up the picnic basket she had packed with the remains of the ham, several slices of bread and some butter she'd wrapped in a cold, wet cloth, and she walked to the door before Mrs. Calhoun could think of any further reason to dally.

Chapter Two

Reverend Calhoun's fondness for sweet tea had left Delia with only an inch or two of sugar in the bottom of the rose-sprigged china sugar bowl, she discovered when she sat down to drink her coffee.

Fortunately, the hens had provided eggs she could bring into town to sell at the general store, then buy sugar with some of the money Mr. Dean paid her, and have a few coins to put aside for another day. But what was she going to do when she needed a sizable sum? If the windmill broke and she had to have it repaired, for example? And she had assumed it might take some time for the town to find a new pastor. If the perfect candidate was available, Llano Crossing's time without a preacher would be brief—leaving Delia without a home. She would have to be able to pay rent somewhere.

Her grandpa had never been a great one for saving, believing that the Lord would meet his needs, even if he gave his meager salary to any down-on-his-luck tramp who showed up at the door. The Lord had always come through, often in the guise of one of the church members who brought them a side of beef or a bushel of peaches. But she couldn't count on that to continue, now that her grandpa had gone on to his heavenly reward.

The Lord helps those who help themselves, she reminded herself. She'd better look into getting a job while
she was in town, so when the time came she could afford to put another roof over her head, even if it was just
a room at Mrs. Mannheim's boardinghouse. Perhaps Mr.
Dean could use another clerk at the general store, or Mrs.
Jackson might need an assistant cook at the hotel. If worst
came to worst, she could offer to clean and cook for Mrs.
Mannheim in exchange for her room and board, though
she had heard the German widow was an exacting woman
who preferred to do everything herself. Or she could write
to Reverend Calhoun and have him check into employment
opportunities in Mason, as he'd offered during his stay.

She hoped, however, that she wouldn't have to leave
Llano Crossing. She'd been living here ever since she was
eleven, when her father had brought her here as his wife
was dying.

Taking a minute to gaze at herself in the cracked mirror, which hung in her room, she made sure the bow of
the black bonnet had even loops and her thick brown curly
hair was still enclosed in a neat knot on the back of her
neck. Black washed out her complexion, making her even
paler than she was, but the walk to town ought to bring
a little color to her cheeks. In the meantime, she pinched
them then picked up her egg basket and went out the door.

Intent on her thoughts, eyes on the path before her, she
almost opened the rusted gate into the horse standing in
the shade of the oak tree at the roadside.

"Oh! I didn't know anyone was there!" she said, her
hand falling from the gate as she took a step back.

It was the stranger she'd seen yesterday, the one who'd
asked directions into town.

He touched the brim of his hat once again. "Yes, ma'am,
you did seem like your mind was elsewhere. I didn't mean
to startle you."

"You…you didn't," she lied, though she knew it was plain as punch he had. He had changed since yesterday; if not for the fact that he was riding the same horse, she might not have recognized him. He had the same wintry gray-blue eyes, but he'd obviously used his evening at the hotel to bathe and shave and have his clothes laundered—or perhaps they were new ones, bought from the mercantile.

Delia was afraid she was staring.

"Can I…can I help you?" She was used to unknown people showing up at her grandpa's door, looking for a handout, or perhaps just spiritual advice, but she didn't want to tell this wolfish stranger she was alone here. "I'm afraid the reverend isn't available right now…."

"I know. Are you Miss Delia Keller?"

She nodded, feeling her heart pounding in her ears. How had he known her name? What did he want?

"I heard about your grandpa's unfortunate passing when I got to town," the stranger said. "I reckon that was his funeral you were leaving yesterday. Had I known who you were, Miss Keller, I would have stopped to talk to you yesterday, not ridden on past." His voice was deep, like the bottom of a slowly flowing Texas river.

Delia blinked. "Who…who are you?"

The man dismounted before he spoke and dropped the reins to the ground. The buckskin seemed used to this action and merely dropped his head to crop at the grass that grew lushly in the shade by the fence.

As the man turned back to her, she got a true measure of his height. Somehow he was even taller than he had seemed on horseback. He would have easily overtopped her grandpa, who had become stooped in his old age, and was probably taller than her father, whom she hadn't seen since the top of her head reached only to his elbow. The stranger would probably have had to duck to enter her house—not that she was even thinking of inviting him in!

He seemed to sense her qualms, for he held his ground and removed his broad-brimmed hat, revealing a headful of raven-dark hair. "Miss Keller, my name's Tucker—Jude Tucker—and the reason I'm here is that your father wanted me to come by and see you."

She could hardly believe her ears, and her eagerness had her rushing forward as fast as she had been backing up. "My father? You know my father? Is he coming? When will he be here? Why didn't he come with you? Oh, I *knew* he'd be back someday!"

A cloud seemed to pass over Tucker's face, and he put out a hand, not to touch her but to stop the flow of her words.

"He…he's not coming, Miss Keller. I'm sorry, I should have made that clear right off. I—I'm sorry to have to be the one to tell you he's dead."

Delia felt the earth shift beneath her feet as if she had been whirled around a dozen times and let loose. She would have fallen if the stranger hadn't put out a hand just then to steady her.

"Easy there," Jude Tucker murmured, his touch gentle. "You're white as bleached bones, Miss Keller. Why don't we step up onto your porch and sit down on those chairs? I've given you a shock, ma'am, but I reckon you'll be wanting to hear the rest once you've had a few moments to think."

She didn't remember giving permission, but with his hand on her elbow, he guided her up the three steps and settled her into the rocker that had been her grandpa's favorite place to while away an evening. He watched as she untied her black bonnet and set it on the small table between them.

"Is there a pump around back? Could I fetch you a cup of water?" Tucker asked.

His voice seemed to come from a long way off, and

Delia had to force herself to make sense of his words before she could answer him. "A pump? Water? No... That is, yes, there's a pump, but no, I don't want any...."

Then, as the result of years of modeling herself after her grandpa, who'd never done the least thing without thinking of other people first, she added, "Oh, but feel free to help yourself, if you're thirsty. There's a cup hanging by a string from the pump."

He looked surprised. "It's mighty nice of you to be askin' at such a time, ma'am. Perhaps I'll do that, after I've told you about why your father sent me to see you."

"What...what happened to my father?" she said, swallowing past a lump in her throat, her eyes burning as she struggled to focus on the stranger.

Jude Tucker looked down at the hat he held between his long, tanned fingers. "He died mining silver out in Nevada, Miss Keller," he said.

When she said nothing, merely waited, he looked up at her, then went on.

"You probably know they struck silver out there in '59, long before he got there, but your father discovered a new mother lode nearby. I'd been helping him mine it. He'd been lucky—luckier than anyone's been since the Comstock Lode. He'd been saying he was going to head back to Texas, but before he could there was a mine collapse. I'd gone to town for supplies with the wagon, and he'd gotten pinned under a couple of big beams for several hours. He..."

Tucker paused, then seemed to think better of what he was going to say. His eyes shifted toward the road, but Delia could tell he wasn't really seeing anything. He was remembering.

"It was clear he was in a bad way when I got there. I pulled the beams off him. I was all for trying to get him to the doctor, but he wouldn't go. He told me he knew he was dying. There probably wasn't anything the sawbones could've done anyway, and the ride would have killed him. He told me just to let him lie there so he could use the moments he had left to tell me where to find you, Miss Keller. He was gone just a few minutes after that."

Delia felt a hot knife of regret stab her. If only her father hadn't been so restless—if only he hadn't felt that need to go seek his fortune. He'd be alive today, and she wouldn't have had to grow up without a father. Mrs. Calhoun had been unknowingly right when she'd quoted that verse from the Bible. The love of money had certainly been the root of evil for Will Keller.

"And now you have," she said, remembering her manners. "It was good of you to come so far, Mr. Tucker, to tell me about my father's death. I… I don't have any way to repay you for your trouble."

Something shifted in the depths of those steely eyes. "You're welcome, but I…didn't come all this way just to inform you of his death. I came to bring you something. You're his only living heir, after all."

"Heir?" Once again, it was as if he was speaking a foreign language.

His lips curved upward slightly. "Well, I suppose *heiress* would be the proper word, ma'am. In my saddlebags I have a certificate from the bank in Carson City that you can have transferred to your bank here in town."

"Certificate? What do you mean?"

"Your father had already mined quite a lode of silver before anyone—anyone besides me, that is—got wind that he'd struck such a big vein. He converted it to cash and put that in the bank. He died a rich man, Miss Keller. And now all his wealth is yours."

He'd been afraid that the news might cause her to faint for real this time. Jude watched, ready to catch her, as the heavy dark lashes flew up and surprise siphoned the blood once more from her cheeks, but Delia Keller remained upright.

A soft gasp escaped her lips. "Rich? *My* father? And he left it all to *me?*"

Her incredulity at being the sole beneficiary surprised him in turn. "You *were* his only child, Miss Keller. Who else should he leave it to?"

"I... I don't know," she stammered in bewilderment. "As long as he'd been gone from here, I thought it possible that he might...well, have married again. Maybe even started a new family somewhere."

Jude wished his friend were alive again, if only for a moment, so he could upbraid him for deserting his responsibility to his only child and making this beautiful woman doubt her importance to her father. Compared to that, even the thousands of dollars Will Keller had left her were fool's gold.

"Or he could have left it to you, his partner." She'd been looking down at her lap, but now he found those green eyes trained right on him.

Jude found himself unable to meet her frank regard. "I... I wasn't his partner," he explained. "I just worked for him. He found the silver all by himself. He gave me plenty for traveling expenses, Miss Keller. That was enough."

"You could have kept the certificate and claimed you couldn't find me. No one would have been the wiser."

Those eyes seemed to bore right through him, straight to his soul.

"No, I couldn't have," he said, wondering what Delia Keller looked like clothed in some color other than black. Green perhaps, to match her eyes. Now, that would be a picture. "Besides, what would I do with so much money? I go where the wind takes me."

"You're a drifter?"

It was phrased as a question, but it wasn't one. Jude

knew she had sized him up when he'd asked for directions yesterday—or if she hadn't, the sour-faced woman next to her had done it for her.

"You don't want to settle down somewhere, Mr. Tucker? Put down roots, make a home?"

He had to quell her inquiries before he ended up saying more than he meant to. Jude gave her a direct look, a look that was a little too bold, a look that said she didn't know him nearly well enough to be asking such a personal thing.

"The question is, what are *you* going to do with it, Miss Keller? That's what you need to be thinking of."

He saw the flush sweep up her neck and into her cheeks and knew she'd gotten the message he intended.

"Oh! I… I suppose you're right…." A parade of emotions played across her face as he watched, from astonishment to thoughtfulness to amusement.

"Well, this *does* change things, doesn't it? I was on the way to town to sell my eggs so I'd have enough to buy sugar, and I thought while I was there I'd see about getting a job. I thought I'd better start saving some money for when the new preacher arrived and I had to find a new place to live."

He laughed. "You won't have to do that now, Miss Keller."

She smiled, a smile of dawning confidence. "No, I won't, will I? I… I can buy a house if I want to, can't I?"

He nodded, amused. She really had no idea, just yet, of just how wealthy she was. "Miss Keller, with the wealth represented by that certificate, there, you can have a house built to your exact specifications. It could be the biggest house in Llano Crossing, if you wanted. Or you could move anywhere you like."

"I—I see," she breathed. "Well! That does give me something to think about, doesn't it?"

A gleam flashed across those clear green eyes. Delia

Keller looked as if she'd thought of something very satisfying. Jude wondered for a moment what it was.

"What do you suggest I do first, Mr. Tucker?" she asked.

"You said you were going to town. You should still go, and right-away. Get that certificate into the bank safe before you tell anyone—and I mean *anyone*—about it."

She looked startled at his sudden grimness.

"Mr. Tucker, this is a small town, full of good people, not swindlers and cardsharps. It's not as if someone would snatch it out of my hand," she protested.

"You asked my opinion, Miss Keller," he reminded her. "All I'm saying is, go to the bank first, before you speak to anyone about what I've told you. After that, you can sit up on the roof of the town hall and call out the news from there, if you've a mind to."

Jude could see his blunt words had splashed cold water on her bubbling excitement, which was as he'd intended. A little caution would serve her well.

"Very well. I'm sure it's good advice," she said. "Would you suggest that I not mention it to anyone afterward, either? Other than the bank president, I mean—he'll have to know because I'll have to tell him how I came by this certificate. But people will guess something has happened when I start looking for property...." Her voice trailed off and she looked at him uncertainly.

He managed not to laugh at her naiveté. "I think you'll find that word will get around as if it had wings, Miss Keller. Be very careful. You're going to find that the way people have treated you is about to change. Don't trust everything that people say to you."

She studied him for a long moment and looked as if she were about to ask him how he knew so much. But apparently, after the way he had responded to her other personal question, she decided against it, for she just nodded.

"I'll do as you suggest," she said, rising. "Perhaps you

would accompany me, Mr. Tucker? The least I could do would be to buy you dinner at the hotel afterward, after the distance you've come to inform me of this…this astonishing change in my situation," she said. She'd have to ask the bank president for an advance of cash in order to pay for the meal, of course, but that shouldn't be a problem.

Chapter Three

He laughed, but this time it was a mirthless sound that stung her pride. "Miss Keller, you're a rich woman now, but you still need to be careful of what people will say. Being seen with a stranger—especially being seen dining with me—would not be good for your reputation."

She hadn't thought of that, but was determined to persuade him. "If I introduce you—if I explain that you were my father's friend and came here to inform me of his death—I'm sure no one would think ill of it."

He shook his head. "That wouldn't make a difference," he said. "In fact, it might make things worse. No, you'd do better to pretend we never met—other than yesterday, of course, when I asked for directions. That wasn't exactly a formal introduction."

"But what will you do? Where will you go from here?" she asked. She'd wanted to hear more from this man about her father—and, if she were honest with herself, she wanted to spend a little more time in the company of Jude Tucker, though she couldn't have said why. There was just something about him. Perhaps it was only because he had brought the news that had just changed her life.

For a moment, he looked as if he was going to ask her why she cared enough to ask. Then he said, shrugging, "I don't know. I'm a fair enough carpenter.... I'll probably stick around town awhile, do some odd jobs to build up a stake so I can go back out West."

"It's honest work," she murmured.

"It'll take a long time to earn enough that way."

"If you're in that much of a hurry, maybe you should rob the bank," she suggested tartly.

"The same bank you're about to go to? Not a very wise suggestion, Miss Keller."

She stiffened at his teasing. "I'm just going to take these eggs back into the kitchen, and then I must be going," she said, going to pick up the basket she had left by the gate. "Good day, Mr. Tucker. Thank you for your kindness in coming, and for your honesty in bringing me my father's legacy."

"Goodbye, Miss Keller," he said, donning his hat again and pulling it low, so his eyes were in shadow. "Remember, if you see me around town, we haven't met."

His unnecessary reminder, and his failure to acknowledge her thanks, irritated her. "That won't be a problem," Delia said, her voice curt.

Tucker had been compassionate in the way he'd informed her of her father's death, but after that he'd done nothing but make her feel like a gullible innocent. Very well! She had tried to show her gratitude and he'd virtually thrown the offer back in her face—even made her feel that, by offering, she had seemed a little forward.

He was gone when she came back out, and she resolved to put Jude Tucker from her mind. With any luck, she wouldn't encounter him again, and she could concentrate on the message he had brought, rather than the messenger.

Her father was dead. It was strange, Delia mused as she walked down the road, but after the initial stab of grief, she felt…nothing. Perhaps, since he'd been gone without a word for so long, he had been dead to her anyway. Of course, Delia hoped he hadn't suffered and that, in the time between the accident and Tucker's return to the mine, her father had thought to pray.

He had believed in Jesus, Delia remembered. She recalled times he'd listened to her prayers and read her stories from the Bible. But that had been before her mother's passing, which had set the wanderlust loose in his soul so badly that he couldn't bide at home and be a father to her.

Delia winced, remembering now how often she'd expressed anger toward her father when talking to her grandpa.

"Delia, darlin'," she could hear him say in his drawling voice, rusty with age, "it's plumb understandable and human that you feel that way, but you'd do better to pray for him, for his safety and his quick return. Let's read that story in the Bible about the Prodigal Son. Maybe your papa will be just like that, and we'll have a feast to celebrate."

Surely it was a sin to be angry toward the dead. Her father was no longer capable of coming back to her.

But what about my prayers, God? I prayed for Papa's safety and his return, and You let him die in a mine collapse, hundreds of miles away.

"God always hears us, child," she could hear her grandpa say, as clearly as if he had been right there by her, "but sometimes his answer is no. And sometimes we won't ever know—this side of Heaven, at least—why that's so."

And now that I'm a rich woman, it's too late for me to help Grandpa with my money. How wonderful it would have been if she could have used some of it to buy him some comfort in his old age. She'd have insisted he move into her new house with her, or if he hadn't been willing, she could have at least had the tumbledown old parsonage fixed so that its roof no longer leaked and its walls were freshly painted.

He'd probably have insisted she send the money to missionaries in Africa instead, Delia mused, and found her cheeks wet with tears. She could mourn her grandpa, even if she couldn't feel deep sorrow for her father.

The town of Llano Crossing lay just around a wooded bend from its church and parsonage. Jude Tucker tied his horse among the cottonwoods that lined the curve of the river and followed Delia on foot, keeping his distance among the trees so she wasn't aware of him. He was pleased to see that true to his instruction, she went straight to the bank without dillydallying to chat with any of the handful of townsfolk who greeted her in passing.

He hadn't expected Delia Keller to be a beauty. Nothing her father had told him while they worked shoulder to shoulder in the mine, or later, when Will lay dying in the wreckage of that same mine, had prepared Jude for those large green eyes, that slender, slightly long nose, that rosebud of a mouth, all set in a heart-shaped face with a faint sprinkling of freckles. He supposed that when Will had last seen his daughter before heading West, Delia had been at that awkward, coltish stage that many girls go through just before being transformed into beauties.

He doubted that Delia even knew she was pretty. There was something unawakened, unaware in those clear green eyes. Her gaze had been direct when she had invited him to escort her to the bank and to buy him dinner. Perhaps it was because he had just told her of her father's death, but Jude was used to women who knew how fluttering their eyelashes just so at a man would get them their way.

There was also a total lack of vanity in the ugly high-necked black mourning dress she wore. Maybe the dress was borrowed. He had known women who looked striking in black, but Delia wasn't one of them. The harsh, flat hue leeched the color from her cheeks—and yet somehow she was still beautiful.

Now that she was wealthy beyond most women's dreams, though, she could at least improve the quality of her mourning. She could buy dresses in finer fabrics, black mourning jewelry and fetching hats to replace that ugly poke bonnet....

Better clothing, along with her change in status from an impoverished orphan to a wealthy heiress, would draw men like flies. He hoped Delia Keller had some shrewdness to go with her comeliness, or she'd find herself the victim of some smooth-talking fortune-hunter who'd treat her to a whirlwind courtship and then, as her husband, exert sole control over the money her father had wanted to benefit his daughter.

Lord, protect her. Make her as wise as a serpent yet harmless as a dove, as the Good Book says.

Will Keller had suggested that Jude be the one to marry and protect her, right after he had struck it rich. "You should go to Llano Crossing and marry my daughter, Tucker. She's a sweet girl, my Delia. You'd be good for one another."

He'd scoffed at Will for saying it. "Will, what does your daughter need with the likes of me? Besides, we'll probably never meet. You'll go home one day, now that you've made your fortune, and I'll keep looking for a rich claim of my own."

"Or a rich widow," Will had joked, wiping the sweat out of his eyes.

Jude had only shook his head. He was done with widows—especially those who claimed to be widows who really weren't at all. He'd settle down with a woman someday, he supposed. He wasn't a good enough man to always resist the clamoring wants of his body forever. But he certainly wasn't worthy of an innocent girl like Delia, a preacher's granddaughter. Not after Nora.

* * *

"This is extraordinary news, Miss Keller," Amos Dawson, the bank president, said, laying aside his wire-rimmed spectacles and the certificate Delia had shown him, and crossing his arms over his considerable paunch. "You're saying you had no idea that your father had amassed such a fortune?"

"Yes," she murmured, feeling uneasy at his staring. His black beady eyes reminded her of her grandpa's old rooster—right before the bossy bird tried to peck at her legs. "I—I mean no, I had no idea. We—my grandpa and I—hadn't heard from him in years, you see. We didn't even know if he was alive or dead."

"How did you get hold of this document? Did it come in the mail?"

Delia wanted to say it had, to avoid questions about Jude Tucker, since he had cautioned her not to claim any acquaintance with him. But it would be easy enough for Dawson to check with the gossipy postmaster of the little town, who knew who was receiving mail from where and didn't mind telling anyone who asked.

"I… That is, the man who had been working for him brought it to me."

Dawson continued to scrutinize until Delia felt a flush creeping up the scratchy neckline of her dress.

"We'll have to telegraph the bank in Nevada to verify its authenticity," he said at last.

Delia felt foolish. The bank couldn't just assume the certificate was real and start issuing her funds based on it. The document could be a clever fraud.

"I… I assumed as much," she said, trying to sound like a woman of the world. "Naturally."

Dawson seemed pleased with her composure. "We'll do so immediately, I assure you, Miss Keller. I would imagine it will take a few days to obtain an answer—but during that time, I regret that I can't…that is, the *bank* cannot act on the basis of this document."

Delia nodded. "I understand completely," she said, rising. It wasn't a problem. She had been poor when she woke up this morning, and she could go on pinching pennies and doing without for a few more days. She only wished she had brought those eggs after all—now she was going to have to walk back to the house and get them or do without sugar in her tea another day.

Dawson rose also. "Assuming this certificate is authentic, Miss Keller, this is very exciting news, isn't it? Just wait until the word gets out!"

Delia felt a prickle of alarm dance up her spine. He was practically clapping his hands together with glee, as if he wanted to be the first to spread the news. "I hope I can rely on your discretion, Mr. Dawson. I… I wouldn't want to be the subject of speculation…especially before the certificate has been proved genuine."

Dawson coughed and took a step back, and his features smoothed out as if an invisible hand had wiped all expression from his face. "Of course not, Miss Keller. Rest assured. But only imagine the possibilities of what you will be able to do with such a sum! The bank will be pleased to be of any assistance to you that you would require."

"Fine. Please let me know when you've received confirmation. Good afternoon, Mr. Dawson."

She swept out, disturbed at the complete transformation in the way the bank president treated her once he had heard the news. No wonder Grandpa had never had much use for Amos Dawson!

Intent on her thoughts as she pushed open the ornate, heavy door of the bank, she nearly collided with Charles Ladley, the mayor's son, who was just coming in.

"Why, hello, Miss Delia," he greeted her, extending a

hand to steady her. "I hope everything's all right? Is there anything I can do for you?"

Delia felt a hidden amusement bubbling up within her at his concerned expression. He must think she was here to ask for a loan!

"Thank you, Charles. Everything is fine," she said serenely. "It's kind of you to ask."

He studied her more closely. "That's good, that's good. You *would* let us know if you needed anything, wouldn't you?"

Us meant the Ladleys, the pillars of the community.

"Of course I would," she said. "Tell your mother I said hello." She smiled and kept moving. It would be interesting to see how this man, on whom she had once pinned all her hopes and dreams, treated her, once he knew she was no longer the poor little church mouse.

Chapter Four

Positioned at a table by the window that faced the bank, Jude was just about to sink his fork into his savory beef stew in the Llano Crossing Hotel dining room when he spied Delia Keller exiting the bank. He straightened, seeing her almost run into the dapper man who then chivalrously kept her from falling. Jude noted, too, how the handsome swell's hand lingered a moment longer than was strictly proper on Delia's elbow.

Jude was surprised by the urge he felt to jump out of his seat and dash out the door, shouting a command for the other man to take his hands off Delia Keller. But then she smiled at her rescuer, and Jude ordered himself to remain where he was.

Obviously Delia knew the man who stared down at her so familiarly, so he needn't interfere. Delia was in no danger, and the richly dressed fellow speaking to her was perhaps the very sort of man she should be associating with from now on.

However, despite the fact that the encounter had taken no more than a minute at most, Jude couldn't quash the primitive stab of jealousy that arrowed through him as he saw Delia gift the man with a warm wave of farewell. Involuntarily his hand clenched into a fist as he watched the other man linger to eye the gentle sway of Delia's hips as she walked down the street away from the bank.

"Care for more coffee, sir?" purred a voice near his ear, and he looked up to see the waitress standing there, steaming pot in hand. She was pretty in a commonplace way, but she grinned as if they were old friends. "I'm Polly. New in town, ain't ya?" She batted darkened lashes at him and he smelled traces of a cheap floral perfume.

"Thanks," he said, deliberately ignoring her inquiry and not giving his name in return. In a small town like this she would already know that he was a stranger, anyway. He extended his cup, his gaze returning to the view out the window. Once his coffee had been refreshed, however, the waitress showed no signs of leaving.

"Who's that fancy gent standing at the bank door?" he asked, the more to keep her from asking him any further personal questions than from a real desire to know.

She put a hand above her eyes to shade them against the glare, then peered through the dusty glass, squinting. For a moment Jude thought she might actually be too near-sighted to answer him. But then she leaned down again.

"Why, that's Charles Ladley, the mayor's son," she said, sighing. "He sure is a good-looking fella. Wish he'd smile at *me* like that, though I doubt it'll do that Keller girl any good neither."

"What do you mean?" Jude kept his voice casual. He knew it was none of his business, but he couldn't seem to keep himself from asking.

Polly gave an elaborate shrug. "Birds of a feather flock together, they say, and the Ladleys have always been as rich as King Midas. The preacher's granddaughter—Delia Keller, that's who he was talkin' to—don't have two pennies to rub together. 'Specially now that Reverend McKinney's gone and died. Wouldn't be surprised if she don't have to come here and work 'longside a' me." There was a trace of satisfaction in her tone as she turned back to Jude.

If only you knew, Jude thought. With Delia's status about to change radically, she and the mayor's son would now be on equal footing. Any impediments to a relationship between them were about to melt like icicles in a Texas summer.

Aloud, he said, "Miss Polly, I'm sure the right man is out there, just looking for you. And when you find each other," he added, trying to sound encouraging, "he'll be so perfect for you, you'll be glad you didn't waste your time with that fellow." He kept his eyes on Ladley, who was finally entering the bank.

The waitress's eyes brightened. Jude realized that if he wanted her to go away soon and leave him to his thoughts, he'd said exactly the wrong thing.

"My, that's an awfully sweet thing for you to say, in spite a' bein' a stranger an' all that," she gushed in that suggestive voice that wasn't nearly as inviting as she apparently thought it was. She glanced quickly over her shoulder in an obvious effort to make sure the hotel owner wasn't watching, then leaned closer. "Where did you say you was from?"

"I didn't say," he said, his gaze swinging back to the window, hoping she got the hint.

But Polly was nothing if not tenacious. "You plannin' on stayin' 'round these parts? I have to work till seven, but after that I could show you around the town."

That would take all of about five minutes, he thought. "Thank you, Miss Polly, but I—"

"Or we could go to the church social next Saturday night," she interrupted. "I know about everyone in Llano Crossing, so that'd be a real nice way to meet folks.…"

He felt a twinge of pity for the girl. He hadn't even given her his name, and here she was laying out the welcome mat. He held up a hand, knowing he had to stem her flow of eagerness. "Miss Polly, much as I appreciate your kindness, I'm not sure what my plans are just yet. I'm not planning on staying long in Llano Crossing, nice as it is. I'm either going to be riding along tomorrow or doing some odd jobs for a while before I head back West."

Polly's face fell and her overbright eyes dimmed. "Sure. I understand—just wanted to be neighborly, that's all. Will you have some peach pie for dessert?"

Jude shook his head and asked her how much he owed. He would have liked some pie, but he thought it best to leave so the waitress could regain her composure. He left her an extra ten cents in addition to the dollar he owed for the meal.

Striding back into the early afternoon sunlight, Jude pondered his options. He could go to the saloon, he supposed.

In the war, he'd spent time in taverns with some of his men—too much time—between the horrendous campaigns that had led to too many lost and shattered lives. Nothing good had ever happened to him, or anyone else as far as he could see, anywhere near such a place. He'd met Nora, after all, as he was coming out of a tavern in Virginia, his judgment clouded with whiskey.

Stop thinking about her. It's over. You have to learn from it and go on.

Resist the devil, and he will flee from you, the Scriptures promised. All very well, but if he wasn't going to seek out a card game, what was he going to do with himself?

The smartest thing, he mused, would be to get his horse, Shiloh, out of the livery stable and ride west out of Llano Crossing. He could stop when he felt tired, sleep under the stars and live off the land between here and Nevada. He wouldn't have to feel responsible for watching over Delia Keller as she navigated her new life of comfort and ease.

It looked like there was an even chance the mayor's son would be more than willing to take over that responsibility.

But didn't he have a moral obligation to his dead friend, Will Keller, to make sure his orphaned daughter was going to be all right, even if he wasn't going to marry Delia?

In any case, it was a waste of money to leave Llano Crossing today when he was paid through tonight at the hotel. Tomorrow he needed to have a plan, but tomorrow was soon enough. In the meantime, Shiloh was standing idle in his stall in the livery stable, no doubt eating his head off the unaccustomed rich grain and hay. Maybe the best thing to do was take the stallion on a run over the hills around Llano Crossing. They'd return in the evening, tired but content, and hopefully the silver buckskin's mile-devouring gallop would have left Jude Tucker's demons far behind.

Within fifteen minutes, Shiloh was saddled and showing his heels to the little town. For the rest of the afternoon and into the early evening, Jude and his mount explored the rolling limestone-and-cedar-studded hills, climbing until the Llano River showed as little more than a winding silver ribbon next to a collection of matchstick buildings of the town. Hawks soared overhead, taking advantage of the updrafts. Mockingbirds and crows darted among the mesquite trees and cedars, and occasionally he spied a roadrunner, darting here and there in search of the insects and snakes on which it fed.

Occasionally he spied a ranch house with outbuildings and a corral, and he knew he ought to stop and inquire if the owner needed another hand, but he felt no strong compulsion. He was enjoying the solitude and the opportunity it gave him to think.

The sun was warm on his back. He remembered, as he paused to let Shiloh drink from a cottonwood-shaded creek, how he had once used such solitary rides to gain inspiration for his sermons. It all seemed like a hundred years ago.

In those carefree days, he'd had no bigger concerns than planning next Sunday's service and wondering and praying about when the Lord was going to provide him with a wife. Every man needed a wife, but a bachelor-preacher surely had more need than most, so as to keep his concentration on the Lord's work. Fully half a dozen unmarried misses plus a widow or two decorated his front pew every Sunday morning, smiling up at him, but none of them had seemed quite right for him. Surely the Lord would shine a special light on the woman who was meant to be his wife, wouldn't He? But as yet, no such illumination had been provided.

Then the shadow of war had cast itself across the land, and Jude sensed this wasn't the time to be marrying and leaving a wife behind, her belly perhaps swelling with his child, a woman who might become a widow. The Lord was calling him to serve as one of His representatives in the army. There was time enough to think about marrying when the war was over, when—if—he resumed his position at the Mount Mulberry Church. A lot could happen during a war, he'd known, but as it turned out, he hadn't guessed the half of it.

And then the war, and the things he'd done during the war, had changed him so completely that there seemed to be no point in even trying to return to Mount Mulberry and its church. He wasn't fit to be its or anyone else's pastor anymore.

With twilight drawing on, Jude and Shiloh had descended the hills and rejoined the road back to town. Jude had been humming "Tenting Tonight," an old Civil War tune, when a shot rang out in the distance, echoing among the hills. The stallion stopped stock-still, his ears pricked forward. He gave a snort and then whinnied as if responding to a call.

Jude stopped humming, listening, too, and then he heard it—the faint cry of a man somewhere off the road among the dense mesquite and cedar. He urged his stallion off the road, navigating carefully among the cacti, the shrubs and the low trees, and after a few moments, he found the old man.

He was sitting alone on a limestone boulder, cradling his right arm, his floppy-brimmed hat shading his features.

"Howdy, stranger. I sure was thankful to hear you coming. I think this arm is broke. I tried walking, but I got to feelin' kinda fainty-like."

Jude dismounted. "What happened?" he asked, going toward the man.

"I rode out here just to have a glimpse at my old spread. Used t' live here afore me and the missus got too old t' be ranchin' anymore and moved t' town. I sold my acres to the neighboring rancher, even though I never thought much a' Dixon Miller. Anyway, I was ridin' along an' someone fired a shot—not at me, I think, but real close t' the road, like. My fool horse was so spooked, he threw me and took off," he admitted with a rueful grin. "Didn't see him run past ya, did ya?"

Jude admitted he hadn't.

"Don't know where he's got to, though it wouldn't surprise me none if Miller's boys find him and put him in with their stock. All I wanted was just a glimpse of our old home," he said wistfully, then he straightened. "James Heston's the name," the old man said, extending his other hand, though he grimaced when he loosed his careful hold on the broken right arm. His face was craggy and lined but his gaze honest and direct.

"Jude Tucker. Let me help you onto Shiloh, here, and

we'll get you into town. Is there a doctor in Llano Crossing?"

The old man gave a mirthless snort. "None I'd send my worst enemy to, let alone go myself. There isn't any need, anyway. Nothing feels out of place." He felt along the forearm as if to demonstrate, wincing as he did so. "My ranch is just over that ridge. If you could just help me get home, Jude Tucker, I'll be fine. And I'm sure my missus will give you supper by way of thanks."

Jude assisted Heston to mount, thankful that Shiloh was even-tempered enough not to mind a strange rider, especially one who trembled slightly with the effort to raise his foot to the near stirrup. Then he walked alongside the buckskin in the direction of town.

They found Heston's horse halfway back. The beast had apparently cut across country and was calmly grazing. Jude mounted him rather than put Heston to the trouble of changing horses, and they rode on to Heston's house.

"That was delicious, Mrs. Heston," Jude said, two hours later, as he pushed himself back from the table and the remains of a dinner of fried chicken, black-eyed peas, corn bread and peach pie—it seemed as if he was fated to have peach pie today, even though he'd declined it at the hotel.

The comfortably plump woman with strands of iron-gray hair coming loose from her bun beamed at him. "My goodness, Mr. Tucker, it was the least I could do after you were kind enough to bring my Jim home," she said, bestowing a smile of immense warmth. "It's such a rare treat to have company, in any case."

"My wife is the best cook in these parts," James Heston bragged. He hadn't eaten that much himself, even though his wife had cut up his chicken and buttered his corn bread so that left-handed eating would be easier. His forearm was splinted now and lying in a makeshift sling of bright yellow calico, so perhaps the pain had dimmed his appetite.

She beamed. "Thank you, Jim. And what brings you to these parts, Mr. Tucker?"

"Just passin' through," he said. "I've been mining out in Nevada, but I had to come here…on some business," he said, deliberately being vague. "I'll be heading west again, soon as I raise a little traveling stake."

Heston's eyes met those of his wife. "Lookin' for work, are you?" Heston inquired.

Jude shrugged. "I might be. I've done some carpentry, but I can turn my hand to most anything."

"I'm going to need some help around here with the chores for a little while, till this bone knits itself back together. And you saw when we came in from the barn that I'm in the midst of addin' on a room to the back."

Jude nodded. Heston was about halfway through framing the addition, from the looks of things.

"We couldn't pay you much, but we'd include room and board for as long as you want to stay. It'd certainly be cheaper than the hotel or the boardinghouse."

Jude was aware that both the elderly man and his wife were holding their breath awaiting his answer. Surely their offer was an answer to a prayer he hadn't even prayed yet.

"Thank you. I'd be pleased to do that for a spell, Mr. Heston," he said, humbled by their kindness to a stranger.

Chapter Five

"Who can find a virtuous woman?" Delia read in the last chapter of the book of Proverbs three mornings later after Tucker had come to see her. She loved to read her Bible there, with the sun just beginning to warm the worn wood of the rocker. Even the raucous cries of the grackles, hunting bugs among the grass, didn't usually bother her, though they could be disruptive when she tried to pray!

She was getting mighty tired of drinking her coffee without sugar, Delia mused as she sipped the unsweetened brew. She had used the very last of the sugar yesterday, so a trip back into town to sell her eggs was a must. And maybe while she was in town, Amos Dawson would see her going by the bank and run out to let her know the certificate had been confirmed by the bank in Nevada.

Delia, time enough for worldly business later. The Lord deserves your full attention right now. She could almost hear her grandfather's cracked voice saying the words.

"For her price is far above rubies." Why, it wouldn't be long until *she* could buy rubies—or at the very least, those garnet earbobs in the window of the mercantile that she had been yearning for forever.

Oh, please, God, don't let anyone buy them before the bank in Nevada releases my money! Wouldn't it be won-

derful to march right over to the mercantile and make the garnet earbobs my very first purchase?

But then in her head she heard, *"For the love of money is the root of all evil."*

The voice was so clear that she had to look around her to make sure Reverend McKinney wasn't standing behind her.

But how could it be wrong to rejoice in the windfall her father had provided for her? Her grandfather and she had had to skimp and save for so many years—surely the only thing she needed to regret was that he wasn't here to be given the comforts she could now provide!

Her eyes skipped down the page of her grandfather's well-worn Bible with his many handwritten notations in the margins to the verse: *She considereth a field, and buyeth it.*

Perhaps *she'd* be considering a field soon, though she'd rather plant a house on it than the vineyard the verse went on to mention. A big, fine, white-painted frame house, with lots of rooms. She'd have one room just to store her clothes in, another for her jewelry, another to entertain her many guests—perhaps even a ballroom on the second floor, with a veranda extending around at least two sides of the structure.

Skimming over the verses that showed the virtuous woman rising early and working long into the night, she read, *"Her clothing is silk and purple."* Well, wasn't that marvelous? She'd love to have a lace-edged silk camisole and pantalets under a purple silk dress with a bustle. It had always been one of her favorite colors. Perhaps she would take a few minutes this very day to study the better fabrics in the mercantile, the ones she'd never even allowed herself to look at back in the hardscrabble days when she and her dear old grandfather had not been sure where supper was coming from.

But you're in mourning, a voice within reminded her, and she felt a twinge of guilt at the greedy path her thoughts had wandered onto. Propriety dictated that she wouldn't be wearing anything but black any time soon. And she would have to graduate from black slowly, lightening the somber hue with gray or lilac.

"Her husband is known in the gates," the text went on, *"when he sitteth among the elders of the land."*

"Miss Delia?" A familiar voice intruded as she read the twenty-third verse. Delia looked up to see a landau parked outside the fence and Charles Ladley coming down the stone-flagged walkway, one hand using a carved mahogany walking cane, the other clutching a bouquet of velvety red roses.

She jumped to her feet, hardly able to believe her eyes. Her abrupt motion sent the china cup clattering off the arm of the rocker. Fortunately the cup didn't break, for it had fallen into the folds of the shawl she had shed as soon as the coffee had warmed her, but it was still half-full. With dismay, Delia saw the brown liquid splash against the hem of her everyday calico dress and soak into the dark folds of the shawl.

"Oh! Charles! I—I'm sorry, I didn't s-see you coming!" she stammered, horribly aware of the untidy picture she made. Her hair was still in the plait she had braided at bedtime last night, with tendrils escaping it and curling wildly around her face. If only she was wearing something better than the dress she had donned to go feed the chickens! She had planned to change before her trip to town. Hopefully she had no feathers clinging to her....

"No, it's I who should apologize for intruding on a lady in the midst of her devotions," he said with that smile that was like a thousand lit candles. "I just came to bring you these," he added, extending the hand that held the roses, "picked from my mother's garden this very morning—with her permission, of course." He winked. As if to testify to the truth of his words, the crimson petals sparkled with dewdrops in the sunlight.

"Thank you so much," she said, wanting to surreptitiously pinch herself to make sure she wasn't dreaming. *Charles Ladley had just brought her flowers.*

"Won't you have some coffee?" she said, accepting the roses with a hand that she prayed wasn't trembling with the delight that she felt. How heavenly it would be to sit on the front porch sipping coffee with Charles Ladley, for all the world to see! Wouldn't it be fun if nosy neighbor Mrs. Purvis peeked out of her kitchen window and saw them!

Charles's smile dimmed with regret. "I'm afraid I can't stay—I must attend the Committee for Civic Improvement meeting that's due to start in—" he reached down and turned the face of the gold pocket watch on his waistcoat so he could see it "—just a few minutes. I only came to bring you these, to let you know we were thinking of you, Father, Mother and I, and to ask you if you'd consent to go with me to the church social on Saturday night. I know it's disgracefully late to be asking you—you've probably long ago agreed to attend with some other *beau*, one of your many admirers…" His voice trailed off as if he was uncertain of her acceptance.

Delia was conscious of an urge to laugh at the very absurdity of his suggestion that she had a string of other *beaux*. "Why, no, Charles, I'm happy to say I haven't," she said, remembering not to admit no one else had asked her. "I always used to go to these occasions with Grandpa.…" Her voice trailed off.

"Ah… I didn't mean to make you sad, Miss Delia," he said, leaning over to wipe away the stray tear from her eye. "If you think it's too soon since his passing to attend a social event, I'll understand." His face was a study of disappointment.

"Oh…oh no!" she said quickly, alarmed that Charles would think she was still too full of grief to be good company. "That is, I think Grandpa would *want* me to go and have a good time."

Ladley's face cleared. "Then we shall go," he said, "and lift our glasses of punch in his honor. I'll call for you at six, if that's agreeable, Miss Delia."

"That would be lovely." Then she had a sudden thought. "Charles, you know that…that is, you won't mind that I—I must wear black, will you?" She had longed forever to be invited out by Charles Ladley—now she had been and she was forced to wear that lifeless color! How she wished she could don some bright, festive color—*anything* but black! But she could imagine how tongues would wag if she violated the ironclad rules that governed mourning.

"Of course not," he responded. "Miss Delia, I've always *admired* your virtuousness, your—" he seemed to struggle for the right word "—moral excellence. I will be proud to be seen with you, even if you choose to wear a flour sack—dyed black, of course."

Delia couldn't help but chuckle with him at the thought. "I solemnly promise I will not be wearing a flour sack when you call for me on Saturday night."

He pretended to mop his brow in relief, causing her to laugh again. "Very well then," he said, bowing, as courtly as any European prince. "Six o'clock on Saturday it is."

He turned to go, and as Delia watched him walk away, she saw that he was favoring his left leg slightly, leaning more heavily on his cane when stepping onto his left foot.

"Charles, you're limping." She was touched to see him pause and turn back toward her, seemingly as loath to leave as she was to see him go. "Is your war wound bothering you?"

Everyone in Llano Crossing knew the mayor's son had marched off to join the first Texas cavalry regiment formed, and that he had been wounded and sent home in the middle of the war.

"Miss Delia, you are kindness itself to notice," Ladley said. "But don't concern yourself. Yes, the old wound aches whenever it's about to rain. With any luck it'll be better by Saturday, and I can leave this cane at home." He waved and continued down the walk to the waiting landau. Delia's heart warmed with compassion as she saw how he strove to conceal a grimace of pain as he climbed up onto the platform.

With Charles's carriage out of sight, she allowed herself a celebratory twirl of delight, hugging herself with sheer joy. Charles Ladley had asked her to the church social! He said he appreciated her virtue and her moral excellence!

Well, she might have to wear black to the church social, but it didn't have to be that borrowed, ugly bombazine she'd worn to Grandpa's funeral! She'd seen a black moire silk dress with satin ribbon trim at the neck and cuffs in the window of Miss Susan's shop, but the price tag had been one that had made her walk regretfully on. Perhaps, if she hinted to Miss Susan that she was about to come into some funds, the seamstress would extend credit to her and agree to make any needed alterations, so that Delia could go to the party, resplendent in a beautiful new dress—even if it was black!

Was it going to rain? Delia studied the sky and was surprised to see clouds forming up in the west. She must have been oblivious to them developing while she and Charles had been talking. Would she have to wait until later to do her shopping?

Absolutely not! That's what umbrellas were for! She was Miss Delia Keller, who was about to become a very rich young woman—what were mere raindrops to her? As happy as she felt, she wouldn't even notice them!

* * *

The dress fit as if Miss Susan had known she would be the one wearing it. It clung to Delia's figure, enhancing her curves without being at all revealing, and the lace trim at the waist emphasized Delia's lithe frame.

"It will only need," the rawboned, horse-faced seamstress opined, "a slight shortening of the sleeves and a few tucks in the waist, since you, Miss Delia, are one of the few ladies in Llano Crossing who don't need to be tightly corseted. It would be a joy to see my creation on you, Miss Delia."

Delia thanked her. "Would you be able to have it ready by Saturday afternoon? I would like to wear it to the church social."

"My dear, I can have it for you by tomorrow morning. Business isn't what it once was, before the war," Miss Susan said, her expression wistful.

Now came the hard part. "Miss Susan, I hate to ask this favor, but would you be able to extend me credit? Only for a week or so, I promise you," she hastened to add, as she saw dismay flash across the old seamstress's face. "I... I could leave Grandpa's watch with you as a guarantee. The truth is, while I'm not yet at liberty to discuss the details, I'm about to inherit some money."

Miss Susan eyed Delia skeptically, and Delia felt a flush of embarrassment creep up her face. Perhaps she had better resign herself to wearing the ugly, old, borrowed bombazine, after all.

"I'm afraid you'll have to give me some hint of what you mean, Miss Keller. I'm only a poor woman trying to make a living with my needle, and as I've said, that's been rather difficult in the last few years. I'd have starved to death long ago if I hadn't been wary of giving credit."

"I—I'm attending the social with Charles Ladley," Delia

said, hoping to distract Miss Susan away from the source of the expected windfall.

Miss Susan's eyes brightened, and she said, "Well, that's real fine, Miss Delia. You two would make a right handsome couple, a handsome couple indeed."

Delia smothered her inward sigh of relief when the seamstress continued. "But I hope you aren't suggesting I extend you credit on the basis of one outing with the mayor's son, are you? I've lived in Llano Crossing since Charley Ladley was teething, and I've seen him squire any number of belles around. I'm sorry, but you'll have to do better than that to convince me you can eventually pay for this dress." Miss Susan held it up, brandishing it as if it were a weapon.

Delia sighed. "All right, but you must *promise* not to say a word if I tell you...." She broke off, her eyes searching the older woman's face, and seeing sympathy warring with practicality in those dark eyes behind her thick-lensed spectacles. Delia knew the moment when sympathy won—along with an honest dose of curiosity.

Miss Susan drew herself up to her full height. "I think you may safely trust in my discretion, especially toward our late preacher's granddaughter." She paused after this prim pronouncement, clearly waiting.

Delia told her the story of her father's untimely death in the mining accident and that she was only waiting to have it confirmed by the Nevada bank that her father had indeed left her a vast sum.

Miss Susan's mouth dropped open long before the end of Delia's recital, and she sank onto a nearby stool. "My, my. So *that's* where Will Keller went—I always wondered. And he left you wealthy—isn't that a wonderment?" she cried. "Why, of course you may pay me later for the dress, Delia—as long as you promise to let me continue to be your dressmaker when you come into your riches! Why,

I can already picture what glorious gowns I can fashion for you, my dear! Of course, it's a pity you're in mourning, but just you wait until that time is up! I've no doubt the mayor's son will have to use that fancy cane of his to beat off your other swains, Delia!"

The two women were smiling with delight at each other when suddenly from the back came the crash of a door being shoved open with such force that it rebounded against the wall. Delia heard the intruder mutter a curse word as a muffled clatter announced that he'd knocked over something heavy.

Miss Susan gave a low cry and seemed to shrink against Delia, trembling.

"Wha—who's that?" Delia demanded, even as a cowboy, his eyes red-rimmed and bleary, shoved the curtain dividing the rooms aside and lumbered into view.

"D-Donley, y-you just wait in the back for a minute until I'm done with this customer—" Miss Susan quavered.

"Gimme it now, woman!" the man roared, lurching forward unsteadily. Even from where she stood, Delia could smell the stale whiskey fumes.

Miss Susan darted a frightened look at Delia. "Please excuse me, Miss Keller—the dress will be ready tomorrow. Now, Donley, come to the back," she said, taking hold of the drunken man's elbow and trying to guide him back in the direction from which he had come.

"I'll knock y-you inta th' middle of nesht w-week!" the man yelled, throwing Miss Susan roughly against the wall. Miss Susan screamed as Donley cocked his fist.

With a shriek of fury, Delia launched herself at the inebriated man, only to be knocked flat on her back by the man's shove. Even as she tried to right herself to go to Miss Susan's defense again, she heard a shout from outside. Then the front door was yanked open and a pair of booted legs dashed past her.

Dazed, she saw that Jude Tucker had seized Donley in a headlock and, despite the man's ineffectual attempts to hit him in the midsection while shouting slurred curse words, was silently dragging him out the door past her. Delia managed to rise just in time to see Jude throw him into the street.

He landed smack in the middle of a new pile of horse droppings. A couple of cowboys, lounging indolently across the street, straightened and strode forward as if they knew him, glaring at Jude while they hoisted the man to his unsteady feet.

"Make sure he doesn't bother these folks again," Jude told them and turned back to Delia and Miss Susan, who by now were standing at the door, openmouthed.

He ushered them back inside. "You ladies all right?" he said, eyeing them each in turn. He gave no sign that he'd met Delia only a few days before.

Delia nodded, staring at Miss Susan, whose face was pale as bleached bones and pearled with sweat. "I'm fine. But she—he shoved her hard…"

"Why don't you sit down, ma'am," Jude said, gently propelling a shaking Miss Susan into a chair by a table stacked with dog-eared *Godey's Lady's Books*. He knelt beside the chair. "I'm Jude Tucker. I'm new in town, just staying a spell before passing on. Any bones broken?" he said, peering at her and smiling encouragingly.

Miss Susan, clearly dazed, stared at him and shook her head.

"I'm Delia Keller," Delia said, playing along. "And this is Miss Susan. It's her shop. Who was that man, Miss Susan?"

"I'm all right. Thank you, Mr. Tucker, for intervenin'. I—I'm sorry you saw that, Miss Delia. Please…"

Delia knew she was trying to find a way to ask them to

go now, to spare her any further embarrassment, but Delia knew they couldn't just leave her like that.

"Who was he?" she asked again. "I want to help you."

Miss Susan's eyes, huge behind her spectacles, blinked back tears. She buried her head in her hands.

"He won't hurt me," she said, "as long as I'm quick to give him money when he wants it."

"But why should you do that?" Jude asked. "What call does he have to demand anything of you?"

Miss Susan stared up at Delia, her lower lip quivering. "I guess the least I can do is explain after you've both come to my aid," she said. "But I depend on your discretion."

"You have it," Jude said, and Delia nodded, too.

"Donley Morrison is my husband, Miss Keller. I left him because he beat me—repeatedly."

"Your…your husband? But I thought you were never married," Delia amended hastily.

"That's what all of Llano Crossing thinks, and I prefer it that way," the older woman said, visibly gathering her dignity around her like a cloak. "I came to town believing I had eluded him, but he followed me and went to work for that rancher, Dixon Miller. Usually he leaves me alone—except when he has no money left for whiskey."

"But you've left him…" Delia stared at Jude, feeling out of her depth.

"He won't let me go. And I haven't the means to flee farther."

"I'll go get the sheriff," Jude said, rising. "He'll put him in jail for assaulting you."

"Sheriff Jenkins is one of Dixon Miller's cronies," Miss Susan told him wearily. "He's the wealthiest rancher in these parts."

"Then you must come and live with me," Delia said, surprising herself. "He won't bother you there."

Miss Susan shook her head. "If I don't leave things as

they are, he'd force me to come back to him. He'd tell everyone he was my lawful husband and I abandoned him, and then who will come to my shop?"

"But if the truth was known—" Delia began.

Miss Susan raised a hand. "Leave things as they are. It'll be all right...though I thank you both for your kindness." She lifted her head then, her eyes pleading with them to understand her need to hang on to what pride she had left.

Delia was silent for a moment, terribly saddened by what she had just heard. "All right, Miss Susan," she said, gathering up her reticule, "but I want you to know you must come to me if anything else happens and you change your mind."

She didn't leave until the seamstress nodded.

Chapter Six

Delia was about to step up onto the boardwalk into the mercantile when Jude caught up to her.

"Are *you* all right, Miss Keller?" His cool gray-blue eyes were warm with concern. "You were on the floor when I ran in. He knocked you flat, didn't he?"

Delia smiled up at him, touched by his earnestness after his dismissive manner at the end of their first meeting. "He only hurt my pride, Mr. Tucker. It's fortunate you were passing by or things might have ended much differently. Do you think Morrison will come back to plague Miss Susan? Should I have insisted she come stay with me?" She didn't know why she expected him to know the answer to these questions.

"I'm going to go in and buy a padlock and install it on Miss Susan's back entrance," he said, with a nod toward the mercantile door. "She had a hook-and-eye latch, but there was a gap between the door and the frame wide enough for a man's hand to fit through, which I'll fix. A better lock should prevent him from surprising her from behind, least."

"Very chivalrous of you, Mr. Tucker."

He shook his head as if to say it was nothing. "And it was good of you to offer her refuge, but I don't believe she's ready yet to admit she can't handle him by herself. There may come a time, though…"

"The offer'll remain open," Delia said. His words seemed based on experience with handling people and their problems, and for a moment Delia wondered about that. But she didn't want to damage the good feeling between them, after their shared experience, by prying.

"Well, now, we've officially met, at least—though we can't exactly say how it came about," she murmured, and waited to see his reaction.

He didn't seem displeased by the idea. "That's true." But just as she hoped he'd feel free to go further with the acquaintance, he seemed to pull himself back. "I'd better not hold you up any longer. After you, Miss Keller," he said, stepping up to open the door for her.

Then they were in the midst of other shoppers in the mercantile and she didn't want to look forward by asking Jude if he'd found work and lodging, so she took her egg basket up to the counter and forced herself not to look to see what he was doing.

It was all right, Delia told herself, if Jude Tucker wasn't interested in her except as an ally in Miss Susan's defense. She was going to the church social with Charles Ladley!

Delia woke in the wee hours of the morning on the day of the church social, unsure what had roused her. Nothing seemed amiss. The only sound was the steady tick-tock of her grandfather's ormolu clock, one of the few possessions of any value that he had not sold or given away from the parlor. With the moonlight streaming in her window, she could see the dark shape of the new black dress as it hung on her wall, pressed and ready to wear tonight at the social with Charles.

Delia tried to imagine how he would look, what they would talk about. She must try her best to be witty and charming, despite the fact that she had no real experience at flirting. Without letting him in on the secret of her inheritance—for Mr. Dawson at the bank had informed her he hadn't heard anything from the Nevada bank yet—she wanted Charles Ladley to realize she wasn't just a timid little church mouse, the preacher's granddaughter, anymore. Delia had seen the succession of belles on his arm just as the old seamstress had, and she wanted to be their equal— no, she wanted to be more enchanting than any of them!

But why had Charles Ladley come around *at this particular time?* She froze as a sudden thought struck her. Miss Susan had assured her of her discretion, and so had Amos Dawson—but could she really trust the banker as much as she did Miss Susan?

About two years ago, it had seemed for a brief time that Charles was sweet on her, but nothing had happened; ever since then he had been nothing more than polite. Yet three days after she had shown the bank president the certificate from the Nevada bank, Charles had come calling, armed with roses and an invitation. *Surely it was only a coincidence....*

Her heart sank within her. Was the mayor's son cozying up to her now because Dawson had whispered in his ear—or perhaps Charles's father's—that she was about to become the richest heiress in the hill country?

Yet Charles's voice had been so courtly, his eyes so kind and full of interest—*genuine* interest, she told herself. He couldn't be merely putting on a show. Perhaps when Charles had failed to follow through in his flirtation with her before, it was because he had realized she was too young and too busy taking care of her grandfather. Now, with Reverend McKinney's unfortunate passing, the time was right and he was stepping forward, having never forgotten her, to show her that she was not alone in the world.

After all, he had never married, despite the numerous ladies he had courted. He had been waiting for her.

Yes, that must be it. And she could always ask him if Dawson had spoken to him about why she had come to the bank that day. If the banker had let her secret slip, Charles would either admit it, or there would be some betraying spark of guilt on his face.

There wouldn't be any such sign, though, Delia was sure of it. But she realized she was beginning to understand that wealth brought a whole new set of worries that she hadn't even had before—even before that wealth arrived.

"You do fine work, son," Heston called from his rocking chair in the shade, just as Jude pounded the last board in place that framed the new addition.

"Thank you, Mr. Heston. That's right kind of you," Jude said, taking a step back to eye his work.

"Kind, nothin'," Heston said with a snort. "Why go back to Nevada? You could probably get all the jobs you want right here in Llano Crossing." When Jude said nothing, he went on.

"You've worked real hard the past few days, Jude. Why not go along with the missus and me this evenin'?"

"Where are you going?" Jude asked, looking up. He'd been planning on taking Shiloh out for a gallop when it cooled off, to make up for all the time the horse had had to spend in his stall while Jude worked, and he was loath to give up the plan.

"The church social. Everybody brings a special dish or two—Lucy's bringin' her fried chicken. It's quite a feast. And there's music and games, and plenty of young ladies…"

Which would mean Miss Delia Keller would surely be there. He hesitated, wanting very much to see her again, knowing he should keep to his resolution to leave her be.

"No thanks. I promised my buckskin a run at sundown."

"Aw, Jude, you got to git out among folks once in a while," Heston coaxed. "Come on, you're too young to become a hermit. Just think, there might be some young filly you'd meet there—if you went, a' course."

That was exactly what he was afraid of—only he'd already met her.

"Yes, son," Heston went on expansively, "you might meet the gal a' your dreams there at this very church social. You could build a house in town and settle down with her—"

"*Whoa,* Mr. Heston!" Jude said, holding up a hand and laughing in spite of himself. "You're getting ahead of yourself, aren't you?" In spite of his words, though, Jude felt oddly touched that the old man had called him "son." Even in the short time Jude had been staying with the old couple, they had treated him with a warmth that seemed wholly beyond what Jude felt he had any right to expect as a mere employee. But how could he explain his ambivalence about seeing Delia again? On the one hand, he knew her wealth was about to put her beyond his touch; on the other, he couldn't imagine anything he wanted more than to see her again.

"If you don't go, how'm I gonna haul that heavy basket a' food one-handed?" Mr. Heston said, pointing to his arm in a sling, with the air of one achieving checkmate.

How could he argue with that? It would be ungracious to refuse to go. It was apparently meant to be. "All right," he said with a grin. "I reckon Mrs. Heston's chicken is worth changing my plans a little."

For one wistful moment, he imagined being free to court Delia Keller without hesitation and bring her as his wife to a house he had built on the edge of town. If only there had been no fortune…

But there was no way Delia Keller, heiress to a mining

fortune, could be expected to live happily ever after in what he'd be able to afford. He was a scoundrel for wishing away her good fortune, even for a moment. And he'd do well to remember that a man who had done what he had wasn't fit to court an innocent girl like Delia, even if she had not inherited a penny.

"Miss Delia, you are the very *vision* of loveliness, even in black," Charles Ladley said as she opened the door to him that evening. "I will be the envy of every man present."

Delia flushed with pleasure. The mirror had told her she looked good, but it must have understated the truth, for the light in her escort's eyes told her she was the fairest of all women.

Enjoying the elation that zinged through her at his open admiration, she gave him a flirtatious smile. "You look very presentable yourself, Mr. Ladley."

And that was an understatement, too. His blond hair and mustache gleamed in the light shed by the setting sun. He wore a black frock coat and waistcoat over pin-striped trousers with a gleaming white shirt and string tie. A gold watch fob across his waistcoat disappeared into a pocket. A single yellow rosebud was pinned to his lapel.

"Here. My mother sent this," he said, bringing his hand, which had been hidden behind him, forward. In it was a small corsage of white roses. "She thought it would be all right if your flowers were white." He meant, she knew that it would be socially acceptable to wear white flowers with mourning.

"They're beautiful," she said. "Thank you so much, Charles." She pinned them in place on her bodice, with the pearl-headed pin that had been included, and nearly laughed out loud. How would anyone dare to openly disapprove of what she wore if she had the endorsement of the mayor's wife?

"It makes me happy to make you happy," Charles said simply.

Happy? It was all she could do not to twirl around in delight in front of him, which would surely have her escort doubting her sanity.

"Shall we go? I just need to grab my wrap," she said, reaching for the wooden peg in the hall from which hung the black *crepe lisse* shawl with the ruffled edges. Miss Susan—who had said nothing about the incident with her husband—had pressed her to take it, too, when she had come to fetch the altered dress, along with the black net gloves that she now wore. The shawl provided an elegant finishing touch to her ensemble.

Delia suppressed a shiver of pleasure as Charles took the garment from her and settled it around her shoulders, then settled her gloved hand on his arm.

Since the parsonage sat only fifty yards or so down the road from the church, they would walk. This would be her last opportunity to ask him the question. She would, of course, be reassured by his answer, and then they could have a blissful evening together—the first of many, she hoped.

"Charles," she began, having rehearsed the question— and the casualness of her tone—aloud not once, but several times, "the other day, you were just about to enter the bank—"

"Ah, you mean when I very nearly knocked you over," he said. "I'm so very sorry about that—"

She cut short his apology. "I only wondered if Mr. Dawson happened to mention why I was there."

Chapter Seven

Ladley turned eyes as limpid as a Texas creek on her and immediately answered, "Why, Delia, are you afraid Amos Dawson would gossip about your private business? I assure you, he's the soul of discretion. The man's mouth is as sealed as a tomb. I should know," he said with a rueful laugh. "I've tried to get him to loosen up about other things!"

"Sealed as a tomb" didn't seem a particularly felicitous description of the banker; nevertheless, Delia felt a lightening of her apprehension.

"So he didn't tell you—"

"The purpose of your visit? I should say not!" Then Charles grew more serious, and faced her again. "I—I assumed you had come—that is, if I may ask, were you there to ask him for a loan? Miss Delia, as we've told you before, the Ladleys would never stand for the preacher's granddaughter being in want if there was something we could do to help. And there's plenty we could do, of course. Your grandfather was always too proud to accept much of what we offered him, you know. *Was* that why you were there, Delia?"

Delia had always thought her grandfather's unwillingness to take any money for his own comforts was more a matter of humility than pride, but she was comforted by Charles's answer, and by the concern in his face.

"It's nothing you need to worry yourself with," she said, making an airy gesture as she faced forward, her voice calm but firm.

"But, Delia, the Ladleys have more than enough financial resources—"

"Charles, you must allow me to have some pride, too," she insisted, her heart singing that her misgivings about him had been for nothing.

He turned to study her as they walked along. "'Pride goeth before a fall,' Delia," he chided gently, and then, before she could give voice to her protest, made a tsk-tsking noise. "Just listen to me, having the gall to quote Scripture to the preacher's granddaughter. I'm only saying my family stands ready to help whenever you have a need. You've but to ask."

"I promise I will, if it's ever necessary," she said in a voice that she hoped made it clear that while she appreciated his kindness, the subject was closed.

He patted her gloved hand on his arm as they turned onto the flagstone path that led up to the church. "And in return for your promise, *I* promise *you* we are going to have a lovely evening, Delia Keller."

The party was being held in the yard on the east side of the church. The same long tables Jude had seen set up for the preacher's funeral dinner were laden with food once again. Paper lanterns, unlit as yet since it was still light outside, hung from ropes around the perimeter of the tables.

In the center of the tables, a fiddler was playing the bouncy tune "Wait for the Wagon."

He couldn't help but scan the crowd as he and the Hestons drew near to the church. *She might not have even come tonight,* he reminded himself, *her grandfather's death being so recent and all.* However, it was as if his eyes had a will of their own.

He saw Delia Keller the moment he stepped within the perimeter of the paper lanterns, laughing and talking to a knot of people standing around her and her escort.

It was Charles Ladley, just as he had been afraid it would be. Jude swallowed acid and fought the urge to clench his fists as he spied the proprietary way Ladley gazed down at Delia as she replied to something said to her.

"Why, there's the preacher's granddaughter," Mrs. Heston cooed. "Doesn't she look pretty, in spite a' all that's happened to her lately? Even dressed in black. And isn't that the mayor's son standin' next to her? My, my, when did that happen? No wonder she's lookin' a little less melancholy than she did before!"

"When did *what* happen?" Heston growled beside her. "Ain't no law against someone standin' next to someone, last I heard. That don't mean they came together!"

"But I was planning to introduce Miss Delia to Jude," Mrs. Heston said, her tone disappointed. "Seemed to me she'd be perfect for our Jude."

"Why, so she would," agreed Mr. Heston. "Introduce 'em anyway. You never know what might happen."

Our Jude? He wondered when he had become that. As much as he cherished the old couple's warmth, he had to put a stop to their matchmaking.

He held back. "Mrs. Heston, I've told you I'm not planning on staying in town long—" he began, but Lucy Heston ignored him like the force of nature she was.

"Now, don't be bashful, Jude. A little acquaintance-makin' never hurt anybody," she said. "Oh, Delia!" she called, moving faster than Jude had known the plump woman could.

There was no avoiding the meeting. Already Delia was watching Mrs. Heston approach, though she had apparently not caught sight of Jude yet, bringing up the rear with Mr. Heston.

"Hello, Mr. and Mrs. Heston. Mr. Heston, whatever happened to you?" she asked, nodding toward his sling.

"Horse threw me." He turned toward Jude, but before he could make the introduction, his wife spoke up. "Delia, how are you gettin' along, dear?" She took Delia's two hands in her own and stood on her tiptoes to kiss the girl's cheek. "I declare, you have never looked better! And, Charles Ladley, how are you?"

She barely listened to the man's murmured answer before her attention swung back to Delia.

"Delia Keller, we'd like to present our new friend, Jude Tucker. He happened along when Jim was thrown and he's been a godsend, helping out around our place."

"Actually, we've already met, Mrs. Heston," Delia said, darting a look at him before going on to say, "Mr. Tucker happened to be installing a lock at Miss Susan's shop the same day I went in for this dress."

It was a neatly formed answer—not a lie, but not the full truth, either, so as to protect Miss Susan's reputation. He sent her an approving look.

A sudden hectic color flooded her cheeks. "Nice to see you again, Mr. Tucker," she said, extending her gloved hand. "Are you planning to stay long in these parts?"

He shrugged as his eyes drank in her appearance. "I don't rightly know just yet, ma'am. I've come from out West—" *as you know* "—and I might only be staying long enough to earn a stake to travel back there."

"But if we could give him some reason, Delia dear, maybe we could talk him into staying.…" Mrs. Heston let the heavy-handed hint dangle in the air.

As if he was determined not to be ignored any longer, Charles Ladley spoke up. "Why, the lovely town and its generous people are reason enough, wouldn't you say,

Mrs. Heston? Charles Ladley," he said, extending a hand
to Jude. "The mayor's my father. If we can be of any assistance to you…"

Ladley's voice trailed off as he shook Jude's hand. His
nails were manicured and looked as if dirt had never clung
to them, but they weren't the smooth hands of a man who
had never done any manual labor. Jude spotted the way
Ladley leaned on his cane without obviously depending on
it and the tightness of his mouth; he knew Ladley was ac-
quainted with pain. Perhaps he'd misjudged the man. Ladley had seen army service, unless Jude missed his guess.

Ladley bent low and murmured into Delia's ear, "Father's beckoning us. I think dinner's about to begin." He
straightened and faced Jude and the Hestons. "If you'll
excuse us…" He swept Delia past them.

"Never you mind, Jude," Mrs. Heston said, patting his
shoulder as if he needed consolation. "I have a notion this
is only the first time they've been out together, so nothing's
set in stone between those two. You still have a chance."

Jude was wondering what he could say to that when the
older man spoke up. "Now, Mrs. Heston, there are plenty
of other fish in the sea for a handsome fella like Jude. And
he can handle those matters himself. We ought t' butt out."

"Nonsense. I think they'd be perfect for one another,"
Mrs. Heston argued, but at that moment the mayor announced that all was ready. He would say the blessing, and
then everyone should line up at the serving table, mothers
and small children first.

His prayer was as practiced a piece of oratory as Jude
had ever heard and went on long enough that Jude could
hear little boys and girls growing restless among the crowd.
The mayor extolled the beauty the Lord had bestowed
upon the river and the hills around them and the twilight
sky above. "Bless those who mourn among us, most no-

tably our own Delia Keller, who has been so recently bereaved...."

Jude was sure that he would have mentioned each townsperson separately if a baby had not begun to wail.

"And thank you for the bounty laid before us of which we are about to partake, amen," he finished hastily.

"*Humph.* I heard the mayor's going to do the Sunday sermons at church until they get a new preacher," Mrs. Heston remarked, and it did not appear to Jude that the prospect made her happy.

"Wordy, pompous old coot," muttered her husband, as he urged his wife forward into the line.

As Heston had indicated, there were a handful of other young ladies present of varying description, and most of them found an excuse to come chat with the Hestons at their table. Mrs. Heston was in her element, introducing Jude.

Jude, standing as he was presented, was pleasant to each one and made conversation for as long as the girl lingered, but after they'd all gone back to their seats, he'd seen none of them that was Delia's equal.

"Maybe you kin eat your chocolate cake in peace if you hurry," Heston said with a chuckle. "But watch out, boy. You're a marked man now, right enough. You'll see that when you come to town, and I wouldn't be surprised if we began gettin' more visitors at the house than usual."

"It's the war," Mrs. Heston explained. "These girls hardly ever see a new fellow in town. Even two years later, it seems all that's left 'round here is graybeards and men who've come back minus a leg or an arm—not that they're not worthy, of course."

Jude pretended to listen, just as he'd pretended to enjoy each introduction. It had been nearly impossible not to look past each girl to where Delia was sitting with Ladley and his parents.

She was only picking at her food, but that didn't seem to distress her. On the contrary, she appeared to be having the time of her life, laughing at Ladley's remarks and chattering away, her graceful, long-fingered hands gesturing as she spoke. Once or twice she leaned past Ladley to answer something Mr. or Mrs. Ladley had asked, and Jude had seen Charles gaze fondly at her bent head.

The sound of a man clearing his throat at the head table where Delia was sitting barely penetrated Jude's consciousness, but then he saw Delia turn her head to look at the older man getting to his feet down the table from him.

"I'd like to make an announcement," the paunchy, well-dressed man said and waited as all around him, the people of Llano Crossing, put down forks and glasses and lifted their heads.

"That's Amos Dawson, th' banker," Heston whispered. "Wonder what he's gonna say. Hasn't the mayor done enough speechifyin' for one evenin'?"

"Now you hush, James Heston, or we won't be able to hear," his wife hissed.

"Our gracious mayor has alluded earlier to those who mourn among us, specifically our own Miss Keller," the banker began.

Jude saw Delia's eyes grow wide and the color drain from her face. Her jaw dropped open as if she wanted to speak. Jude realized at once that she knew what Dawson was about to say and that if she could have stopped him, she would have. But the man only smiled beneficently as she made a move as if to stand, and he gestured for her to remain seated.

"Now, Miss Delia, let me speak. You've always been the very essence of humility, not wanting any attention for yourself," he said. "But there are people who have been worried for you, and now you must allow them to share in your joy at the news I am about to bring."

"No, please, I don't think—" Jude heard her say. All at once Jude also knew what the banker was about to announce and why Delia wanted so desperately to keep him from speaking.

"The longtime residents of this town will remember that many years ago Miss Delia's father, Will Keller, rode off to seek his fortune out West after the tragic loss of his wife, Miss Delia's mother. When time passed and he did not return, most of us thought something ill had befallen the man and that Delia would likely never see her papa again, alas." Dawson paused to look over the crowd, avoiding Delia's pleading gaze. Satisfied that every eye was trained on him, he opened his mouth again. "But recently Miss Delia received some news that is bittersweet. Sadly, it is true that her father is dead, but he died only recently. In dying, however—and this is the sweet part, folks—he has left her the sole heiress to a fortune in silver mining profits."

Chapter Eight

Delia's cry of horror at the news being blurted out was drowned in the collective gasp of the crowd.

Succeeding at last in rising on legs that shook as if she was standing on stilts, she stared at Dawson, stammering, "You…you had no r-right…" But her words were smothered in the thunder of applause and cheers from the townspeople around her.

Dawson ducked his eyes, making motions with his hands to encourage the crowd to keep clapping and cheering.

Charles had risen, too, and had an arm around her shoulders. "Delia, dear, what an amazing thing! That is to say, I'm so sorry to hear about your father's passing, of course, but how wonderful he has left you this legacy!" His surprise seemed real enough.

"But, Charles, Mr. Dawson shouldn't have—"

He made a tsk-tsking noise. "Such news was bound to leak out soon enough," he said into her ear as he squeezed her shoulder bracingly. "And rumors would have been flying if folks had learned the news by word of mouth—you know how facts get distorted that way."

"My son's right," chimed in Mayor Ladley. "You would have been plagued with everyone's curious questions as to whether it was true. This way, everyone has heard the truth at once."

"Dear, you must allow them to rejoice with you," Jane Ladley urged. "They all wish you well."

Cries of "Speech! Speech!" and "Miss Delia, what're you going to do with all that money?" rose from the rows of tables, aimed right at her, like small stones. Every eye was on her, each person holding his or her breath to hear what she would say.

Delia opened her mouth to speak. "I... I..." She faltered. "This...all this is so n-new to me. I've hardly had time to take it in...especially since it comes with...very sad news. I hope you'll all believe me when I say I'd rather have my father back than one penny of this inheritance." She shrugged, not knowing what else to say.

As the crowd applauded again, their faces sympathetic, Delia turned to her escort, imploring, "Charles, please, would you take me home?"

"Of course, sweetheart," he murmured.

A respectful silence fell over the crowd as Delia settled her shawl around her shoulders, and Charles held out his arm to her.

"I'm sorry, Miss Delia," Dawson said, stepping forward as if to intercept her. "I meant no disrespect to the dead, you understand. I just thought everyone would want to celebrate with you."

"We will speak later, Mr. Dawson," Delia said, keeping her tone level but quickening her steps as she passed by the banker. This wasn't the appropriate setting to discuss such a matter, and she was so angry with the banker that she couldn't have trusted herself to talk with him anyway.

So angry that she had forgotten that Jude Tucker was sitting somewhere in the crowd and had seen the whole embarrassing fiasco unfold—until her eyes met his as she approached where he and the Hestons had been sitting.

He stood as she drew near and gave her a barely perceptible nod. The look in his pale eyes was one of rueful sympathy, as if he understood her dismay even better than she did. Delia felt at that moment that he comprehended her feelings perfectly.

Hardly realizing she was doing it, Delia straightened her spine and lifted her head as they left the churchyard.

Charles was silent for the short time it took them to walk down the moonlit road to her house. Then, as they reached her gate, he cleared his throat.

"Delia, I understand that you are mourning a tragic loss. Why, I can't even comprehend losing a parent...."

Delia turned her chin to look at him, but in the shadows, Charles's face was guileless.

"But I hope you will forgive me if I ask you a question." He waited until she had nodded her assent before speaking. "Don't you think your father would want you to be happy and enjoy your good fortune, not feel guilty that you're receiving it because he is no longer with you?"

She seized upon the euphemism in his question. "My father hasn't been 'with me,' as you put it, for a good part of my life. Why should I feel guilty?"

He studied her for a moment. "A poor choice of words, sweet Delia, but you know what I meant." He had stopped outside her gate and stood to face her, leaning his cane against the low stone wall.

"You meant he is *dead,*" Delia said with deliberate emphasis. "I don't know why everyone is too careful to say that word around me." She was astonished at the bitterness that had flown out of her and wished she hadn't spoken so to Charles, of all people. What must he think of her now?

"I'm so sorry, Charles, I can't imagine what made me speak so sharply...." Delia began, but then tears drowned the rest of her apology.

Suddenly Charles was pulling her into the circle of his

arms. She felt safe as the storm of her emotions broke across her.

"My poor dear, you've had such a difficult time," he murmured, his voice and his touch soothing. He let her cry for a few minutes, then he lifted his head as if hearing something from the direction of the church.

"Perhaps we should step inside your parlor, Delia dear," Charles said. "It sounds as if the party is breaking up, and—"

She didn't want the good folk of Llano Crossing to pass by on the way to their homes and see her weeping on Charles Ladley's shirtfront.

"I suppose you're right," she said, and led the way up the porch and into the house. She felt a little strange about what she was doing—she had never been alone with a man before, except for her grandfather or Amos Dawson at the bank, if that counted.

Once inside, however, she strove to calm herself by lighting the lamp on the table. When its soft glow filled the room, she turned back to Charles. "Please, sit down," she said, pointing to a threadbare horsehair couch while she sank onto the ladder-back chair nearby. "May I offer you a glass of tea?"

He waved away her offer. "No, thank you, Delia, but I'm as full as a tick that just fell off an old hound's back, as my colonel used to say back in the war."

The folksy way of speaking made her smile, as he must have known it would, since it wasn't his usual correct style of speaking. Then Delia saw a pensive expression cross his face. Of course—he had suffered in the war, and had returned with chronic pain and a cane.

"I won't stay long," he said. "It wouldn't be proper, I'm well aware. I just wanted to say that I think I know why you're distressed at what that fool Amos Dawson said."

"You do?"

He nodded. "Delia, you're used to being a very private person, and now everyone knows your business. That is the lot of the wealthy, you know," he informed her. "Everyone knows, or thinks they know, everything about you. I've experienced it since I was just a boy, Delia, and despite the Yankees' attempts to ruin the South's gracious way of living, the Ladleys still enjoy a comfortable life. But you've had that change thrust on you without warning, and you feel a bit...*uncovered,* if I may be forgiven for such an indelicate description. Isn't that right?"

She blinked in surprise. Yes, that was *exactly* how she felt. How wise, how understanding Charles was! Surely he had been sent by God to help her.

As if he could read her thoughts, Charles smiled and cupped her cheek in a caressing hand. "Don't you worry, Delia Keller. You're not alone any more, struggling to find your way. I hope we're going to see a lot more of each other, for I'd like to be there every step of the way to help you in your new life."

"You're so kind," she said. Hadn't this been what she'd dreamed of all along, having Charles at her side? Only now there would be no inequity of social position between them. It was too perfect!

"I'd best be on my way," he said, picking up his cane. "But before I go, I have something for you to think about, Delia."

Was he going to invite her out again? Where would he suggest going? "And what's that, Charles?" she asked, smiling up at him. She could hardly wait to hear what his question would be.

"What's the very first thing you would like to do with your money?"

His question was so far from what she had been thinking he would say that for a moment she was disappointed. But she wanted him to admire her for having a businesslike approach to her wealth, so she forced herself to refocus her thoughts.

"I would like to buy land and build a house," Delia told him. "A fine house, one of the best in Llano Crossing. I have to admit I'm tired of living with a leaky roof in a tiny building that lets in all the cold in the winter and all the heat in the summer."

Charles laughed. "That's the spirit! Nothing's too good for you, Delia Keller. You've been a poor little church mouse long enough."

His approval washed over her like a balm. So why did she hear the voice of her grandfather in her heart, asking what she was going to do for the Lord with her money?

But Charles was speaking again, and his voice drowned out her grandfather's. "But, Delia, why don't you wait awhile and see what the future has in store for you? Why, some handsome prince is apt to happen along, complete with his own castle, and sweep you off your feet. Then you would have spent a large chunk of your money for nothing." A small smile played about Charles's perfectly formed lips.

Delia stared at him. Was his high-flown way of speaking a way of hinting *he* wanted to be her prince?

She felt suddenly more sure of herself and decided to test Charles a bit.

"Why, who says I'll even *want* a husband, Charles Ladley? If I'm to be a woman of means, perhaps I won't even need someone to rule over me and tell me what I may spend my money on."

He seemed amused by her assertion. "No wise man would ever dream of doing so, Miss Delia. He would just count himself lucky he could share your life. And now good night, my dear."

Holding both her hands between his, he allowed himself a sigh of regret as he headed for the door. "Until we meet again…"

* * *

"Gonna get some shut-eye, Jude?" Mr. Heston asked, after they returned to their little house in town. Jude had just turned toward the barn. Although the Hestons had offered him their spare room, he'd fixed up a pallet in the small barn's tackroom and that suited him just fine.

Jude shook his head. "I reckon I'm too wide-awake to sleep just yet. I think I'll give Shiloh that gallop I promised him earlier. We'll be quiet when we return, I promise."

Heston considered that, looking out the window to peer at the full moon. "I s'pose it *is* pert' near bright as day out there, ain't it?" He turned back to Jude. "Goin' t' ride by the parsonage, to see if Miss Delia's light's still on?"

Jude paused, with one hand on the back door, then forced himself to reply casually. "No, why would I do that?"

"I got eyes in my head, son," came the old rancher's quick reply. "I saw how you were lookin' at her."

Jude sighed. He was going to have to find some polite way to deter Heston from reading his mind.

"I told you, Mr. Heston—"

"Why don't we stop the 'Mr. Heston' stuff and call me Jim? We're friends, ain't we?"

"All right, then—Jim, I told you I don't intend to court any ladies here," Jude said evenly. "I took this job so I could raise a stake to go back out West."

Now it was Heston's turn to sigh. "I'm sorry, Jude. Lucy tells me I need to learn t' tend my own knittin', and that's a fact. Forgive a curious old man, won't you? But there was somethin' about the way you were watchin' her…and watchin' Ladley watchin' her," he added frankly. "Just thought you might be goin' to see if Ladley had left her house yet. Yeah, I spied him goin' into the house with her as we left the social, same as you did," he said when Jude peered more closely at him. "And for what it's worth, I think you'd be a darn sight better man for her than the mayor's boy."

"He's hardly a boy," Jude countered. "He's been a soldier, after all."

"Aw, I remember when that pup was knee-high to a bumblebee," Heston retorted. "But what about you and Delia?"

"You heard the same news about her that I did tonight."

"That she's livin' in tall cotton now? Yeah, so what?"

"So I've got as much in common with the young lady now as I have with that moon up there," he said, nodding toward the sky. "She'll have enough fortune hunters beating a path to her door without me getting in line."

"You ain't no fortune hunter," Heston insisted, his chin jutting out stubbornly. "You were lookin' at her that way afore the announcement was ever made. I'll shut my mouth now an' let you get on with your ride. See you in the mornin'."

Jude made short work of saddling Shiloh. Minutes later, he was galloping up the road on the stallion's back, savoring the smooth play of the powerful beast's muscles beneath him and the sight of the horse's moonlit shadow eating up the ground beside him.

He deliberately rode away from town for a while, as if to deny even to himself that Heston's guess had been right about his destination. But a couple of miles up the road from where he'd first encountered the old man, the road began to climb steadily upward. Jude was too good a horseman to tax his mount by running him uphill, so he reined Shiloh around, slowed the stallion to a lope and headed back to Llano Crossing.

Most of the buildings in the town were dark, though the saloon was doing a roaring business, to judge by the tinkly music of the piano and the bright lights spilling from its dusty windows and over the batwing doors.

He might as well go ahead and do what he had really come for. Jude slowed the stallion to a trot in the direction of the far side of town and Delia Keller's house.

He hadn't realized he was holding his breath until he rounded the bend in the road. The shadowy outline of the old preacher's former abode appeared as a rectangular mass under the oak trees that blocked much of the moon's brilliance. Not one tiny candleflame shone through the drawn calico curtains at the windows.

So Delia had gone to bed, Jude thought, relieved.

"Love bears all things, believes all things, hopes all things, endures all things," a Voice suddenly reminded him, and he realized that this was the Voice he should have been listening to all along.

He smiled ruefully as he continued to gaze at the house. *Love?* Why on earth would that verse have occurred to him? On what crazy basis could he say he *loved* Delia Keller? He hardly knew her—or she, him. He had just been a messenger to her, a bearer of mixed tidings at best. His role in her life was already over, no matter how pleased she had seemed to be tonight when she saw him.

But there it was, as sure as the moon hung over his head. He loved her. *Lord, what can you be thinking?*

My ways are not your ways, the still small Voice reminded him.

He studied the house again. There was a quietness, a peace to it that somehow didn't seem possible if two people had been inside it, awake and doing things he wouldn't allow himself to think about.

Jude sighed. It was time to get home and get some rest, even if he couldn't sleep—

"Jude, is that you?" a voice said from deep in the shadows of the porch.

Chapter Nine

Jude almost fell off his horse in astonishment as a small, shawl-swathed figure detached itself from the rocker and took a step or two forward.

"Delia?" he said, hardly sure if it was really her or just wishful thinking on his part. He was barely aware of dismounting and going toward her. "What are you doing, sitting out here in the dark?" As he drew closer, he could see her more clearly. She wore some sort of flower-sprigged everyday wrapper in place of the elegant black dress he'd seen her in earlier. Bare feet peeped out appealingly from beneath the wrapper's hem. Her hair had been taken down and hung in luxurious curls nearly to her waist. He longed to touch it.

He noticed also that she had dropped the formality of calling him "Mr. Tucker," nor objected when he called her by her first name, too.

"I could ask you the same thing," Delia retorted. "At least I'm not out riding around in the dark."

"Dark? It's pert' near bright as day," he said, smiling as he quoted the old rancher. "Couldn't you sleep?"

Delia shook her head.

He could hardly believe that Delia wasn't already beating a hasty retreat inside her door. Her neighbors wouldn't think it proper for them to be visiting like this.

He took a step closer. "Are you still upset about the banker spouting your news like he did?"

Her gusty sigh stirred the ruffle along her neckline. "Yes," she admitted. "I suppose in the end it'll be easier than having to tell all the details over and over again, but I wish Mr. Dawson had asked me first." She sank down on the top step, and amazingly, patted the area next to her, clearly inviting him to sit.

Jude did as she bid, but he was careful not to sit too close.

"Charles thinks I'll have a lot to get used to now that my situation has changed," Delia said, not looking at him.

He hated having to agree with anything Ladley said, but he could hardly disagree. "He's right. Everything will be different now," he said carefully, wondering where this was leading.

Her face was lovely in moonlit profile. "I want to buy a house," she said, surprising him yet again. "A large house. A really nice house. Do you think that's silly?"

He didn't know why she was asking, but the answer seemed very important to her.

"No," he said, choosing his words carefully. "You can hardly go on living here forever—"

"That's what I was thinking," she broke in in a rush. "The church will call a new pastor, sooner or later, and I'll need a new place to live. I…" Her voice trailed off as if she would've said more but didn't think it wise.

"If you're asking me, I—I think you should pray about it, and ask God to find you the right place. But then go ahead. You've got a lot of money, Delia. Your father wanted you to be able to live well."

His answer seemed to please her, and she smiled tremulously at him. "Yes, it seems he did, didn't he? You don't…

that is, you don't think I should wait until I am married to have a house, do you?"

He tried to hide his amazement that she was asking him this question. "I think," he said, praying that the Lord would give him the right words, "that the same God who would find you the right house will be able to arrange all other aspects of your life for the best."

"Thank you, Jude," she said, eyes lit with appreciation. "How did you get to be so wise?" Impulsively, she leaned forward and kissed him on the cheek.

He was still for a few seconds, absorbing the fact that Delia Keller had just kissed him, and then he let his lips turn toward hers, his heart singing with joy. He lowered his head…

The snapping of a twig outside the gate seemed as loud as the crack of a gunshot, startling them away from each other. Jude was on his feet in a flash, the wariness of the war years causing him to instinctively shield Delia from whoever had been trying to sneak up on them.

"Who is it? Who's there?" he called, reaching for a pistol he no longer wore.

"It—it's only me," called a quavery female voice from the road. "I'm sorry…sorry to intrude."

Delia recognized her first. "Miss Susan?" she cried, leaping to her feet and running down the walk to the woman who stood outside her gate in a patch of silvery moonlight.

She was inches from the woman when the ethereal glow illumined the woman's disheveled hair, the scrape on one cheek, the swollen-shut eye and the ragged tear in her sleeve. At her feet lay a worn, stuffed carpetbag.

"Miss Susan, what happened to you?"

"I… I waited as l-long as I could.…" the woman stammered, still hesitating. "I d-didn't want anyone to see me… wanted to make s-sure *he* didn't see me… I'm sorry to intrude," she said again, looking from Delia to Jude and back again.

"Don't give it a thought," Jude said, coming forward to join Delia now and usher the woman into the house. "Did your husband do this?"

Shoulders sagging, Miss Susan nodded and let them help her inside. "He was all liquored up. He didn't really even know what he was doing."

"When did he do this?" Delia asked grimly, settling Miss Susan into a chair in the parlor.

The woman nodded. "I... I was late leaving the shop, and he caught me between it and my room at the boardinghouse. Mrs. Mannheim thought...that is, she helped me pack and said perhaps I'd better take you up on your promise to take me in."

"Of course you must stay here with me," Delia said, kneeling by Miss Susan and stroking her arm. Her eyes met Jude's.

"And tomorrow morning I'll go with you to make a complaint at the sheriff's office," Jude said.

"Nooooo!" moaned the woman.

Jude was firm. "He has to know that decent people won't allow him to treat you that way, Miss Susan—"

"But tomorrow is Sunday," she pointed out. "Everyone will be passing through town on the way to church. I can't stand for them to see me like this!"

Delia's face was sympathetic. "You know, I'd forgotten tomorrow was Sunday," she admitted. "Sheriff Jenkins will be at church. I'll ask him to call on us here in the afternoon."

"If you need me to confirm what happened at the shop, just have him call on me at the Hestons'," Jude said.

Assured that Delia could help the woman bathe her scrapes and bruises and would make her comfortable in her spare bedroom, Jude took his leave a few minutes later.

He'd had a feeling that Miss Susan's abuser would strike again, but even he hadn't thought it would be this soon. He hoped that Delia's taking the woman in wouldn't expose her to danger, too. And they'd have to be sure, Jude decided as he remounted his buckskin and headed back toward town, that one of them was available to escort the seamstress to and from her shop.

The saloon was still full of noisy drinkers, though the piano player had evidently taken a break, because no music drifted toward Jude as he neared the establishment. But as Jude drew abreast of the far side of the building, where a stairway on the side of the building led up to the second floor, he heard the sound of a footfall at the top.

During his time in the army, an unexpected sound might have meant a sniper was taking position to fire. Jude halted Shiloh in the shadow of the saloon and peered upward.

He saw Charles Ladley outlined in the moonlight at the top of the stairs, holding the door open, and heard a woman's voice. Then a bare arm reached out, handing Ladley his silver-headed cane.

Jude prayed Ladley wouldn't see him—and that the stallion didn't betray Jude's presence by snorting or stamping.

The two at the top of the stairs shared a chuckle.

"Thanks, honey, I'd have forgotten that," Ladley murmured and leaned back into the doorway a moment. Then, grinning, he resumed his descent and disappeared into the far alleyway behind the building.

Jude was thoughtful about what he had just seen, well aware that the upper floor of the saloon was where the saloon girls took the customers who wanted to spend private time with them, so to speak.

The impulsive kiss Delia had bestowed upon Jude's cheek may have only been meant in a friendly way—he didn't know, for Miss Susan's arrival had interrupted him just as he was about to kiss her in return. He didn't know how she truly felt about Charles Ladley.

What if she was smitten with Ladley? Jude was sure she didn't know the man secretly liked spending time with women of ill repute. Did Jude have an obligation to tell Delia what he had seen?

He listened for the still small Voice, but at the moment it was silent.

Even if it hadn't meant leaving Miss Susan alone at the house, Delia would have dreaded going to church. It had always been the highlight of her week before. Now, however, not only was her beloved grandfather gone, but there would be no preacher in the pulpit. Also, last night's revelation of her new fortune would still be uppermost in the minds of many of the townspeople. She would have to face their questions after the service.

But Charles will be there, she reminded herself, humming a hymn as she dressed. She'd have to find a time to tell him about Miss Susan staying with her.

What about Jude Tucker? Would he attend? Last night, he hadn't mentioned going. What had he thought of her kiss? She was almost certain he had been about to kiss her—and not only on her cheek as she had done, either— but then Miss Susan had arrived and the moment had ended.

Charles was waiting for her at the church door. He led her to the front pew where his mother was sitting. His father was already standing by the pulpit. Jane Ladley was all graciousness in her greeting as Delia took her place between her and Charles. Delia, who had always used the time before the opening hymn to quiet her heart and turn her mind toward worship, hoped she wasn't expected to make lively conversation with the mayor's wife.

She was in luck. She had no sooner settled herself when

Mrs. Purvis struck up the first notes of "Shall We Gather at the River" on the aged organ. Those already seated stood and began to sing while stragglers filed in.

During the second hymn, Delia spotted the Hestons in one of the middle pews. Jude Tucker, however, was not among them.

So he isn't a churchgoer. It's none of your concern, anyway, she told herself, wrenching her attention back to the words of the song and Charles's pleasant tenor.

Charles Ladley Sr. read one of the Psalms and then expounded on it in a resonant, formal voice. Fortunately he kept his remarks brief, ending modestly with a hope that a new pastor would soon be obtained to replace him so he could return to "merely" being the mayor. Everyone smiled in sympathy and a few chuckled.

Afterward, Delia found the presence of the Ladleys as good as a fence. She was greeted, but no one aimed any inquisitive remarks her way. She took advantage of the Ladleys' being drawn into conversation with Barton Jeffers, the mill owner, to ask Sheriff Jenkins to come speak to Miss Susan that afternoon, and he rather grudgingly agreed.

"Delia, dear, will you join us for dinner at our home this afternoon?" Mrs. Ladley asked her when she rejoined them.

Delia regretted having to explain why she must decline the gracious invitation. "It's so nice of you to ask, but Miss Susan is staying with me for a few days, and I don't want to leave her alone."

She saw Charles raise an eyebrow. "Oh? When did this come about?" he asked. She knew he was thinking that he'd seen no sign of her the night before when he'd come inside.

"Why not bring her along? The more the merrier!" boomed the mayor, standing behind his son.

Delia cleared her throat. "She…ah… I'm afraid she isn't feeling very well right now. Perhaps another time." She was aware of Charles's curious gaze, but she didn't want to explain more fully in front of his parents.

Delia was pensive as she prepared to leave the house the next morning. Prior to the church social and its aftermath, she had thought she might go into town Monday morning, stopping at the bank to make her first withdrawal from her account—not a large amount, but enough to pay for what she wanted. She'd then stop at Miss Susan's, where she would commission some more dresses, as well as several camisoles and petticoats of the softest lawn and the finest lace trim the seamstress could lay her hands on.

Then she would go to the general store and buy some provisions. This time she wouldn't have to limit herself to only necessities, such as flour and sugar and cornmeal. Why, if she chose, she could buy fancy jellies some *other* woman had put up or a whole sackful of peppermint sticks. And if Mr. Dean still had that lovely paisley shawl in his window, the one with the long, silky black fringe, why, it wouldn't be hanging there any longer than it took for her to snap it up.

It would be so much fun, she'd been thinking, being able to do as she wanted, rather than having to hoard every cent and pester her hens for eggs to sell. She stared in the cracked mirror in her room and thought it would be nice to buy a new mirror, one that reflected faithfully the elegant lady she was becoming. Perhaps she could find some scented cream there, too, to rub into her dry, work-worn hands, so that they became smooth like those of a woman of means, who had other people scrub her floors and wash her dishes.

Miss Susan's presence had changed her carefree mood.

The seamstress had announced this morning that she wasn't going to her shop until the swelling and bruising went down around her eye, and she asked Delia to insert a note on the door that the shop was closed until further notice. Despite the sheriff's gruff assurance that he would order Donley Morrison to leave his wife alone, Delia could understand the woman's reluctance to face the curious and pitying glances of the townspeople. It would take a week, at least, before the bruising faded. How much ought she to encourage Miss Susan to trust the townspeople's compassion and return to her regular routine?

Just as Delia inserted her final hairpin, a knock sounded at the door. Who could be calling so early? Peeking out the bedroom window, she saw that it was Jude Tucker.

She assumed he had come to check on Miss Susan, but, still, his unexpected appearance had her flying to the door as if her feet had wings.

"Good morning, Jude. My, you're up bright and early today," she said, beckoning for him to enter. "Would you like some coffee? Have you had your breakfast? We've eaten, but I could scramble some eggs, and I believe there's some jam left."

"And good morning to you, Delia," he said. "Don't you look pretty this morning? No thank you. Mrs. Heston already made her husband and me a huge breakfast."

"Are you here to check on Miss Susan?" she said, lowering her voice. "She's in the other room dressing, but I'm sure she'll be out in a minute—"

"She's doing all right? Jenkins came and listened to her account?"

"He did," she said. "And he swears he'll make sure Miss Susan won't have to worry about Morrison bothering her again. But she's still not feeling up to going to work."

"I'd give her a few days," Jude said, his eyes thoughtful. "And yes, I came to see about her, but also I'd like to take you to see something."

She stared at him. "What? Where?"

He grinned. "It's a surprise," he said. "You'll see when you get there."

Chapter Ten

"You're not going to tell me before we get there?" Delia asked as they left her house. He'd borrowed the Hestons' buckboard, she noticed.

His eyes danced teasingly as he settled himself on the seat next to her. "No, ma'am. That's why it's called a surprise."

Jude directed the horse west down the dusty road. "You haven't been out this way lately, have you?"

She shook her head. "I've been pretty much a homebody since Grandpa got so frail. Everything we needed was in town."

The buckboard rolled on for a couple of miles until it came to a bend in the road, and then Jude pulled to a halt and said, "Now close your eyes, please, to get the full effect."

Obediently, Delia complied. She felt the wagon roll go around the turn in the road, and then Jude called, "Whoa."

"Now you can open your eyes," he said beside her.

There before her, on a gentle rise above the Llano River, sat the wooden frame of a large, unfinished two-story house. It was flanked by cottonwoods and a barn, with a couple of venerable, gnarled oak trees shading the front.

Delia blinked. "Whose place is this?"

Jude's smile broadened. "Yours, if you choose to make it so, Delia. It includes five acres, too."

She continued to stare at him in confusion. "But who started this? Why didn't they finish it?"

"I'm told a couple of Yankee speculators bought the site from an old couple—did you know the Delaceys, who moved to Houston? The speculators razed the smaller old house and started to build."

Delia searched her memory. "I remember the Delaceys moving. They were two of the oldest members of the church. And I heard about two Yankees coming to town, trying to buy up land right after the war, but I never heard what became of their project. Grandpa didn't keep up with such things. Do you know what happened to them?"

"Mr. Heston said some men in the town convinced them they wouldn't be happy here after all...."

"'Convinced them'?" Delia echoed.

"That's all he would say, but he didn't sound like he approved of whatever their tactics were. The Yankees sold the property back to the bank and left."

Delia stared at the unfinished house, which was big enough to hold four or even more buildings the size of the parsonage, then back at Jude. "So you're saying that I—"

"Might be able to buy this place for a very fair price. It's not completed, obviously, so it would be a while until you could move in, but that's also its great advantage, Delia. You could have it finished to your own specifications."

Delia felt a rising sense of excitement. "So I could..." she murmured, continuing to gaze at the building. "Oh, Jude, could I see the inside?"

Jude grinned. "I rather thought you'd want to." Setting the brake, he stepped down from the wagon and held out his hand to assist her. She took it, feeling the calluses of hard manual work.

Too exhilarated to be ladylike, Delia ran the few yards

into the house. Inside, there were no room divisions, only a rock chimney on one side and a plank stairway in the middle that led to the second story.

"This could be the drawing room," she said, pointing to the chimney side of the first floor. "And the kitchen, back there, and perhaps a parlor, over there," she added, gesturing in each direction in turn. "Can we go upstairs?" she asked.

Jude, clearly pleased at her enthusiasm, offered his hand again. "Allow me to assist you, ma'am. In place of this," he said, indicating the rough-hewn railing, "you could have a polished pecanwood banister and stairs."

"Oh, Jude," she said, as they reached the top. "This is so wonderful. Why, there's room for at least *six* bedrooms up here, even if I make mine large." She gazed out one of the framed openings for a window and gave a laugh of pure joy as she took in the view of the Llano River flowing close by, the rolling, tree-dotted countryside beyond it and the blue hills in the distance.

"You want it, don't you?" he said, as they descended the stairs once more. It was more a statement than a question.

Delia paused. "Can I…can I afford it?" she wondered aloud. Jude knew the amount of her inheritance.

Jude said, "I believe so, but of course you should think about it carefully."

"And pray about it, my grandpa would say," she mused.

Jude nodded.

Delia closed her eyes. She could imagine living here— no more leaky roof and drafts and the parties she could hold here, with guests spending the night upstairs if they chose. And someday, maybe some of the bedrooms would hold her children… *But who would be her husband—and their father?*

What would Charles say about this place? She imagined showing it to him. When she had spoken about wanting to buy a house, he had suggested she wait and let a husband provide it for her. Would he change his stance on the subject when he saw this place?

She felt a blush creeping up her neck and looked away from Jude. She felt so confused. She had been attracted to Jude on the day they met, but he had actively discouraged her on that score. Yet he had found this place for her. Charles, meanwhile, had made it clear that he was quite interested in her. If only she knew what Jude had been thinking about her kiss and what would have happened next.

"I'll have to meet with Mr. Dawson," she thought aloud, gazing at the unfinished house. "If after meeting with him, he confirms I can afford it—considering the cost of finishing it, too, of course—I'll take it."

"Very businesslike, Delia," Jude said.

"My grandfather had always taught me to count the cost of a project before beginning it," she replied modestly, but then had a sudden thought. "Speaking of which, where on earth will I find someone to finish this place for me?"

Jude grinned innocently. "Well… I *am* a carpenter. And the work I'm doing for the Hestons won't take much longer—"

"You could do this all by yourself?"

"There's some parts I might have to find a couple of fellows to help me with," he agreed. "But that shouldn't be hard."

"So finding this place for me was a scheme to get work?" Delia asked. She was unable to subdue a pang of disappointment that this might have been his sole motive.

His eyes under his broad-brimmed hat were hooded, unreadable in the bright sunlight. "Seemed to me I could kill two birds with one stone," he said. "I found a source of employment—a reason to stay for a spell, rather than riding on—and something you were wanting, Delia."

Delia resolved to go to the bank this very day and

speak to Amos Dawson and get the paperwork started if he thought it was feasible for her. And she would speak to God about it, too, when she said her bedtime prayers.

"How soon could you finish it?" she asked as they got back into the wagon and headed back toward her house. "The only difficulty would be if the deacons find a new pastor before you do—but I suppose if that happened I could take a room in the hotel for a time."

"It's September now. With good weather, I reckon you could be in there by Thanksgiving, maybe sooner," Jude said.

Another thought came to her as they rolled along. "I think with some of my money I'll pay for some improvements to the old place, and you could do those, too. A new preacher and his family deserve a new roof and new paint throughout, at the very least."

Jude looked at her with approval. "You are quite a generous lady, Delia Keller. Quite a lady indeed."

After checking on Miss Susan, whose spirits seemed a bit brighter than they had been earlier, Delia decided to go straight to the bank. No one else had any interest in the half-finished house, as far as she knew, but she didn't want to take any chance of losing it to another buyer. That house was meant to be hers.

Amos Dawson was pleased to see her, judging by the promptness with which she was ushered into his private office by the same wispy young teller who, before the news of her fortune, had acted as if her entering the bank was an imposition. Now, before leaving Delia with Dawson, he offered Delia a glass of lemonade and freshly baked cookies. Delia accepted both with a gracious smile.

"Miss Keller, how might the Llano Crossing Bank serve your needs today?" Dawson said, beaming after the teller had left them alone.

Delia told him of her interest in the Delacey place, without mentioning how she had learned of it.

"Ah, splendid!" the banker cried, clapping his hands together. "The property would be eminently suitable for you, Miss Keller."

"It would be if the price is right," Delia responded, injecting briskness into her voice. It wouldn't be wise to show just how much she wanted the place. "I've no intention of being foolish with my money."

"Of course not," Dawson responded, his face bland as buttermilk. He took up a sheet of paper and, dipping a pen into the inkwell above his blotter, scratched something on it and handed the sheet across the desk to Delia. "This is what the bank is owed for the property and the house."

Delia, studying the amount he had written, was careful to keep her features as blank as the paper had been moments before. Sure the cost had been inflated at least a little, she named a sum several hundred dollars less.

Mr. Dawson hesitated. "You drive a hard bargain, Miss Keller, but it's been on the bank's books for a long time. Very well, the bank accepts your offer."

Delia just smiled. "Excellent."

"We'll begin drawing up the papers immediately," Dawson went on. "I'm delighted you are planning on remaining in Llano Crossing. Oh, and may I suggest a group of fine German craftsmen from Gillespie Springs to finish your house?"

"Thank you," Delia said, "but I have someone in mind already for that." She saw a curious gleam in the banker's eyes and decided not to satisfy it. "He thought I would be able to move in by Thanksgiving, if all goes well."

"Of course, you may not have acquired all your furnishings by then," the banker pointed out. "It'll take time to select quality pieces and have them shipped to Llano Crossing."

"I had thought of seeing what Mr. Dean had at the mercantile," she said aloud, while wondering if Jude's talents included furniture-making.

Dawson sniffed his disdain. "As a stopgap measure, perhaps. But I am in touch with craftsmen who know how to make furniture fit for a lady in your position. Why, I've even assisted Mrs. Ladley in such purchases."

"I'll keep that in mind," Delia murmured noncommittally. She would have to be careful not to place herself too thoroughly in Dawson's hands or she would drain her legacy in a matter of months.

She rose. "Thank you, Mr. Dawson. When will the papers be ready for my signature?"

"Tomorrow, Miss Keller. Shall we say nine?"

Delia nodded, already thinking ahead. After she signed, she might do some of that shopping she had been contemplating.

"Oh, and there's another matter you might give some consideration," he added before she could reach the door.

Delia turned back reluctantly. Property, workmen, lodging, furnishings—didn't she have enough to ponder already?

"Investments," he said, scuttling toward her as if he feared she might take wing before he could utter the word. "You must consider putting the balance of your money to work for you, so it can grow. There are a myriad of ways—stocks, real estate, and the Committee for Civic Improvement has been investigating some ways of improving the town as a whole."

"Of course," she said, feeling her head beginning to ache. Her life had been so uncomplicated before this.

He must have seen that she was growing weary. "But I have taken enough of your time, Miss Keller. There is no need to discuss such a detailed subject today. Once construction of your house is under way, and you can spare me an hour or so, perhaps then..."

"Certainly, Mr. Dawson," she said, and made her escape before he could bring up anything else.

Outside, she was surprised to find Charles Ladley sitting in his landau, as if he were waiting for her.

"I saw you go in," he said, taking off his hat to mop his brow. "I must say, I didn't think you'd be in there as long as that. Conducting weighty business, Miss Keller?"

"You might say so," she said with a wink. "Charles, if you have time, I want to show you something."

He looked intrigued. "My carriage is at your disposal, milady," he said, reaching down a hand to assist her to get in.

Minutes later, they reached the site. "I'm buying this place," she told him. "That's why I was at the bank. Would you like to see the inside?"

"Of course." He followed her into the building, listening impassively as she described what she planned to do with it. Leaning heavily on his cane, he followed her up the crude stairway to see the upper floor, gazing in all directions, admiring the view as she had.

"It's perfect for me, don't you think?"

"It could be pleasant, once a lot of work is done," he said. "How did you find it?"

Delia had known the question would come. She knew she could just say she'd been out exploring and come across it, but it wasn't in her to lie. "Jude Tucker thought I might like it," she said, watching him carefully to see how he would react.

His jaw hardened and his expressive eyes went flat. "Oh? So you've been confiding your dreams to Tucker, have you?"

He was hurt, she thought with a guilty pang. "I wouldn't say that," she said carefully. "He's looking for work, and he knew I was in the market for a house, that's all." She wouldn't blush if she didn't think about how she had told Jude of her need on her shadowy porch at midnight.

"I see."

"It could be done by Thanksgiving, he thinks. But I'll need your advice in choosing furniture and drapery and such things," she added, hoping that would appeal to him, "since most of the furniture in the parsonage is pretty old and worn. The only difficulty will be if the church board finds a new pastor before the house is finished, but I could take a room at the hotel." She became aware she was chattering to fill the heavy silence.

"You know you can count on my assistance," he said. "And you must do as you please, of course. But it all seems so unnecessary."

She blinked, uncertain of his meaning.

"My parents wouldn't hear of your staying alone at a hotel when we have several guest rooms at Ladley House," he explained impatiently. "You could move in tomorrow, if you wanted. And you should. It's hardly fitting that you stay in that tumbledown old shack in the current circumstances."

Delia opened her mouth to defend the old parsonage. She knew every nook and cranny of it. It had known all her grandpa's and her joys and sorrows and had been home to them for many years. It wasn't such an awful place. But soon it wouldn't be hers anymore.

Charles raised a hand and went on. "Don't you see, if you moved into Ladley House, we could spend more time together—all under strictly proper circumstances. I—I hadn't meant to speak about it so soon, with you in mourning, but I have great hopes for a future with you. And I had thought that finding a house would be something we did *together*."

Chapter Eleven

She couldn't stifle her gasp. "I—I didn't realize you were thinking of such things...." She felt as if she were being swept along in the middle of the Llano River at floodstage.

Charles looked crestfallen. "I think I've tried to move things along too fast, Delia. It's a failing I have. I'm sorry."

The sight of his downcast face distracted Delia from her doubts. "Oh, Charles, I'm not saying no. It's just...just too soon for me to make such a big decision."

Charles smiled unexpectedly. "Delia, you are as wise as you are beautiful. And brave and hospitable, too. It's kind of you to offer shelter to Miss Susan."

Shelter? He seemed to know more than what she had told him and his parents on Sunday.

"I saw Dixon Miller earlier today, and he mentioned the sheriff had spoken to him about his cowhand Donley Morrison," Charles explained. "Does she plan to stay with you long? Mightn't they reconcile sooner if...if she wasn't avoiding him?"

He couldn't know the whole story if he was asking that, she reasoned. "What she's avoiding are his fists, Charles— and his demands for her money so he can buy whiskey."

He looked shocked. "I see. Very well, but be careful,

won't you? Men who would abuse their wives are dangerous, and they wouldn't scruple at harming those who try
to stop them, either."

Delia and Miss Susan were just doing their dinner
dishes the next night when Jude showed up at her door.

"Evening, Delia. Miss Susan, how're you feeling,
ma'am?"

Delia saw the older woman's face turn pink with appreciation that he'd asked.

"Better, on the whole. It's fascinating watching this—"
she indicated her bruised eye, which she could now open
"—turning from black to purple to green," she said with a
wry twist to her lips. "I think I'll go back to work tomorrow, just for the pleasure of watching folks goggle at it."

"That's the spirit." Jude smiled. "Delia, I brought these
drawings over for you to see." He handed her several sheets
of paper with detailed drawings of how he planned to finish her house and a sketch of the house as he imagined it
would look from the outside when completed. It was obvious he'd put considerable thought into it, and she said so.

"Make any changes you'd like," Jude said, gesturing toward the drawing. "It's going to be *your* house, after all."

"Well, how about a larger window, here," she said,
pointing to the parlor area. "And could there be a veranda?"

"You're the boss, ma'am," he said agreeably. "I'll be
finished with what I'm doing for the Hestons by the end
of the week, so I can start immediately after that. I'm
going to be staying with them, at least till Mr. Heston's
arm is fully mended, so you can let me know if you think
of anything else."

After Miss Susan had admired his work also, she excused herself, saying she had some mending to do, leaving Jude and Delia together on the porch.

There was a pleasant breeze, with a hint of coolness

to the air, now that the heat of the day was over. Fall was indeed imminent.

Jude felt in no hurry to leave, and Delia seemed pleased at that. The silence between them was companionable.

"Jude, what was your occupation?" Delia asked, after a while. "Before the war, I mean. Did you work as a carpenter then?"

Jude sighed, his eyes on the rolling blue hills just visible over the tops of the mesquite trees. He'd figured Delia would get around to this question eventually, and he cared too much about her to try to fob her off with some vague answer.

"You don't have to tell me," Delia said, before Jude could speak. "If you'd rather not. It's not polite to pry. You just didn't seem like you're running from the law or anything."

"No, I'm no desperado on the loose," Jude said, smiling to show her he didn't mind her asking. *I'm just running from myself.*

"Nor like some man who left a wife and seven children back East," Delia added.

Jude's smile broadened. "No, I didn't do that, either. I've never been married—nor a father." He sighed again, shifting his gaze to the drawings she still held. "All right, but I have to say before I tell you anything more—that part of my life is over now."

Delia lifted her hands in a gesture to indicate Jude's terms were understood.

"I learned carpentry at my father's knee, but then I became a preacher," Jude said. "I had a church in the little town of Mount Mulberry, Tennessee."

Delia's eyes flew open in astonishment. She seemed to be waiting for him to say something else, but when he didn't, she finally asked, "So why aren't you one now?"

Jude thought about the blood and noise and the senseless losses of a battle. And he thought of Nora and the way she'd scarred his soul. He wanted to be honest with Delia, but she'd never look at him the same if she knew. And some pains were just too private to expose.

"War changes a man," he said at last, hoping Delia would leave it at that. "I've done things that make going back to preaching impossible."

He saw puzzlement cloud her green eyes. "But, Jude, the Lord will forgive anything. The Bible says so. You just have to ask Him."

"I have. And I believe He's forgiven me. But…" *But I can't forgive myself.*

Delia gave him an exasperated look. "Jude, the pulpit's standing empty right here in Llano Crossing."

"I told you, that part of my life is over."

"I don't mean being a carpenter can't be serving the Lord, too," she said, her tone conciliatory. "Jesus was a carpenter, after all."

"Besides," Jude argued, "I thought you said the mayor was taking over the preaching until a preacher could be found."

Delia looked down at her hands for a moment. "Mr. Ladley tries, but he's no pastor—which you would know if you came to church," she finished tartly, her eyes returning to his. "Why weren't you there Sunday? Maybe if you came it would give you a calling for it again."

Now it was Jude's turn to look away. Mr. Heston had asked Jude to attend with them yesterday, but he'd declined with some vague excuse. But there was some truth in Delia's last words, too—Jude was afraid that, inside the sanctuary in the midst of a church service, he'd feel that desire to preach the Word again, only to know he was no longer worthy.

And he hadn't liked the possibility that he'd see Delia Keller sitting with the mayor's son.

"Okay," said Delia, when he said nothing more, "but please consider coming next Sunday."

Her appeal made him suddenly irresolute. He wanted to please her, but what would be the outcome?

"Maybe I will," he said.

"Knowing you were a preacher explains a lot," Delia said, surprising him. "Your compassion with Miss Susan, for example. I imagine you were very good at it—at pastoring, I mean."

He had been, until war had challenged his basic assumptions about the goodness of men—and his own ability to withstand temptation.

"Please...you won't tell anyone what I told you, will you?" he said.

She sighed. "All right, but I warn you, I'm going to be praying that you feel the calling again," Delia informed him. "After you finish my house, of course," she added with a smile.

She was going to pray about him. The idea mattered to him more than he wanted it to.

"I hope you're praying for rain, while you're at it. We could use some," he said lightly, to defuse her seriousness. He nodded toward the dried grass in her yard.

"That's a good man," Miss Susan murmured, coming back onto the porch after Jude had ridden off in direction of town. "He's worth ten of Charles Ladley."

Delia wondered if she'd overheard what he'd told her, but Miss Susan didn't seem the type to eavesdrop.

"You've met Jude...what, three times now? What makes you say that?" Delia asked, not in an argumentative way, but in a tone that showed she really wanted to know.

"It's something a body can just *tell*, that's all. Especially when you get to be my age."

"I think Charles is a good man, too," Delia put in mildly.

"He's been very kind to me—not only him but all his family. I've liked him all my life—and at last he seems to like me, too." She wondered what Miss Susan would say if she knew Charles had asked her to stay with his family so they could get to know each other better, all but saying it was a prelude to marriage—and that he said he preferred that they buy a house together someday soon.

"Humph!" Miss Susan snorted. "There's kind and there's kind that expects to *get.* I don't like to tell you your business, Delia. Just look deep, before you make up your mind."

"Make up my mind?" Delia repeated. "Jude's made it perfectly clear that he's not interested in me that way or in settling here. I need a house, and he wants work. It's as simple as that. And Charles and I have more in common now..."

Miss Susan put her hands on her hips. "Jude Tucker's not *interested?* Delia Keller, open your eyes! He may say he's not, but look at what he *does.*"

Delia could only stare at her while Miss Susan's words echoed in her soul. "I'll think about it," she promised.

"I wish Reverend McKinney were still here. He'd tell you the same thing I am. And you know he'd tell you to pray about it."

"I wish he were here, too," Delia said bleakly and not only because of those two men.

"How's your courtship of the lovely young Delia going?" Charles Ladley, senior, asked his son over port and cigars in a private room off the hotel's dining room. "Things moving right along?"

Soon the other members of the Committee for Civic Improvement would be walking in, but for now it was pleasant to lean back and chat with his father after a sumptuous meal.

The younger Charles grinned at his father through a haze of aromatic blue smoke. "It's going well, I'd say. Of course, I'm having to proceed slowly," he admitted, thinking of their conversation after he'd seen the house she was buying, "her bein' a preacher's granddaughter and all. Don't want to spook the filly before she's saddled—with matrimony—do I?" He didn't want his father to know how he'd nearly scared Delia away by pressuring her too soon.

The elder Ladley chuckled at the image. "Boy, you're a chip off the old block, indeed you are! But don't go *too* slow and let some other man catch her eye. Be a little bold. The ladies like that, now and again."

His son quirked a brow. "What do you suggest, Father?"

The mayor blew a smoke ring and thought about it for a long moment.

"An expensive gift might be just the thing. Something so valuable she knows she really shouldn't accept it since you're not betrothed but something so delightful that she really can't bear to let it go."

Charles was hesitant. "But don't we need to save money for…our project? It doesn't seem the time to be spending—"

"Boy, sometimes you have to spend money to make money, haven't I taught you that? If you can gull that girl into marrying you—the sooner the better—we'll have even more money to achieve our goal than if we only fleece the town, you see?"

Father and son smiled together in perfect accord.

"Hmm… I think I've thought of the perfect thing," Charles murmured.

Chapter Twelve

"That was such fun, Charles!" Delia said a few days later, as they walked their mounts back to town to cool them down after an exhilarating gallop on the road south of town. "I'd forgotten how wonderful it felt to go so fast and feel the wind in my hair! I felt like I was flying!" She reached down and patted the glossy neck of the gelding she'd borrowed from the Ladley stables.

"You're a natural horsewoman," Charles praised. "Even though you weren't used to a sidesaddle."

"You're very tactful—and Midnight's very forgiving of my rustiness," she said, patting the horse again. "Papa used to take me up on his horse, and we never told Mama how fast we'd go, but after he left all I had to ride was Grandpa's mule that passed on long ago."

"Mother told me to tell you to keep her riding habit and the hat, since she doesn't ride much anymore. The habit fits as if it were made for you," he added, his gaze frankly admiring.

"How kind of her!" Delia said, flushing with his praise. She was aware that the habit emphasized her trim waist and that the deep green hue flattered her coloring.

"Sure you won't change your mind and come back to the house for a cold drink?" Charles coaxed, as they drew up in front of the mercantile. "Cook makes the best iced tea in Texas, and Manuel got fresh ice from the ice house this morning."

"I'd like to, but now that I've played this morning when I should be planning for the new house, I'd better stop in here as I'd planned," she told him, handing him the reins and dismounting. "Oh! I'd forgotten how stiff one gets when one doesn't ride often!" she said, self-conscious about the awkward way she was walking.

"We can soon remedy that," he told her. "You have to remember, you're a lady of leisure now."

"Wonder if you'd mind goin' with Lucy on some errands?" Heston said that morning. "She had her heart set on gettin' supplies at the general store today—says she's out a' flour an' cornmeal an' everything, but Doc Jones says my arm won't be ready t' carry loads for a spell."

Jude had pronounced the room addition finished just an hour ago, and he'd actually planned to visit the mill and check out their lumber supply that morning, but it could wait till later. "Just let me stick my head under the pump handle." He was hot from his exertions, and he hadn't shaved, but he supposed he looked respectable enough to be seen with Mrs. Heston.

Once they'd picked up supplies at the general store, though, Mrs. Heston confessed that she also had a hankering to visit the mercantile and perhaps then the seamstress's shop. She hadn't had a new Sunday go-to-meetin' dress in five years, and her eyes were getting too bad to sew her own.

Jude groaned inwardly as he lifted the brown-wrapped packages and prepared to follow Mrs. Heston to the mercantile, realizing that by the time they'd visited two more places, the mill might be closed. He'd learned it closed at noon on Friday. He'd hoped to have the wood and other supplies delivered Saturday morning, but he reminded himself how good the Hestons had been to him, providing him with a roof over his head and three square meals a day. He could go to the mill on Saturday morning and maybe even talk Barton Jeffers into delivering the same day.

Jude climbed up the three stone stairs to the boardwalk, following Mrs. Heston, and stepped into the mercantile.

"Why, look who's here, Jude!" Mrs. Heston's voice rang out before his eyes had even adjusted from the bright sunlight to the pleasant dimness inside the store. "Just look who I've found in here!"

Delia shifted her gaze from the shorter Mrs. Heston to the lean figure backlit by the doorway. He strode toward them, his boot heels thudding on the flooring.

She was surprised to feel her pulse accelerate. Goodness, she had forgotten Jude Tucker was so tall—he had to be at least a head taller than Charles. She felt almost tiny as he stopped in front of her, those pale wolf eyes studying her as his mouth relaxed into a smile.

"Looks like you're too late, Mrs. Heston," he said in that gravelly voice of his. "Miss Keller's already bought out the store." He gestured toward the mound of parcels of various sizes and shapes, to which Mr. Dean, the proprietor, was still adding. There was also a carved wooden vanity table and matching stool that stood next to Delia, which she had apparently purchased as well.

Mrs. Heston chuckled.

Delia smiled back at Jude. "Oh, no, I've only bought a few things I've been needing," she said, trying to keep her voice light and carefree. She couldn't imagine why this man affected her the way he did—his appearance was so rough and uncouth next to Charles's polished gentility. From what she had seen, Charles never had left his house unless he was immaculately groomed.

Today, unshaven and dressed in a worn shirt and trousers, Jude Tucker looked almost dangerous—like an out-law on the run.

"I see you've been riding, dear," Mrs. Heston was saying, gesturing toward the riding habit Delia was wearing.

Jude peered over his shoulders to the empty hitching rail outside. "Where's your horse? I didn't know you had one—did you just buy it?"

"No, Charles loaned me one of their geldings, and he took him back to their stable," Delia explained, not missing the way Jude's smile faded, his eyes becoming remote, wintry.

She turned back to Mrs. Heston. "I'd forgotten how enjoyable it was!" she went on. "I think I'll have to make a good saddle horse one of my next purchases."

"I'm sure Jude could help you with that," Mrs. Heston told her, beaming at Jude. "That Shiloh of his is so gentle for a stallion. Why, he eats sugar lumps right from my hand."

"She's spoiled him for good—me, too, for that matter," Jude said, though his smile somehow didn't reach his eyes as he looked at Delia. "They've made me so welcome, it'll be hard to leave when it's time to go back West."

"Well, *we* hope he'll never leave," Mrs. Heston put in. "He's become indispensable to Jim and me—like the son we never had."

Jude was clearly touched by the old woman's praise, Delia noted, but then Mrs. Heston was speaking again and Delia was forced to wrest her gaze from Jude.

"I hear you bought the old Delacey place, Delia, and Jude's going to finish it for you."

"Yes, it's going to be wonderful. A palace, compared to the parsonage. I still have to pinch myself to make sure I'm not dreaming!"

"How exciting, Delia! I'm sure your grandpa would be so pleased for you," Mrs. Heston gushed. "Or I should say, I *know* he's lookin' down from Heaven, and he's tickled p—"

Delia wanted to beat a hasty retreat from the now grim-faced man in front of her. Seeing that Mr. Dean had finished wrapping her purchases, she interrupted the older lady's flow. "Yes, I'm sure you're right. But I mustn't hold you up, Mrs. Heston," Delia said. "Give your husband my best."

"And how are you planning on getting all those things home, Delia?" Mrs. Heston asked. "You can't possibly carry all that."

"I'm not. Mr. Dean is going to deliver it. Of course, he can't do that until he closes at the end of the day—"

"Nonsense," Lucy Heston cut in. "Jude could borrow the wagon to take those things now, couldn't he, Mr. Dean?"

The mercantile owner agreed.

"You go on with Jude, Delia. I know Jude's bored to death, keeping an old woman company."

"But what about your purchases, Mrs. Heston?" Delia asked, not at all certain she wanted to be alone with Jude after his disapproving looks.

"I still need to visit Miss Susan's, and Mr. Dean will hold those things till you come back. Take your time, mind," she added, when Jude looked as if he was going to protest.

"But, Mrs. Heston, it's not necessary, really," Delia said. If Jude didn't want to help her, she certainly didn't want his assistance—Lucy Heston didn't know what she was getting Delia into.

"It's no problem, dear," Mrs. Heston insisted, and Delia was sure she saw a twinkle of mischief in the old woman's eyes.

Jude said nothing throughout the process of loading the buckboard and wordlessly assisted Delia to climb aboard.

Nor did it seem like he planned to speak on the short drive back to the parsonage.

"Nice weather we're having," she said at last, desperate to break the silence. "Mild for September…"

"I reckon."

She was going to have to be more direct. "I—I'm sorry Mrs. Heston got you into this," Delia said, "even though it'll be nice not having to wait on the things to be delivered."

"It's nothing." He unloaded her purchases and brought them into the house with the same silent efficiency as when he had loaded them onto the wagon. Finally he wiped his brow with his handkerchief.

"That's it, then." He took a step toward the door.

"Would you like some cold lemonade from the springhouse?" Delia offered, then wondered why she was trying to delay his leaving. He'd done her the favor he had come to do.

"There's no need to trouble yourself, Delia." His gaze was fixed at some point slightly above her head.

"It's the least I can do to thank you for helping me get these things home," she said.

He shrugged. "All right, if you're sure it's no trouble. And if you're sure Charles Ladley won't mind," he added, those pale eyes on hers.

At first she couldn't believe he had said it.

She felt a spark of anger. "Why would Charles mind me offering a glass of cold lemonade to a friend who did me a favor?"

He shrugged, avoiding Delia's gaze.

"Charles doesn't own me. He's a *friend,* too."

His head snapped up at that. "Oh, he wants to be much more than your friend."

"What's that supposed to mean?"

"Has he asked you to marry him, Delia?"

Delia felt herself blushing, furious with Jude for asking because she couldn't exactly say no—Charles *had* admitted he was looking forward to a future with her. "It's much too soon for me to be thinking of such a thing—even if I weren't in mourning," she reminded him, with a pointed glance at her black dress. She was angry at herself, too, for blushing, knowing that Jude would take that for an admission, no matter what she said.

"Taking refuge in vagueness, Delia?" His words were like a slap.

She gave him a bitter laugh. "I guess you won't care if he courts me since you *won't!*"

The gleam in his eyes went dangerous. "I'll show you how much I 'don't care,' Delia," he said, then crossed the room in two quick strides, catching her face between his two hands and kissing her until neither of them could breathe. Delia was too shocked to struggle.

Then he let her go just as quickly, and all they could do was stare at one another while they tried in vain to catch their breath.

Jude looked just as angry as he had looked before.

Finally, Delia drew herself up in icy dignity. "Perhaps that lemonade wouldn't be a good idea after all."

Jude had gone very still. "I reckon not, Miss Keller. Please excuse me." He stalked toward the door, grabbing his hat up off the table where he'd left it.

She whirled away from him, praying she wouldn't start crying before he was gone.

Chapter Thirteen

"Well, ain't that a nice sight," commented James Heston, coming into the tackroom that Jude used as his room in the barn. Jude looked up from the Bible that lay open on his knees.

In the week since his confrontation with Delia, he'd kept busy with odd jobs for the Hestons and their friends around town. But he hadn't done anything further about buying the lumber for Delia's house, nor had she sent word that she'd found someone else for the job. Pretty soon he would be out of excuses for remaining in Llano Crossing.

Every time he dreamed, it was of Delia Keller, her green eyes hot with anger at him. Charles Ladley was always present, sometimes smirking in the background, sometimes with his arm around Delia. In the illogical way of dreams, all three of them stood at the pulpit of the Llano Crossing Church. On the pulpit, where the open Bible usually lay, was a coiled rattlesnake. Seemingly Delia couldn't see her danger because she leaned trustingly into Ladley, just inches from the snake, and told Jude to go away.

At this point Jude would wake up, drenched in a cold sweat, and sleep was over for the night.

It had been during these predawn morning hours that he'd dug out the worn leather-covered Bible that had lain forgotten in the bottom of his saddlebag for so long. He'd begun to read it again and had been doing so when his boss entered.

"Yessir, that purely is a beautiful sight, you readin' the Good Book," Heston said again, nodding at the Bible in Jude's lap. "Maybe this is a good time t' ask you the same thing I ask you at the end of every week."

Jude feigned confusion, though he knew what was coming.

"Are you goin' to go to church with the missus an' me on Sunday mornin', or are you gonna stay here like a heathen? An' don't be tellin' me you've got jobs t' make up because of the rain, neither."

Jude took a deep breath. Maybe it was time.

"All right, you win," he said and a sudden lightness within him told him he'd made the right decision.

"Well, hallelujah!" Heston cried. "Wait'll I tell Lucy!"

Then both men became aware of a sound, or rather the absence of a sound. It had stopped raining, and now a beam of sunlight came lancing through the window next to Jude's bunk.

Jude studied it. Well, if he was going to go to Sunday worship in the morning, there was something he had to do now. He'd just been reading the part of the Gospels where it said something about mending one's fences before taking one's gift to the altar.

"Think I'll take a walk," he said.

Delia, her brown curls pinned up under by a scrap of calico folded triangularly into a kerchief, hummed as she dived into the deep cleaning that had never gotten done this spring because of her grandfather's illness. She hadn't wanted Miss Susan to feel like she had to offer to help, but once she had walked Miss Susan to the shop, it had seemed like a good day to tackle the job at last. There hadn't been any news of a new preacher coming, but if she suddenly had to move into a hotel, having this chore done would make the move that much easier.

And it would keep her—at least for a few hours—from wondering what she ought to do about her new house. She had received no word from Jude after their angry parting last week. She had no idea whether he still planned to finish it for her or not. She'd thought, perhaps, he had even left town, until Miss Susan had mentioned seeing him enlarging the corral at Mr. Pierce's livery.

Delia knew she ought to walk down to the Hestons' and ask him point-blank whether he was going to complete the house or not, so if he wasn't, she could go ahead and hire the German workers from Gillespie Springs Mr. Dawson had suggested. Was she being a coward? All she knew right now was that her dusty closets were a lot more appealing than braving those cold gray-blue eyes of Jude's. Maybe tomorrow she'd be up to the task. She had to know sooner or later, after all.

"Anyone home?" called a deep male voice from the front door, just as she started back to work.

Charles had mentioned something about a ride, but he hadn't said when, exactly, and she didn't think it was him. The voice was too deep, too gravelly... *Too like Jude Tucker's.* But Jude wouldn't come here, after the way they had left matters between them.

"I'm coming—"

It *was* Jude Tucker standing there, looking completely different from the unshaven cowhand who had left her home so precipitately after their harsh words. He wore a fresh shirt and clean denim trousers, and he appeared to have stopped at the Barber and Bath shop in town, for he smelled faintly of soap. Even his boots looked freshly brushed, she noted absently. In one hand he held his broad-brimmed hat; in the other, he held a small bouquet of wildflowers, though where he'd found them in the early September heat she had no idea.

"Hello," he said, and held out the bouquet. "Did I catch you at a bad time?"

Those light gray-blue eyes roamed over her kerchief and old dress, and she felt sure there must be as many smudges of dust on her cheeks as there were on her dress.

"N-no, it's…it's all right," she stammered and took the bouquet with hands that were visibly shaking.

"It's a peace offering."

She looked from him to the flowers and back again. "Uh…th-thank you. Come in. But that wasn't…n-necessary," she said.

"I thought it was. You might want to put those in water," he suggested, crossing her threshold.

"I will.…"

"You're in the middle of cleaning," he said. "You're busy. I won't stay."

He looked as though he was going to turn around and leave. "No, come in and have that lemonade I owe you," she said quickly, gesturing for him to enter and smiling to show that she had forgiven him. "Cleaning is thirsty work, and I was just getting ready to take a break." She reached for a pair of glasses in her cupboard. "Sit down, please," she said, indicating the kitchen table. "I just have to go out to the springhouse and get the pitcher."

When she returned, she poured them each a glass of the cold liquid and then watched as he took a sip.

"I've been trying to decide what to keep and what to leave for a new preacher," she said, pointing at the furniture, once again feeling she had to fill the silence. "Most of these things are still good, and preachers never seem to have much. I'm buying mostly new things, just taking the things that had been my mother's. Of course, if he came soon, I'd have to put some of these things in storage at Mr. Pierce's livery. Mrs. Purvis next door would take the chickens. It'd be so odd not to wake up to the rooster crowing...."

He let her talk, saying nothing, just watching her.

She had a sudden pang of fear at his silence. "Are you— that is, did you come to tell me you were leaving? That you aren't going to finish my house?"

Jude looked down at his hands. "I wasn't sure if you still wanted me to," he admitted.

"Of course I do."

He seemed to take encouragement to speak from that. "I... I wanted to apologize," he said. "I was out of line when I was here last week."

Delia gathered her courage. "Are you apologizing for kissing me, Jude? Because I don't want you to—apologize, that is. I think I'd like to try it again—kissing—only not with you angry at me." Then she held her breath to see what he would do.

She only had to wonder for the space of a few heart-beats. Then he was out of his chair and kneeling in front of hers, then he kissed her again, and this time he was definitely *not* angry. While he kissed her, he pulled off her kerchief and somehow the pins got loose and her curls were cascading around her neck.

"I've wanted to touch your hair for so long," he mur-mured, raising his head just long enough to say the words before his lips touched hers again.

Then a knock sounded at the front door, and they sprang apart.

Jude's eyes bored into Delia's. "You expecting some-one?"

"No. Yes. I—I don't know," she said, suddenly flus-tered. Charles would have questions about Jude Tucker's presence there—especially if he saw the flowers. She was not about to try to hide them, though, not with Jude watching. They lay where she had left them on the kitchen table, near where she had been sitting.

"I'll just go see who…" Her voice trailed off as she walked quickly down the hall away from the kitchen.

As she'd feared, it was Charles.

"Why, hello, Delia, whatever have you been doing?" He studied her messy hair and her rumpled appearance with amusement, but his eyes slitted when he spotted Jude coming down the hall from the kitchen.

"I've been cleaning," she explained again. "Charles, you remember Jude Tucker…"

"Tucker," Charles said tightly, nodding. His knuckles had tightened around his cane.

Jude nodded back. "Ladley."

Delia sensed that Charles was waiting to be informed about what Tucker was doing here, but she felt she had told him enough already. Oh, glory, she could smell the flowers clear out here in the parlor.

"I was just leaving," Jude said at last. "As I said, Miss Delia, I'll be buying the lumber tomorrow and starting to work on the house bright and early Monday."

"That will be fine. Goodbye, Jude."

Delia watched Charles watch through the window as Jude strode down the steps. He smiled with a certain grim satisfaction at one point, and after the sound of retreating hoofbeats he turned back to Delia.

"I have a surprise for you, Delia. Too bad Tucker saw it before you did, but come look."

Puzzled, and still shaking a little from the feeling of an averted confrontation, Delia came to the window and looked where Ladley was pointing.

Next to where Charles's bay saddle horse was tied to the back of the Ladley carriage stood a tall coal-black horse. It pawed the ground restively. On its back sat a lady's sidesaddle.

"She's a thoroughbred, Delia," Charles told her. "She's yours. Go put on your riding habit, and you can try out her paces."

Delia felt her jaw drop in astonishment. "Mine? But, Charles, I couldn't possibly accept such a gift...." But she was already flying out the doorway, and a moment later she was stroking the mare's inky, velvety muzzle. "Oh, you're *beautiful,*" she breathed, inhaling the mare's scent.

"Her name is Zephyr, though you can rename her anything you want, naturally," Charles said. "And of course you can accept her. In your position, you'll need a mount worthy of you."

Could she find the words to refuse this wonderful creature? The mare seemed to be trying to persuade her by butting her shoulder.

"Charles, I have nowhere to keep a horse."

"You'll keep her in our stable, of course, until you move to your new house."

"How do you know I'm a good enough rider for a horse like this?" she asked him. There was a hint of fire and mischief in the mare's eyes, a promise of speed in the supple muscles that rippled under Delia's hand as she stroked the mare's high shoulder.

"You've seemed a competent enough horsewoman when we've gone riding," Charles told her. "And having a horse like this will make you even more so in a short time."

Delia studied the mare as she considered his words. She and Charles had gone riding several times, early in the morning when it was still cool, and she'd loved flying over the roads on the borrowed gelding. But he was docile and perfectly trained. She knew she had a lot to learn about riding a horse like this spirited creature.

"Darling Delia, please say you'll accept her," Charles pleaded, the entreaty in his dark eyes weakening her rapidly melting resolve. "You know you want to."

She took a step back from the mare and from Charles. "But what would it signify to you?" she asked, amazed at her own temerity.

Ladley seemed to struggle to formulate an answer. At last he said, "As much or as little as you want it to, Delia."

"That's clear as mud."

He smiled down at her. "At the very least, a demonstration of my regard for you."

"And at most?"

"A betrothal present. But only if you want it to be," he added quickly, as she opened her mouth to protest.

"I… I couldn't," she said. "I'm sorry. I'm not ready for that, not yet. I'll enjoy riding her, but I think she should remain yours unless—"

"Say 'until,'" he interrupted, but his face remained bland and unconcerned. "All right, Delia. You're a prudent lady. I saw her, and I just wanted you to have her, regardless of whether *I'm* part of the gift or not. I love you, Delia, but I'm willing to wait. When the time is right, I'll merely have to think of another betrothal present."

He loved her. And he didn't seem to expect her to say it back right now. Did that make it all right to accept his gift?

Delia took a deep breath. "All right," she said, "as long as we're clear about that. How very kind and understanding you are to me." She opened her arms to him and stepped into his embrace.

Chapter Fourteen

Even though he had never attended services in the Llano Crossing Church, Jude felt a sense of coming home when he sat down in a middle pew with the Hestons. He watched the townspeople striding in in their Sunday best, smiling at each other—farmers, shop owners, laborers and their families—all of them God's children.

Even Charles Ladley, Jude supposed, as he caught sight of the mayor's son sitting proudly in the front pew next to Delia.

Yesterday, when Jude had spotted the exquisite thoroughbred mare outside Delia's house, he had guessed it was intended as a present for Delia—the beast might as well have had a big red satin bow around its neck. And what would induce Ladley to be giving Delia such a costly gift?

Delia had said Ladley didn't own her and had kissed Jude with every indication of sincerity and genuine feeling, but she and Ladley appeared very cozy together up front. Jude wondered if Ladley had been able to persuade Delia he was the better man. He hadn't thought Delia so changeable, but he must have been wrong. His heart ached with a crushing sense of loss.

But You didn't bring me to church to spend my time en-

vying Ladley, did You, Lord? Help me to concentrate on You, to hear what You have to say.

Jude resolutely wrenched his eyes and mind away from the couple. He opened his mouth to sing along with the rest of the congregation and felt a soothing peace descending upon him like a blessing. Even in the midst of the mayor's rambling attempt at a sermon, Jude knew he'd done right to come.

"All right, you spent a pretty penny on that nag," Mayor Ladley growled almost three weeks later. It was once again time for the Committee for Civic Improvement to meet, and as usual, the two Ladleys had come early so they could discuss things they didn't want Mrs. Ladley overhearing. "And why you didn't make the gift conditional on her agreeing to marry you, I don't understand—"

"Because I know that this way I'll get what I want more easily in the end," Charles Ladley told his father. He wasn't about to admit that Delia had told him she wasn't ready to consider his proposal any time soon and wouldn't accept the gift of the mare yet.

Ladley Senior harrumphed. "Time to move the project along, son. We need control of Delia Keller's money, and the only way that's going to happen is if you're her husband, not merely her adoring beau. What's next in the plan?"

The younger Charles took a sip of the rich port his father favored. He'd have preferred whiskey, but this stuff wasn't bad.

"Perhaps we'll go for a surprise moonlight picnic out at Ladley Hall one night, before it gets too cold. Very romantic, eh?" He winked. Calling Delia's new home "Ladley Hall" was a private joke between him and his father, a reference to when it—and Delia—would be firmly under his control.

"Capital, capital! To success then—" his father said with a wink and extended his glass to clink with his son's "—and control of the fortune. No woman should ever have control of that much money, eh? No long engagement. Appeal to her romantic notions, and get her to elope with you." He leaned closer to his son. "Compromise her, if you have to."

Charles was saved from the necessity of a reply by the door opening and their fellow committee members striding into the room.

"Ah, here are the fellows now," the mayor said, looking up as the others strode into the room. "Friends, why not be the first to congratulate my son, the future husband of Llano Crossing's own heiress? Of course, the news can't leave this room—he hasn't asked her yet."

The other men of the committee—Amos Dawson, Dixon Miller, Barton Jeffers, the mill owner, and Sheriff Jenkins—guffawed, pledged secrecy and slapped Charles on the back, calling him a sly dog.

Then Dawson, always the most impatient man on the committee, asked, "Does that mean we're about ready to seed the creek?" The phrase was a code for the plan shared only by the committee. "I'm tired of this one-horse town. I can't wait to be sippin' tequila on my *estancia* with a doe-eyed *señorita* fannin' my brow."

Ladley smirked at the banker's fantasy. "Dawson, your patience is about to be rewarded. I think the time is nearly upon us. Miller, ready to play your role?"

"Yeah, I've been keepin' the entrance to that cave well-hidden—which ain't easy, as many hands as I've got workin' on my spread."

"Excellent, excellent," purred the mayor. "Of course, our biggest source of investment money will come from Miss Keller—assuming my son's suit is favored," he added, with a meaningful look at his son.

"Trust me, Father, it will be," Charles said, stroking his mustache. "She loves me a little more each day."

"And once he gets a ring on that gal's finger," Jeffers demanded, "what's to keep you Ladleys from just runnin' off to Mexico on your own? You'll have plenty of money then."

There was a chorus of agreement from the other two men.

"Why, I'm hurt you would think such a thing," the mayor said, looking it. "We have our honor as Southern gentlemen, so we would never dream of leaving you men holding the bag. Besides, there's greater money to be made if we're able to get all those gullible fools to invest. Never fear, gentlemen, we're in this to make as much money as possible."

"You have the gold in a safe place?" Dawson asked, still sounding suspicious.

"Of course," the mayor said.

In the last fortnight, Delia had seen Jude only at the site of her house. He was all business, and since the finishing process was at the stage where he needed help to complete the interior walls, he was always surrounded by men he'd hired to help him. The Jude who had kissed her so tenderly and smiled so winningly at her might never have existed.

Delia guessed Jude must have decided that because of the appearance of the horse, she had chosen Charles. She didn't want to let him continue in that mistaken notion, but all her efforts to speak to him alone had failed. She had tried going by the Hestons' house once in the evening, but Jude and his horse were gone, and she had spent a fruitless half hour chatting with the Hestons and pretending she'd just been out for a stroll.

She'd even thought of leaving him a note somewhere in the house where he'd be sure to find it, but finally, pride had taken over. Jude was apparently determined to believe what he wanted to believe, she decided, so she spent more time with Charles, who was never moody and prickly. She came to depend on his unfailing charm and ability to make her laugh. He always seemed to have a compliment at the ready, and every few days he came up with some small gift for her—a pair of onyx earbobs, a crystal vase to hold the flowers he picked from his mother's garden…

As for his mother, Jane Ladley had made it only too clear that she was delighted with her son's choice of sweetheart and couldn't wait to officially welcome her into the family. Her approval made up for the overheartiness of her husband, who nevertheless always seemed to be sizing up Delia—for what, she didn't know.

Charles kept telling her that he loved her. Could she love him? She enjoyed his gentle embraces that had never gone beyond what was proper between a courting couple. Was that enough? Many couples had less. They were now social equals, and he would fit into her world in every way—especially since Jude Tucker apparently didn't want to.

Shouldn't you pray about it? Now where had that thought come from? Delia glanced guiltily at the Bible sitting on her bedside table. She hadn't been reading it very much lately, as the dust that had settled on the worn, cracked leather cover attested.

"Señorita Keller, Mr. Charles says to tell you he will have to skip his ride with you this morning," the wizened old groom said when Delia arrived at the Ladley barn at their usual riding time. They'd ridden together almost every day, and Delia had become quite confident in her horsemanship.

Delia wrinkled her nose in disappointment. She was wearing a new dove-gray riding habit, which Miss Susan had finished for her only yesterday. It was among her first new garments of "half mourning" rather than full, solemn black.

"He said to tell you he was sorry, but he had to go to Mason on business," Manuel told her as he continued to curry her mare's gleaming black coat.

"That's fine, Manuel, but would you saddle up Zephyr anyway?" Delia asked.

The old groom's brow furrowed in uncertainty. "Señorita Keller, I do not know about thees.... You have not taken her out yet by yourself, *si?*"

"*Si*—I mean, no, I haven't!" Delia gave him a sunny smile. "But thanks to Charles's expert teaching, I'm sure I'll have no problems. There has to be a first time, right? He'll be so proud of me! Don't worry, we won't go faster than a sedate trot, I promise."

Manuel still looked dubious, but at last he shrugged. "You should ride around town *solamente, si?*"

"Only around town," Delia repeated, nodding. She would do that for the first little while, at least—and then she and the mare would head out of town. She'd give Zephyr her head, and they'd fly! The few times she and Charles had galloped their horses together, it had been delightful beyond words.

All went well while they remained in Llano Crossing. Delia felt the cynosure of all eyes as she rode the mare at a decorous walk down Main Street. She was so proud of the way the beautiful creature arched her lovely neck and picked her way delicately, as if she were walking on clouds.

Then all at once the mare shied at a puppy that came yipping out of an alleyway. Snorting, she gave a little half buck that nearly unseated Delia.

"Sorry, Miss Delia, didn't mean for Skippy to frighten your horse," Billy Dean, son of the mercantile owner, yelled, running out to scoop up his pup.

By that time Delia had succeeded in calming the mare somewhat with her voice. "No problem, Billy," she assured him, though the mare continued to sidle and curvet, her nostrils flared as she eyed the little dog as if fearing it might leap out of his young master's arms at her.

"Sure is a pretty hoss, Miss Delia."

There was nothing to this, Delia thought, as she bade Billy goodbye and rode on. She was ready to feel the wind in her face right now. She nudged the mare into a trot and headed her west. She would let the mare trot until they reached the site of her new house and see how the workmen were progressing, and then once she rode around the bend, she'd give Zephyr her head. That would show Jude Tucker how much she was pining for him!

When she arrived at the site, Jude, shirtsleeves rolled up, was directing two fellows who were carrying in a stack of fresh-cut two-by-fours. Shiloh was cropping grass in the shade of one of the big trees.

"How's it going, Mr. Tucker?" she called, being formal since there were a couple of laborers painting the outside of the house.

"Fine." Jude eyed her and the horse with hands on his hips, seemingly impatient at the interruption. "We'll be painting the walls by the end of the week. You'll be able to move in by Thanksgiving, as I promised."

"That's not so far away," she called, riding around in a circle because the echoing of hammers from within was making the mare more restive than before. "Are you sure?"

"Promised you, didn't I?" His gaze shifted to Zephyr, who was now sidling and pawing the ground. It was as if the mare had guessed her rider's intentions to let her run, and she was impatient to feel the wind in her mane. "Miss Delia, are you sure you're ready to be riding that horse without—by yourself?"

First he was curt, then he announced he doubted she

could control the mare? She'd show him what a horse-woman she had become! "Perfectly sure," she informed him and nudged the mare with her heels.

"Delia, rein her in!" she heard Jude call after her, but she ignored him.

Chapter Fifteen

There was truly nothing to compare with the feeling of flying over the hard-packed clay road on the back of a fine horse. The wind had blown Delia's hat off half a mile or so back, and now her hair had come loose from its pins and was blowing loose behind her. The rolling mesquite-and-cactus-dotted hills raced by.

Delia laughed aloud from the sheer joy of it. This was living! The only thing she could imagine being better would be to be riding astride rather than sidesaddle. She knew it wasn't considered ladylike but perhaps if she did it only out here where it wasn't likely she'd be seen...

She'd ridden a mile beyond her house when the road grew rougher, and she decided she'd better rein in. It was then Delia realized she was in trouble, for Zephyr wasn't ready to slow down. Delia sat back in the saddle and pulled back on the reins, calling, "Whoa, girl. Easy, Zephyr."

Seizing the bit in her teeth, Zephyr lowered her head and galloped even faster. She'd been named for the wind, but a gentle western wind, not like this! Delia felt icy fingers of apprehension grip her—

Didn't she know she could fall off that horse and break her neck? He'd tried to warn her, and she'd ignored him,

Jude told himself as Delia and the thoroughbred disappeared around the bend in a cloud of dust. *She had chosen to become Charles Ladley's problem, hadn't she?*

Does that give you an excuse not to do what's right? The Voice wasn't still or small at all this time.

"All right, Lord," he murmured, then cupped a hand around his mouth to call out to one of the painters. "Will, I'll be back in a few minutes." He ran over to where Shiloh was hobbled under one of the oak trees.

A minute later, he had vaulted onto the stallion's bare back and had kicked him into a gallop, gripping him with his knees and clutching a fistful of the buckskin's mane.

Please, Lord, let this worry be all for nothing. Let me find her cooling her mare down farther along the road, he prayed desperately as Shiloh's hooves devoured the road.

His hopes were dashed when he spied the black horse up ahead, riderless, blowing with her head down. Nearby lay a still, crumpled gray form.

"Delia!" He jumped his horse even as Shiloh skidded to a halt and ran to her.

She was unconscious but stirred slightly, moaning, as he touched her. There was a lump the size of a hen's egg already rising on her forehead, and a scrape where her cheek had collided with a stone. "Delia, you have to wake up!" he yelled down at her. *What if she never came to her senses again?*

Then he spied the canteen attached to her mare's saddle. *At least Ladley had taught her that much.* Wetting the handkerchief he yanked from his pocket, he bathed her forehead, all the while praying harder than he had ever prayed in his life.

Delia awoke to the feeling of a wet, cool cloth on her forehead and the trickling of water down the back of her neck. Wincing at the pain that lanced through her skull, she tried to open her eyes, only to be blinded by the sunlight shining directly into them. She tried to put a hand up to block the brilliant glare but felt a hand on her forearm, restraining her. She cried out in fear, struggling to rise to see who was keeping her down.

"Thank You, God," she heard Jude say. "Lie still, Delia. You've had a bad fall." He shifted himself so that he blocked the sunlight.

She lay still, squinting as she looked up into the pale eyes in that hard, angular face shadowed by his wide-brimmed hat. He ran his hands down her arms, probing.

"Do your arms hurt? Can you move them?" His tone was gentle and soothing, but his eyes hadn't yet lost their anxiety as he studied her.

"*Everything* hurts," she said, but flexed her fingers and bent her forearms experimentally. "I—I don't think anything's broken. Where's Zephyr?"

"What about your legs? Can you feel them? Can you move them? No, *don't try to get up*," he said again. "Just tell me."

She knew she should remind him it wasn't proper to call them *legs* instead of *limbs* to a lady, but now wasn't the time to be prim. "Yes, I can feel everything," she said, wiggling them to demonstrate. "H-how did you know to come?"

"I tried to go back to work, but then I just *knew*," he said simply. She saw Shiloh standing beyond him, saddle-less. He'd been so worried, he hadn't even taken the time to saddle his horse. He'd ridden after her bareback.

"Where—where's Zephyr?" she asked, hardly bearing to hear the answer.

He moved again so she could see the mare for herself.

"A jackrabbit ran right out in front of us," Delia murmured. "It wasn't her fault."

"No, it wasn't," he agreed, but his eyes were compassionate as he said it. "Didn't you hear me call out to rein in? You could have been *killed,* Delia."

Again, his tone was gentle, but she could hear the barely relieved fear in his voice and closed her eyes against the stinging truth of his words. He was right; she knew it. She'd been foolhardy beyond all measure, and her willfulness could have cost her her life—or that of the beautiful mare.

"Do you think you can sit up?" Without waiting for permission, he slid one arm under her shoulder while the other cradled her neck and assisted her into a sitting position.

Every bone in her body felt bruised, and her lower back throbbed in tune with her throbbing head. Nausea churned in her stomach. *Don't let me be sick in front of this man, I beg of You.*

To distract herself, Delia looked back at her mare and saw now the way Zephyr stood so that her weight was shifted from the off foreleg. "Is her leg…*broken?*" she finally dared to ask. "Please—see if Zephyr's all right."

Jude got to his feet and strode over to the mare. Zephyr raised her lovely head as he approached, but she stood still, trembling, as he took hold of her trailing reins and ran a hand gently over her legs. Delia saw her flinch as his hand reached her off foreleg. Straightening, he spoke softly to the mare, leading her to take a few steps.

Delia saw the horse dip her head every time she put weight on the off foreleg. Jude tied her reins to a nearby mesquite before turning back to her.

"Nothing's broken, but she's lame."

"She'll recover?"

He nodded. "After a while. She'll have to be on stall rest until her leg heals. I'll take you home on Shiloh, and lead her. Maybe the doc should check you over."

"That's not necessary—" Delia began, but he was already lifting her to her feet by scooping one hand under her backside while keeping the other around her shoulders.

As soon as she put her weight on her left foot, however, pain zinged up her leg and she sagged against Jude, stifling a cry.

"Looks like that mare's not the only one who's lame," he said, and before she knew what he was about, he had picked her up and was carrying her toward his stallion.

"You'll have to ride astride," he told her, "and hold on to Shiloh's mane. He'll just follow me." He boosted her onto the silver buckskin's back as if she weighed nothing.

Delia felt her face flame scarlet as she looked down at the length of stockinged leg and lacy petticoat showing above her short riding boots. But Jude, leading the mare slowly beside his stallion, either didn't notice, was unmoved by the sight or perhaps was saving his energy for the long trek back to town.

When they reached her house, Delia kept her head down, embarrassed, as Jude informed the workmen who came to see them that he'd be back as soon as he had her situated at home and the mare back in the Ladley stable.

"You p-poor d-dear!" Miss Susan cried sympathetically, red-faced and panting as she ran into the house minutes after Jude had left. "Mr. Tucker stopped at the shop to tell me what had happened, and he looked so worried I thought I'd better leave the shop early. Does it hurt very badly?" she asked, pointing to the leg Delia had propped on another chair, with a cold cloth wrapped around it.

"You didn't have to do that," Delia said, but in truth she was glad to see her. "It's sprained, Jude says. I deserve every ache I've got and worse. I know I could have killed that horse."

"Don't be so hard on yourself, honey," Miss Susan said sympathetically. "You're going to mend—and so will the mare, Mr. Tucker said. We'll wrap your ankle, and I'll fix you some willowbark tea that'll help the pain. You've got a lump on your forehead and a scraped cheek, too, did you know? And didn't I see your grandpa's cane under my bed? You'll be needing that for a while."

"I'd forgotten it was there," Delia murmured, but she was thinking about what Jude had said before he'd left—

"Delia, I know you love that horse, and it's true she's a beauty, but please, if you've ever believed me about anything, ask Ladley to get you a horse that's less high-strung."

"She's not my horse, Jude," she had told him. "He tried to give her to me, it's true, but I told him I couldn't accept such a gift. I—I'll tell him I'm not ready for her yet—maybe ever."

He gave her an astonished look. "Then she wasn't a—a betrothal present? You're not engaged to wed Ladley?"

"No." She saw him start at her answer. "I told you it was too soon to commit myself to Charles—or anyone, for that matter. A beautiful horse didn't change that."

He blinked, and suddenly his features relaxed and he looked almost happy. "All right then. I—I reckon that's good. I'll just take your—the—mare on to the Ladley stable and check on you later."

Chapter Sixteen

"Delia, sweetheart, I came as soon as I heard...." Charles rushed past Miss Susan, into the parlor and over to where Delia sat with her foot propped up on an adjoining chair. He glanced outside, where dusk was drawing in. "I'm sorry, my business took longer than I'd thought it would. I arrived home minutes ago, and Mother told me what happened. Are you in pain, my dear? Why, that bruise, and that scrape on your face! And your poor ankle. That blasted nag!"

She'd been half-afraid he would be angry—justifiably—with her for laming the valuable horse, but he was only concerned for her. "Charles, I'm *all right,*" Delia said, trying to stop his flow of regret. "My ankle's only sprained, and these will fade in a few days," she added, pointing to the wounds on her face. "It's not the horse's fault, it's mine, as Jude Tucker told me when he found me. He was right—I shouldn't have been out galloping alone. Thank God nothing worse happened. I'd never forgive myself if Zephyr had broken a leg."

"Delia, I'm much more concerned about your safety than about a horse or anything in this world," he told her. His voice was a caress in itself. "Tucker will be rewarded for assisting you. He wasn't too stern with you, was he? I'd have to thrash him if he was!" He was almost jovial now.

"No, of course not. I—I think perhaps Zephyr's too much horse for me."

Charles moved to cup her cheek in his hand, seemingly oblivious of Miss Susan standing by the door. "Nonsense, darling," he reassured her. "We'll have some more lessons, and by the end of them, you'll be riding like a cavalryman, I promise you! Just think, we're both using canes now, although thankfully yours is only temporary.

"It's too bad this happened," Charles went on. "I'd thought to take you on a picnic tonight, out at your future house, the weather continuing so mild for fall."

"That is too bad," Delia agreed. "I would have enjoyed that. Perhaps we can do that another—"

"Ah, but we can still have a picnic of sorts, though in your yard here, not out there," Charles interrupted. "Cook had already packed it for us, and it's sitting out in the landau. There's no sense in wasting it because of a sprained ankle. I'll set everything up on the grass, and then I have only to help you outside."

Delia's eyes met Miss Susan's as he made his way back outside.

"He expects you to hobble outside, just so he can call it a picnic?" Miss Susan groused. "Plumb foolishness, I say."

Inwardly, Delia also wished they could eat at her table so she wouldn't have to make an additional painful effort of negotiating the steps, but she didn't want to spoil Charles's attempt to provide a romantic evening. But she felt awkward about going outside to eat with Charles, leaving Miss Susan inside by herself—as if she were a servant and not a guest in her house.

"Everything's ready," Charles proclaimed, returning inside. "Here's your shawl, in case it gets chilly, and your cane, Delia. You can lean on my arm."

"Miss Susan, join us, please," Delia said.

"Oh, no, I wouldn't dream of intruding on your picnic—"

"And we wouldn't dream of leaving you out, would we, Charles?" she said, meeting his eyes.

Delia thought she saw a flash of frustration streak across Ladley's handsome, agreeable face before he chimed in, "No, of course not. There's plenty of food. If we could merely borrow a table service from your kitchen, Delia, since Cook didn't know we'd have anyone joining us..."

"Thank you both—it's very kind of you—but I'm not hungry," Miss Susan said. "You two go ahead and enjoy it. Please, Delia."

Delia watched her go, aware of Charles's almost palpable relief that it would be only the two of them. She sighed and decided she had done her best. She might as well enjoy the meal Charles had brought.

Once she had made her way outside with some difficulty to the "picnic spot" in her front yard, and was assisted to sit at the edge of the linen cloth Charles had spread out, Delia sighed with pleasure and discovered she was hungry. Maisie, the Ladleys' cook, had indeed outdone herself. There were roasted quail, new potatoes, green beans almondine, chocolate cake and a large jar of cold tea, with delicate cut-glass tumblers set in front of heirloom china. Charles had even brought a pair of candelabras, which he lit with great ceremony.

The food was as delicious as it looked. But Charles was abnormally quiet, his words stilted when he did speak. Delia wondered what was troubling him. Was he merely disappointed that they couldn't be having this picnic out at her house site?

"What a lot of trouble Maisie went to, Charles," Delia said. "Please thank her for me. It was thoughtful of you to

think of this, too. I'm so sorry to have ruined it by going
and getting myself injured as I did."

"Not at all, Delia. I had hoped this evening... But
there'll be another time. I guess I just have a lot on my
mind. Forgive me for being poor company." There was an
uncharacteristic strain to his mouth.

Delia wondered what he had begun to say about his
hopes for this evening. Surely after their talk the other
day, he hadn't been going to propose under the moonlight
this evening or try to push their relationship further than
she was ready for it to go? Perhaps her injury had really
been a blessing in disguise.

"Heard some news in town today," Lucy Heston said
from across the table as she passed her husband a plate of
corn fritters with one hand, while handing Jude a bowl of
buttered biscuits with the other.

"Oh? What's that?" James Heston asked. "Don't tell me,
Llano Crossing's going to become the new state capital instead of Austin, and Mayor Ladley's running for governor."

"No, silly," Lucy Heston said, giving her spouse a loving but exasperated look. "The mayor's calling a big meeting to be held next Sunday night, and he wants everyone
there."

"Humph," he snorted. "Wonder what he's up to? No
good, probably."

"Now, Jim," his wife reproved him in her gentle way,
"you don't know that."

"Maybe not, but speaking of Mayor Ladley, while you
were out gallivantin'—" he winked at his wife to show he
was joking "—he paid me a call and asked me to read the
Scripture at church come Sunday. He says he's tryin' t'
share the responsibilities a' leadin' the worship service,"
Heston explained, but he looked skeptical. "Huh! If ya

ask me, he'd do better to go beat the bushes an' find us a new preacher."

"Maybe that's what he's going to announce at this Sunday-night meeting," Jude suggested.

"No, they say it's got nothing to do with church, rather some plan the Committee for Civic Improvement has developed."

"Guess we'll have t' wait and see."

"What passage are you supposed to read?" Jude asked.

"The part about the Good Samaritan. Jude, I kin read, I reckon," Heston said, "but I'm all slow and stumbly when I have t' read out loud. It's you who should be doin' it—you have a fine reading voice."

Jude shook his head, wishing now he hadn't read to the old couple out of the Psalms a few times in the evenings, but the Hestons read the Bible every evening after dinner, and when he was around, he'd taken part. "I'm just a carpenter. And besides, he didn't ask me." He wanted to help the kindly old man who'd become his friend, however. "Why don't you come out to the barn, and you can practice reading the passage in front of me?"

Mr. Heston reluctantly admitted that might work.

Five days had passed, and Delia found that Miss Susan had given good advice about her ankle. By wrapping it firmly in linen strips, keeping her foot propped up on a cushion and staying off of it as much as possible, using her cane and drinking willowbark tea three times a day, the ankle had gotten progressively less painful and swollen.

The high point of her day was when Jude stopped by at sunset every day on his way home from the worksite, ostensibly to report on his progress and ask how her injuries were healing, but he stayed and chatted with both Delia and Miss Susan. He always asked the latter if Donley Morrison had bothered her any further, and the seamstress always replied in the negative. Once, Jude even took supper with them, since he had finished late that evening, and they were just sitting down to eat when he arrived.

Miss Susan seemed to always have an excuse to leave them alone during part or all of his visit, but while Jude seemed in no great hurry to leave, neither did he say or do anything that indicated any wish to deepen their friendship. He seemed as if he was waiting for something, but what?

Mystified, she'd mentioned it to Miss Susan one night after Jude left. "Maybe he's waiting for you to make up your mind about Ladley," the older woman said tartly.

Delia sighed. If she was honest with herself, she already had. She valued Charles's friendship, and didn't want to hurt him, but she had nothing in common with him but social position—certainly not enough on which to base a marriage. She loved Jude, she knew that now. But for all she knew, he was still planning to return to Nevada once her house was built.

Show me what to do, Lord, she prayed each night.

Now it was Sunday morning, and as Delia waited on the porch for Charles to stop by in his carriage, she found she was able to put weight on her ankle without too much discomfort. She'd keep the cane with her for now, though, just in case.

Jude sat with the Hestons in their usual pew in the little church and did his best not to stare at Delia sitting up front next to the mayor's son. Perhaps while they waited for the service to start, he ought to say a little prayer for his boss that his reading would go smoothly. Oddly enough, Heston didn't seem nervous about it anymore, but surely a little prayer wouldn't hurt.

Three hymns were sung, as was the usual pattern. Then,

instead of the mayor leaving the front pew and heading to the lectern, he kept his seat and his son got up.

"I have an announcement before Mr. Heston reads the Bible passage. My father asked me to inform you that along with a bit of a sore throat, he seems to have lost his voice this morning and can't speak above a whisper. He's hoping to be able to lead the meeting tonight if he rests his voice, but if not, I will take his place. So once the Scripture is read…why, I suppose we can all just sing another hymn and go home to our Sunday dinners a bit early," he concluded with a genial laugh.

"Couldn't you read his sermon notes?" an old man in the crowd asked.

Charles gave a self-deprecating smile of regret. "I'd be happy to, but being the gifted speaker that my father is, he always speaks extemporaneously. He never makes any notes."

There was a murmuring among the congregation, and Jude saw Mr. Heston and his wife exchange a look.

"Mr. Heston," Charles said, beckoning to the open Bible on the lectern.

James Heston stood, smoothing the frock coat he only wore on Sundays, then reached into his breast pocket. "Soon as I get my spectacles…" He began to look worried, then patted both trouser pockets. His weathered, gnarled hands dived into them and came up empty.

"Lucy," he said, looking down at his wife, "do you by any chance have my spectacles?"

She looked back at him, bewildered. "No, Jim, of course I don't have them. Didn't you bring them?"

He clapped a hand to his forehead. "Oh no!" he exclaimed. "I must have left them on the bedside table, after goin' over the passage this very mornin'! Folks, I'm sorry, but I don't have it memorized, so I can't read this mornin'."

Was it Jude's imagination or was Heston avoiding his

eyes? There was something almost *practiced* about his distress.

Charles Ladley looked nonplussed. "I suppose I—"

"But Jude Tucker, here, can read it," Mr. Heston interrupted quickly.

Jude shot a look at the wily old man, sure now that he'd been set up. He thought about refusing, but then Jude saw that Delia had turned around and was staring at him, her eyes wide at this surprising turn of events.

Chapter Seventeen

Ladley began to demur, saying, "Oh, but I could certainly…"

Go read the story, Jude.

Jude rose and made his way to the pulpit, aware that members of the congregation were whispering and poking one another. Both Mr. and Mrs. Heston were grinning.

Jude walked up to the pulpit on shaky legs. He found the Bible already open to the correct place. "Our reading this morning is in Luke, chapter ten," he began, looking out over the sea of faces. It had been so long since he'd done anything like this. *Help me, Lord, if You want me to do this.* "A certain man went down from Jerusalem to Jericho, and fell among thieves.…"

His voice started out unsure, like a key being inserted in a lock that was rusty from disuse. He stumbled over a word or two. Then Jude felt peace sweeping over him— and certainty—and by the time he reached the part about the Samaritan finding the wounded man and taking him to the inn to recover, his voice was ringing with confidence. When he finished the passage, *"amens"* were popping up all over the congregation.

He closed the Bible with a soft thump and started to step away from the pulpit, but now Mr. Heston spoke up.

"That was right fine, Jude! Why don't you expound on that a little, tell us what you think it ought t' mean to us?"

"Oh, no, I don't think—" Jude started to say, just as the younger Ladley said, "Mr. Heston, surely we oughtn't to put Mr. Tucker on the spot...."

"Yeah, why don't you say a few words?" Mrs. Dean, wife of the mercantile owner, called out. "Man who reads th' Bible as nice as that prob'ly has some thoughts to go with it!"

There was an answering chorus of agreement, though Mayor Ladley sat there looking uncomfortable, as if he'd just swallowed a horny toad.

But it was the surprise of seeing Delia's green eyes, sympathetic and encouraging, and the swift nod she gave him that made Jude believe he could do as they were asking and *should* do it. He sent up another quick prayer that he be given the right words to say.

"And occasionally," he concluded some twenty minutes later, "we need to look beneath the surface to see that someone is hurting and not assume that it's someone else's role to help him. Do as the Samaritan did."

He looked up from the Bible and saw the Hestons beaming at him like proud parents and Delia, as well as the rest of the congregation, looking thoughtful.

"I... I reckon that's all that needs to be said about the Good Samaritan, at least by me this morning," Jude concluded, humbled at what had just taken place. It was as if he had never left his little church in Tennessee, as if those war years, and all the wrong things he had done during them, were wiped away. "Why don't we sing another hymn like Mr. Ladley said, and then perhaps Mr. Heston would like to give the final blessing." He grinned triumphantly at James Heston, who accepted Jude's getting the last laugh with good grace and managed to do a fine job.

Afterward, it seemed to Jude as if he was the center of a

whirlwind. Most of the congregation came up and shook his hand and complimented him on the fine little sermon he'd done with no prior notice. Several asked him if he'd ever thought about becoming a preacher, and a few even urged him to consider becoming the pastor of this church, even though as far as they knew he'd never been to seminary.

"You did a fine job. I knew you could do it," Delia praised him, when it came to her turn to shake his hand on the way out. Ladley, right behind her, nodded curtly at him and muttered something that might have been approval. Delia looked as if she wanted to say something more, but then Charles touched her elbow, reminding her they were to have Sunday dinner with his parents, and steered her on.

Jude, turning to greet the next person who wanted to shake his hand, missed the rebellious set to Delia's mouth after Ladley's high-handedness.

"You sure did yourself proud, son," Heston told him on the way out of the church, and his wife murmured her agreement. "You've been a preacher before, haven't you?" It was a statement, not a question.

Jude frowned at Heston, putting his finger over his mouth, hoping no one among the stragglers had overheard Heston. "Thanks, but let's talk about it later."

Heston nodded. "Mum's the word."

"Delia Keller sure looked lovely today," Mrs. Heston said, and looked meaningfully at Jude.

"She'd look a lot better standin' next to Jude than with that polecat Charles Ladley," growled Heston, before Jude could form an answer. "Don't think I didn't notice how often you glanced her way," he said to Jude.

What was he supposed to say to that? Was he supposed to admit that he lay awake every night, thinking of her, wondering why her eyes said she cared about him whenever he came to see her, but around town, he kept seeing her with Ladley?

* * *

Delia knew as little as anyone else in Llano Crossing about the subject of the meeting that evening. She only knew Charles was like a coiled spring, filled with a suppressed excitement that caused his eyes to dance with the secret they held. His father seemed possessed by the same energy, and at the Sunday dinner table, while she and Mrs. Ladley had talked about her new house, Delia saw father and son exchange looks that seemed charged with meaning.

"Thank you all for coming," Mayor Ladley said, still hoarse, but managing to get the words out as he arose from his chair in the front of the church. Alongside him sat his son, Amos Dawson, Dixon Miller, Sheriff Jenkins and Barton Jeffers. "I know all of you have been wondering about the subject of this meeting. We will keep you waiting no longer."

Miss Susan, sitting next to Delia, said in a stage whisper, "It's about time!" and everyone chuckled—even the mayor, who said, "Yes, it *is* about time. About time Llano Crossing's citizens begin to enjoy the prosperity they so richly deserve, a prosperity that was beginning to dawn until the War Between the States robbed us of the flower of our youth, left many others grievously wounded—" Ladley paused to glance meaningfully at his son behind him "—and beset many of us with ruinous taxes."

"You ain't plannin' on us secedin' from the Union, are ya?" called a man in the crowd who had lost an arm in the war. "'Cause I've already done that once, and once was enough."

The mayor smiled again and made a gesture for quiet. "Never fear, fellow citizens of Llano Crossing. As your duly elected mayor, as much as I would have liked to see our boys in gray prevail, I would not countenance anything so foolish as a new rebellion. No, what the Committee for

Civic Improvement had in mind was a way of bringing prosperity to our town and its citizens, and our town only."

He paused, until it was so quiet Delia could have heard a pin drop in the little church, then cleared his throat. "Several months ago, our own Miss Delia Keller—" the mayor gestured toward her "—was the recipient of a windfall, which has transformed her life. I am telling you now that all of you who participate will also be receiving a financial bounty that will transform yours."

A buzz of excitement rose from the pews. The mayor tolerated it for a moment before lifting a hand for silence.

"Before I ask Dixon Miller to come forward and announce the plan, I am going to have to ask that everyone present pledge themselves to maintaining secrecy. This plan will not succeed if rumors start flying and others not of our town start flocking in to take the hard-won riches that the committee seeks to share with all of you good citizens of Llano Crossing."

Mayor Ladley's eyes roved over the attendees. "I cannot stress the need for discretion enough, good citizens. I am going to ask those of you who are able to commit a sum of money. I want to assure those who feel they do not have any spare cash that they need not despair, for a role can be found for you, too. A rising tide floats all boats, does it not? You need not indicate how much you will invest at this time. That is a matter for reflection and discussion at home and, of course, prayer," he added unctuously. "Do I have your solemn promises of secrecy? All those willing, stand now and raise your right hands to pledge your commitment. All those who feel they cannot so pledge, please leave now."

Everyone stood, glancing at each other, wondering what the plan was. No one left.

"Please repeat after me—"

The attendees dutifully stood and repeated phrase by

phrase as the mayor rasped it out, pledging support of the plan and utmost secrecy, with a penalty of having to leave the county if they should break faith. Neighbors exchanged uneasy glances but completed the pledge, eager to hear what was going to make them rich.

Delia had stood with the rest, but she had not raised her hand nor repeated the words. No one seemed to notice. She couldn't help wondering what her grandpa would have thought of all this or, for that matter, what Jude Tucker was thinking. She had seen him sitting with the Hestons in their usual place when she'd come in with Charles.

The mayor clasped his large, meaty hands together and beamed at everyone. "Congratulations on your willingness to enter into this adventure with us. I had hoped you would, and I have not been disappointed. I knew I could trust all of you. Dixon Miller, will you please come now and explain the plan?"

There was a renewed hum of talk as the rancher stepped forward. "Some of you may know," he said, "that there is a small, spring-fed creek on my land that waters my southeast pasture before emptying into the Llano River. Not long ago, one of my ranch hands, Donley Morrison, was watering his horse at this creek when he spotted something in the water that made his heart beat quite a bit faster. Donley, come up here and show the folks what you found."

From the back of the room, the barrel-chested man Delia hadn't seen since that day in Miss Susan's shop ambled forward, grinning self-consciously. Delia felt Miss Susan move closer to her.

Donley faced the audience, reaching into the pocket of his worn, patched trousers. He raised his clenched fist and then opened it, palm upward, to reveal an irregular lump about the size of a robin's egg.

Even from where she sat, Delia knew she was looking at gold. The townspeople gasped as one.

"Yes, it's gold," Miller said, "discovered in my creek. But I care about this town, so I'm not seeking to keep the profit to myself, surprising as that may be. After Donley made this discovery, I followed that creek to its source in a little cavern, a cavern that's so well-hidden I had never suspected its presence. You wouldn't find it, either, unless I showed you. This cave's only big enough for a couple a' men to stoop over in it, but there's tiny passageways leadin' off from that that're only big enough for a wiry feller to crawl into. He tells me there's veins a' gold so rich in this cave that you can't begin t' imagine the wealth to be had if we could just get to 'em. And that, my dear fellow citizens of Llano Crossing, is where you come in. Mr. Jeffers, would you mind explainin' the rest?"

Barton Jeffers, a big, imposing man with jowly, florid cheeks, stepped forward as Dixon Miller took his seat.

"What we're proposing is an association, I suppose you could call it. Obviously, money will be needed to pay for development of the mine—enlarging those narrow passages, paying miners to dig it out, and so forth. There would be various levels of membership, in accordance with how much investment money you're willing and able to put in. And your profits would be reaped accordingly."

"So the more money you put in, the more you make?" a man in the back called out.

Jeffers smiled like a teacher pleased at his class. "Exactly. But everyone who puts in anything will see a handsome return. What we in the committee envision is a way to keep the profits within the community, rather than having gold-hungry prospectors pouring into Llano Crossing and turning it into a boomtown, with all the accompanying evils that go with it—more saloons, gamblers, unsavory women... With the profits from the mine, our prosperity will, in turn, attract quality settlers who value a safe, civilized community."

"Sounds good to me," someone called out from behind Delia. "Where do I sign?"

Jeffers held up a hand. "I appreciate your eagerness, but as Mayor Ladley said, we want y'all to think about the plan, discuss within your families how much you feel able to contribute. Come back here Wednesday night, prepared to commit yourselves wholeheartedly, if you agree. Meanwhile, remember you've pledged yourselves to secrecy. If you should happen to encounter anyone from outside Llano Crossing, you cannot speak of this plan. And now I think it's time to end this meeting. Mayor Ladley, will you dismiss us in prayer?"

Chapter Eighteen

After the meeting, Charles, Delia and Miss Susan drove back to the parsonage, but when Delia would have followed the seamstress inside, Charles put a hand on her wrist.

"Why don't we go for a drive, Delia? It's a nice night, and I'd like to hear what you thought of the sche—the plan."

She hesitated. "Could we just sit in the parlor and talk for a while, Charles? I—I'm a little tired, but I *do* want to discuss what they said."

His mouth drooped sulkily. "I suppose," he said with a heavy sigh, "though I must confess I liked it better before *that spinster* came to live with you. I feel as if we have no privacy with her in there." He nodded toward the house. "She's probably always got her ear to the keyhole. She isn't planning to live with you forever, is she?"

Delia stared at him, surprised and annoyed at the peevish tone she'd never heard him use before. "Miss Susan," she said carefully, "would never *dream* of listening at keyholes, and she's welcome in my house for as long as she cares to stay."

"I'm sorry," Charles said hastily, taking hold of her hand. "I suppose I'm a little fatigued myself, after working with the committee for so long to bring this plan to the town. Friends again?"

Delia nodded, still inwardly uneasy. She had just seen a side of Charles he'd never shown before, and coupled with her earlier misgivings about committing herself to him and her growing love for Jude Tucker—no matter what his feelings were for her—made her more sure than ever that she needed to make a clean break with Charles Ladley.

"Don't you think the plan is marvelous, Delia?" he said, as they settled themselves on the horsehair couch. "Just think, you and I'll be among the primary shareholders. We'll be richer than the proverbial Croesus!" Even in the flickering lamplight, his eyes gleamed and his grin was exuberant—amazing, since he had been so petulant only minutes ago.

"Primary shareholders?" she echoed. "You have money to invest?"

"Some, though not as much as you, of course," he admitted. His eyes had left hers and seemed to focus on a point across the room. "But, darling, one of these days I'll be your husband. What's yours becomes ours, right? Just as what's mine becomes yours," he added quickly, glancing at her. "We can use the money to make more money— that's the way it's done."

"I… I see." Delia pulled her shawl closer around her, as if the October evening chill had penetrated the cozy little house. She hadn't thought about it much before tonight, but whoever she married would be the one who had the final say in how her money—*their money*—would be spent. Charles, she sensed now, would always assume that as the man his opinion was the only one that mattered in how the money was spent, no matter where the money had come from.

"Don't look so worried, sweetheart," Charles said, slipping his arm around her shoulders to pull her close. "Ah,

Delia, that's what I love about you. In your heart, you're still a poor preacher's granddaughter, and even now, the idea of fabulous wealth still makes you a bit nervous, doesn't it? Don't ever change, darling. Stay as innocent and sweet as you are."

Delia turned toward him just as he leaned closer to kiss her cheek. She pulled hastily away.

He pulled away and studied her. "I-is something wrong?"

"I—I..." She didn't want to say the words that would hurt him, but she must. "I guess it's true that talking about vast sums of money makes me nervous," she agreed.

"I understand, sweetheart. How much were you thinking of contributing? Maybe just saying it aloud to me will make it easier to get used to the idea."

She swallowed hard. "A thousand dollars..."

Charles's jaw dropped. "A thousand dollars? *That's all?* Delia, I thought you supported the committee's plan! A thousand dollars from one with a fortune such as yours is...well, it's paltry."

Oh, dear, she had offended him after all, and that would make the other matter she had to discuss that much harder to broach.

"Charles, I am willing to support the project, but think about it—*I* don't need the money the mine would make, do I? I already have more than enough—I don't want to be greedy."

Charles's lips compressed to a tight, bloodless line. For a long moment he said nothing, and then he let out a breath and his features relaxed again. "Of course, you're right. I had forgotten how generous and unselfish you are. You want the people who have not experienced your good luck to enjoy the profits."

As she had thought so often, Delia wanted to say that she'd rather have her father back than all the luck in the world, but she thought better of it. "Something like that, yes. It's good of you to understand."

"I love you, Delia. Why wouldn't I?" he said. "All right, a thousand it is." He started to rise. "Maybe I should go. It's been a long day."

Don't love me, she thought. *That will make this so much harder.*

"There's more I need to say, Charles," Delia said and watched as he sank back onto the couch, his confidence faltering now.

"I've valued—that is, I *value* our friendship, Charles," she said. "I always will, and I hope you will do the same. But…" *Help me, Lord.* "I can see you want it to become something more than that. I thought I just wasn't ready, but it's become more and more clear to me that…that I don't think you—that is, *we*—are right for each other. We value different things," she said, her eyes stinging as she saw his eyes widen with pain. "No matter how used I grow to my new wealth, I think I will always be, deep down, the preacher's poor granddaughter, a—a church mouse."

"Don't say that, Delia, don't!" he cried, and then astonished her by kneeling at her feet and taking both her hands in his while he stared up at her, his eyes pleading. "Don't tell me you can never love me!"

Her stomach clenched with compassion as she saw a tear snake its way down his suddenly pale cheek. She hated hurting him.

"I *do* love you—as a friend, Charles. I'll always be that, as I said. You—and your family—have been very kind to me. But I can't love you as a wife should, I know that now. I… I also know the right woman is out there for you."

"The right woman for me is *you,* Delia," he insisted. "Please, think about what you're doing! How can I te—" He broke off, and once again Delia was left wondering what he'd been about to say.

She stood up, letting her hands slip from his. "I *have* thought about it, Charles—believe me, I have."

"Is there…is there someone else, Delia? Has that Jude Tucker been making you promises, telling you lies about me?" He stood up, and now his eyes glittered with something that made Delia cold all over.

She had to set him straight. "No, Charles. We don't talk about you. Mr. Tucker is building a house for me, and mostly that's what we speak of. I'd better say good-night now, Charles. Please remember I'd like to continue being your friend, if you're willing."

"We'll always be friends, of course," he said stiffly, but he did not meet her eyes.

"See, Jude, you won't even have to go back to Nevada to be a miner again," Heston groused, once they had returned home from the meeting at the church. "I suppose after you finish Miss Delia's house, you'll sign on with the committee as soon as it starts hirin'."

Jude turned to his boss. "It might be a good idea."

Heston snorted. "What d'ya mean by that?"

"It might be wise to keep an eye on what they're doing."

"So *you* think there's a fox in the chicken coop, too!" Heston exclaimed, slapping his knee. "Dadgum it, but I knew you were smart, son! You think these old boys're up t' something like I do, don't you?"

"I don't know," Jude said thoughtfully, rubbing his thumb and forefinger over his chin. "But there's never been any gold found anywhere in these parts before, has there?"

"Not so much as a glimmer," Mrs. Heston supplied from her rocking chair, and Heston nodded in confirmation.

"It's *possible* that Morrison really found gold," Jude pointed out.

Heston gave a skeptical snort again. "I wouldn't trust him far's I could throw him, any more than I do his boss.

I'm pretty sure that's the same fella that fired a shot and spooked my gelding that evenin' we met, Jude. That cave he's talkin' about used to be on my property. I had to go down into it once to rescue a calf that fell in there, but I can't say I looked around much—too busy keepin' that bawlin' calf on my shoulders and climbin' back out at the same time."

Jude was thoughtful for a minute. "Have you ever heard of pyrite, Jim? Fool's gold?" Jude asked. "Looks just like the real thing."

"But it ain't. You think that's what it is?"

"'All that glitters isn't gold,'" Mrs. Heston quoted, picking up her crocheting.

Jude shrugged. "I sure couldn't tell from a glimpse of that nugget so far from me. It would take an assayer to say for sure. Now, pyrite's not always a bad thing. Sometimes it's mixed up with copper or iron."

"But it ain't valuable as gold, is it?"

Jude shook his head. "And we only have Morrison's— and the committee's—word that what he was showing us was really found where he said it was." *A man who'd beat his wife might do anything else, especially if he was paid enough.*

Heston gave a low whistle. "Jude, you're smart as a tree full a' owls, you know that? So you're plannin' to hire on t' see what they've found?"

"Thought I might, for a spell. I promised Delia I'd be done with her house by Thanksgiving, and there's not much for me to do outside with winter coming on, anyway. I heard someone say they're planning to start hiring in November, though they don't plan to start working in the mine till the end of winter. Once they've enlarged those passages, though, it shouldn't take long for me to figure out if it's the real thing. Were you planning to invest?"

Heston gave a bark of laughter. "Even if I *had* a passel

a' greenbacks, which I don't, I wouldn't put 'em into anything Dixon Miller or the mayor're involved in."

Jude grinned. "You might be passing up your chance to be rich, Jim."

"I'm already rich, boy, in the things that matter. Got me a good wife," he said, jerking his head toward Mrs. Heston, "got some good land, my health, a good relationship with the good Lord. And good friends." He nodded at Jude. "What else does a man need?"

"Well said," Jude murmured. Silence fell over the three, and Jude found his thoughts straying to Delia. He'd caught glimpses of her lovely profile as she listened to the committee's plan, and there hadn't been the avid excitement there that he'd seen on the faces of many of the other townspeople. Perhaps it was because she already had plenty of money, but Jude had thought she'd seemed troubled rather than detached.

Chapter Nineteen

"You look a mite wilted," Miss Susan said the next morning as she and Delia washed and dried their breakfast dishes. "Did you get any sleep last night?"

"Not much," Delia admitted, wondering if the older woman guessed why. Her eyes felt heavy and her brain foggy, but she was also aware of a dawning sense of relief.

"Stop me if you don't want me meddlin', but I could hear Charles's voice raised through my door last night. Couldn't tell what he was saying, but he sounded upset."

"He was," Delia said. "I'm not willing to contribute enough money to the committee's project to suit him."

"Good for you for havin' backbone! Don't you let him sweet-talk you into changin' your mind, either."

"Oh, I don't think he'll be doing any more of that," Delia said, then told her the rest of what she had said to Charles.

Miss Susan dropped her dish towel and clapped her hands. "Delia, that's the best news I've heard in a year of Sundays! I never, ever thought Charles Ladley was worthy of you. Well, I'll make myself scarce when Jude stops by tonight after work so you can tell him."

Delia's hands stilled in the soapy water and she stared at Miss Susan. "You think I should *throw* myself at him? I couldn't do that!"

"Why ever not? Don't you love him?"

The question caught Delia off guard. She'd never said it aloud before. "Yes," she whispered; then, "Yes, but what if he rejects me again—what if he tells me again he's going back to Nevada as soon as possible?"

"What if he *doesn't?*" Miss Susan countered. "All I'm saying is, tell him what you just told me, and unless I miss my guess, he'll be happy to take it from there."

Delia found she couldn't stop the smile from spreading across her face. She felt like dancing for joy, even with her still-touchy ankle. "One way to find out," she said. "Oh, how I *wish* I had a horse—I'd go out there this morning!"

The thought reminded her of Zephyr and made her wistful, in spite of her happiness. She hoped the affectionate, spirited mare was recovering from her lameness. Charles would probably sell her, and she'd never see her again.

"That's the spirit," Miss Susan approved, hanging up her dish towel. "Well, I'd better get to the shop."

"I'll walk with you," Delia said. After her fall from the horse, she hadn't been escorting Miss Susan to work because of her sprained ankle, but after intercepting the glare Donley Morrison had sent Miss Susan's way when he'd been standing in the front of the church last night, Delia thought she'd better resume doing it.

"There's no need," Miss Susan tried to tell her. "If Donley was going to do something, I think he'd have done it by now—"

Delia wasn't convinced, after seeing the expression in the big cowboy's eyes last night. Grabbing her cane, she followed her out the door. "It's no trouble. Doc Jones told me I needed to start using my ankle again, a little at a time."

They were halfway to the shop when Miss Susan suddenly said, "Delia, be careful about Charles."

Delia paused in midstride. "What are you saying?

Charles may be disappointed about us, but I know he'd never hurt me."

"It's just a feeling I have, Delia. I don't think anyone really *knows* Charles. And I can tell you this now—you didn't know Charles spent a good deal of time above the saloon, did you? You understand what I'm saying?"

"How do you know this?" *Charles consorted with saloon girls?*

"My shop's right across from the saloon," Miss Susan reminded her. "Many's the time I'd work late on a wedding dress or some such, and I'd see Charles coming down those stairs from the rooms above the saloon where those girls—"

"I know what they do. And I've heard men can smoke opium up there…" Her head was reeling with the idea of Charles going there—and with the idea that she might have married such a man.

It was nearly noon before Charles Ladley descended the stairs at Ladley House.

"About time you showed your face," his father said, from his desk in his study, which faced the landing. "Been out late celebrating?"

Charles started at the voice, freezing at the bottom of the stairs, and rubbed his eyes. His head felt like someone was hammering horseshoes inside it. "G-good morning, Father. I thought you'd be out at Miller's ranch."

"Your mother said she heard you come in at dawn, and I thought I'd wait and ask you what happened. You look like the dickens, boy. Do I take it you and Delia finally—" he sniggered "—sealed the deal, so to speak? Did you set a date?"

He'd hoped his father would be out of the house and he wouldn't have to tell him yet. "I didn't stay at Delia's.

I went to Flora," he said, knowing his father was well-acquainted with the saloon girl.

His father's eyes narrowed. "There's more."

Charles's stomach twisted. "Delia's only putting in a thousand. And she told me she won't marry me."

His father's jaw dropped, his face turning blotchy. "Won't marry you? She adores you! You merely haven't been persuasive enough, boy."

Charles shook his head, remembering the finality of Delia's words. "She told me she doesn't—can't—love me that way."

The mayor's eyes bulged in their sockets. "You can't just *accept* that like a meek little lamb! We need her money!"

Charles's eyes clenched shut in misery at the contempt in his father's voice. "I—I'm sorry, Father...."

"Sorry won't get us control of her fortune!" Charles Ladley Senior's voice was like the crack of a whip.

"I'll get her back, Father, I swear it. I'll find a way...."

Delia was sitting on the porch when Jude rode up. Dressed in pearl-gray silk with contrasting bands of charcoal-gray at the hem and wrists, her hair curling loosely down her back, she looked so lovely that his throat tightened.

"New dress, Delia? It's very pretty," Jude said, dismounting. *Was she wearing it to go to dinner with Ladley?*

"Thank you. Yes, it's new." She stood, watching him intently as he strode up the walk.

"Were you...going somewhere?" he said, pausing at the top of the steps. "I won't stay if you were... I... Mrs. Heston's probably got dinner ready...."

Her eyes were luminous in the early evening light. "I saw her in town today, and told her you might be late. Come inside—I have something I want to tell you."

Was he going to have to listen to her tell him she'd accepted a proposal of marriage from Ladley? Was she so oblivious to his feelings that she'd expect him to wish her happy?

Climbing the last step and following her inside seemed like scaling the highest mountain. His heart beat like a trip-hammer.

Closing the door behind them, she took his hand in hers. "I want you to know I told Charles last night I couldn't marry him."

Could he have heard her right? "Why?" was all he managed to say, drowning in the green, fathomless depths of her eyes as she looked into his face.

"Because I love *you,* Jude Tucker. I… I don't know what you'll do about it—maybe it won't change your mind about going back to Nevada, but that's the reason."

"Oh, Delia, I love you, too." Afterward, neither of them were ever sure which of them opened their arms first, but it was some time later when he said, "I was a fool not to have started courting you the day we met. But why would you have trusted *me,* a man you'd just met, who came to tell you your father was dead and you were rich? I'd have sounded like nothing more than a fortune hunter."

Delia looked thoughtful. "I did trust you, though. I don't know why. Maybe it's why I was so forward, inviting you to dinner at the hotel. I wanted to hear more about my father, yes—but I wanted to get to know *you,* too."

"I *wanted* to accept," he admitted, cupping her cheek. "I didn't think it would be good for you…that *I* would be good for you. I'm still not so sure, Delia. The good Lord's been working on me, but I'm still a poor man—"

"That doesn't ma—"

He interrupted her before she could say that his lack of money didn't matter, because she had to know the rest. "And a minister who very nearly committed adultery with another man's wife."

Delia's eyes widened.

He gestured for them to sit down on the couch. "I didn't know Nora was married when I met her," he said, watching Delia's face, hoping he wouldn't see the glorious new love for him fade. "She told me she was a widow, and I began helping her out at her farm, which she was barely keeping going by herself. I would have done anything for her. She kept dangling herself as the prize...." He looked away then, shamed anew. "Then her supposedly dead husband returned from the war."

Delia's eyes never left his.

"She said if I'd kill him, she'd not only give herself to me that very night, but she'd marry me. For a few moments, I was actually tempted," he admitted. "But then it was as if I suddenly woke up. I left that farm that very night."

She'd gone pale, taking it in.

"That's why I told you I can't go back to being a preacher. You can still love me, knowing what I almost did?" he asked, and was shaken to see her nod.

"The important thing was you *didn't* go through with it," she told him. "I'll love you, no matter what you choose to be, but I still think you ought to go back to preaching—right here in Llano Crossing. Oh, you'll have to tell the church board what you told me," she said, holding up a hand when he would have protested. "But God's forgiven you, and I believe He still wants you preaching the Word."

"I—I'll have to think about that, Delia—*pray* about it," he said. "But do you really think a board headed by Charles Ladley Senior is going to accept me?" he asked.

"Especially if you're marrying the woman his son was courting, you mean?" she asked, sobered at the thought, but she stopped as she saw him grin. "What's so funny?"

"Why, Delia Keller, I believe you just proposed to me," he drawled.

Her jaw dropped open, but then she began to smile.

"Why, Jude Tucker, I believe you're right. It seems I can't stop being forward around you."

He kissed her again. "And I accept. But we're going to do this properly. I'm going to court you, Delia Keller, and we're going to pray about it, and about whether I should be a preacher again, and—"

"I wouldn't have it any other way."

Chapter Twenty

Delia awoke at dawn smiling. Her world had changed completely last night, and now she knew what joy really meant. It hadn't consisted of having enough money to buy anything she wanted or being able to move into the house of her dreams soon. It had nothing to do with being worthy of marrying into a socially prominent family like the Ladleys. She had achieved those things, and they had left her empty and uncertain inside, because she had forgotten about depending on God.

It had everything to do with knowing she had the love of a good man, a man who was finding his way back to serving God and who would help her to do the same. Whether Jude became a preacher again, remained a carpenter or whatever he did, the Lord would be the head of their house.

She only had one unpleasant task to do before she felt entirely free to enjoy her happiness. Rising before she heard Miss Susan stirring in the other bedroom, she gathered together the things Charles had given her—earbobs, a crystal vase, a gold brooch and the riding habit Mrs. Ladley had lent her. She had to return these things to him, and she wasn't looking forward to it. Perhaps she could leave them with his mother? But had Charles even told her what had happened?

She regretted that ending her relationship with Charles would probably mean the end of her burgeoning friendship with Jane Ladley. The mayor's wife seemed to be a genuinely nice, motherly lady, and because she loved her son, she might well see Delia now as the woman who had hurt Charles.

"Don't put yourself through that, Delia. I'll walk over to the Ladley house and drop those things off before I open the shop," Miss Susan offered as they walked to town, when Delia explained what was in her poke. "You know he'll try to wheedle his way back into your good graces."

Delia feared exactly that—or that he might have grown angry and say rude things to her, especially if they were alone together at his home. "Thanks, but it would be cowardly of me."

"Well, you won't have to walk to his house, Delia," Miss Susan said, as they neared her shop. "He's coming out of the bank. Want me to stay?"

Charles had spotted her and was walking toward her. He'd probably not appreciate a witness to their conversation. "No, and don't let him see you watching from the window," Delia said. Shrugging, Miss Susan went around to her back entrance.

"Delia! You're looking beautiful this morning. I'm glad to run into you," he said, smiling at her as if nothing had happened. "See, everyone's buzzing about the gold-mine project," he added, nodding toward a knot of men talking excitedly in front of the saloon across the street.

"Good morning, Charles," she said, taken aback by his cheery demeanor. She kept her voice pleasant, even. "I... I have some things to give back to you."

He froze. Some of the color faded from his face, and for a moment she thought he wouldn't take the sack from her. He looked inside. Pain swam in his dark eyes as he lifted them to her.

"Delia, sweetheart, these were gifts. I wanted you to have them. I still do."

"I can't keep them, Charles. It wouldn't be right. And please thank your mother for the loan of her riding habit."

He took her hand before she realized what he was doing.

"Delia, I'm not giving up on us. You loved me—I know you did—and you will again. Please keep these things, and let them remind you of me," he said, trying to hand the sack back.

She took a step back, freeing herself. "I can't, Charles. And please believe that I won't be changing my mind. Again, I'm sorry, Charles, but I—"

"You will change your mind," he told her with a brittle confidence. "And don't forget about the meeting at the church Wednesday night, when everyone is bringing their pledged money. I'll see you there, right?"

Delia blinked. After the conversation they'd just had, he expected her to attend?

"I—I'll write a draft at the bank and leave it there for you," she told him stiffly. "Goodbye, Charles." She was shaken at the way he'd seemed determined to ignore her resolve. Hoping he didn't see her trembling, she walked into the bank. He was gone when she came out.

Having decided to bake a cake for Jude, she went into the general store for baking chocolate. Just as Charles had said, everyone inside was chattering about the Llano Crossing gold mine and what they were going to do with their shares of the profits. She heard boasting about how much some would pledge—or how hard their men would work to mine the gold. Delia was glad it was none of her concern.

"I'll be painting the rooms inside your house for the next few days," Jude told Delia as she sliced the chocolate cake into pieces for him, Miss Susan and herself.

"Can you borrow the wagon and pick me up at Miss

Susan's shop? I can help you paint," Delia told him, delighted that the house was so near completion.

"Pick us both up here," Miss Susan said. "I reckon I can close the shop for the day and wield a paintbrush."

"We can bring a picnic lunch, too," Delia said.

Jude grinned. "Sounds like a good deal to me."

"Remember, we're not painting the dining room or the parlor," Delia reminded him. "I have wallpaper on order from the mercantile. Oh, what if it doesn't arrive in time for Thanksgiving dinner?" she said and fretted.

"We're having wallpaper instead of turkey?" he asked, so seriously that both women giggled.

"Jude, a bare wall in the dining room just wouldn't be very festive. Oh, and tell the Hestons they're invited to Thanksgiving dinner," she told Jude.

"Lucy will want to bring something, so I'll tell her to discuss that with you."

"Tell her I'm making the pies," Miss Susan chimed in. "It's so nice to have folks to bake for."

Later, as Jude and Delia sat together on the porch, realizing it would soon be too chilly to sit outside, Delia asked, "Am I doing the right thing?"

"Sitting out here holding hands with me? Absolutely, I believe you are, Delia honey."

"I love it when you call me that. No, I mean the house. If you're going to be the preacher, maybe I should sell it, and we'll just stay here," she said, nodding toward the house behind her. "I can't believe I ever let *things* become so important to me. All I want now is to be the very best preacher's wife that ever was."

"And you will be," Jude said, smiling at her in approval. "But, honey, God doesn't disapprove of His children using the blessings He sends, including money. I'm thinking that big house could be a blessing, not only to the Tucker family," he said, smiling at that, "but to others in need—travelers, folks in need, orphans—whoever the Lord sends. Not to mention the babies I hope the Lord will bless us with. If we do even half of that, this two-bedroom parsonage would soon seem very small." He grinned as Delia smiled shyly, sensing she was blushing in the dark. His heart swelled with love and thankfulness that God had seen fit to bless him with this woman's love.

"That all sounds wonderful," she agreed. "Will it be all right if Miss Susan continues to live with us for as long as she wants?"

"Of course," he said, surprised she even thought she had to ask. "Delia, you're a good woman."

Then she told him about her encounter with Charles that morning, her brow furrowing as she described it.

"Try not to worry, honey," Jude told her. "Today he may not believe you mean it, but as the days go on and you don't change your mind, he'll understand—especially when he sees us at church together and so forth."

"But is that wise?" she said. "You're going to speak with the church board about becoming the new preacher, and his father is the chairman—"

Jude laid a finger on her lips. "Delia, I'm not going to pretend I don't love you. The Lord will work all these things out. If He means for me to be the preacher here, I will be. But there's something I have to investigate first." He told her he was going to apply for a job as a miner as soon as the committee started hiring after Thanksgiving.

"Why?"

Then he told her about his suspicion that there was no genuine gold in the cave. "I'm going to find out. Who better than someone who's been a miner? I know the difference between fool's gold and the real thing."

Her eyes widened with alarm. "You think the committee's out to defraud the town? How could they get away with it? They'd be found out sooner or later."

"And by then they could be miles away with the money. I hope I'm wrong," he admitted. "But does it seem logical that a man like Dixon Miller, whom Heston says has never cared a lick about anyone but himself, suddenly wants to share wealth with everyone in Llano Crossing?"

"No, nor any of the others," Delia murmured, her eyes troubled. "Oh, I *wish* I hadn't pledged anything! I wonder if it's too late to get it back?"

"I'd leave it as it is," he advised. "We don't want them to get wind of the fact that anyone's skeptical. If this *is* fraud and we can catch them at it, I'm hoping everyone can get their money back."

"Oh, Jude, be careful," she said, knowing she couldn't dissuade him from his investigation. "These men could be dangerous—especially Miller and his cowboys."

"I will be," he promised her. "Remember Who we've got on our side."

Chapter Twenty-One

October blended seamlessly into November. Sumac bushes turned red as Moses' Biblical burning bush as Delia's house neared completion. Jude had secured the loan of the Hestons' carriage horse, which was also saddle-broken, and Delia spent almost each day there with Jude, painting, wallpapering and supervising the placing of the new furniture as it arrived. She left in time to accompany Miss Susan home from work and fix supper for the three of them—or sometimes they would go to the Hestons', for the old couple seemed to have appointed themselves as honorary grandparents.

Miss Susan had taken her aside at one point and told Delia that she'd be moving back to the boardinghouse when Delia moved into her new house. "For you'll be getting married soon after that, I don't wonder, and newlyweds need their privacy."

Delia urged her to change her mind. The new house was a big one, she reminded her, and she and Jude wanted it to be a blessing for others, too. They would have room for her for as long as she wanted it.

The older woman's eyes had welled up and she'd hugged Delia, saying she'd stay until Delia and Jude married, at least, for she didn't want Delia to be lonely in that big house by herself.

Delia heard nothing from Charles. He looked away from her whenever their paths crossed. Jude's reading of the Scripture passage and commenting upon it had become a regular part of Sunday services, and Jude had told her that Charles never looked up when Jude was in the pulpit. Mayor Ladley was frigidly civil to both of them. Much to Delia's amazement, Mrs. Ladley never failed to greet her with a kind smile, but her husband always tried to hurry her past.

Delia would have felt complete relief that Charles had accepted her decision to end their relationship, except that she never saw him with another girl—and there had been times when, alone in town or outside both the parsonage and her new house, she had felt the sensation of being watched.

She never saw anyone, of course, just felt that prickling at the back of her neck....

Delia moved into her new house on the Monday before Thanksgiving and had barely had time to get her kitchen arranged before the day of the big feast.

Thanksgiving dinner was a hearty success. With a little guidance from Lucy Heston and Miss Susan, the turkey was roasted to perfection, and the table groaned under the weight of it and all the traditional side dishes—and all of them groaned with satisfaction afterward. There had been enough food for a battalion, and all that was left of the turkey was bare bones.

Jude pushed himself away from the table after politely declining a second slice of pumpkin pie. "Thanks, but I've let my belt out to its last notch now."

"Yep, I reckon that was the best meal we'll eat this side of Heaven," Mr. Heston chimed in.

"The committee's going to start hiring for the mine

tomorrow," Jude reminded them, as they sat in the parlor later.

"Still plannin' to ride out there and apply, are you?" Heston asked.

"Oh, Jude, be careful," Delia said, unconsciously twisting a fold of her skirt of dark purple silk.

Two of Dixon Miller's cowboys lounged indolently on the front porch of the big house, looking harmless enough except for the gun belts they wore. Jude joined the line of applicants that snaked into the house and out onto the winter-brown lawn. Known to most of them now from church, Jude chatted with them while they waited. He learned that most of them had not been able to pledge much, if any, money for the project at the meeting run by the Committee for Civic Improvement, and were hoping to help their families by signing on as miners, but no one except Jude had ever actually done any mining before.

"You're sure t' be hired, then," a wiry graybeard said a little enviously, after hearing Jude had mined silver out in Nevada. "They'll want a man with experience. Mebbe they'll even make you foreman."

But Jude was not made foreman, when it came his turn to be interviewed in Dixon Miller's study. As he stood facing Miller, Amos Dawson, Barton Jeffers and both Ladleys, all seated behind a gleaming pecanwood desk, and another of Miller's henchmen, standing with a gun belt slung low on his hips, he was told his services weren't needed.

"But…but I have experience," Jude protested, allowing himself to look shocked, though he wasn't completely surprised about being rejected. It only strengthened his conviction that something was amiss. "I'm the only one in that line who can say that. Wouldn't you gentlemen like to hire someone who's actually *been* a miner?"

"Mr., ah… Tucker, was it?" Miller made a big show of peering through his spectacles at the application paper Jude had filled out. "Yes, that's it, Tucker. You have to understand, this project was meant to benefit the Llano Crossing residents. You're an outsider."

"But…but you know I've been living here since August," Jude protested, though he already knew it was futile. Charles Ladley was already smirking.

"And did you invest in the project?" Mayor Ladley retorted, reaching for a list on the desk and studying it. "No, your name's not on here."

"I'm a carpenter, not a wealthy man. Most of the men out there aren't on that list, either," Jude argued, jerking a hand in back of him to indicate the line of applicants outside. His sudden motion had the armed man standing behind the seated men straightening and fingering the handle of his pistol in its holster meaningfully. Jude ignored him. "That's why most of us are applying for jobs—we need work."

"But they're longtime citizens," Ladley told him with a sniff. "Whereas *you* drifted into town only recently."

"I've worked for several of the townspeople, including James Heston—a longtime resident—and Mr. Miller's former neighbor," Jude shot back. "Doesn't that count for something?"

"I'm afraid not," Dixon Miller said, with a deprecating smile.

Jude let his shoulders slump in apparent defeat. "I don't know how I'm going to make it through the winter."

"Perhaps you ought to consider riding on…to greener pastures, shall we say?" Dixon Miller suggested with insincere concern.

Charles Ladley snapped the reins over the carriage horse's rump with unnecessary sharpness as they pulled away from Dixon Miller's grand house. Startled, the horse half reared, then lurched into a trot.

"Take it easy, Son!" his father, next to him, snapped. "I certainly taught you to drive better than that!"

Charles bit back a sharp reply. "Sorry, Father. It's been a long day."

So it had. As the sun sank behind a pair of blue hills in the distance, all the men needed for the gold mine had been hired—the ones to construct the timber shoring, the dynamiters, the excavators, the ones to pan the creek and the river, the ones to guard the creek and the river from outsiders. Panning would start immediately, to take advantage of the milder pre-Christmas weather, but the actual work in the mine had been set to start in February, once the ground had thawed.

"Cat got your tongue?" Charles Ladley Senior said, interrupting his son's thoughts. "You ought to be feeling some satisfaction, giving Jude Tucker his comeuppance. Or are you still riled because Delia Keller showed you the door in favor of a mere jack-of-all-trades? There's plenty of women for you, my boy—you might as well wait for a spicy little *señorita* in Mexico."

Charles glared at his father's bare-faced bluntness.The old man's condescending tone grated on Charles's nerves. "I don't think you realize Tucker could do more than just wreck my chances with Delia Keller," he snapped. "I think we ought to get rid of him."

"What're you saying?" his father demanded uneasily. "You can't mean…"

"What I *mean,* Father, is that Tucker is the only man who's got the knowledge to blow this whole plan up in our faces! Like he said, he's been a miner! And guarding the mine to keep him from snooping may not be enough. If we don't get him out of the way, we won't be sitting pretty on our *estancia* in Mexico—we'll be languishing in a cell in Huntsville Prison."

"But…*murder?* Son, it's too risky. I know you're a good shot—the Yankees certainly had reason to rue your skills—but I'm not sure I trust the committee enough not to open their mouths."

Honestly, the old fool was heading into his dotage! "We don't need to inform them. All I have to do is set up an ambush for Tucker—something I did all the time when I was a sniper in the war, remember. Easy, neat, no loose ends."

His father harrumphed. "I don't want to know anything about it," he said.

Chapter Twenty-Two

November had given way to December, and one afternoon nine days before Christmas, Mrs. Ladley surprised Delia by paying a visit to her new home.

"I hope I'm welcome, Delia. Charles and his father don't know I'm here, but I've missed you and I don't know why we shouldn't continue to be friends, even though I'm not to be your mother-in-law." Her face was sad as she said the last thing, but Delia was warmed by the fact that she'd wanted to come and welcomed her into the parlor, which was now decorated for Christmas. Branches of red possumhaw berries wove themselves among candles on the mahogany mantel, and a sprig of mistletoe Delia had plucked from a mesquite tree hung from the doorway. Jude had dug up a juniper tall enough to touch the high ceiling as their Christmas tree and they had decorated it only the night before.

"Were those ornaments your grandfather's, Delia?" Mrs. Ladley asked as she sipped the cup of tea Delia had poured for her.

Delia shook her head. "A couple of them were my mother's," she said, pointing to a small, carved angel of wood and a cobalt-blue glass ball with only a tiny crack in the back. "When Grandpa was alive, we usually just made paper chains and popcorn string decorations. Most of the ornaments are from the mercantile. Mr. Dean was kind enough to order them for me from Fredericksburg."

"Those German immigrants make the loveliest ornaments. I suppose it's because the Christmas tree came from their country," the mayor's wife said and sighed. "I guess it's up to the women and children to make Christmas what it should be this year—every man in town is so wrapped up in this gold-mining project. It's all they talk about. You can't imagine how much time the committee's spending in meetings these days."

"I hear there's to be improvements for the town with all the money the gold will bring in," Delia said. "A public park with a bandstand, a new town hall, and they'll enlarge the church…"

"I'm thinking they'd better wait until that money starts rolling in, don't you?" Mrs. Ladley said, rolling her eyes. "Men! Well, hopefully when all these things start happening, we can finally get a new preacher. I just can't understand why all our inquiries haven't brought us one," she fretted. "Especially since you're having the parsonage renovated at your own expense. That's so generous of you, dear."

"I'm honored to be able to do it. And I suppose the right man just hasn't offered himself yet," Delia murmured, forbearing to tell her that Jude was going to offer himself for the position one day or that he'd had plenty of time to work on the parsonage since he'd been turned down by the mine hiring committee. She wondered how much of his rejection had been pure spite on the Ladley men's part, and how much because there was no real gold that would be found—the committee realized Jude would know that as soon as he went down into the cave.

"Are you going to the Nativity play Wednesday night?" Mrs. Ladley asked.

Delia nodded. "It'll be fun to be just a member of the audience this time, not directing it as I always did when Grandpa was alive. I'm so grateful Mrs. Purvis took over the rehearsals this year since I was so busy with building the house."

The grandfather clock in the corner of the room began to chime.

"Dear me, look at the time," Mrs. Ladley said, rising. "Four o'clock already! I must be going, dear. Charles will be wanting his supper before you know it."

Delia bid her a warm goodbye, suspecting that neither Mr. Ladley nor his son knew that she had come.

Sitting in the darkened, crowded church with Jude by her side and watching the story of Christmas being played out before them was like seeing it for the very first time herself, Delia thought.

There were cries of delight as a young girl appeared onstage, stumbling over the long hem of her white cotton angel dress, her golden wings and halo wobbling dangerously as she announced, "Fear not, Mary, for thou hast found favor with God…"

Delia and Jude chuckled along with the rest of the audience as one of the sheep, borrowed from a local farmer, bleated and tried to escape from the stage, which set the burro braying, which in turn made the heifer tethered to the leg of the piano begin to bawl. But everyone howled when three other boys dressed in improvised Magi robes (which looked suspiciously like Mrs. Purvis's old brocade curtains) and turbans made of towels, complete with borrowed jewels stuck in the centers, marched in leading calves to whose backs had been fixed makeshift humps of burlap to make them look like camels.

"Where is the newborn King that we may worship Him?" the oldest boy, whose voice was beginning to crack on the edge of manhood, asked. "For we have seen His star in the east and bring him gold, frankincense and…and…"

"Myrrh!" Mrs. Purvis stage-whispered from the front row.

"And myrrh!" the boy completed his question triumphantly to another boy playing Herod. Herod had been rendered sinister by a scary-looking fake mustache and beard. It was the same Christmas story, ever wonderful, ever new, ever inspiring.

If only there wasn't that shadow on the horizon caused by the possibility that the committee was arranging an enormous swindle to bankrupt most of its trusting citizens. Jude had told her that he was going to find a way to sneak into the cave some night soon to find out for himself just what, if anything, was down there.

What if he was caught by the committee's henchmen? They could kill Jude and no one might ever be the wiser. Delia shuddered at the possibility.

"Are you all right, sweetheart?" Jude asked solicitously, his face turned toward her in the flickering shadows formed by the row of lanterns that made the stage lighting.

"Sure. I… I just felt a draft," she said, not wanting to tell him about her fears and spoil the magic of the age-old story of Jesus' coming.

"Fear not, for I bring you tidings of great joy," an angel, whom Delia recognized as one of the Dean girls, announced.

Fear not. The words resounded in Delia's heart. God would protect Jude, and he *would* succeed. All the Christmases to come would be more peaceful in Llano Crossing because of Jude's brave investigation.

The sun had already begun to sink into the western hills in late afternoon. Jude was thoughtful as he rode Shiloh along the fence line that separated the road from Miller's ranch, eyeing the fencing that now circled a thick grove of cottonwoods and oak trees on Miller land.

A tough-looking pair of grim-faced, rifle-toting *hombres* stood guard at the entrance. Miller was taking no chances, Jude mused, that someone might want to come explore the mine on his own—and maybe pocket away some of the alleged gold. Jude would have given much just to be invisible for the few minutes it would take to shimmy down into the cave with a pickax and a lantern and see for himself what was down there. Of course, his tools would have to be invisible, too.

Originally, the cave entrance was in the grove that had been on the edge of Miller land where it bordered the Hestons' ranch; now it was all Miller's.

The nugget Morrison had displayed at the meeting had been assayed and proven to be genuine gold, but Jude figured it had been planted, along with a few other nuggets and flakes that some of the investors who had been hired as panners had found in the creek.

Shiloh sidled and pawed the ground. Jude felt that same tingling down his spine Delia mentioned she'd been feeling lately. He knew the guards were watching him, but this was closer—

A shot rang out and Jude crumpled in the saddle. Consciousness ebbing, feeling the warm blood dripping over his face, he clung to Shiloh as the horse plunged and whinnied in alarm.

Help me, God! Then he felt a scorching pain in his shoulder a heartbeat before the second report blasted his ears. He grabbed desperately at Shiloh's mane as a wave of dizzying blackness washed over him, and he went boneless as a sawdust doll over his horse's neck.

"Got him!" Ladley leaped from his concealed perch in one of the thick-leafed oak trees. "And about time! I knew he'd show up sooner or later, nosing around, but I was getting tired of sitting up here waiting like a vulture."

"Looks like ya did," Donley Morrison said, from a sturdy nearby branch, peering through a spyglass. "But there goes his horse with him," he said, as the buckskin whirled and took off back toward Llano Crossing. "Shouldn't we follow and make sure he's dead?"

"No need. Did you see all that blood? Tucker's dead, all right—or will be in minutes. He'll probably collapse off his horse before he reaches town, and if the bleeding doesn't kill him, exposure will. This couldn't have happened better—when he's found he'll be off Miller land and no one can prove who shot him. I'm heading for the saloon—can I buy you a drink? Killing's thirsty work."

Chapter Twenty-Three

Church mouse no more, Delia thought as she stared into the mirror. The image that stared back at Delia from the mirror was that of a confident woman whose eyes and face were lit with the radiance of love. Her hair was parted in the middle and clusters of curls were held back from her face with ivory combs.

"You've outdone yourself, Miss Susan," Delia said, gazing down at the dress she wore of dark green bengaline with scarlet satin piping, then back at the older woman who stood at the doorway of her room.

"Thank you." Miss Susan beamed with pride at her work. "You look so Christmassy. Jude's going to say you're pretty as a picture."

"If he ever gets here," Delia said with a sigh, as the grandfather clock chimed the hour downstairs. "I thought he'd be back by now. He said he had something to do, but he didn't say what."

"Christmas is coming," Miss Susan reminded her. "Don't fret, I'm keeping dinner warm on top of the oven. That ham's going to be tasty. You and Jude have something special planned for tonight?"

Delia felt her cheeks flush. "We were going to talk about setting a date."

"Oh, sweetie, I'm so happy for you," Miss Susan said, coming forward and embracing her, then she straightened. "I hear someone coming," she said, and both women went to the window that faced the road.

In the gathering dark they could see not Jude on his horse, but a man in a buckboard wagon pulling to a stop in front of her house and clambering down from the driver's seat.

"It looks like Mr. Heston," Delia murmured. "What on earth…"

As she hurried for the stairs, she heard pounding at her door, and Heston's voice calling through it, "Delia? Anyone home?"

"Yes, I'm coming!" she called back. "What is it, Mr. Heston?" she asked as she threw the door open.

The old man's face was grim in the lamp-lit foyer. "Delia, you need to come with me. Jude's horse showed up a few minutes ago with Jude hanging over his neck, passed out. He…he's been shot."

The words made no sense. "*Shot?* Jude's been shot? Who did it? Why?"

"I don't know, but I have my suspicions. We can talk about it on the way. He's asking for you," Heston told her. "I've already stopped to summon the doctor, so he should be there by now."

"Oh, dear Lord," Delia said, feeling the floor shift beneath her feet. For a moment she thought she might faint, and then she felt Miss Susan holding on to her, bracing her.

"I'm coming, too," the seamstress said. "Let me just grab our wraps…"

"Where is his wound?" Delia demanded, as Miss Susan helped her into her coat and threw on her own.

"He has a graze wound to his head and a bullet went through his shoulder. He's lost a lot of blood from that one, Delia," Heston said, as he assisted her and Miss Susan up onto the buckboard. Miss Susan sat in the wagon bed behind them.

The chill that raced through Delia had nothing to do with the brisk winter wind. Would Jude die before she could reach his side? *Lord, please save him!*

"Where did this happen?"

Heston snapped the reins and the two carriage horses took off. "He told me he was riding along the road that runs past Miller's land, in front of the cave entrance, and all of a sudden shots rang out. He didn't see where they were coming from."

That meant he'd regained consciousness and was able to tell Heston what happened.

"It's a wonder he was able to hold on long enough for that stallion a' his to carry him back to our house," Heston told her, almost shouting to be heard above the drumming of the horses' hooves. "Or he'd be lying out there somewhere, still bleeding—or Miller's men woulda finished him off," Heston told her, keeping his eyes on the road as he snapped the reins to speed up the horses.

They managed to get though town without passing anyone. It seemed like an eternity before the wagon pulled up in front of the Hestons' little house. Delia spent it praying. *Please, God, let him live! Oh, Lord, why would they want him dead?*

"You go on in, Miss Delia—he's in the back bedroom," Mrs. Heston called from the doorway. Delia jumped down and ran inside, barely aware that Miss Susan remained behind with Mrs. Heston in the kitchen.

Jude was lying on his back in the shadowy room, his unshaven face looking drawn and almost as bleached of color as the bandages around his head and the top of his left shoulder. His eyes were closed but flew open as Delia ran into the room and up to the bed.

"You…you came," Jude said, as if it were a miracle.

"Of course I came," she said, spotting Doc Jones sitting on the other side of the bed as she sank onto her knees. "Oh, Jude, you might have been killed," she cried, staring at him, seeing the tiny splotch of dried blood that had come through the layers of bandage on his shoulder.

He shook his head at her last exclamation. "God's not finished with me yet."

Doc Jones stood. "He should recover, if infection doesn't set in," he said. "I'll just step out into the kitchen for a minute while you talk. But not for too long," he cautioned.

"Mr. Heston told me you didn't see who shot you," she said, still staring at his pale face. "Jude, you have to stop this investigating. The committee's apparently so determined to keep their secret they're willing to kill. I think you should leave town—"

"It's too late now," he said. "They know I'm onto them. No, I have to find a way into that mine when it isn't guarded. Get a sample somehow. I can tell in a minute if it's fool's gold or not—pyrite flakes into crystals, for one thing, and there's black streaks running through it, where real gold has yellow streaks. Maybe there's nothing down there at all, unless it's more planted nuggets."

Her mouth dropped open. "Jude, you're *badly wounded,*" she said, wondering if the doctor had given him some laudanum that was making him talk out of his head. "You're in no shape to be exploring caves."

"I'll mend in a few days," he told her. "Well enough to get down there, anyway. I've got to see for myself before we can report this to the state police," he said, referring to the force that had taken the place of the Texas Rangers in the state's Reconstruction government. "Sheriff Jenkins is on the committee, you know, so we can't trust him."

She saw that she wasn't going to change his mind. "Could you get down there at night?"

"If it's guarded during the day, it's probably guarded at

night, too," Jude countered. "Particularly now that they've shot me for getting too close."

"We've got to tell everyone you're shot worse than you are, that you'll probably die," Delia said, her mind somehow operating very clearly in spite of the shock that made her tremble like a sapling in a windstorm. "If they think you're going to be up and around in a few days, they might try again," she said flatly. "They might come here—can we trust Doc Jones?"

Jude nodded. "I've already sounded him out on that, and we can. Seems he was doubtful about this gold mine from the start. He's going to let it be known I'm still unconscious, hovering between life and death, and there's nothing he can do but pray," he said in a mock-dramatic tone that failed to bring a smile to Delia's lips.

"What are you planning?" she asked, hardly daring to breathe.

"I'm thinking there'll be guards out there on Christmas Eve just like every other night, but I'm betting they'll be celebrating—" he pantomimed drinking from a bottle "—sure that everyone will be snug in their beds that night," Jude explained. "I'll wait until they're all dead drunk, then sneak past them into the mine."

"I can't let you do that," she said, her chin jutting forward with her determination. "If they catch you, they'll finish killing you! No, I'll call a town meeting and insist the committee hire an official assayer to confirm that there's real gold in the mine. If they refuse, it's as good as an admission of fraud."

He shook his head. "Most of them have gold fever so bad they probably wouldn't believe you. The committee will say that hiring an outsider will bring claim-jumpers. The Llano Crossing folks want so badly to believe they're going to be wealthy just as soon as the mining begins— as wealthy as you."

Chapter Twenty-Four

The congregation's mood was festive, and the church was decorated in fresh greenery on this last Sunday of Advent, Mrs. Heston reported when she returned from church. Delia had stayed at their house along with Mr. Heston, ostensibly to keep vigil by Jude's bedside but also to stand guard in case the committee's henchmen thought to take advantage of the church service and come to finish Jude off. Heston had loaned Delia his pistol; he had his carbine close to his hand.

"Mayor Ladley led the congregation in prayer for your recovery, Jude, and the capture of whatever bandit waylaid you," Lucy Heston told him.

"The blasted hypocrite," growled Heston.

"Part of his prayer is already being answered," Jude said, flexing his injured shoulder experimentally and trying to hide his wince. "It hurts a lot less. I'll be ready to explore that cave Christmas Eve."

"Oh dear," fretted Lucy Heston. "I wish there were some safer way, Jude dear. Maybe we should telegraph the state police instead."

"How do we know the telegraph office isn't controlled by the committee?" Delia pointed out.

"Time enough to telegraph them when we have the Ladleys and their cronies corralled in the jail," Jude said.

"Is Mr. Tucker better?" Mr. Dean asked as Delia paid for her purchases. Mrs. Heston had sent her to the mercantile to buy a few staples she was running short of, and since Delia had been spending most of her time at the Hestons' with Jude, she was happy to run the errand for her. It would allow her to buy a few Christmas presents for the old couple.

"There's no change," Delia said and sighed heavily, keeping her eyes down.

Mr. Dean was studying her sympathetically. Not wanting to meet his gaze, she looked instead down the counter at an elegant black frock coat with matching trousers, a black string tie and complementing gold-figured waistcoat hanging tantalizingly behind the counter. How easily she could imagine Jude, tall and handsome in such an elegant ensemble, preaching from the pulpit, but of course she couldn't tell Mr. Dean that.

"Does he need any laudanum, perhaps?" Mr. Dean suggested, holding up a small dark bottle of the liquid from underneath the counter.

Delia shook her head. "Mrs. Heston still has some for him, thanks," she said, gathering up the rest of the things Dean had wrapped up. "Have a nice Christmas."

"Merry Christmas," Mr. Dean called after her, as she walked out the door.

She hated having to deceive the shopkeeper she'd known forever, but she couldn't admit Jude was nowhere near death's door and risk that he would tell others. Mr. Dean was one of those who'd invested heavily in the gold mine.

It was nearly dark and shops were closing. Delia had only to collect Miss Susan, and they'd walk down to the Hestons' and have dinner with them and Jude. She was going to have to find a way to thank the old couple for taking such good care of Jude and for their hospitality to her, when this was all over.

Passing the bank, Delia stepped off the boardwalk into the narrow road between the bank and the seamstress's shop.

"Hello, Delia," said a voice out of the shadows at the side of the bank. She looked up into the face of Charles Ladley.

"Oh! Charles…" Delia hoped he hadn't seen how he'd startled her, though every nerve had turned to threads of ice at the sight of him. "G-getting close to Christmas, isn't it? Please wish your parents a merry Christmas for me. I have to go—Miss Susan's expecting me," she said, pulling back.

"Is that so?" he asked, his voice on-the-surface pleasant, but something far from pleasant lurked in his dark gaze—something soulless and lethal, like the unblinking stare of a snake.

Delia looked past him to the shop, hoping to see Miss Susan watching for her from her window, but she wasn't there.

"Let me go, Charles," she said levelly, her eyes darting in all directions to see if someone—anyone!—was nearby. But it seemed everyone had gone home for their suppers and the streets were deserted. No one was going in or out of the saloon right now. If anyone was dining at the hotel restaurant, it seemed they weren't sitting near the window.

"Put down your packages and come with me, Delia." He took them from her and dropped them in the dirt.

"Why?"

"I have a little surprise for you. 'Tis the season for surprises, isn't it?" He pulled at her hand, urging her down the narrow road that led toward the river and Jeffers's mill.

Balking, she stared at him, her mind racing. She thought

of pretending to faint or, better yet, screaming at the top of her lungs that she was being robbed. Miss Susan would have to hear her and come running—and maybe Mr. Dean, too. Charles wouldn't dare stay and have them find him there.

Pushing her against the building with one hand, he let her see the pistol he had been concealing under his coat. "Come on, Delia," he said. "Don't make me use this."

How had she ever found him handsome? Or kind?

"You are as faithless as you are beautiful, Delia," he went on in a strange singsong. "Do you think I don't know you aren't plotting with Jude Tucker to bring down all we've planned? Is he your lover?" he asked casually, but his eyes bored into hers, glittering.

"No," she said, answering his last question first. "Let me go, and we'll say no more about it, Charles," she said, trying to sound as emotionless as he did. "We won't expose your crooked plot. We'll leave town quietly, this very night," she said, desperately searching his face for some sign of agreement and finding none.

She tried again. "Let me go and we'll go to the bank, and I'll sign over every cent to you. You'll never hear from us again."

"'Us' meaning you and your *carpenter*." Charles sneered. "You must think me quite a fool to imagine I'd let you run off to Austin and bring the state police down on our heads, Delia, but I'm no fool. You'll be leaving town, all right, but not with Tucker. You'll be departing with me, right now. I took the liberty of going to your house and packing a few things—easy since you've hardly been there of late—and placing them in the landau. We'll head for the border, along with my entourage," he drawled, now nodding toward the two men who stood at both ends of the alleyway, their pistols drawn and cocked. One of them, Delia saw, was Donley Morrison, who smirked at her from the shadows.

"We'll be married right across the border in Matamoros," he told her. "We'll tell everyone we've been reunited, and our love couldn't wait any longer."

"You can't force me to marry you," she said, horror-struck.

"Oh, I think I can," he said. "You think some Mexican *padre* who doesn't speak English will listen to your pleas? My parents will be there, too—we'll have our own little Ladley palace down in Mexico, with the aid of your money and all that's been fleeced from the gullible folk of Llano Crossing."

"Your mother won't agree to this," she hissed. "She's good and kind, everything you're not. How she could ever have given birth to a son like you is a mystery to me."

"She didn't," Charles told her. "I'm the product of my father's liaison with a saloon girl. But Mother's never had to fend for herself, and she'll agree to anything to keep Father and me happy, even moving to Mexico. Once Father brings the money from the 'gold mine'—and the sale of your house—we'll all be one big happy family, far from the reach of the pigeons we've plucked."

Delia could only stare into the face of the man she had once tried to convince herself she loved. That time seemed years ago. Now there was something not quite sane about the way he talked.

Charles lowered the gun and pressed it insistently into her ribs. "Now march down the road here to the carriage like nothing's amiss, or I swear I'll shoot you right here like the faithless woman you are."

There was nothing she could do but comply. She walked to the landau, her legs like jelly. Absently, she noticed that Zephyr and Charles's bay had been tied to the back of the carriage.

He saw her looking at her mare.

"Yes, I'm not leaving a valuable beast like your thoroughbred behind for these yahoos. But abandon any hopes of running away on her, sweetheart. I wouldn't hesitate to put a shot right between her ears and bring her down. And I can do it—I was a sniper in the war. I killed hundreds of Yankees."

While the cowboy-guards mounted their horses, Charles got in beside Delia, keeping his Colt leveled at her but out of sight.

Busy with Christmas preparations, no faces appeared in windows to mark her passing. Llano Crossing might as well have been a ghost town. They would take the road leading south out of town—not the east road that led past the Hestons' house. Jude would not even know she had been taken.

She was numb with terror and hopelessness. If she resisted, he'd kill her. If she complied and allowed him to force her into marriage, her life would be misery beyond imagining.

And call upon Me in the day of trouble: I will deliver thee, and thou shalt glorify Me.

All she could see were the faces of her captors. But she heard the voice in her heart, an echo of all those times her grandpa had her read aloud in the Psalms: "I will call upon God; and the Lord shall save me."

You told me to call if I needed Your help, Lord. You see the danger I'm in. Please do as You promised, and Jude and I will spend our lives glorifying You.

Jude was restless as a red ant under a magnifying glass. He and Heston had talked endlessly about the plan.

"I'm goin' out to the mine site with you Christmas Eve," Heston told him. "It's too dangerous, you goin' alone."

"It's too dangerous for you to go with me," Jude retorted. "No hard feelings, Jim, but do you really think you could crawl under the barbed wire with me?"

"No, I know I can't," Heston shot back. "But what if those guards *ain't* drunker'n boiled owls? You're assumin', son, but what if you're wrong?"

Since it was the same objection Delia had made, it silenced Jude for a minute.

"You wouldn't shoot 'em to get your look in the mine, would ya?"

"No," Jude admitted. He'd give his own life, if need be, to save the woman he loved, but no matter how bad these men were, it wouldn't be right for him to get his evidence that way. "What did you have in mind?" he asked Heston.

"If they ain't three sheets to the wind, I'll stage a diversion. I'll make some noise and draw 'em off, and while they're chasin' after me, you can shimmy down and get your ore samples."

Jude sighed. He'd really hoped Heston had a scheme better than the one *he'd* racked his brain to come up with. "Sorry, but there's no way I'm going to let you do that. Mrs. Heston won't thank me if I get you killed."

Heston's shoulders sagged. "That's what I really hate about getting old," he said. "No one thinks you can do anything."

Jude laid a comforting hand on his boss's shoulder. "You can do a lot of things," he assured him. "And I'm counting on you, if something happens to me, to ride to the next town and telegraph the state police."

"Of course," Heston said. "Hope it doesn't come to that."

"It's up to the Lord to make this succeed," Jude reminded him. "I don't like waiting till Christmas Eve, either. But if my plan doesn't work, or the Lord doesn't want us to wait that long, He's going to have to show us another way."

Together, they bowed their heads.

They had been praying for only a few minutes when Jude was seized by a restlessness he could not explain. Lifting his head, he interrupted Heston in midsentence. "Jim, I've got to go into town and check on Delia. Something's wrong. I can feel it." He pushed the sling down off his shoulder and grabbed for his shirt. He might not be able to use the arm very well, but at least it was his left one. Shiloh was well-trained enough to be guided by his master's knees if Jude had to use his hands. "Lend me a pistol."

"Gimme a minute to load my old Colts. You're not goin' alone, and that's that."

Chapter Twenty-Five

Miss Susan was locking her shop when Jude's stallion, followed closely by Heston's sorrel gelding, slid to a stop in front of her.

"Did you see Delia?" Jude demanded without ceremony.

The middle-aged seamstress goggled up at him, clearly astonished to see him out of the house and on his horse. "An hour ago she poked her head in to say that she was going to buy some things for Mrs. Heston at the mercantile, and she'd stop by to get me afterward. We were coming down to see you. But she never showed up, and the mercantile's closed. I thought maybe she forgot to pick me up, and I was going to walk down to the Hestons' and see—"

"Do you think she might've gone to her house instead?"

The seamstress's brow furrowed in thought. "I can't think why—she'd said we were invited to dinner, right, Mr. Heston?" All at once she peered into the darkness and pointed. "Oh, look," she said, pointing to some small wrapped bundles lying by the side wall of the bank, and before Jude could dismount, she went over and opened them.

"Flour, eggs, sugar...a shaving mug...a crystal dish... She said Mrs. Heston was out of some essentials, and she wanted to buy them some little Christmas presents...."

"Then those things might be hers," Jude said.

"But why would she leave 'em there?" Heston asked.

Both men turned in their saddles to look down the mill road and up the street that led out of town. There was no one outside, and every business but the saloon was dark.

"Where could she be?" Miss Susan demanded. "I saw Charles Ladley walk by sometime before she stopped in here, and he had Donley with him, that scoundrel, and some other cowboy—" The older woman stopped, her eyes widening in horror, just as Jude reached the same conclusion. "Oh, Jude, you don't think he...he..."

The two men exchanged looks.

"I think we'll ride on over to the Ladleys' house and see if they're there," Jude told her. "Can you walk on down and stay with Mrs. Heston?"

Miss Susan nodded, and both men reined their horses around and kicked them into a lope in the opposite direction. Jude was surer than ever that Delia was in danger. But if Charles hadn't brought Delia there, would his parents know where they were—and if they did, would they tell them the truth? Maybe they'd try to steer them wrong deliberately.

No groom came outside to inquire if he could take their horses when they pulled up in the Ladley courtyard. The house was unlocked; no one answered their halloos when they went inside. Then Jude heard a faint thumping coming from the attic. Following the noise, they ascended the stairs and found Mrs. Ladley and Maisie, the cook, trussed up like Christmas geese, gags in their mouths. The two women had been rocking the chairs that they had been bound to against the wall.

Mrs. Ladley's eyes went wide with fear when Jude burst into the attic room. They went wider still when he ran up to her. She whimpered, clenching her eyes shut, clearly almost hysterical with fright, shrinking away from him but unable to scream because of the gag in her mouth as he bent over her.

"I mean you no harm, Mrs. Ladley," he assured her, working at the tight knots to untie her gag. "I'm Jude Tucker, and I only want to know if you've seen Delia. Did your son bring her here? I have reason to believe she's in trouble. Why are you tied up?" he asked, when he was able to pull the knot loose at last.

"Please... I'm dry... Water..." she croaked. Jude ran back downstairs and fetched a pitcher of water and two glasses, while Heston bent to free her and the cook from their bonds.

"Thank God someone finally came," she said, after drinking a glass of water straight down without pausing, while Jude poured another for the cook. "Maisie and I were tied up because I dared to argue when Charles came in here and told me he was going to elope with Delia. He was wild-eyed—crazy-looking. I raised that boy, and I know when he's lying. When I wouldn't shut up, he *pulled a gun on me and Maisie* and herded us up here and tied us up!"

"Where's your husband, Mrs. Ladley?" Heston asked.

She shrugged. "I don't know. He hasn't been here all day. I know my husband and his son think I'm a witless fool," she went on, "and merely a decoration in this house," she added, chafing her abraded wrists, "but I'm not. I've suspected for a long time that there was something crooked about that so-called gold mine."

"Miz Ladley's right. Dat boy looked crazy as a horned toad with a sunstroke," the cook chimed in.

"Mrs. Ladley, where do you think your son took Delia?" Jude asked her, letting her see his urgency. "Delia wouldn't go with him willingly for any reason, let alone marry him. She was expected at the Hestons' house. I'm afraid Charles may have taken her against her will."

"I don't know," she said, staring up at him, "and that's

the honest truth. But my fool of a husband's been careless enough to keep records of the committee's meetings, and I know what they're plotting. There's no gold, Mr. Tucker— unless you count what they planted there and fool's gold enough to keep the townspeople thinking they've found the real thing for a while longer. My husband and his cursed committee are planning to take the money they've stolen from the honest citizens of this town and run off to Mexico and live like kings. But I think my husband and his son have stolen a march on the rest of the committee and taken the money—yes, and maybe Delia—and left his cronies to face the music. And they thought I'd go with them!"

Jude felt no sense of victory at having his suspicions confirmed, only a desperate need to cut through the mayor's wife's tale to get to a clue about Delia.

"So you think Charles and his father have taken Delia with them to Mexico?"

Mrs. Ladley, however, was not to be hurried. Now that she finally had an audience, she seemed determined to tell her story her way. "Charles and his father have been more and more fearful of discovery as the date of the mine opening drew closer. Yes, I don't mind admitting I listened at keyholes," she said with a bitter laugh. "They realized it was only a matter of time before someone noticed they'd been swindled, and they were determined that Charles would wed Delia first, so they'd have her money, at least, if everything else about the plot failed. This is a fine old house, yes, but I don't mind admitting to you that we haven't had a nickel to spare since the war. We've just been keeping up appearances."

"Mrs. Ladley—" Jude said, trying to interrupt her.

"Charles rather fancied Delia Keller all along," she went on, oblivious, "but of course she was poor as the proverbial church mouse. Charles and his father had decided that in order to resume our proper place in society again, Charles had to marry a rich woman. But when Delia inherited all that money, Charles decided she was good enough for him now, the poor girl! I know I should have warned her," she said sadly, "but I'd hoped she might persuade Charles to become a better man...."

A tear made its way down her wrinkled cheek.

"Mrs. Ladley, I'm sorry that all this happened to you," Jude said, as patiently and kindly as he could despite the exigency that gripped him. He felt pity for this woman, who had apparently endured years of emotional abuse. "But is there anything you can tell me that will help me find Delia? Is your husband with them? Every minute may count, ma'am."

Mrs. Ladley could only shake her head. "I don't know where my husband's gone, Mr. Tucker. But I suspect that his son—" Jude noticed she'd referred to him as "his son," not "our son" "—is going to head for the border and force Delia to marry him in Mexico and set up a home down there where the officials can be bribed to ignore their presence."

Jude turned to Heston. "What lies between here and the border?" he asked. When he'd traveled from Nevada to Llano Crossing, he'd come from the northwest, not the south.

The old man thought for a moment. "Fredericksburg, but other than that, nothin' much between here and San Antone but more little towns like Llano Crossing. After San Antone, though, there's just one main road and not much but cactus and mesquite till the Rio Grande. But if they decided to stop at San Antone..." He shrugged. "There's lots a' places to hole up there, and we'd go right past, thinking they'd gone on south past the city."

"So I've got to catch them before they reach San Antonio, if at all possible."

Heston nodded. He understood without asking that Jude

would have to go alone. At his age, he wasn't up to such an arduous fast ride, and Jude couldn't afford to be held back by him.

"Go with God, son. While you're gone, we'll call the townspeople together and tell 'em what's been going on. After I tell them Ladley's kidnapped Delia, they'll believe the whole gold-mine scheme's a fraud, I promise you. We'll round up any of those scalawags from the committee that are still left and stick 'em in the jail."

"I'll be happy to testify against my husband when he's caught," Mrs. Ladley said with quiet dignity. "God keep you safe, Jude Tucker."

"And we'll find some young fella to ride for the law in Mason, since our own sheriff will be in the jail with the rest," Heston added.

Jude was impressed by their determination, but even so, he felt a jab of despair. Ladley had several hours' head start on him, and darkness had fallen as they reached the Ladleys' house. There wouldn't be enough of a moon out tonight to light his way. Shiloh wouldn't be able to gallop all night, and what if he put a leg into a hole in the road that he couldn't see?

Lord, if You want Delia and I to be together, we're going to need Your help now. You gave the three Wise Men a star to follow so long ago—please, help me, too. Give my horse swift and sure legs. Help Delia not to be scared. I'm not worthy to ask You for anything, but You've assured us that You listen to Your children's cries for help.

Chapter Twenty-Six

While Donley put up the folded bow top on both ends of the landau, Charles wrapped her up warmly with a buffalo robe, every inch the loving beau, then settled himself opposite her with his gun hidden beneath the folds of his own buffalo robe.

Delia said nothing at first, as the landau bowled along over the hilly roads south of town. What was there to say? Begging would do no good. Charles had no heart to be reached. She couldn't bear to look at him. Instead, she kept her eyes on the endless parade of mesquite, cedar, cactus and rolling, rock-studded hills. The sun was fast disappearing behind a mesa on her right side; soon it would be completely dark.

Be strong, and of a good courage.

After another mile or two, she said, "We can't drive all night, you know. The horses won't last. And it looks mighty cloudy up there." She pointed at the sky. "I think it's going to rain."

"Father's meeting us with a brougham—and a fresh team," he told her, laughing at her dismay. "We'll be at the meeting point soon."

A brougham? It was going to be more than a little crowded with the two of them, the mayor and the luggage, too. Perhaps Charles was planning to ride his horse some of the time. But if she was right about the weather, at least she would be more protected from the elements than in his landau.

About half an hour later, they pulled up in front of a black hulking shape in a grove of oak trees. As they drew nearer, the shape revealed itself as the promised brougham hitched to two fresh horses. Charles Ladley Senior got out of it, holding up a hand in greeting.

"You made good time," Mr. Ladley praised his son. "And how's your lovely bride? Good evening, Delia," he greeted her with such effusive cordiality that Delia wanted to spit at him. "Such a romantically thrilling elopement, eh?"

Delia's smoldering anger vented itself in sarcasm. "Not too many eloping grooms have to bring their fathers along for reinforcement. And I see you couldn't talk your wife into joining us on this little romantic getaway, Mr. Ladley."

She wasn't quick enough to avoid Charles's slap, or to control her own instinctive reaction. Fingers curled into claws, she launched herself at him.

Anticipating her fury, he caught her wrists before she could strike him and held her as she thrashed wildly against him while the hired guns swiftly and expertly bound her wrists and ankles then hauled her to the brougham.

Quick tears welled up in her eyes, but she averted her face, not about to let any of them see her cry.

"Mind your tongue, you little shrew," the mayor said, "or I won't let my son sully the Ladley name by giving it to you."

Chilled to the bone by the elder Ladley's threat, she nevertheless couldn't help but retort, "You've sullied your own name, Mr. Ladley."

For a moment, she thought the mayor was going to

strike her, then he turned to his son and snarled, "Let's get going."

Delia sat hunched in despair as the carriage rumbled on through the night. How much did Mrs. Ladley know of the plot, if anything? She hadn't been brought along, but when her husband and son didn't come home, would she raise the hue and cry? Or was she so beaten down by years with her husband that she would wait tamely for her chance to join them in Mexico?

How soon would the town realize they'd been duped and demand to see what was in the mine?

Had Jude realized yet she'd been kidnapped? He'd be out searching for her, regardless of his recent wounds, but he wouldn't know where to look unless Mrs. Ladley had guessed her husband and son's intent to escape to Mexico and told what she knew. How soon would that be? She had no way of knowing.

"Jude Tucker will catch up," she said, as though she believed he was minutes away. "He won't let you get away with this."

"Your lovesick carpenter won't have any idea what's happened to you," Charles said. "And even if he ever figures it out, he'd be too far behind to catch up."

"Yes, he will," she insisted.

"Even if he did, he'd be rather outnumbered, don't you think? Ace and Donley are more than a match for one miner-carpenter," Charles retorted.

Just then Delia heard the first plops of rain fall on the carriage roof, and even inside the carriage she could hear the wind pick up.

"We'd better stop in Fredericksburg and spend the night at the hotel," the mayor told his son, as the plops became more steady.

"I'm not stopping for a little rain," his son snapped.

"Fredericksburg's too close to home, if they figure out where we're going!"

"They won't," his father said. "Everyone's so wrapped up with Christmas coming and gold fever, they won't notice if we're missing," he said with a chuckle. "My dear wife's going to be mad as a wet hen when Manuel finally finds her and Maisie all tied up, but she might be so embarrassed she's been left behind that she won't say anything till they come looking for us."

The rain became a drumming, and still the carriage rolled on through the night.

The rain had been falling in spattering, tentative drops that slid down the oilskin duster Jude had dug out of his saddlebag, but a few yards ahead of them, it was falling in undulating sheets of water. In a moment, Shiloh would be running in the thick of the downpour.

Lord, I thought You were going to help me, he thought, despondent as thunder rumbled somewhere behind them. *A downpour will only slow me down.* Shiloh had been making good time, eating up the miles with his far-reaching stride, but Jude knew he'd have to rest his valiant stallion soon. And soon would come sooner in this cloudburst.

If the rain slows you down, Jude, don't you think the rain is going to delay Ladley more? the Voice within him said. Jude had seen Ladley's landau was not in the stable, and Mrs. Ladley said their brougham was missing as well, so he could guess they were in one or the other, rather than on horseback. No carriage could travel as fast as a horse and rider. "Lord," he said aloud, "Shiloh's just about exhausted."

He can go a little farther. Ride on till you find shelter.

Minutes later, horse and rider came to a bend in the road caused by a limestone crag jutting out. Just then lightning flashed and Jude spotted a rocky overhang high and big enough for his horse to stand under. It wasn't much, but it would keep most of the rain off of them while they rested.

"Son, we've got to stop! We can't keep going through this storm all night!" Mr. Ladley said, right after a jagged bolt of lightning struck the ground in the distance and caused the tired team to shy.

His son scowled but gave in. "Find someplace to stop, Ace!" he called to the cowboy up on the driver's seat.

"There ain't no place, Mr. Ladley!" Ace called back in a disgusted voice. "We ain't yet to Fredericksburg, and we're in the middle a' nowhere!"

"Then we'll just have to stop on the road till the worst blows over," the mayor shouted over the drumming of the rain. "We don't dare stop under a tree, with all this lightning!"

"Ain't nothin' around but scrubby little mesquite, anyway!" Ace called back.

The carriage rattled to a stop at the bottom of a hill, the horses blowing and miserable, as wet as if they'd been swimming underwater. Behind the carriage, Charles's bay and Zephyr were in an equally wretched state.

"What about *us?*" Donley demanded, peering into the brougham's window from the back of his horse. He'd been riding behind them, leading Ace's horse. Just like Ace on the driver's seat, he was drenched to the bone.

"Well, there's hardly room in *here,*" Charles said, curling his lip. "Get under the carriage or something!"

Delia saw the cowboy gaze up at his cohort in the driver's seat. A moment later, Ace jumped down from his high perch, but rather than taking Charles's suggestion, he took the reins of his horse from Donley and mounted.

"Hey!" Charles cried as the men reined their horses away from the carriage. "Where are you going?" He pulled out the pistol he'd been clutching all this time. "Stop, or I'll shoot!"

Donley paused long enough to shout over his shoulder, "Ladley, you're *loco!*" Donley and Ace galloped into the inky cascade of rain and disappeared.

"Don't fire, you fool!" his father cried. "The horses will spook and stampede! You can't hope to hit either man anyway!"

Father and son glared at one another, dumbstruck. Delia turned her face away from them, afraid she would laugh and they would turn on her.

"We don't need them, blast their hides," Charles fumed. "We can make it just fine without them." He pulled out his pocket watch and peered at it. "I can't even see what time it is!"

"Got to be after midnight," his father said. "Let's try to sleep until the rain lets up."

Sleep? Delia's muscles were cramped from having her hands and legs tied and not being able to shift and stretch, but she knew it was futile to ask to be untied. Settling herself against the upholstery, she closed her eyes and waited.

Please, Lord, send Jude.

Then, amazingly, she slept.

Chapter Twenty-Seven

Delia woke in the gray light of dawn to the sound of men cursing. The carriage lurched forward, then backward, but didn't move.

Stretching as much as her bonds would allow, Delia blinked and opened her eyes. She was alone in the carriage. Above her, in the driver's seat, she could hear Charles's father swearing at the horses and cracking the whip above them; behind the brougham, Charles groaned and lunged against it.

No one had to tell Delia they were stuck in the mud. Ace had parked the carriage at the bottom of a hill, and the water had soaked into the depression, creating a mire that now held them fast.

"I can't budge it!" Charles grunted, coming past the window to glare accusingly at his father.

"Whip them up—they've got to pull us out of here!" Charles cried, desperation edging his voice. "Maybe if I get Delia out it would be easier for them to pull us free?"

"I've been whipping them! They've been trying, but the beasts just can't do it!" his father snapped back. "And I don't think moving Delia would make a difference. We're going to have to leave the carriage and go on!"

Charles stared up at his father and then in at Delia.

"Come on," he said, opening the carriage and pulling her out, heedless of the way her numb, bound legs made her sag against him and nearly fall. "You're going to have to ride the rest of the way."

Righting herself, Delia faced him and felt her mouth turn up in an impudent grin. She didn't care if he slapped her again—it was worth it to see the frustrated rage on his face.

Instead, however, he took hold of her chin and bent over so that they were practically nose to nose. "Delia Keller, when we get to Mexico, I'll make you pay for every insolent word," he vowed, eyes bulging and red-rimmed. "You will rue the day you were born."

She wasn't about to let him cow her. "Maybe, but first we have to get there, don't we? If you expect me to ride, you're going to have to untie me."

He couldn't argue that. After he'd used a pocketknife on the rope binding her legs, though, Delia held out her hands, but he only shook his head and pointed at his bay.

"I'm riding your thoroughbred, Delia, so abandon any hope of racing away from me."

"And what about *your father?*" the mayor demanded in an indignant voice.

"Sorry, Father, but you're going to have to ride one of the carriage horses," Charles told him. "Here, take my knife, and cut the harness to make yourself reins."

"You're out of your mind!" Charles Ladley Senior roared. "The thoroughbred can carry double, and I'll ride your bay."

"The mare can't carry two. She's too skittish. Especially with me loaded down with money," his son argued, reaching into a heavy canvas bag and coming out with both hands clutching fistfuls of gold coins, stuffing them into his pockets until they bulged and sagged. He tied the bag, which still sagged with weight, onto Zephyr's saddle. "That's only a part of your inheritance that Dawson was good enough to draw out for me," he assured Delia. "He'll have the rest transferred, along with the profit from selling your house. We've got to get going. By now we're probably being pursued."

"So leave Delia here, if you're suddenly yellow," his father shouted. "They won't chase us if they can rescue her."

"Sorry, Father, but I've come too far to give Delia—and especially her fortune—up now," Charles told him, cool as the ice that rimmed the nearby puddles of water. "It's your choice—you can either follow on one of the team or you can stay here and wait for Tucker to catch up."

Delia watched, incredulous, as Ladley glared at Ladley. At last, the older man's body slumped. "I should have left you in the saloon with your crazy mother," he growled, glaring at Charles. "You're as mad as she was. Take the girl and go. I won't stay here, but I won't be a part of your insanity, either."

Charles boosted Delia up onto his bay. Beneath her stocking-clad legs, the leather of the saddle was wet and cold.

Taking the bay's reins, he mounted Zephyr. As they rode away, Delia saw that the mayor had cut his mount out of the traces and was struggling to pull himself onto the carriage horse's bare back.

Charles and Delia trotted for perhaps an hour in the bone-chilling damp, the only sound the occasional twittering of birds and the sucking noise as hooves landed in mud and were pulled out again. Try as she might, Delia couldn't hear the sound of any horses behind her.

So Jude wasn't coming or at least he was too far behind them to help her. But they'd have to stop and buy food, but surely she could manage to run away or cry out to someone along the way who would help her. It was still a long, long way to Mexico.

"We're going to avoid the towns," Charles muttered then, almost as if he could read her mind. His eyes gleamed with a light that was no longer reasonable. "When we're hungry, I'll tie you up and go buy food. Between here and the Rio Grande it's mostly poor greasers, anyway, and they'll be happy to earn a few coins."

As if her money mattered now. "What *about* the rest of your committee?" she asked him. "You don't seem very concerned about them. Aren't you worried Dawson won't send the rest of the money to Mexico? And they'll turn state's evidence on you? Or come after you for running out on them with the money?"

He shrugged. "They'll slip away, if they have any sense, my dear Mrs. Ladley."

I'm not your wife yet, and I never will be, she wanted to remind him, but she didn't have the energy. She needed all the strength that remained to keep her knees gripping the bay's sides.

"Ought to be coming to the Guadalupe pretty soon," Charles said conversationally, after they skirted Fredericksburg. They might have been two friends out for a canter in the spring sunshine. "Hopefully there's a bridge, or we'll have to swim for it."

Sure enough, around the next bend, the green water of the Guadalupe River appeared before them. There had been a bridge, all right, but all that remained of it lay in collapsed wreckage on either side. The rain-swollen, rushing river had apparently flooded beyond its banks during the night and taken the bridge with it.

Charles shrugged again, saying with maniacal cheerfulness, "Ah well, it's not as if we could get any wetter by swimming, eh, my love?"

Delia's jaw dropped. Even a madman couldn't imagine they would be able to swim across this river, could he? As she watched, the splintered remains of a ferry platform bobbed past them in the raging torrent.

"Charles, the horses can't swim that," she pointed out, keeping her voice logical and calm. "If we wait awhile and hide out back in the town, the river will go down. A day—maybe less—you'll see."

"But we can't wait, Delia," he responded, just as reasonably. "He's coming."

She paused, listening, but she could hear nothing but the rushing water. Was paranoia consuming Charles?

And then she heard it—distantly, muffled at first, but then she was sure. The sound of a horse's hooves was coming up fast behind them.

"Come on!" he shrieked, as both of them spotted the silver buckskin, with Jude on his back, at the same moment. "We've got to go right now!"

"No!" she screamed, desperately trying to wrench the reins away. "There's no way we'd survive! Charles, I don't want to drown!"

"We can't let him catch us!" he shouted back frantically, trying to kick the mare into plunging into the swift current. He seemed to have forgotten that Delia didn't have the same goal he did—she desperately *wanted* to be "caught."

The bay she rode dug in his heels, pulling away from the other horse. Charles had too much to do to stay on Zephyr to keep hold of the bay's reins, and at last the bay jerked free.

Zephyr continued to resist Charles's commands, bucking and rearing as her crazed rider desperately raked her sides with his spurs. She was struggling to keep her hooves planted on the muddy bank, but it had been weakened by the raging river, and clods of clay kept breaking away into the water.

Just then a report of a gun shook the air, and Delia

whipped her head around to see Jude firing, not at Charles but straight up into the air.

The report set the already terrified thoroughbred rearing and plunging, but while she managed to keep from falling into the river, Charles did not. Delia screamed as Charles was catapulted headfirst into the swirling greenish-yellow water.

Charles surfaced almost immediately, yelling and grabbing at branches but weighted down by the coins in his pockets—he couldn't hold on. She had to help him! Dismounting with clumsy haste because her hands were still tied, she tried to grab on to one of the splintered timbers of the bridge, but it was stuck in something beneath the surface of the water and she couldn't pull it loose to extend it to him. She could only watch in horror as he was swept on past.

Jude was still too far away. By the time his stallion slid to a stop beside the shivering mare, Charles Ladley had gone under again. She thought she saw his arm raised, yards down the river, but it may have only been a branch.

And then Jude was pulling her against him, shielding her from what she had just seen, holding her while she wept as if he would never let her go again.

Zephyr was too spent to ride, so Delia rode Charles's bay back to Fredericksburg while Jude, back on Shiloh, led the mare at a walk. Once they reached the town, they went straight to the sheriff's office and told him what had happened, including the fact that Mayor Charles Ladley was still on the loose, probably riding a carriage horse bareback.

The sheriff listened carefully, promising to ride out with his deputies to look for him.

"There's a hotel in town, if you want to rest the horses for the night," the sheriff went on. "Mister, you look plumb played out, if you don't mind my sayin' it, and it *is* Christmas Eve."

Delia blinked. With all that had happened, she had forgotten Christmas was so close.

"Played out" didn't begin to cover it, as far as Jude was concerned. He hadn't slept while waiting out the storm last night, and his wounded shoulder throbbed like a fiery toothache. But as he gazed at Delia, all he wanted was to be at home on Christmas Day with her.

"Reckon we'll push on," he told the sheriff. "We need to notify Charles Ladley's mother about his death. Would it be possible to rent a light carriage at the livery and leave our horses there for a few days?"

"Good idea. One of you can drive while the other sleeps. And if I could make another suggestion, you might take a few minutes to stop over at the mercantile and buy something dry to wear, ma'am. You both look like drowned cats, and it's right nippy out there today after that rain."

Jude smiled, thinking that even with her curls plastered against her face and neck and her dress spattered with mud, Delia still looked beautiful to him.

"You need to borrow some money for the clothes and carriage?" the sheriff asked. "I got some in the drawer here for emergencies."

Jude shook his head and thanked him, explaining that while Charles Ladley's pockets had been weighted down with gold coins, there was still a goodly sum in the bag that had been tied to the thoroughbred's saddle.

"Poor greedy fellow," the sheriff said, shaking his head.

An hour later, having eaten and wearing newly purchased and blessedly dry clothing, Delia and Jude had just reached the edge of town in their rented carriage when they spotted a pair of deputies riding toward them, one of them leading a horse with the remains of a harness still on him, the other leading another horse with an old man in torn, soggy clothing slouching on his back.

Delia gasped, recognizing Mayor Ladley. He looked up at the faint sound, but his eyes were empty and seemed not to recognize her.

At least Charles had taught her to drive a carriage. Now she was thankful that he had, so Jude could doze at her side while she drove into the afternoon.

Jude took over as the early twilight of December darkened the road ahead of them. With the storm having blown eastward, the sky was soon blanketed with stars.

Chapter Twenty-Eight

Llano Crossing seemed as deserted early Christmas morning as it had been when Delia had left. Delia and Jude longed to go to the Hestons' house first to let them know they were safe, but it seemed wrong to pass by Ladley House on the road from the south without going in to tell Mrs. Ladley about her son's death.

When they pulled into the courtyard between the mansion and the stable, however, it was not Mrs. Ladley but Jim Heston who came out to greet them.

"I'm so thankful you're safe," he cried. "Lucy, Miss Susan and I thought it best to wait with her so she wouldn't have to be alone, it bein' Christmas and all." He hesitated, peering at their faces. "I see by your sober faces that you've got some bad news to tell her."

"We do," Jude confirmed. "I'm glad you've been here."

They found Mrs. Ladley waiting at the door, flanked by Lucy Heston and Miss Susan. There were welcoming hugs all around. "Come inside, my dears," she said. "I've got coffee ready, and Maisie's making breakfast. Let's just go to the parlor, shall we?" Her worried eyes betrayed the fact that she was already prepared for bad news. As everyone found a seat, with Jude sitting next to Mrs. Ladley and Lucy Heston on her other side, Delia took a deep breath, knowing one of the most painful parts of their ordeal would take place now.

Gently, Jude told Mrs. Ladley a carefully edited summary of what had happened, that the son she had raised as her own would never be coming home and that her husband was in custody in Fredericksburg and would likely be spending time in prison.

She took the news bravely about Charles, murmuring, "Poor lost soul, poor lost soul…" as she wept. "Oh, Delia dear, I'm just glad you're safe." About her husband, she said nothing at all. Mrs. Heston held her while she cried, and after a few minutes, she and Miss Susan helped her to go lie down in her room.

"Jane and I did a lot of talking while the men were at their meeting last night," Lucy Heston said. "I think she already knew that this was going to end badly for her husband and that boy, and she'd accepted whatever was going to happen. She said she had already decided she wasn't going to join them in Mexico, no matter what."

Over breakfast, Jim Heston told them what had taken place while they were gone.

"After you rode after Delia and Ladley, Jude," James Heston began, "I sent for the sheriff in Mason, and he and a deputy and Doc Jones and I went out to the cave. The Mason sheriff arrested the guards there, and while the deputy was standin' guard over them, he and I went down to the cave and had a look around with a lantern. I'm pretty sure you're right—what I saw embedded in the walls down there looks like pyrite to me. I hit it a coupla whacks with a little hammer I took with me, and it chipped off in crystals, just like you said fool's gold would. There's an assayer on the way to prove it, though—along with the circuit judge to put that pack of scoundrels away for as long as the law allows."

"The rest of them were all still here?" Jude asked, surprised. "Not only the sheriff, but Dawson and Miller and Jeffers, too?"

Heston nodded. "Yup, they were, and wonderin' where the two Ladleys had gone. I think they were just beginnin' to get wind a' the fact they'd been swindled just like the rest a' the townspeople."

Jude and Delia shook their heads in amazement.

"Sheriff Jenkins agreed to testify in exchange for a lighter sentence," Heston went on as Miss Susan and his wife returned to the room. "I called a short meeting the same day, and the whole town was there. Once I told 'em all about the conspiracy, and the fact that both the Ladley men had kidnapped Miss Delia, they were ready to tar an' feather the fellows in jail. But once I told them Dawson said that most of their money was still sittin' in the bank, they calmed down a lot. They're mighty grateful to you, Jude—as I'm sure they'll be tellin' you."

Delia saw Jude duck his head in embarrassment at the praise.

"And that ain't all," Heston said. "Donley Morrison showed up on a lathered nag as we were leavin' the meetin', demandin' Miss Susan go with him—tellin' everyone she was his lawful wife all this time—and the sheriff from Mason arrested him on the spot for bein' an accessory to kidnappin'. He's in the jail with the rest a' the plotters."

"You're safe now!" Delia said to Miss Susan.

"I know," the older woman answered with a smile. "I'm grateful to you for giving me a safe place for so long. I hope you won't mind, but I think I'll be stayin' with Mrs. Ladley for a while. Poor soul, she's going to be so lonely."

Delia assured her she understood.

"I hope you won't mind too much, Jude, but I went ahead and told 'em all you were a preacher," Heston added with an unrepentant grin. "The church board took a vote right then and there and authorized me to tell you the job's yours if you want it."

Jude's face was dismayed. "Jim, there's things I need to tell them that may make them want to change their minds—"

"I doubt it, but they're meetin' early New Year's Eve, so you can speak to 'em then. I'll be there—I've been appointed to the church board to take the mayor's place. 'Course, the sheriff's job is open, too—from the sound a' things, you could take your pick."

"And why don't you be the new mayor?" Jude suggested, only half joking. "As for me, I think I'll do what God wants for a change and be a preacher here, if they'll have me. And Delia's husband, too, of course," he said, smiling and embracing Delia.

"How soon?" Miss Susan asked. "I need a little time to sew the wedding gown, you know. It just so happens I've got some sketches I've been drawing for your consideration, Delia...."

"Is Valentine's Day too soon?" Jude asked Delia.

"Not for me," she said, beaming at him. "Miss Susan, does that give you enough time?"

"Plenty."

Delia gave them all a watery smile. "Is it right to feel so happy when Mrs. Ladley is grieving?"

"She said you'd feel that way, and she doesn't want you to," Miss Susan told her briskly, and Lucy Heston nodded in agreement. "She said Charles threw away his chance at happiness with you, and she was happy that you had found the man who wouldn't ever do that."

Jude pulled her into his arms for a kiss, which left her flustered in front of everyone.

"She also said she wants you to have Zephyr as a wedding present," Mrs. Heston said.

Delia looked uncertain. "She's a beautiful horse and

very affectionate, but Jude's right—she *is* a bit too much for me to ride."

"I could work with her," he said. "I've got to admit, I'd been picturing what fine colts we could get if we bred Zephyr to my Shiloh. We could raise fine saddle horses as a sideline."

Delia pondered that. "Maybe we could offer Mrs. Ladley a three-way partnership?"

"Susan, Jim, I think it's time we took these dirty dishes in the kitchen and redded them up," Lucy Heston said, rising and pulling on her husband's hand. "These two have some plans to make, and they don't need a couple of old folks gawking!"

When they were alone, Delia went into his arms, as naturally as a bird returning to its nest. "All I want now is to be your wife—and the very best preacher's wife that ever was."

"Delia, you're the woman God made for me. And that's the best I could ever ask for."

"I like the way you think, Jude Tucker!" she cried, lowering her lips to his for another of his delicious Christmas kisses.

Epilogue

Jude rode on to Delia's house as soon as he left the meeting of the church board on New Year's Eve. They were to have a late dinner, and he would stay until just after the clock chimed midnight and the new year. They would both be glad, Delia knew, when they could begin their married life and he would never have to leave.

"Whew! That Norther's sure made things cold in a hurry," Jude said, coming into the house after he had put Shiloh in the barn. "We may see snow by morning." As if to agree with him, the wind slammed the door shut behind him.

"You're looking at the new preacher of Llano Crossing Church," he told her.

Delia flew into his arm with a whoop of joy. "I knew it!"

He smiled down at her. "It was amazing, Delia. I told them what I'd done in the war, how my faith had been shaken by all the senseless tragedy around me, and afterward—how I'd nearly sinned with that woman—and they said that what mattered was not that I had sinned—we all do, to one degree or another—but that I'd repented. They all laid hands on me and prayed for me, Delia. I feel so good, so blessed...."

"*We're* blessed, you and I," she said. "What does the board plan to do with the parsonage?"

"They plan to keep it as church property—rent it out for a nominal fee, perhaps, to someone down on his luck. Someday when we pass on, maybe a preacher will live there again."

He kissed her then, and sometime later, she pointed outside. The snow had already begun to fall, and soon the lawn would be white.

"Like a new beginning, the slate has been wiped clean. A new year—in a few hours," she said, as behind them the grandfather clocked chimed the hour. "A new life for the two of us—and for the whole town." She could practically hear her grandpa's—and her papa's—applause.

* * * * *

A *USA TODAY* bestselling author of over forty novels, **Lyn Cote** lives in the north woods of Wisconsin with her husband in a lakeside cottage. She knits, loves cats (and dogs), likes to cook (and eat), never misses *Wheel of Fortune* and enjoys hearing from her readers. Email her at l.cote@juno.com. And drop by her website, lyncote.com, to learn more about her books that feature "Strong Women, Brave Stories."

Visit the Author Profile page
at Harlequin.com for more titles.

HER CAPTAIN'S HEART

Lyn Cote

Blessed are the peacemakers
for they shall be called the children of God.
—*Matthew* 5:9

I can do all things through Christ
which strengthen me.
—*Philippians* 4:13

Dedicated to my Sunday school teachers,
the women and men who first taught me
about God, His Son and His Spirit. Florence Brauck,
Ruth Silovich, Beatrice Sladek née Nilsen,
Gordon Zoehler and others whom only God recalls.

Chapter One

Gettysburg, Pennsylvania, September 1866

Verity Hardy loathed the man, God forgive her. She stood looking down at her late husband's cousin, she on the top step of her wide porch, he on the bottom. The unusually hot autumn sun burned just beyond the scant shade of the roof. Her black mourning dress soaked up the heat that buffeted her in waves, suffocating and singeing her skin. The man had been haranguing her for nearly a quarter of an hour and she didn't know how much more she could take.

"I can't believe you're going through with this insane plan." Urriah Hardy wiped sweat from his brow with the back of his hand and glared at her, his jowly face reddening. He held the reins of his handsome gelding, fidgeting just behind him.

Pressing a hankie to her upper lip, she looked past him to the golden fields beyond. Memories of wounded soldiers—their agonized screams and soul-deep moans—shuddered through Verity. She'd never forget those bloody July days three years ago. She couldn't let them count for naught. Still, her deep uncertainty made her hands tremble. She clasped them together so he wouldn't see this sign of weakness. "Thee knows," she said in a final attempt at politeness, "I've packed everything, and we leave at dawn."

"You're a fool, woman. That renter you've found won't make a go of it. He lost his own farm."

Yes, because he was drafted into the Union Army and thy younger brother, the banker, wouldn't give him more time to pay the mortgage. "That's really none of thy business," she murmured, adding a warning note to her tone.

"You should have rented to me. I'm family."

His reference to family stung her like rock salt. Urriah had cheated on every business deal she'd ever known him to make. "So thee could have cheated me instead?"

After the brazen words popped out of her mouth, conscience stung Verity instantly. *Judge not, lest ye be judged.* But she couldn't—wouldn't—take back the words. She stood her ground, her face hot and set.

He swore at her, vulgar and profane, something no man had ever done in her presence.

Her frayed temper ripped open. "I don't expect thee to understand," she shot back with a disdain she couldn't hide. "Not a coward who bought his way out of the draft."

For a moment he rocked on his toes and she thought he might climb the steps to strike her. Instead, an evil, gloating leer engulfed his ugly face. "Well, since you won't listen to reason, I guess you'll just have to take what comes, down in Dixie. You'll be lucky if the Rebs just run you out of town on a rail. If they lynch you, I'll inherit the land and you know it." He chuckled in a mean way and turned his back to her. "The day a woman bests me will be the day hell freezes over," he taunted as he mounted his horse.

His parting shot drew her down the steps and into the dusty lane. "I've made out a will and thee's not the beneficiary!" she called after him. "Roger's father inherits the land as guardian of Beth."

"I'm a patient man, Quaker." He pulled up the reins,

stopping his horse. "I can wait till Roger's father dies and then the court will name me, your daughter's next of kin, guardian of her assets." He doffed his hat in an insolent way and cantered off.

Stiff with disapproval, she watched until she could see only the dust his horse's hooves kicked up in the distance. The hot anger drained out of her, leaving her hollow with regret and worry.

Letting anger rule the tongue was never wise. But his cutting words had prompted her own doubts. Was she up to the task she'd taken for herself?

Out of the blue, a memory—vivid and as fresh as today—caught her by surprise. Five years earlier, she'd stood in this very spot as her husband had left for war. She could see the back of his blue Union uniform as he marched away from her.

Then he halted in midstride and ran back to her. Pulling her into his arms, he'd crushed her against the rough wool of his jacket. His kiss had been passionate, searching, as if drinking in the very essence of her. "I'll come back to you," he'd promised. "I will."

But he hadn't. Thousands upon thousands had broken that same promise. She'd watched many soldiers die, both gray and blue. And many had keepsakes from wives or sweethearts in their pockets. It broke her heart to think of it.

She wrapped her arms around her. In spite of the scorching sun, the loneliness she'd lived with for the past five years whistled through her like an icy winter wind. "Now I'm leaving, too, dearest one," she whispered.

She'd asked God's blessing on her plans but how had she behaved the day before she left? Shame over her unruly tongue deepened. She covered her face with her hands as if she could hide her hot tears from God.

"I'm sorry, Father, for my temper. I shouldn't have spoken to Urriah like that. But he's…it's such an injustice. He lives and prospers while Roger lies somewhere in an unmarked grave in Virginia." She pressed her hands tighter against her face as if pushing back the tears and her un-Christian words, feeling as if she couldn't get anything right today.

"Again I must apologize, Father. It is not my job to decide who is worthy of life and who deserves to die." Lowering her hands, she turned back to the house. Her father-in-law and her daughter would be back from their last-minute trip to town anytime now and she had to get a cold supper ready for them.

At the top step, she paused and leaned against the post. "God, I've felt Thy spirit moving within me, Thy inner light. I'm sorry I'm such a weak vessel. Please use me. Let me reflect Thy light in the present darkness."

Fiddlers Grove, Virginia, October

In one routine motion, Matt rolled from the bed, grabbed his rifle and was on his feet. In the moonlight he crouched beside the bed, listening. What had roused him from sleep? He heard the muffled nicker of a horse and a man's voice. Then came knocking on the door. Bent over, Matt scuttled toward the door, wary of casting a shadow.

Staying low, he moved into the hall and ducked into an empty room. He eased over to the uncurtained windows overlooking the front porch. From the corner of the window sash, he glanced down. A buckboard stood at the base of the porch steps. A man wearing a sad-looking hat was standing beside it and a little girl sat on the buckboard seat.

"Verity, maybe there is a key under the mat," the man said quietly to a woman hidden under the front porch roof below Matt's window.

Verity? A key? A woman was knocking at his door and looking for a key? And they had a child with them.

"But, Joseph," came her reply from out of sight, barely above a whisper. "This might not be the Barnesworth house. I don't want to walk into some stranger's home uninvited."

She spoke with a Northern accent. And this was or had been the Barnesworth house. Wondering if this was some sort of diversion, he listened for other telltale sounds. But he heard nothing more.

He rose slowly and walked back to his room. He pulled his britches over his long johns and picked up his rifle again. Just because they looked like innocent travelers who had turned up after dark didn't mean that they actually were innocent travelers. Caution kept a man alive.

He moved silently down the stairs to the front hall. Through the glass in the door, he glimpsed a shadowy figure, dressed in a dark color, facing away. He turned the key in the lock, twisted the knob and yanked the door open. "Who are you?" he demanded.

The woman jerked as if he'd poked her with a stick, but did not call out. She turned toward him, her hand to her throat.

"What do you want?" he asked, his rifle held at the ready.

Her face was concealed by shadow and a wide-brimmed bonnet and her voice seemed strangely disembodied when she spoke. "Thee surprised me, friend."

Thee? Friend? "What's a Quaker doing at my door at this time of night?" he snapped.

"No need to take that tone with her," the older man said, moving toward the steps. "We know it's late, but we got turned around. Then we didn't find anywhere to stop for the night and the full moon made travel easy. So we pressed on."

"Is this the Barnesworth house?" the woman asked.

"It was," Matt allowed. "Who are you?"

"I am Verity Hardy. I'm a schoolteacher with the Freedman's Bureau. Who are thee?"

He rubbed his eyes, hoping she would disappear and he'd wake up in bed, wondering why he was having such an odd dream. "Why have you come here?"

"Why, to teach school, of course." Her voice told him that she was wondering if he were still half-asleep. Or worse.

Not a dream, then. His gut twisted. Something had gone wrong. But he forced himself not to show any reaction. The war had taught him to keep his cards close to his chest. He rubbed his chin. "Ma'am, I am—" he paused to stop himself from saying Captain "—Matthew Ritter." But he couldn't keep from giving her a stiff military bow. "I am employed by the Freedman's Bureau, too. Did you come with a message for me? Or are you on your way to some other—"

"This is the Barnesworth house?" the woman interrupted.

He didn't appreciate being cut off. "This was the Barnesworth house. It belongs to the Freedman's Bureau now."

Something moved in the shadows behind the strangers. Matt gripped his rifle and raised it just a bit. He searched the shadows for any other telltale movement. It could just be an opossum or a raccoon. Or someone else with a rifle and lethal intent.

The woman turned her head as if she had noticed his distraction. "Is there anything wrong?"

The older gentleman said, "I think we need to shed some light on the situation." He lifted a little girl with long dark braids from the buckboard and drew her up the steps. "I'm Joseph Hardy. Call me Joseph, as Verity does." He offered Matt his hand. "I'm Verity's father-in-law. Why don't you invite us in, light a lamp and we can talk this out?"

Matt hesitated. If someone else were watching them, it would be better to get them all inside. And he couldn't see any reason not to take them at face value. Four years of war had whittled down a good deal of his society manners. "Sorry. Didn't mean to be rude."

Matt gripped the man's gnarled hand briefly and then gave way, leading them to the parlor off the entry hall. He lit an oil lamp on the mantel and set the glass globe around the golden point of light. Then he set a vase in front of it, making sure the light was diffused and didn't make them easy targets. He knew what Fiddlers Grove was capable of doing to those with unpopular views.

Turning, he watched the woman sit down on the sofa. She coaxed the little girl, also dressed in black, to sit beside her. Joseph chose a comfortable rocker nearby. Matt sat down on the love seat opposite them, giving him the best view of the front parlor windows. He rested the rifle on his lap at the ready. Now that he had more light, he saw that they looked weary and travel-worn. But what was he supposed to do with them?

He was still unable to make out the woman's face, hidden by the brim of her plain black bonnet. He glanced at her hands folded in front of her. Under her thin gloves he saw the outline of a wedding band on her right hand. Another widow, then. Every town was crowded with widows in mourning. He knew they deserved his sympathy, but he was tired of sidestepping the lures cast toward him.

He watched the woman untie and remove her bonnet. The black clothing, Quaker speech and the title of teacher had misled him. He'd expected mousy brown hair and a plain, older face. But she looked to be around his age, in her midtwenties. Vivid copper-colored hair curled around her face, refusing to stay pulled back in a severe bun. Her almost transparent skin was illuminated by large caramel-brown eyes. The look in those eyes said that, in spite of her fatigue, this widow was not a woman to dismiss. A vague feeling of disquiet wiggled through him.

Why are you here? And how can I get you to leave? Soon?

As if she'd heard his unspoken questions, she began explaining. "I was told in a letter from the Freedman's Bureau to come to this house this week and get settled before I start my teaching duties next week. But I was not told a gentleman would be at this house also." The cool tone of her voice told him that she would not be casting any lures in his direction. In fact, he'd been right. She sounded as disgruntled to find him here as he felt in confronting her.

Good. But what had happened? Matt frowned as he added up the facts. He should have expected something like this—everything had been running too smoothly. The Freedman's Bureau was part of the War Department. And after serving four years in the Union Army, he didn't trust the War Department to get anything right. "There's been a mistake."

"Obviously," Joseph said dryly.

"Would thee mind telling us what thee is here for?" Mrs. Hardy asked him.

He did mind, but he thought an explanation might help resolve the problem. "In general, I'm here to help former slaves adjust to freedom in any way that I can. Specifically, I am here to form a chapter of the Union League of America and to prepare the former slaves to vote. I expect the amendment that will give them that right will be passed in Congress soon. And I'm to get a school built."

Mrs. Hardy quivered as if somebody had just struck her. "The school isn't built yet?"

"Did they tell you it was?" Matt asked, already guessing the answer. His gaze lingered on those caramel eyes that studied him, weighing his words.

Suddenly he realized how wild he must appear to her. He was shirtless with bare feet and uncombed hair, and his rifle still rested in his hands. Yet she sat prim and proper, appearing not the least intimidated by him. One corner of his mouth rose. The woman had grit.

But now he had to deal with this mixup. This was the second unexpected wrinkle in his plans. The first had been his sharp feeling of regret when he arrived here. To fulfill a promise, after he'd joined the Freedman's Bureau, he'd asked to be assigned to this part of Virginia. He'd expected to feel better coming here—he was, after all, coming home in a way. But upon arrival, he'd felt quite the opposite.

"If the school isn't built yet, what am I to do?" she asked. "I'm supposed to begin lessons for former slaves and their children as soon as feasible. But how can I do that if the school hasn't even been built yet?" A line of worry creased the skin between her ginger eyebrows.

His mouth twisted, a sour taste on his tongue. "It's easy to see what happened. Somebody sent you a letter too early. I'll telegraph the War Department and get this straightened out. You'll just have to go back to where you came from until the school's built."

"We can't go back," she objected. "I have rented out my house for a year."

I work alone, Mrs. Hardy. That's why I took a job where I'd be my own boss. "You can't stay. The school isn't even started—"

She interrupted him again. "We've driven all the way from Pennsylvania."

Joseph cut in, "We're not going to drive all the way back there unless we're going home for good." He'd set his dusty hat on his knee, wiping perspiration from his forehead with a white handkerchief. The little girl stared at Matt like a lost puppy.

Matt frowned at them. They frowned back. He really did not want to deal with this. He rose and walked toward the front window to peer out. Again he detected that subtle shifting in the shadows in front of the house. He stepped near the window and raised his rifle so it would be clearly seen by anyone outside.

Returning here had been a foolish, ill-considered notion. Upon arrival, he'd realized that who he was would just make all the work he had to do here more difficult, more unpleasant, more personal. He muttered too low for anyone else to hear, "I should have gone to Mississippi, where I could have been hated by strangers."

Mrs. Hardy cleared her throat, drawing his attention back to her. She moved to the edge of her seat. "I'm certain that the Freedman's Bureau would not expect an unrelated man and a woman to live under the same roof. Even with my father-in-law living with us…" Her voice drifted into silence.

He couldn't agree more. He heard the nicker of their horses outside again. Did the animals sense something that shouldn't be here? He parted the sheer curtains with his rifle and gazed outside once again.

"I would say that I could find somewhere else in town to stay." He brushed this possibility aside. "But I doubt any of the former Confederate widows would want a Yankee boarding in their homes." *And I wouldn't like it either.* He didn't want to live with others. He hated having to make polite conversation. He hated it now. He continued peering out the window.

"What is distracting thee?" she asked.

He held up one hand and listened, but heard nothing unusual outside. Still, he asked in a low voice, "You're Quaker, so you didn't come armed, right?"

Joseph spoke up. "Verity's family is Friends. Mind isn't. I brought a gun. Do I need it now?"

Matt watched the shifting of the shadows out in the silver moonlight, concentrating on listening.

"A gun?" she said. "Why would we need—"

Rising, Joseph cut her off. "What's going on here? Haven't the Rebs here heard that Lee's surrendered?"

The woman continued, "Thee didn't tell me thee brought a gun, Joseph."

Matt spoke over her. "Where's the gun?"

The older man came toward him. "It's under the seat on the buckboard, covered with canvas. I wanted it handy if needed."

"Maybe you should go get it now." Matt motioned with his rifle toward the front door. "I'll come out and cover you. And stick to the shadows, but make sure the gun's visible and be sure they hear you checking to see that it's loaded."

Verity stood up quickly. "Wait. Who does thee think is watching us?"

Matt shrugged. "Maybe no one, but I keep seeing shadows shifting outside. And your horses are restless."

"That could be just the wind and the branches," she protested. "I don't want rifles in my house."

"This isn't your house," Matt said, following Joseph to the door. "And some of the Rebs here haven't surrendered. We're from the North and they don't want us here."

She followed them, still balking, "I didn't expect it would be a welcome with open arms—"

He didn't listen to the rest. He shut the front door, closing her inside, and gave cover to Joseph, who collected his gun, making a show of checking to see that it was loaded.

When they reentered the house, the widow stood there with hands on her hips and fire in her eyes. "We don't need guns. We are here to bring healing and hope to this town."

"No, we're not." His patience went up in flames. "We are here to bring change, to stir up trouble. We've come to make people here choke down emancipation and the educating of blacks. The very things they were willing to die to prevent. We've brought a sword, not an olive branch. If you think different, just turn around and leave. No white person is going to want us here. Many will be more than willing to run us out of town. And if they could get away with it, a few would put us under sod in the local church-yard."

His words brought a shocked silence. Then the little girl ran to her mother and buried her face in her mother's skirts. Mrs. Hardy cast him a reproving look and began stroking her daughter's head. Ashamed of upsetting the child, Matt closed and locked the door. Maybe he had been imagining something or someone lurking outside. But he'd survived the war by learning to distrust everything. "I'm sorry. I didn't mean to…scare her."

"You only spoke the truth," Joseph said. "Christ said He came to bring a sword, not peace. And you knew that, Verity. We discussed it."

"But guns, Joseph," she said in a mournful tone, her voice catching. "The war is over."

Her sad tone stung Matt even more than the little girl's fear. "Why don't we discuss this in the morning?" he said gruffly.

The little girl peered out from her mother's skirts. And then yawned.

Right. Time for bed. A perfect excuse to end the conversation. "It's late," Matt said. "Why don't we just get you settled for the night—"

"But how can we if you're here?" The woman actually blushed.

The solution came to him in a flash. "There is a former slave cabin back by the barn. I'll stay there until this is sorted out. That should fulfill propriety until one of us is moved to another town. We could just take meals together in the house till then. I plan to hire a housekeeper." He felt relief wash over him. He'd keep his privacy and she'd probably get a quick transfer to a more sensible post.

Verity and her father-in-law traded glances. "Are thee sure thee won't mind?" she asked in a way that told him she wasn't just being polite.

He shrugged. "I lived in tents through the whole war." Images of miserably muddy, bone-chilling nights and cold rain trickling down his neck tried to take him back. He pushed the images and foul sensations aside. "Don't worry about me. The cabin's built solid and has a fireplace. I'll be fine."

"You served in the Union Army, then?" she asked solemnly.

He nodded, giving no expression or comment. *I won't talk about it.*

"My husband served in the Army of the Potomac."

Silence. Matt stared at them, refusing to discuss the war. *It's over. We won. That's all that matters.*

Again, her eyes spoke of her character. Their intensity told him she took very little about this situation lightly. She inhaled deeply, breaking the pregnant moment. "Then we have a workable solution. For now. And tomorrow we'll compose that telegram to the Bureau about this situation. Will thee help us bring in our bedding?"

"Certainly." He moved toward the door, thinking that he didn't like the part about them penning the message together. *I'm quite capable of writing a telegram, ma'am.*

Out in the moonlight, they headed toward the buckboard. Mrs. Hardy walked beside Matt, the top of her head level with his shoulder. She carried herself well. But she kept frowning down at the rifle he carried. And he in turn found his eyes drifting toward hers. "Let's get started carrying your things in, ma'am."

Verity looked up into Matt's eyes. "Thank thee for thy help. I'm sorry we woke thee up and startled thee."

Her direct gaze disrupted his peace. But he found he couldn't look away. There was some quality about her that made him feel... He couldn't come up with the word. He stepped back from her, unhappy with himself. "No apology necessary."

Laying his rifle on the buckboard within easy reach, Matt began helping Joseph untie and roll back the canvas that had protected the boxes and trunks roped securely together on the buckboard.

Maybe this would all be for the best. Maybe he, too, should ask for a transfer in that telegram. It would be wiser. Then he could leave town before Dace and he even came face-to-face. Blood was the tie that had bound them once. But now it was blood spilled in the war that separated them.

His thoughts were interrupted by the gentle sound of Mrs. Hardy sharing a quiet laugh with her daughter. The nearby leaves rustled with the wind and he nearly reached for his rifle. But it was just the wind, wasn't it?

Unsettled. That was the word he'd been looking for. Mrs. Hardy made him feel unsettled. And he didn't like it one bit.

Chapter Two

In the dingy and unfamiliar kitchen, Verity sat at the battered wood table. Her elbows on the bare wood, she gnawed off a chunk of tasteless hardtack. Trying not to gag, she sipped hot black coffee, hoping the liquid would soften the rock in her mouth. Her daughter was too well-behaved to pout about the pitiful breakfast, but her downcast face said it all. Their first breakfast in Fiddlers Grove pretty much expressed their state of affairs—and Verity's feelings about it.

She leaned her forehead against the back of her hand. The house had looked more inviting in moonlight. Gloom crawled up her nape like winding, choking vines. And yet she couldn't keep her disobedient mind from calling up images from the night before—a strong tanned hand gripping a rifle, a broad shoulder sculpted by moonlight.

She gnawed more hardtack. Why had Matthew Ritter behaved as if he'd expected someone to attack them? The war is over. The people here might not like the school, but there is no reason for guns. Her throat rebelled at swallowing more of the gummy slurry. She gagged, trying to hide it from Beth.

Joseph came in the back door. "Ritter isn't in the cabin out back." He sat down and made a face at the hardtack on the plate and the cup of black coffee. Joseph liked bacon, eggs and buttered toast for breakfast, and a lot of cream in his coffee. "Slim pickings, I see."

She sipped more hot coffee and choked down the last of the hardtack. "Yes, I'm going to have to find a farmer and get milk and egg delivery set up. Or perhaps that store in town stocks perishables."

"Do you think we're going to be here long enough to merit that?" Joseph asked. "I'm pretty sure Ritter has gone to the next town to send that telegram."

At the mention of Matthew Ritter, Verity's heart lurched. She looked away, smoothing back the stray hair around her face. Last night when Matthew had opened the door, shirtless and toting a rifle, she hadn't known which shocked her more: his lack of proper dress or the rifle. Of course, they had surprised him after he'd turned in for the night. But he hadn't excused himself and gone to don a shirt or comb his dark hair.

Men often shed their shirts while working in the fields, but he'd sat with them in the parlor shirtless and barefoot. And she couldn't help but notice that Matthew was a fine-looking man. She blocked her mind from bringing up his likeness again. Her deep loneliness, the loneliness she admitted only to the Lord, no doubt prompted this reaction.

As if Joseph had read a bit of her thoughts, he said, "Ritter is probably more comfortable in the company of men. You know, after four long years of army life."

No doubt. She willed away the memory of Matthew Ritter in dishabille. "He might be sending the telegram, but we don't know what the answer will be. Or when it might come." She tried to also dismiss just how completely unwelcoming Matthew Ritter had been. And how blunt. "And we need food because, after all, we're here." *And we can't go back.*

Joseph grunted in agreement. "Well, I'm going to do

some work in the barn. This place must have sat empty for quite some time. The paddock fence needs repairs before I dare let the horses out."

Verity rose, forcing herself to face going into a town of strangers. After Matthew's dark forebodings last night, all her own misgivings had flocked to the surface, pecking and squawking like startled chickens. *If we're on the same side, he shouldn't be discouraging me. How will we accomplish anything if we remain at cross-purposes?*

"Joseph, I'm going to walk to the store and see about buying some food. We'll eat our main meal at midday as usual. I'm sure I'll be able to get what I need to put something simple on the table." *I can do that. This is a state of the Union again. No matter what Matthew said, I will not be afraid of Fiddlers Grove.*

With a nod, Joseph rose. "Little Beth, you going with me or your mom?"

"I want to help in the barn," Beth said, popping up from the table. "May I, Mother?"

"Certainly," Verity said. *Better you should stay here, my sweet girl. I don't want you hurt or frightened. Again.* Last night Matthew's harsh words had caused Beth to run to her. She shivered.

I will not be afraid. Not until I have good reason to be.

With her oak basket over one arm, Verity marched down the dusty road into town. Fiddlers Grove boasted only a group of peeling houses with sagging roofs, two churches and a general store. With the general store looming dead ahead, her feet slowed, growing heavier, clumsier, as if she were treading ankle-deep through thick mud. This town was going to be her home for at least a year. Starting today. *Lord, help me make a good first impression.*

On the bench by the general store's door lounged some older men with unshaven, dried-apple faces. Matthew's warning that some here would welcome her death made her quiver, but she inhaled and then smiled at them.

Grime coated the storefront windows with a fine film and the door stood propped open. Flies buzzed in and out. Her pulse hopping and skipping, Verity nodded at the older men who'd risen respectfully as she passed them. She crossed the threshold.

A marked hush fell over the store. Every eye turned to her. Drawing in as much air as she could, Verity walked like a stick figure toward the counter. The townspeople fell back, leaving her alone in the center of the sad and bare-looking store. She halted, unable to go forward.

She began silently reciting the twenty-third psalm, an old habit in the midst of stress. *The Lord is my shepherd; I shall not want. He maketh me to lie down in green pastures: He leadeth me beside the still waters.*

Near the counter, a slight woman in a frayed bonnet and patched dress edged away from Verity, joining the surrounding gawkers. Verity tried to act naturally, letting everyone stare at her as if she hadn't fastened her buttons correctly.

She forced her legs to carry her forward. "Good morning," she greeted the proprietor. Her voice trembled, giving her away.

The thin, graying man behind the counter straightened. "Good day, ma'am. I'm Phil Hanley, the storekeeper. What may I do for you?"

She acknowledged his introduction with a wobbly nod, intense gazes still pressing in on her from all sides. Her smile felt tight and false, like the grin stitched on a rag doll's face.

"Phil Hanley, I'm Verity Hardy and I need some of those eggs." She indicated a box of brown eggs on the counter. "And, if thee have any, some bacon. And I need to ask thee who sells milk in town. I require at least two quarts a day.

And I'm out of bread. I'll need to set up my kitchen before I begin baking bread again." Her words had spilled out in a rapid stream, faster than usual.

In the total silence that followed, the man stared at her as if she'd been speaking a foreign language. People who weren't used to Plain Speech often did this, she told herself. They would soon grow accustomed—if she and her family stayed here longer than Matthew hoped.

She waited, perspiring. As the silence continued, Verity blotted her upper lip with a handkerchief from her apron pocket. More of the twenty-third psalm played in her mind. *For Thou art with me; Thy rod and Thy staff they comfort me.*

"Ma'am." A slight, pinched-looking woman edged nearer and offered in a hesitant voice, "I just baked this mornin'. I have a spare pan of cornbread."

With a giddy rush of gratitude, Verity turned toward the woman. "Thank thee. I'm Verity Hardy. And thee is?"

"Mary. I mean, Mrs. Orrin Dyke, ma'am." Mary curtsied.

"I'm pleased to meet thee." Verity offered her hand like a man instead of curtsying like a woman, knowing this would also brand her as an oddity. *Well, in for a penny, in for a pound.*

Mary Dyke shook her hand tentatively.

"Mary Dyke, I'm living at the Barnesworth house. Could thee drop by with that cornbread later this morning?"

"Yes, ma'am. I can do that," Mary said with a shy blush, curtsying again.

Verity reached into her pocket and then held out a coin. "Here. I'll pay thee in advance."

"No." Mary backed away, one ungloved hand up. "You just give the money to Mr. Hanley to put on my account. I'll bring the bread over right away. 'Sides, that's way too much for a pan of bread. I couldn't take more than a nickel."

Sensing a stiffening in the people surrounding her, Verity wondered how she'd given offense. Still, she held out the dime, her mind racing as she tried to come up with a way to make her offer acceptable. "But I'll owe thee for delivery, too."

"No, no, ma'am, I can't take anything for bringing it. Or in advance." Mary scurried from the store.

Verity appeared to have offended the woman by offering to pay too much and in advance. But what could she do to amend that here and now? Nothing. Her mind went back to the psalm. *He restoreth my soul.* Yes, please, Lord, she thought. She took a deep breath and said through dry lips that were trying to stick together, "Two dozen of those fine brown eggs, please, Phil Hanley?"

"Of course." He set the offered oak basket on the counter and carefully wrapped the eggs in newspaper, nestling them into it. His movements provided the only sound in the store other than Verity's audible rapid breathing. She fought the urge to fidget.

"Anything else, ma'am?"

"Well, now that I'm going to have cornbread—" she smiled "—I'll need butter. And the bacon, if thee has some. Two pounds, please?"

"Just a moment." He stepped out the back door, leaving Verity on display. While she gazed at the nearly empty shelves, the crowd surrounding her gawked in stolid suspicion. The feeling that she was on a stage and had just forgotten her lines washed through her, cold then hot. *Thou preparest a table before me in the presence of mine enemies.*

In the persistent silence, the storeowner reentered and wrapped the butter and slab of bacon with the rustling of more newspaper. He tucked them into her basket. "Anything else, ma'am?"

"Not right now. How much do I owe thee?" The thought that her ordeal was almost over made her fingers fumble. But finally, out of her dangling reticule, she pulled a leather purse. She struggled with the catch, and then opened it. The taut silence flared and she sensed their disapproval distinctly. She glanced around and saw that everyone was staring at the U.S. greenbacks folded neatly in her purse.

She pressed her dry lips together. A show of wealth was always distasteful, especially in the presence of such lean, ragged people. She tasted bitter regret. At every turn, she appeared unable to stop offending these people. *Lord, help me. I'm doing everything wrong.*

The proprietor spoke up, breaking the uncomfortable silence. "After Mary's nickel for the bread, that's just two bits then, ma'am."

She gave him the coins. "I'll bid thee good day then, Phil Hanley." She offered him her gloved hand.

He shook it and nodded farewell. Still smiling her rag-doll smile, she walked out into the bright sunlight.

Cool relief began to trickle through her. She'd gotten food for the midday meal and let Fiddlers Grove know she'd arrived. It said much about the suffering of Virginia that she, who'd always lived a simple life, should suddenly have to be concerned about flaunting wealth. Wounding Southern pride wouldn't help her in her work here. She'd have to be more careful. *I'd never had been this jumpy if Matthew Ritter hadn't tried to scare me off. It won't happen again, Lord, with Thy help.*

Later that warm, bright morning, Verity stood at the door of her new home, her pulse suddenly galloping. "Won't thee come in, Mary Dyke?" *Lord, help me say the right things.*

"No, ma'am. Here's your pan of bread, as promised." The small woman's eyes flitted around as if she were afraid. She handed Verity the circle of cornbread, wrapped within a ragged but spotless kitchen cloth. A sandy-haired boy who looked to be about eleven had accompanied Mary Dyke.

Verity needed information about the sad-looking town and its people to get a sense of how the community would really react to the new school. In spite of Matthew's warning, Verity refused to assume the possibility of community cooperation was impossible.

Verity smiled. "Mary, I've never moved before—at least, not since I married and left home to move into my husband's house. I was wondering if thee…and is this thy son?"

"Yes, ma'am." A momentary smile lit the woman's drawn face. Mrs. Dyke patted her son's shoulder. He was taller than his mother already and very thin, with a sensitive-looking face. "This is my son, Alec. Son, make your bow."

The boy obeyed his mother and then Verity felt a tug at her own skirt and looked down. Evidently Beth had been drawn by the lure of another child. "This is my daughter. Beth, this is Mary Dyke and her son, Alec." Her seven-year-old daughter with long dark braids and a serious face made a curtsy, and stole a quick glance at the boy.

"What is it you are wondering about, ma'am?" Mary Dyke asked, sounding wary.

"I could use some help opening boxes and putting away my kitchen things." Verity gestured toward the chaotic room behind her. "Would thee have time to help me unpack boxes? I'm sure company would make the work go faster." *Please, Lord, help me make a friend here.*

The woman appeared uneasy, but then bit her lip and said, "I can stay a mite longer."

"Excellent. And perhaps thy son would like to help my father-in-law with the horses in the barn?" All children loved horses—and Joseph.

"Yes, ma'am." Alec bowed again and started toward the barn at the back of the property. Beth slipped from her mother's side and followed the boy, keeping a safe distance from him.

Verity smiled and ushered Mary into her disordered kitchen. Wooden boxes with straw and crumpled newspaper packing covered the floor. "Thee sees what I mean?"

"Yes, ma'am."

Soon Verity and Mary were working side by side. Unwrapping jars of preserves swathed in newsprint, Verity was cheered by Mary Dyke's companionship. She already missed her six sisters back in Pennsylvania and her kind neighbors. If she were to be able to accomplish both her public and private reasons for coming here, she needed to begin to learn about the people here. And she couldn't forget that she'd come with a personal mission, too.

Then Verity asked a question that had occurred to her on the way home. "Where is the school? I didn't see it in town. I want to get Beth enrolled." Verity paused to blot the perspiration on her forehead with a white handkerchief from her apron pocket.

Mary didn't glance up. "Ma'am, we don't have a school in town."

"No school?" Verity couldn't keep the dismayed surprise out of her tone.

"I've heard that there are free schools in the North," Mary commented in a flat tone, not meeting Verity's eyes.

Verity realized she'd just insulted the town again. She racked her brain, trying to think of some way to open up this timid woman—not to gossip but merely to provide Verity with helpful information.

Perhaps honesty would suffice. "I'm afraid that I offended many at the store this morning. I didn't mean to, but perhaps I should have been less forward with my offer of payment. I hope I didn't offend thee by offering to pay thee to deliver the bread."

When no reply came, Verity's face warmed with embarrassment. "It's just that I don't know anyone here yet and I didn't want to… I don't know exactly how to say what I mean. I just didn't want thee to think thee owed me anything. If we were back in Pennsylvania, I would probably have known thee all my life…" *Why can't I stop babbling?* "Oh, I'm doing a terrible job of explaining."

Mary finally glanced her way. "No, ma'am, I think I understand and I wasn't offended—or maybe I should say not much. You're a Yankee, and I know Yankees don't have Southern manners." Then the woman colored red. "I mean—"

Verity chuckled. "Now thee knows how I feel. And thee hasn't offended me."

The back door swung open and Matthew Ritter stepped inside. "Mary!" he exclaimed.

In the midst of lifting a jar of peaches to the shelf, Mary dropped it. The glass shattered, the yellow fruit and syrups splattering the floor, wall and Mary's skirts. "Oh, ma'am, I'm so sorry!"

Matthew stood apart, saying nothing. Seeing Mary prompted scenes from childhood to flood his mind—playing hide and seek among the ancient oaks around Mary's house, fishing at the creek, running in the fields with Dace and Samuel. Why did the widow have to be here as witness to the first time he encountered an old friend who was now probably an enemy?

When the mess had been cleaned up, he took a deep breath and said, "I'm sorry I startled you, Mary." He wondered for a moment if she would try to act as if she didn't know him.

Mary turned toward him, but looked at the floor. "That's all right, Matt. I just didn't expect to see you here. Someone said they thought they'd seen you, but…"

A strained silence stretched between them. A string of odd reactions hit him—his throat was thick, his eyes smarted, he felt hot and then cold. To break the unbearable silence, he nodded toward her simple gold wedding band. "You're married, I see."

She still wouldn't meet his gaze. "Yes, I married Orrin Dyke. We have one son, Alec."

Orrin Dyke? Sweet Mary McKay had married that shiftless oaf, Matt hoped his low opinion of her husband didn't show on his face. He forced words through his dry throat, "I'm happy to hear that."

Mary looked up then. "Are you… Have you come home for good?"

Home for good? The thought sliced like a bayonet. He grimaced. "Probably not. I doubt I'll be welcome here." He made himself go on and tell the truth, the whole truth. "I'm working for the Freedman's Bureau. I'm here to help former slaves adjust to freedom and prepare them to vote."

Mary simply stared at him.

He'd expected his job to be offensive to his old friends, but he was who he was.

The Quaker widow watched them in silence. Her copper hair and air of confidence contrasted sharply with Mary's meek and shabby appearance. Meeting Mary after all these years was hard enough without the widow taking in every word, every expression. His face and neck warmed—he hated betraying his strong reaction to the situation.

"Your parents?" Mary asked.

He swallowed down the gorge that had risen in his throat. "My parents died during the war."

"I'm sorry." And Mary did sound sorry.

"Your parents?" he asked, wishing the widow would excuse herself and leave them. But of course, it would be almost improper for her to do so.

"My mother died, but Pa's still alive. It's good to see you again, Matt, safe and sound after the war."

He imagined all the prickly thoughts that might be coursing through Mary's mind about his fighting on the Union side and the reason his family had left town in 1852. Just thinking of leaving Fiddlers Grove brought back the same sinking feeling it had that day in 1852—as if the floor had opened and was swallowing him inch by inch.

Mary turned to the widow. "Ma'am, I must be leaving."

"Of course, Mary Dyke, I thank thee for thy help." The widow shook Mary's hand as if she were a man.

Matt held on to his composure as he bowed, wishing Mary goodbye.

Mary curtsied and then she was out the back door, calling, "Alec!" Her son, Orrin's son.

That left him alone with the widow as they faced each other in the kitchen. Again, he was struck by her unruly copper curls, which didn't fit her serene yet concerned expression. He wanted to turn and leave. But of course, he had to deal with her. He took himself in hand. *I faced cannon so I can face this inquisitive woman and my hometown where I won't be welcome.*

She went to the stove and lifted the coffeepot there. "Would thee like a cup?"

He wanted to refuse and leave, but he was thirsty and they needed to talk. He hoped she didn't make good coffee. He didn't want to like anything about this woman. He forced out a gruff "Please."

She motioned him to sit at the table and served him the coffee. Then she sat down facing him. "I take it that thee went to send the telegram about our situation?"

He'd braced himself for her expected interrogation. "Yes, I did, and I bought some chickens for the yard and a cow for milk."

She raised her eyebrows at him. "I'm surprised that thee made these purchases. Thee sounded last night as if thee didn't think my family and I would be here long enough to merit the purchase of any stock."

He sipped the hot coffee. It was irritatingly good. "I'll be here long enough to do what I signed on to do." That much he'd decided on his ride to send the telegram. "And whether you're here or not, I'll need eggs and milk. We need to hire a housekeeper. Would you do that? Hire her?"

The woman considered him for a few moments. "I could do that. But perhaps I should just do the housekeeping until I start teaching."

He shook his head. He didn't want this woman to become someone he'd come to depend on. With any luck, she'd be gone soon. "When you're busy teaching, it would be better to have household help." It wasn't shading the truth, since the decision as to whether she would stay or go was not up to him. After all, he might end up stuck with this woman indefinitely. With her early arrival the Freedman's Bureau had demonstrated that it could make mistakes.

"Very well. I'll see about hiring a housekeeper."

He sipped more of her good coffee, brooding over all he couldn't change in the situation. After four years of following orders, he'd wanted to be free, on his own. And then here she was. And then the question he dreaded came.

"Thee didn't tell me that thee had ever lived here before."

Yes, I didn't, and I don't want to tell you now. "I lived here with my parents until I was around twelve. Then we moved to New York State." *And that's all you need to know.*

"I see."

Was she too polite to ask why? He waited. Evidently she was. *Good.* Feeling suddenly freer, he rose. "I'm going out to settle the stock. I see your father-in-law is already working on that fence that needed fixing."

"Yes, Joseph is very handy to have around. When it's time for dinner, I'll ring the bell. I bought only bacon, eggs and cornbread, so the menu will be somewhat limited. But soon I'll have the kitchen completely stocked, and with a cow and some chickens, we'll only need to buy meat and greens from a local farmer."

Matt nodded and walked outside into the hot sunshine. As he stood there, the muscles in his neck tightened. He remembered the look on Mary's face when she'd recognized him. Well, the fat would sizzle soon. Word that he was indeed back in town would whip through Fiddlers Grove like a tornado. It couldn't be avoided. But he'd given his word and he'd stand by it.

The concerned look the widow had given him poured acid on his already lacerated nerves. He wanted no sympathy—just to do his work and move on. Oh, he hoped that telegram would come soon. He wanted this disturbing Quaker widow anywhere but here.

Later that afternoon, Verity was putting the final touches on the freshly hemmed and pressed white kitchen curtains she'd had sense enough to bring. When someone knocked on her back door, she started. Scolding herself for lingering jitters, she went to open the door and found a tall, sturdily built black woman looking back at her.

Her visitor appeared to be in her middle years with the beginning of silver hair around the edges of a red kerchief tied at the front of her head.

"May I help thee?"

"I'm Hannah. I've come to meet y'all Yankees."

The woman's directness made Verity smile, and some

of the tightness inside her eased. "Please come in, Hannah. I'm Verity Hardy."

"Are you a Miss or Mrs.?" The woman looked at her pointedly.

"I'm a widow, but I'm a Quaker and prefer to be called by name." Verity opened the door and gestured the woman in. *Please, Lord, help me do better with this new neighbor.*

"Yes, ma'am." The woman entered the kitchen.

Footsteps sounded in the hall and Beth ran into the kitchen. She halted at the sight of Hannah.

"Hello." Beth curtsied. "I'm Beth."

"You can call me Aunt Hannah, you sweet child." The woman's face and voice softened.

Beth looked to her mother for direction. Verity nodded. "If the woman wishes to be called Aunt Hannah, Beth, thee may address her in that way." Then she turned Hannah. "Won't thee sit down? I have coffee on the stove."

Hannah stared at her and then at the table. "This Virginia. Whites and blacks don't never sit down together."

Verity did not know what to say to this. It made her stomach flutter.

"But we're not from Virginia," Beth explained earnestly.

Hannah laughed. "You sure ain't, honey. I know that. Tell you what, I go back outside and set on the top step and you can bring me that cup of coffee. And y'all can sit on chairs on the back porch. And that would look all right. How's that?"

Verity nodded in agreement. Why had Hannah come? Was she bringing more bad news? Very soon, the three of them were seated in Hannah's suggested manner on the small back porch. Verity waited for Hannah to speak. She hated this awkwardness, this unfamiliarity—hated being the stranger. Odd tremors had coursed through her on and off ever since her trip to town. Now they started up again, making her feel off balance.

After several sips of coffee, Hannah began, "I hear you folks come from the North and you talk like Quakers. And I figure if you be a Quaker, then I think afore the war you was abolitionist, too."

"Yes, my whole family was very active in the abolitionist movement," Verity replied. *Where was this leading?*

Hannah nodded. "I figured so. What're y'all doing here in Fiddlers Grove, then?"

Only God knows the full answer to that. "I came to teach school."

"What school?"

"The school Matthew Ritter is here to build."

Hannah stared at her. "I heard the Ritter boy come back."

"Yes, he has." So Matthew was generally known here. Verity tried to discern what Hannah's attitude was toward the man's return, but Hannah's reaction was not apparent.

"What you two living here together for? Are you married?"

Verity sighed silently and tried to quell the trembling that wouldn't leave her. The close living arrangement with Matthew would be a topic of gossip and speculation, so she might as well tell this woman. She explained the mistake about her coming too soon and Matthew moving to the cabin. Hoping to sidestep the queries and pick up some information, Verity continued, "May I ask thee a question?"

Hannah nodded.

"Soon it will be First Day. And I see that thee has but two churches in town—"

"First day, what that?" Hannah looked puzzled.

"Quakers use Plain Speech, meaning we try to speak simply and truthfully. We do not use the same names for the days of the week as other Christians do because each one of them is named after a pagan god."

"I never knew that."

Beth piped up, "Wednesday is from Woden. He was a Nordic god."

"Do tell," Hannah replied with a grin.

Verity chuckled, but pressed on, "I was inquiring about the churches—"

"We got St. John's and Fiddlers Grove Community," Hannah said.

"Which church does thee worship at?" Verity asked, setting down her cup carefully so as not to let it rattle on the saucer.

"Neither. I attend Brother Elijah's preaching on the Ransford place on Sunday afternoons. Elijah is the Ransford butler and my husband."

Verity nodded. "I see. Does either town church have an evening service?"

"Fiddlers Grove Community has 6:30 p.m. service. But St. John's only meet at 9:00 a.m. sharp. They got a bell. Y'all hear it, all right."

"Thank you, Hannah." Verity waited, sensing the woman was finally about to reveal her reason for coming.

Hannah put her empty cup down on the step. She bowed her head for a moment and then looked up at Verity. "I can't read or write. Can you write me a letter? I know the name and a place to send it. I can pay."

The request pricked Verity's heart. *How awful not to be able to read and write. Lord, help me get this school started here or wherever Thee wishes.* "I have time to write a letter. And I would take it as a kindness if thee would let me do it for thee without pay. I don't think it's right to charge a neighbor."

Hannah grinned. "I thank you. Will you write that letter for me now?"

"Certainly." Verity rose and dragged her chair back inside, leading the way for her daughter and Hannah to follow. "Who am I writing to?"

"The name's Isaiah Watson and he live in Buffalo, New York."

"Is this a matter of business?" Verity asked.

"Don't know if you'd call this business or not. There be someone I want to find. And I think Mr. Isaiah Watson might know where that person be."

"Aunt Hannah," Beth asked, "who is the person that you want to find?"

"Miss Beth, I want to find my boy."

Chapter Three

In the dazzling light of First Day, Verity gazed at St. John's Church, which sat on a gentle rise in the midst of an oak grove at the edge of town. It was small but impressive with its tall steeple and golden marigolds along its cobblestone path. Her father-in-law and Beth walked beside her, through the red door and into the sudden dimness of the church foyer. Matthew brought up the rear. A very grim and reluctant Matthew.

She hoped that three visits to three churches would remind the people of Fiddlers Grove that they shared a common faith in Christ. Still, her spine had become a tightly wound spring she couldn't relax. She feared that this would be worse than visiting the store. Quakers never called attention to themselves—never. And worst of all, the fear Matthew had sparked within her lingered.

Inside St. John's, a pipe organ began playing. Beth did a little jump. "Music."

Verity smiled, though her lips felt stiff. Beth shared her late father's love of music. Verity waited until the congregation had finished the first verse, then she nodded at Joseph and Matthew. Joseph led them down the center aisle to seats in an empty pew near the back of the church. Matthew removed his hat and stood beside Verity, taking the aisle space. He hadn't brought his rifle, of course, but he looked as forbidding as if he had. It was almost as if he expected someone to attack them.

As expected, many heads swiveled to watch them enter. Verity smiled, her lips wooden. Then Beth began to sing along, as did Joseph. Their voices—the high wispy soprano and the low bass—blended in with the singing. "'Lord, as to Thy dear cross we flee, and plead to be forgiven.'" She hoped the people singing were listening to the words coming from their mouths. "'Kept peaceful in the midst of strife, forgiving and forgiven, O may we lead the pilgrim's life, and follow Thee to heaven.'"

Quaker meetings were composed of silence, praying and speaking, not singing. Though Verity didn't feel comfortable singing, she enjoyed the music, which calmed her wary heart and lifted her spirit. Still, Matthew stood beside her as stiff and silent as a sentinel. Waves of infectious tension wafted from him. But his formidable presence also managed to reassure her. No one would antagonize Matthew Ritter without good reason.

Verity looked up over her shoulder and saw what must have been a slaves' balcony. It was empty now, showing that—after emancipation—the black population must not want to come to the white man's church.

The hymn ended. There was a general rustling around the church as books were put back into their holders and ladies gathered their skirts to sit down. Verity concentrated on the vicar, who in his clerical collar and vestments looked about the same age as her father-in-law. Then she noted that one man, who looked to be about Matthew's age, kept glancing back at her and Matthew.

Throughout the rest of the service, Verity tried to ignore the surreptitious glances from the people of Fiddlers Grove. It was no surprise that people would be curious about them; still, it made her uneasy. Who was the one man who looked at Matthew over and over?

After the final hymn was sung, the congregation rose and made its way into the aisle. Verity, Joseph, Beth and Matthew made their way toward the clergyman, standing at the doorway and shaking hands with everyone as they left.

She was very aware of the same man who'd kept glancing at Matthew. Was he planning on making trouble? Matthew, on the other hand, pointedly ignored the man.

When it was finally her turn to offer her hand to the vicar, it felt as if the whole congregation on the steps and in the foyer paused and fell silent, listening. Verity swallowed and tried to smile.

"Good morning," the vicar said. "I am Pastor Savage."

"That's a scary name," Beth said.

Verity touched her daughter's shoulder. Beth hung her head and then curtsied. "I beg your pardon."

"Mine is an unusual name, especially for a clergyman." Pastor Savage smiled. "You are new to Fiddlers Grove."

"Yes," Joseph responded, and shook the pastor's hand.

"Everyone has been wondering why you have come to our little town. Many believe you are one of those meddling Yankee schoolmarms we've heard of." His tone was friendly but uncertain.

"It is hard to be a stranger in a small town," Verity said without giving him an answer. She liked the pastor's eyes. They were good eyes. But very sad ones, too.

"Maybe our new family moved to Fiddlers Grove for their health," a pretty woman in a once stylish but now faded dress suggested in a sly tone. She stood beside the man who'd been watching Matthew.

Verity smiled, though a frisson of fear went through her. Had there been a veiled threat in that statement? Would it be "unhealthy" here for them? There was a pregnant pause while everyone waited for Verity to reply.

When she did not, the man beside the woman said, "May I make myself known to you? This is my wife, Lirit, and I'm Dacian Ransford. I wish to welcome you to our town."

Mr. Ransford must have served in the Confederate Army. He had that "starved and marched too long" look she'd seen so often in '63. "I am pleased to meet thee," she murmured, for once not really sure she meant her proper words. It was obvious in the way Dacian dressed that he was a prominent member of society here. Hadn't Hannah said that her husband was the Ransford butler?

Joseph accepted Dacian Ransford's hand and Beth curtsied. Then before Joseph could introduce the fourth member of their party, the man faced Matthew. "Hello, Matt."

"Dace." Matthew nodded, no emotion visible on his face.

"I didn't expect to see you in Fiddlers Grove again." Neither Dacian Ransford's tone nor his expression gave any clue as to whether he thought it good or bad to see Matthew here now. Yet neither offered a hand to the other.

Verity tried to behave as if she were unaware of the heightened tension that ran through the milling congregation. Matthew's expression became stony.

"Oh?" Matt replied. No emotion. No inflection.

Perhaps war did this to men; perhaps it "closed" them. Suddenly she wondered why Matthew's family had left Fiddlers Grove.

As Verity studied the two men, a forceful wind moved her skirts. Overhead, large white clouds glided across the blue sky.

"How is my aunt Samantha?" Dacian asked Matthew. "My mother died of cholera in '62. She had been widowed for a year then. And my aunt Sarah Rose?" Matthew asked.

"My mother passed just after Lincoln was elected. A fever. My father survived her by two years."

"I'm sorry to hear that," Matthew said, sounding sincere.

"And I'm sorry also about your parents passing." The two men were silent for a moment, and then Dacian nodded and took his wife's elbow, steering her down the church steps.

Verity tried to make sense of this exchange between first cousins, as well as the shocking news she'd gathered—the fact that Matthew hadn't mentioned Dacian. Why hadn't Matthew just told them he had relatives in town?

Later that day, Matthew trailed after Verity and her family, heading toward the singing coming from a maple-and-oak grove on the Ransford plantation. Why had the Quaker insisted they attend three church services today? She'd only smiled when he'd asked her. He was tempted to stay behind, but he hadn't wanted her going without him. And of course, he'd come face-to-face with Dace this morning. His emotions from that meeting continued to bubble up inside him. He crammed them down. *Forget it. Forget all of it.*

The singing drew them closer and he began to recognize many of the black faces as people from his childhood. He tightened his defenses against all this remembering. Yet he still searched for Samuel's face. From him, he might get a genuine welcome.

Before emancipation, slaves had been required to attend church with their masters. Now they were holding their own service and singing a popular freedom song he'd heard in the streets of Richmond and Washington D.C.

Mammy, don't yo' cook and sew no mo'.
Yo' are free, yo' are free.
Rooster, don't you crow no mo'.
Yo' are free, yo' are free.
Old hen, don't yo' lay no mo' eggs.
Yo' are free, yo' are free.

At sight of them, the whole congregation broke off in
the middle of a note and fell silent. Abashed, the widow's
little girl hung back, hiding within the folds of her mother's
skirt. The boisterous wind that had come up this morning
was now picking up more speed. The black ribbons of the
Quaker's bonnet flared in the wind. Verity smiled, looking
untroubled and genuine. But was anyone that cool? What
would stir this woman enough to pierce her outward calm?
Or did it go straight through to her very core?

Matt had eaten the cold midday meal with them, but
hadn't offered any explanation about his past in Fiddlers
Grove. Why couldn't he just tell her why his family had
left and why he'd come back? Somehow, explanations remained impossible.

He recognized Hannah in the shade of a twisted old oak
and felt a pang. Samuel's mother had survived. She hurried to him and hugged him. "Mr. Matt, welcome home."

"Mr. Matt!" Hannah's husband, Elijah, grasped both
Matt's hands. "I heard that you had come back to town.
As I live and breathe, sir. As I live and breathe."

"It's good to see you, too, Elijah." Matt swallowed down
all the memories that were forcing their way up from deep
inside him. He wanted so much to ask about Samuel, but
he found he couldn't say the name.

Elijah visibly pulled himself together. "Yes, welcome
home, Mr. Matt." The man's genuine warmth had been so
unexpected that Matt glanced skyward, hiding his reaction.

It struck him that Elijah wasn't quite as tall as Matt remembered him. Perhaps because Matt had been a child the last time he'd seen Elijah. Elijah looked gaunt, and his closely cropped hair and bushy eyebrows were threaded with silver. He was dressed in a good-quality but worn suit and spoke with a cultured cadence. After all, he was the Ransfords' butler.

Again Matt felt the urge to ask where Samuel was. But what if Samuel had died? He couldn't bring himself to stir those waters.

"Y'all come just like you said you would." Hannah approached Verity and offered her a work-worn hand. "I told everybody about how you wrote that letter for me."

What letter? To whom? Matt's heart started throbbing in his chest. *What was the woman up to now?*

Verity shook Hannah's hand. "It was a pleasure to help thee. Hannah, thee remembers my daughter, Beth. And this is my father-in-law, Joseph Hardy."

Hannah introduced Verity and her family to Elijah. "Sister Verity, we're glad to have you and your family. Welcome," he said.

"I ain't glad," declared a large woman wearing a patterned indigo kerchief over her hair. "Do the Ransfords know this Ritter boy back in town? And what a white woman and her folks doin' comin' here? I want to know if she with the Freedman's Bureau. And when we going to get our land? That's the only reason I stayed in this place—to get what's due me."

"I told you they was Quakers and abolitionists afore the war." Hannah propped her hands on her ample hips. "And why shouldn't the Ritter boy come home?"

Come home. Matt was undone. Blinking away tears, he stared up into the gray clouds flying in from the northeast.

The woman with the indigo kerchief demanded, "Are they are our side or master side?"

"We are on God's side, I hope," Verity said. "I wish thee will all go on with thy singing, Elijah."

Matt glanced at her out of the corner of his eye. *Thank you.* Hannah urged the widow and her family to take seats on the large downed log in the shade. Matt hung back, leaning against an elm. The brim of the widow's bonnet flapped in the wind, giving him glimpses of her long, golden-brown lashes against her fair cheek.

Soon, the congregation was singing and clapping to "O Mary."

"O Mary, don't you weep, don't you mourn
O Mary, don't you weep, don't you mourn,
Pharaoh's army got drowned."

Matt wondered if, in their minds, Pharaoh's army was the Army of the Confederacy. It had gone down in defeat like Pharaoh's army. But it hadn't been an easy defeat. Why was it that he could stand here in the sun listening to beautiful singing and yet still be on the battlefield, with cannons blasting him to deafness? Why wouldn't his mind just let go of the war?

"O Mary, don't you weep
Some of these mornings bright and fair
Take my wings and cleave the air
Pharaoh's army got drowned.
O Mary, don't you weep.
When I get to heaven goin' to sing and shout
Nobody there for to turn me out."

The little girl was singing and clapping with the gathering. Her mother sat quiet and ladylike, her gloved hands folded in her lap. Her serenity soothed something in Matt.

He tried not to stare, but drew his gaze away with difficulty.

He repeated the words of the song in his mind. *Some of these mornings bright and fair, Take my wings and cleave the air.*

Though his heavy burden of memories tried to drag him down, he fought to focus on the present. The work his parents had begun must be completed. The laws of the land must be the same for white and black. He must not lose sight of that.

The widow glanced over her shoulder at him. How long could he hold back from telling her the story of his family and Fiddlers Grove? The simple answer was that he could not ignore Dace—not just because Dace was his only cousin, but also because Dace had the power to sway others. The Ransfords had run this town for over a hundred years. Matt came to a decision. He'd have to talk to Dace. There was always an outside chance that Dace wouldn't be hostile to the school, wasn't there?

After the evening meal, Matt trudged through the wild wind into the white frame church with Verity and her family. The church sat at the end of the town's main street. It was surrounded by oaks, elms and maples and was much larger than St. John's. The wind tugged at Matt's hat. A storm was certain. Matt looked forward to it, hoping for relief from the stifling, unseasonal heat of the past few days.

On the other hand, Matt dreaded walking into this church. Most of its members had been vocal enemies of his parents. And Matt wondered which of them had been responsible for that final night that had sent his family north. His gut clenched. He reminded himself that that was all past and his side had won the war. Not theirs.

Again they entered during the opening hymn. They elicited glances, some surreptitious and some blatant. Toward the front, Mary and her son, Alec, sat with her father, Jed McKay, who looked like an Old Testament prophet. Orrin was nowhere in sight—an unexpected blessing.

When the hymn ended, the preacher looked straight at them and demanded, "What are you people here for?"

For once, the widow looked startled. "I beg thy pardon?"

"We don't want Yankees coming down here and telling us what to do with our people. If you're here to do that, you might as well leave in the morning. We won't tolerate any Yankee meddling."

Matt waited to see what the Quaker would say before he entered the fray.

"Friend, I am not a meddler. But anyone who thinks nothing here is going to change after secession, four years of bloodshed, Lee's surrender and emancipation is deluding themselves."

Matt's eyes widened. The widow's tone was civil but her words broadsided the congregation. He felt the angry response slap back at them. *Whoa.* The woman had nerve, that was for certain.

Jed McKay leaped to his feet and pointed a finger at her. "We're not going to let a bunch of Yankees tell us how to run things in Fiddlers Grove."

"What things are thee talking about, Friend?" the widow asked, as if only politely interested.

Matt's respect for her was rising. A grin tugged at a corner of his mouth.

Jed swallowed a couple of times and then came back with, "We won't have our darkies learning how to read and such. And they'll never vote in Virginia. Never. Blacks voting is just as far-fetched and outlandish as letting women vote. Won't happen. No, sir."

"Does thee not read the papers?" the widow countered in a courteous voice. "The Congress is waiting for the amendment for Negro suffrage to be passed by the states, and when it is, Negroes will vote in Virginia."

"Over my dead body!" Jed roared.

"I believe, Friend," the widow replied in a tranquil tone, "that there has been enough bloodshed. And I hope many will agree with me."

Matt drew in a deep breath at her audacity. *Whoa.*

Her words left Jed with nothing coherent to say. He grumbled mutinously and then looked at Matt. "Ritter, you should never have come back here. That's all I got to say to you." With this, Jed sat down.

"I think it would be best if you all leave our service," the preacher said. "Now."

"Mother, can he make us leave church? I thought anybody could go to church," Beth said in a stage whisper, tugging at her mother's sleeve.

Matt looked to Verity, leaving it to her whether they stayed or left. After all, this had been her idea. But he'd take on the whole congregation if she wanted him to. In fact, his hands were already balled into fists.

"I bid thee good evening, then," Verity said, taking Beth's hand and walking into the aisle like the lady she was. Matt followed her to the door of the church. Then he turned back and gave the congregation a look that declared, Everything the lady said is true. We'll leave now. I don't listen to a preacher who speaks hate. This isn't over.

The wind hurried them all home, billowing the widow's skirt and making Joseph and Matt hold on to their hats. At their back door he paused for a moment, thinking yet again that he should say something about Fiddlers Grove and his family, but he could come up with nothing he wished to say. So he bid them good-night and headed for the cabin. Behind him, he heard Verity and her father-in-law closing and latching the windows against the coming storm.

Just before Matt closed the cabin door, he gazed up at

the storm-darkened sky. Jed McKay's words came back: "Ritter, you should never have come back here." Opposition was a funny thing. Initially, he'd felt the same way as McKay—that he shouldn't have come back. But now that he'd been run out of one church, rebellion tightened in his gut. *No one's running me out of town. Not again.*

The thunder awakened Verity. And Beth's scream. Verity leaped out of bed. Lightning flashed, flickering like noonday sunshine, illuminating the room. Beth ran into the room and threw her arms around her mother. "Make it stop! Make it stop!"

Verity recognized the hysteria in her daughter's voice. Thunder always brought back their shared fear of loud noises that had begun with the cannon at Gettysburg and the terror of war. Verity knew from experience that words would not help Beth. She wrapped her arms around her daughter, hugging her fiercely. That was the only thing that ever helped. Verity's own heart pounded in tune with the relentless thunder.

Then the house shook. And exploded.

Or that was what it sounded like. Felt like.

Joseph charged into her room, trousers over his nightshirt. "I think we've been hit by lightning," he shouted over the continuing din. "I'm going outside to see if anything caught fire."

Verity glanced out the window and shrieked, "The barn! The barn's on fire!"

Joseph ran from the room. Verity settled Beth in her bed and pulled the blankets up over the child. "Stay here, Beth. I must help thy grandfather!"

Verity snatched up her robe, trying not to hear her daughter's frightened cries as she ran. Outside, the storm shook the night. Lightning blazed. Thunder pounded. Barefoot on the coarse wet grass, Verity ran with her hands over her ears. It seemed impossible that anything could burn in the downpour, yet flames flashed inside the open barn loft.

Ahead, Joseph and Matthew were opening the stalls to get the horses out of the burning barn. Between thunderclaps, the shrieking of horses slashed the night. Verity raced over the soggy ground. Somehow she had to help put the fire out.

One of their horses bounded out of the barn. Galloping, it nearly ran her down. She leaped out of the way and fell hard. Another thunderbolt hit a tall elm nearby. Brilliant white light flashed, followed by a deafening thunderclap. She covered her eyes, as well as her ears. The ground beneath her shook.

When she could, she looked up. In the open barn doorway, Joseph was waving both arms, beckoning her. She dragged herself up from the ground. Slipping on the wet grass, she hurried toward him. With the lightning flashing, she didn't need a lantern to see what had upset her father-in-law. Mary Dyke's son lay on the dirt floor of their barn.

"What happened to him?" she called over the continuing thunder.

"I don't know!" Joseph shouted back at her.

Matthew yelled, "I think he climbed the ladder in the hayloft and opened the door so the rain could douse the fire."

Verity looked up and saw that the fire was out. "What's he doing here? In our barn?"

"Don't know," Matthew said, "Joseph, help me get him into the house."

Within minutes, Matthew laid the boy on the kitchen table. Verity asked Joseph to check on and reassure Beth so she could examine Alec. Verity listened to his heart and felt for a fever. No fever. But the boy had a black eye, bruises and a split lip. Had he been fighting? Why was he hiding in their barn? Sodden and chilled from her own wet clothing, she tried to rouse him but had no luck.

The thunder still boomed outside, but it was more distant now. "The boy worries me." She looked toward Matthew and gasped. His hand was pressed against his forehead, blood flowing between his fingers. "Thee is hurt. What hurt thee?"

"Blasted horse knocked the stall door into me on his way out. Don't worry about me."

Wasn't that just like a man? Blood pouring from his head, but don't worry about him. Her exasperation moved her past her fear of the storm. She moved quickly to the pantry and collected her nursing equipment, a wash basin, a fresh towel and soap. "Sit." She pointed to the chair.

Grumbling, Matthew sat. She lit an oil lamp on the table and leaned close to him, examining the gash.

"This will need a stitch or two. I've got some experience nursing. I'll take care of it."

"Just clean it and use some sticking plaster to close it."

Ignoring him, she gently washed away the blood. It felt odd to be touching a man. His wet hair released the distinctive scent that was Matthew Ritter. She forced herself to focus on the gash on Matthew's forehead. He sat very still, probably as uncomfortable with this nearness and touching as she was.

Finally she was able to turn away, drawing in a ragged breath. She'd nursed other men without this breathless reaction. Matthew should be no different. She emptied the basin out the back door and returned the medical supplies to the pantry.

The chair behind her scraped as Matthew rose. "What are we going to do about Mary's boy?"

She looked out at the pouring rain. "This is not a night to go afield. We should get him out of his wet clothing and into a warm bed."

Matthew swung the thin boy up into his arms and carried him upstairs. Hearing the creak of the rocker in her room and realizing Joseph was rocking Beth, she directed Matthew to lay the boy down on Beth's empty white-canopied bed. Beth and Verity could share a bed as long as Alex needed to stay.

Verity gathered a clean nightshirt from Joseph's room and brought it back to Matthew. "Here, put this on him. It will be too big, but it will be dry." A pile of soaked clothes sat on the floor.

Matthew had lit the bedside candle and stood, looking down at the boy. His expression caught Verity's attention. "What's wrong?

Matt hesitated and then folded back the top edge of the blanket covering the boy. Verity gasped.

Chapter Four

The boy was covered in harsh purpling bruises—hardly a spot of skin had been spared. Matt felt a wave of anger wash over him.

The widow turned away, shuddering as if fighting for control. "That couldn't have happened to him just from the storm," she finally said in a low voice laced with revulsion.

Matt had to stop himself from putting an arm around her. No woman should have to see something as cruel as this. "No, but it explains what he was doing in our barn." Matt's low words scraped his throat. "He was hiding. This isn't a normal whipping of a boy. Somebody has beaten the living daylights out of him. Somebody bigger and stronger." Anger steamed through Matt. He had no doubt who'd done this. He met the widow's eyes across the bed. But he couldn't, wouldn't tell her who he thought was responsible. *Poor Mary. I have to think what to do to help, not make matters worse. But what? If I confront Orrin, he'll just beat the boy worse or turn on Mary.*

"What are we going to do?" Verity asked, echoing his thoughts.

"Let me think." This was a sticky circumstance. Going over to Orrin Dyke's house and beating the thug into the mud wouldn't help Mary or her son. But Matt had to fight himself to keep from doing just that. Dyke was lucky enough to have a son, and he treated him like this?

Matt glanced up at the rustling of the bedsheets. The widow was very gently and thoroughly checking each of the boy's limbs for movement. The candle cast her face in shadow. And for once, she was without her armor, her widow's weeds and tight corseting. In her muslin wrapper and slippers, she looked slender and almost frail. Very feminine.

This reaction rolled through him like the thunder in the distance. He throttled it and asked harshly, "Are any bones broken?"

"His legs, arms and shoulders move in the normal ways. But I'm sure that he has bruised or cracked ribs. Is there a doctor nearby?"

Her compassion touched him. He fought against showing this. "Not near. About eight miles from here. Do you think he is in need of a doctor?"

"I don't know. I can't get him to wake up. See here." She brushed back the boy's bangs and showed him an especially nasty bruise. She had long slender fingers and her hands showed signs of honest work.

For a moment the woman looked down, a soft expression on her face as she stroked the boy's cheek. Matt felt her phantom touch on his own cheek. He was conscious of both the sound of steady rain against the window and of the scent of lavender wafting from the woman. He dragged his gaze from her, forcing himself to study his surroundings. This must be her daughter's room. Pinafores hung on pegs by the door and a canopy covered the bed—it was a homey place that contrasted with the ravaged boy.

She reached across the bed and gripped his damp sleeve. "What can we do about this?" she whispered.

He shook his head and then, unable to stop himself, he laid his hand over hers.

A moan startled him. She released Matt's sleeve, breaking their connection. "Mama." The boy was waking.

"Alec, it's Verity Hardy."

The boy tried to sit up and groaned. The sound spoke of such deep pain that Matt found himself gritting his teeth.

"Don't try to sit up yet," she cautioned. "You're hurt."

Alec still struggled, trying to get up as the widow tried gently to hold him back.

Matt leaned forward. "Alec, I'm Matt Ritter, an old friend of your mother's. Lie back down. It's all right." He carefully pressed boy back down.

The boy looked up wide-eyed in the candlelight. "You're that Yankee. What happened? Why am I here?" Before Matt could answer, he saw fear flash in the boy's eyes. "I shouldn't be here." Again the boy thrashed feebly under the blanket, trying to get up.

"Alec, you must lie still." The widow held his shoulders down. "Mind me now."

At her quiet but insistent words, the struggle went out of the boy. He went limp. "What's happening, ma'am?"

"Thee helped us keep our barn from burning down," Verity answered. "Thee must have been hit in the head somehow. I couldn't wake thee. So we brought thee into the house."

"Ma'am, I should be getting home."

"No, I think it would be best if thee stayed the rest of the night here."

"But, ma'am, my mother needs me. Please."

Alec's words struck Matt like a blow to his breastbone. Was Orrin beating Mary right now? The urge to run to her rescue made Matt's heart gallop. He added his hand on the boy's shoulder over one of the widow's. "All will be well. You'll go home in the morning."

Panic widened the boy's eyes. "But my father—"

The widow touched the boy's fair wet hair. "Thee must lie back and rest. Trust us."

The boy appeared to want to argue, but fatigue and weakness overcame him. He whispered something that Matt could not understand and then his eyes closed again.

The widow touched the boy's forehead. Then she looked over at Matt.

When their eyes connected, he saw deep concern. Suddenly he felt his solitary bachelor state as he never had before. He looked away. "I think he'll sleep the rest of the night." He turned toward the door, wanting to put distance between them.

"Matthew Ritter," she asked again, "what can we do for this child?"

Her soft voice beckoned him to remain. "I'll think of something," he rumbled. He left her, his mind churning as he thought of Alec. And of how much longer he'd have to wait for the telegram that would whisk this woman—so dangerous to his peace of mind—out of his life.

Matt and the widow and her family stared at the telegram sitting open on the breakfast table. A military courier stationed at the railroad and telegraph depot had brought it just as they were sitting down to breakfast.

The telegram had been short and to the point. "Mrs. Hardy stay and start school wherever possible STOP Ritter move forward with school construction STOP Signed, The Freedman's Bureau." Matt had wanted to say STOP himself and had tried to hide his irritation, but he didn't think he'd done a very good job. The widow had merely read it aloud and then made no comment. Clearly she wasn't a gloater.

Then he thought to ask about Alec. "Is our visitor staying for breakfast?" The telegram had made him forget momentarily that there were more important things to deal with. His will hardened. An honorable man couldn't just ignore what had been done to the young boy—he had to act today.

The widow looked strained, glancing sideways at her little girl. "Our visitor left before I was able to invite him to stay for breakfast."

Beth glanced up at her mother with obvious curiosity. "We had a guest?"

"Alec stopped by for a bit, but he had to get home."

"Oh," Beth said, sounding disappointed.

Matt didn't like that Alec had left. Would he suffer for running away?

"I was wondering, Matthew, if we should drop by and visit Alec's parents." The widow gave him a pointed look.

"I don't think that's something we should do," he replied, aware that she didn't want her daughter to know of Alec's situation. Orrin would lash back unless the right person spoke to him. Men like Orrin only listened to those they dared not disregard, those they feared. And there was only one man in Fiddlers Grove Orrin might fear.

"But something should be…" Her voice faltered.

"Perhaps we should talk about this later," Matt said, nodding toward her daughter.

"Yes, we'll discuss it later."

Beth looked at both of them and then went back to eating her oatmeal.

Matt cleared his throat. "The surveyor will be here this morning to survey the school site before we start building, so I'll be busy with that today. Have you had a chance to hire us a housekeeper?"

"I will attend to that today," the widow replied, offering him a second helping of biscuits.

It was hard to stay annoyed that Mrs. Hardy was remaining. She brewed good coffee and made biscuits as light as goose down. He might as well just get over the aggravation of having someone—this woman—working with him. *We're here for the duration.* He forced a smile. "Good biscuits, ma'am."

She smiled her thanks and offered him the jar of strawberry jam.

He took it and decided not to hold the excellent jam against her, either. She couldn't help it if she was a good cook. All in all, it could have been worse. She wasn't much for nagging. He'd just go about building the school and signing men up for the Union League of America, and she'd start teaching school. They need meet only for meals.

He let the golden butter melt on the biscuit and blend with the sweet jam, and inhaled their combined fragrance. Army rations weren't even food compared with what Mrs. Hardy put on a table. He hoped she was as good at hiring a housekeeper as she was at cooking.

He wondered briefly where she was supposed to start the school in Fiddlers Grove. Did the Freedman's Bureau think the locals would rent her space? *Not a chance.* Well, that was her job. He had enough on his plate, starting with Alec and Mary. His conscience wouldn't let him pass by on the other side of the road.

After breakfast, the widow sent her daughter out to feed the chickens and give the leftovers to the barn cats, who, along with the horses and the barn, had survived the night's storm. Joseph rose from his place at the table and asked without preamble, "What was wrong with the boy?"

"He had been beaten unmercifully," the widow replied.

Matt heard the mix of concern and indignation in her voice. His nerves tightened another notch.

"Disciplining a boy is one thing. Beating him is another." Joseph looked concerned, his bushy white brows drawing together. "Alec is a good boy, too."

"I don't know what to do. I've never dealt with anything like this." The widow lowered her eyes and pleated the red-and-white-checked tablecloth between her fingers.

Matt wished he could save her from worrying over this. "What can anyone do? A father has control over his children, absolute jurisdiction." The bitter words echoed Matt's frustration over his inability to take direct action. The world was the way it was and good intentions never went far enough.

Matt had decided he wouldn't tell the widow or Joseph what he planned to do. He didn't want to give her hope when there probably wasn't any. He had to admit to himself that he also didn't want her to know he'd tried and failed. He ground his molars, irritated.

"I will pray about this," the widow said. "All things are possible with God."

Matt gritted his teeth tighter. Prayer didn't help. He'd learned that while watching the life leak out of friends on the battlefield. He'd been the one who closed their eyes in death. Either God didn't hear prayers in the midst of cannon fire or Matt didn't rate much with God.

Knowing his opinion would shock the Quaker, he pushed up from his place. "I've got things to do. See about hiring that housekeeper and find a laundress. I think you'll find a lot of former slaves who will be happy to get work." He regretted sounding so brusque. But he couldn't help it. He was a captain—he was used to giving orders.

"Thank thee, Matthew."

Joseph gave him an approving look. "You show you understand how much work it takes to run a household. You must have had good parents."

Uneasy, Matt looked at the older man, wondering where this comment had come from. "Yes, I had good parents."

Joseph nodded and walked outside, whistling. Matt hurried out after him, not wanting any more discussion about Alec. He'd deal with the surveyor and then he'd do what

he'd known he must do sooner or later. Deathbed promises were a burden he couldn't ignore. And Alec could
not be ignored.

Verity had left Beth at home with Joseph because, once
again, she didn't know what kind of reception she'd receive. And she didn't want Beth troubled. Verity had a
formidable errand this morning and could only hope that
she was following God's prompting.

The memory of the battered young boy from last night
haunted Verity. She had tried to turn Alec over to God,
but the image of his injured body lingered in her mind.
Some images were like that.

She had seen many sights during the war that she
wished she could erase from her mind. But that wasn't
possible. She wondered what images Matthew carried with
him day after day, after four years of soldiering. What a
burden. No wonder he was brusque at times. *I will be more
patient with him.*

Her steps slowing with her reluctance, she walked
around St. John's Church to the house behind it. Like all
the other houses in Fiddlers Grove, the parsonage looked
as if it had had no upkeep for a long time. White paint was
peeling and green shingles needed replacing. She said a
prayer for boldness to help conquer the uncertainty she
was feeling, and walked up the steps. Then she lifted her
suddenly unusually heavy arm to knock on the door. It was
opened by a black girl of about thirteen in a faded blue
dress with tight braids in rows around her head. "Good
morning," Verity greeted her. "Is the vicar in?"

"Yes, ma'am." The young girl eyed her as if wanting to
say something, but unsure if she should.

"May I see him, please?" Verity smiled, her lips freezing in place.

The girl stepped back and let her in. "Wait here, please, ma'am."

Verity waited just inside the front door.

Within short order, the pastor emerged from the back of the house. He looked shocked to see her in his house—just what she'd expected. In everyday clothing, he appeared shorter and slighter than he had in his white vestments. He was rail-thin, like most everyone else in town, with gray in his curly brown hair.

"Good morning," she said, greeting him brightly with false courage. "I was wondering if I could have a few moments to discuss something with you."

The man looked caught off guard and puzzled. "I... I don't know what we'd have to discuss."

She tried to speak with the boldness of the apostle Paul. "I have come with funds and the authority from the Bureau of Refugees, Freedman and Abandoned Lands to open a school in Fiddlers Grove."

He gaped at her.

"And I need thy help." Her frozen smile made it hard to speak.

"My help? I've read about that infernal bureau in the paper. I'm not helping them. Bunch of interfering..." He seemed at a loss for words to describe the Freedman's Bureau in front of a lady.

"I hope you will listen to what I have to say." She swallowed to wet her dry throat.

"You are mistaken, ma'am. We lost the war, but that does not mean that we want Yankees telling us how to live our lives and taking our land." He moved forward as if ready to show her the door.

"I beg thy pardon, but how is having a school in Fiddlers Grove telling thee how to live thy life?" she asked, holding her ground.

"If it doesn't affect me, then why discuss it with me?"

"Please let me at least explain what I propose. Does thee have an office where we might discuss this in private?" *I will not be afraid.*

Maybe her calm persuaded him or the Lord had prepared her way, but he nodded and showed her to a den off the parlor. He left the door open and waved her to a chair. He took a seat behind a fine old desk. "Please be brief. I am studying for my next sermon."

Verity nodded, drew in air and said, "I did not realize that there was no free school here. I was a schoolteacher for two years before I married. It grieves me to see children growing up without education."

He glanced at the clock on the mantel. "I, too, wish there could be a free school in town, but there wasn't one before the war and there won't be one now that everyone is in such difficult financial straits."

She pressed her quivering lips together, knowing that her next words would shock him. "I have come to set up a school to teach black children and adults. But I think that it would be wrong to set up a school for only black children when the white children have no school. Doesn't thee agree?"

He stared at her. "Are you saying that you could set up two schools?"

"No. Why not one school for children of both races?" She forced out the words she knew would provoke a reaction.

"You are out of your mind. This town would never accept a school that mixed black and white children."

Praying, she looked at his bookshelves for a few moments and then turned back to him. "I don't understand. Is the offer of free education something to be refused?"

"The kind of free education you are talking about is not even to be considered. If you build such a school, they will burn it down." He stared hard at her, underlining his point with a scowl.

Her face suddenly flamed with outrage. They were poor and defeated, but still rigidly committed to the past. She tried to use reason. "There is great want here. Wouldn't men welcome the work of building a school and the cash it would bring?"

"You're a Yankee. You don't understand Virginia. White men farm, but Negroes do the laboring. They are the carpenters, plasterers, coopers and bricklayers."

"Well, that will change. It must, because no longer can Negroes be told what to do. They will choose what they wish to work at. Just as thee did. The old South is gone. It died at Appomattox Courthouse. Slavery has ended. And nothing will ever be the same here again." The truth rolled through her, smoothing her nerves.

He stared at her, aghast.

Now that she'd said what she'd come to say, she felt calm and in control. "It may be of no comfort to thee, but the North has changed, too. No people can go through the four years that we've been through, suffered through, and be the same on the other side. Doesn't thee see that?

"A school would be good for the whole town," she continued. "Why not let progress come? Why not let me rent thy church to use as a school until the new school is built? And the Freedman's Bureau may pay thy church rent, money that I'm sure thy church could use. Why not leave bitterness behind and be a part of a brighter future?"

After the surveyor had finished, Matt made himself head to the Ransford plantation to have the meeting he'd dreaded since he'd arrived. With imaginary crickets hopping in his stomach, he knocked on the imposing double door and waited for the butler to answer. When the door opened, he managed to say, "Good morning, Elijah." Looking into the familiar face yanked Matt back to his childhood.

"Did you wish to see the master of the house, sir?"

Even in his distraction, Matt noted the change from "the master" to "the master of the house." Matt appreciated Elijah's assertion of his freedom. He wondered again about Samuel. Did Elijah know where Samuel was? This wondering about Samuel chafed at Matt, but he couldn't speak of Samuel here and now. "Elijah, I need to speak to… Dace on a matter of importance—"

"Elijah, is that Matt Ritter?" Dace's gruff voice came from the nearby room.

"Yes, sir, it is."

"Bring him on back, please."

Elijah bowed and showed Matt into the small study that Matt recognized as the room Dace's father had used for business. Memories flooded Matt's mind—coming in here and snitching toffees from the candy jar that still sat on the desk, the scent of his uncle's pipe tobacco.

After Elijah left them, Dace said, "I was wondering when you would come."

Matt sat down in the chair across the desk from his cousin, his only living blood relative, and looked him in the eye. Dace showed the telltale signs of war. He was gaunt, with deep grooves down either side of his face, and tired eyes.

"What brings you here?" Dace said over the rim of a coffee cup, sounding neither pleased nor displeased.

"Three matters, one from the past and two from the present. Which do you want to hear first?" Matt kept his tone neutral, too.

"Let's deal with the past first. I still like to do things in order."

This took Matt back to childhood also, to the many times he, Dace and Samuel had been planning on doing something daring like swim across the river at flood stage. It had always been Dace who planned out each test of their courage. "On her deathbed, my mother asked me to come back here and try to reconcile with you after the war."

"So that's why you came back?"

"Yes." *And with the foolish hope of coming home.* But of course, Dace had never been forced to leave town, so he would not understand the feeling of not belonging anywhere or of having lost a home. Matt made sure none of this showed on his face. He would give Dace no chance to see that the events of their shared childhood still had the power to wound him.

"How do we reconcile? Shake hands? Remain on speaking terms?" Dace asked with a trace of mockery.

Matt's neck warmed under his collar. "I don't think real reconciliation can ever take place. There was hardly a chance before the war. Now there is even less hope."

"So why did you come?"

Matt's taut spine kept him sitting stiffly. "To fulfill my promise and to be a part of making the South change, even though it doesn't want to. That is the present matter I came to discuss."

"How will you make the South change? By force?"

"Force has already been used. My side won. Congress is moving forward, granting citizenship to former slaves and giving them the right to vote as citizens."

Dace just stared at him, tight-lipped.

"I'm hoping that it won't come to the point where I must ask for Union troops to put down opposition here. But I'm here to form a Union League of America chapter and to get a school built for former slaves and—"

The sounds of the front door slamming and rapid footsteps alerted the men, and then Dace's wife rushed into the den. "Dace, you won't believe—" She broke off at the sight of Matt.

Matt rose, as did Dace. Of course, he remembered Lirit as a pretty girl, spoiled by her doting father on a nearby plantation. Though around the same age as the Quaker, Lirit looked older, somehow faded and thin and thread-bare. "Hello, Lirit."

She drew nearer her husband as if Matt were unclean or dangerous. "Dacian, I'm sorry, I didn't realize that you weren't alone."

Matt ignored her obvious rejection. Lirit had never been one of his favorites, unlike Mary, whom he'd adored as a child. The thought of Mary started a fire in his gut. *Alec.* Where was he now and what had he suffered for running away and hiding?

"Matt and I were just discussing why he's come back to Fiddlers Grove," Dace said.

Lirit glanced at her husband. "You know that he's build-ing a school for the children of former slaves?"

Dace nodded.

"Where did you hear that?" Matt demanded. He'd only told this to Mary, and he doubted Lirit and Mary were on speaking terms.

Lirit looked at him. "I was just at the parsonage. Your Mrs. Hardy had been there trying to talk the vicar into renting our church building as a school. She actually sug-gested that white children attend with black children."

Matt frowned. White children? "The school is to be only for black children and former slaves."

"The Quaker said that she didn't like to see the white children going without an education." Lirit's scathing tone made her opinion of this clear.

Matt began to leave the room. "I should go—"

"Wait," Dace said, stopping him. "You said you had come on three matters. We've only discussed two."

Matt sent a doubtful look toward Lirit.

Taking the hint, Dace touched his wife's shoulder. "May I have a private moment with Matt?"

"Certainly." Lirit walked out, haughtily pulling off her gloves. She snapped the pocket door shut behind her.

Matt and Dace stared at each other for a few heavy moments. "Last night our barn was hit by lightning. When we went to put out the fire, we found Alec Dyke unconscious and hiding in our barn. He'd been beaten mercilessly, and had bruises and cuts all over him. Were you aware that Orrin is probably abusing the boy?"

Dace looked worried and rubbed his chin. "I don't know what I can do about it."

"I know I can't do anything about it, but you might say something."

"It could just make matters worse."

"I hope you'll think this over, Dace. If anyone can stop Dyke, it would be you."

He turned to leave.

"Matt," Dace said, stopping him. "Where is the Quaker from, do you know?"

Matt thought this an odd question, but replied, "Pennsylvania."

Dace folded his hands in front of his mouth and stared out the window opposite him. "I don't like the idea of Yankees coming here and telling us how to live our lives. But it's like we are already in the coffin and they're tossing dirt on our heads and we don't even object."

Matt looked directly into Dace's eyes. "Change is inevitable." He didn't think he needed to say that even in the aftermath of the disastrous war, Ransford Manor was still the largest plantation for miles. And if Dace Ransford were in favor of something, people paused before they opposed it.

"Well, I've taken care of my obligation to my mother.

The next time we meet, I'll just be the Yankee working for the Freedman's Bureau." Matt left without looking back, something he should have done fourteen years ago.

Chapter Five

In the autumn afternoon with golden leaves fluttering above, Verity turned to see Matthew coming toward her on the road back to town. She waited for him to catch up. Her mood lifted at the sight of him; after all, Fiddlers Grove didn't abound with friendly faces. And there was something so competent about him, so focused. He was not a man who sought the easy path. Or who would give up easily.

She knew he wished she had arrived after he'd left Fiddlers Grove, but having him here was a great comfort to her. Of course, she wouldn't embarrass him by saying that. The wind had ruffled his dark hair, giving him a raffish look. She turned away so as not to betray her reaction.

"What are you doing here?" he asked, breathing a bit fast from his short sprint.

"I came here to hire our housekeeper. I asked Hannah if she could recommend someone and she said she could recommend herself." Verity smiled. She valued frankness in a world where people rarely told one another what they were really thinking. *Like this man.* She turned his own question back on him, asking, "What is thee here for?"

"Mrs. Ransford overheard you at the parsonage," he

said, ignoring her question. "The whole town will know now what we're here for."

The wind had loosened the ribbons on her bonnet. Turning her back to the wind, she retied them tighter. "Was our work here to remain a secret?" *Like thy reasons for returning to a town that wouldn't welcome thee home?*

"What did you mean trying to rent the church for the school?" he scolded. "Surely you knew what the vicar's response would be."

"And what was his response?" she asked, a smile tugging at the corner of her mouth. Much better to be amused by his overbearing behavior than to take offense. Men always liked to think that only women gossiped, but men did it, too, as Matthew had just demonstrated. If he continued scolding her, she'd go ahead and ask about his cousin and this town. *It's not just nosiness, Lord. I need to know so I don't say things I shouldn't, assume things I shouldn't and cause trouble I could avoid.*

He scowled at her. "I'm sure it was not favorable."

From the corner of her eye she glimpsed movement behind her. She glanced over her shoulder and saw a stray dog following them. He looked like some kind of hound, with drooping ears, a long face with large brown eyes and a brown matted coat. The sight of his ribs almost pushing through his hide wrung her heart. *Poor creature.*

"No one is going to rent you space to teach in. I don't think you're really aware of the extent of anti-Yankee feelings here yet." A gust nearly took Matt's hat and he clamped it down with a frown.

She gave him a look and then turned around to the dog. She'd much rather help this poor animal than argue with Matthew Ritter. "Here, boy," she coaxed in a low voice. "Here, boy."

The animal stopped walking and sank to its belly, whimpering.

"What are you doing? Ignore the cur or he'll follow you home."

Ignoring his brisk order, she smiled. "That is my hope, yes."

He said something under his breath that sounded uncomplimentary about fool women.

She glanced up at him. "What was your rank in the army?"

"Captain. Why?"

Because thee still acts like a captain. But I didn't enlist in the army. She chuckled to herself. Stooping, she smiled and cooed to the stray again, holding out her hand, palm up.

"What do you want a dog for?" he asked.

"Beth needs a friend. And since I am quite aware of the anti-Northerner bias here, I know she may not find a child who will befriend her. Strays always make the best pets." She crooned more loving words to the dog while Matthew huffed in displeasure. Men often behaved like this to cover a tender spot. Had Matthew had a dog when he was a boy? Or had that been denied him?

Matthew made a hasty gesture and the stray slunk behind a bush.

She rose, gave Matthew a pointed look and repeated, "What brought thee out here?"

"So Hannah is going to be our housekeeper?" He walked along beside her, ignoring her question as he ignored the stray.

I won't forget my question, Matthew Ritter. "Yes. I don't think that the Ransfords are paying them."

"Dace probably doesn't have anything to pay them with. It's funny—not really funny, but odd. Before the war, he had money and could have paid his people. Now he's supposed to pay them and he doesn't have any funds."

She quickened her pace to keep up with his longer

strides. "It's an interesting twist, yes. Is that what thee discussed with thy cousin?"

"The surveyor staked out the site for the school. I can start hiring workers as soon as I get the wood and nails."

"I see." She decided her inquiries about his visit to his cousin didn't go far enough. *In for a penny, in for a pound.* "Why did thy family leave Fiddlers Grove?"

Matthew walked on, acting as if he hadn't heard her.

She glanced over her shoulder and saw that the stray dog was still warily following them. She paused and coaxed, "That's right, boy. Come home with us. I have a little girl who will love thee and then will love thee some more. And I have delicious leftovers that thee will enjoy." She decided to try Matthew once more. "Did thee visit thy cousin?"

He began whistling and kicking a rock along, completely ignoring her question.

So he must have, and the visit didn't prosper. Verity glanced back at the stray, still keeping up with them, and was touched by how dogs and humans both longed for family.

After supper, Verity and Beth sat on the back steps and watched the dog creep forward on his belly. Beth had put out a pan of leftover scraps and then retreated to the porch so that the dog would venture out to eat it. When he finished the scraps, she put out a pan of water between the porch and the flaming spirea bushes.

"Take a step back," Verity said in a low voice. Matthew had ignored the dog and gone to his cabin for the night. There was something in Matthew that needed healing, but she could see that he didn't want to admit that yet. The war had damaged them all. Why hadn't the South just given the slaves their freedom? Slavery had never made sense to her. Why had so many thousands had to die to end it?

Why had her husband had to die? And why did thinking of Roger still hurt so?

Beth obeyed, stepping back and waiting. The dog snuffled the ground, crept over to the bowl of water and began to lap it—still with one wary eye watching Beth and Verity.

"I'm going to call him Barney," Beth confided.

"Oh, a very good name. He looks like a Barney." Verity squeezed her daughter's shoulder.

The beat of horses' hooves entering the yard scared the dog and he streaked into the bushes. A stranger dismounted and stepped up to her back porch. "Your servant, ma'am." He swept off his gray, worn Confederate officer's hat and bowed to her.

Verity recognized him then and a tingle of warning shot through her. He was Matthew's cousin, whom she had met at St. John's on Sunday.

"Mama, the doggy ran away," Beth lamented, rising.

The gentleman bowed to her. "Ma'am."

"Dacian Ransford, how good to see thee." Swallowing with difficulty, Verity offered him her hand, which he shook briefly. Then she looked down at Beth. "Dacian and I will go into the kitchen, and then thee can coax the dog out again. Remember to speak softly, move slowly and offer him thy open hand to sniff. But don't hurry him. He's been a wanderer for a while and is afraid of being hurt."

"Yes, Mama." Beth knelt down near the water dish, watching the bushes.

"Please, Friend, won't thee come and sit?" Maybe he wouldn't want to come into her home. If whites didn't sit with blacks in Virginia, did ex-Confederates sit with Yankees?

He nodded and motioned for her to take the lead, his expression polite, even curious.

Sensing his watchfulness, she became wary. She walked into the kitchen and went to the stove, where a pot of water simmered. She forced herself to go on as if ex-Confederate officers often visited her. "May I offer thee a cup of tea?"

"That would be quite welcome, ma'am."

Verity motioned him toward the chair nearest the door. She felt his gaze on her as she made his tea. After a few awkward moments she handed him a cup and broke the silence. "And to what do I owe this visit?"

He held the cup up to his nose and sniffed it. "Real black and orange pekoe." His voice was almost reverent.

"Yes, I prefer it to Darjeeling." She put some oatmeal cookies on a plate and sat down across from him. Was he going to fence with her, as his cousin had done on their way home today?

"You are a lover of tea then, ma'am?"

She nodded and had no trouble believing that this man appreciated the finer things of life. After all, she'd seen his wife. But after four years of the Union blockade, the South only had items it could produce on its own. Now that the blockade had ended, Confederate money was worthless. *Why is thee here? What could thee possibly want from me?*

She took a sip, trying to ignore his intense concentration on her, though it sent a shiver down her spine. She could wait for him no longer. "Pardon me, but I do not think that thee came to discuss tea with me."

He chuckled. "One can always tell a Northerner. Always the direct approach."

"I am afraid that thee is correct." She held her cup high. "But I hope I have not been impolite."

"No, I think it best that I come to the point." He paused and sipped his tea. "I've heard about your plans to teach at the Freedman's school my cousin is planning to build here."

She nodded. Was this the real reason he'd come? It didn't seem to ring true. He continued to study her face.

"Ma'am, your goal may be laudatory, but I do not think

you will meet with success. Not enough time has passed since the hostilities ended. Passions are still running high here."

She set down her cup and leaned back, considering him. Why not be bold? "And it is not easy bearing defeat."

He grinned ruefully at her. "The direct approach. Again."

"In one way I agree with thee, Dacian Ransford." She traced the rim of her cup with her index finger. "The times are unsettled. But it is in turbulent times that great change can be made. And great change is what the South needs." He started to speak, but she held up a hand, asking for his indulgence. "I don't know if thee realizes it but this war has changed the South and the North and the West. Or maybe it has shown how the world is changing," Verity continued in measured tones, folding her arms around her to ease the chill her own words gave her. "The East and the West Coasts are now linked by railroad. The Atlantic Ocean has been spanned by telegraph cable. The North abounds with factories, industry and all manner of inventions. Our lives on the farm are passing away." She stared at her tea.

He set down his cup. "That may be true, but what if many in the South do not want to change?"

She looked him in the eye. "Wasn't that the issue that this war settled?"

"Touché." He acknowledged the hit with a slight nod. "We must change. But I fear that there are many who will not." He continued to study her face.

"I am not taking the danger to myself lightly. But I must remind you that I am used to going against common prejudices. I am a Quaker—or I should say, I was a Quaker until I married. I belonged to and was raised by people who did not go along with whatever was popular at the time. We did not mind dressing and speaking and thinking differently. We even defied the law that said we must return runaway slaves to their masters. My family were abolitionists even before the American Revolution. I was an abolitionist before *Uncle Tom's Cabin* was published and the cause became popular."

He looked over the rim of his cup at her. "I can only repeat that the South is unready for such sweeping change."

"I told thee I did not expect to be welcomed here with open arms. But the change will come whether people want it or not. There will be a school in this town for black children and freed slaves. The Thirteenth Amendment has passed and former slaves are now freemen."

Dacian looked pained.

She continued, "The Fourteenth Amendment will give them citizenship and the right to vote. The North is absolutely committed to making sure that slaves were not set free only to be enslaved in some other form. If former slaves are citizens, they can vote and defend themselves."

"The South will never ratify the Fourteenth Amendment," he countered, his voice hardening, "and I am afraid that educating Negroes will meet with limited success. Most do not have the intelligence."

She shook her head, sorry to hear his words. "I am afraid that the two of us will always disagree upon that issue. I have known educated black men and women and they are equal to us in intellect. Black skin does not announce inferiority."

"I'm afraid that the two of us will always disagree upon that issue," he said, using her words. "But I do see that the Freedman's Bureau will have its way here. And I do thank you for thinking of the white children, but I doubt that any white parent would allow their child to go to such a school."

"I'm sorry to hear that." She liked the man's honest face and wished he would see things differently.

He nodded to himself as he rose, as if he had decided

something. "I think that you have come with the finest intentions, but the South is not ready."

"Then I fear for the South." She rose also and folded her hands, looking up into his eyes earnestly. *Let him hear me, Lord.* "The North will not have lost thousands and thousands of lives to achieve nothing. If the South will not change willingly, the Radical Republicans will jam these changes down Southern throats. President Johnson, a Tennessean, has been able to hold off the inevitable for a time, but his protection will not last. The Radical Republicans hold power in Congress and they will not hesitate to use it."

"I have never before discussed politics with a woman." He gave her a wry half smile. "But I do not doubt the correctness of your assessment. You see, ma'am, the war continues." He bowed to her and walked toward the door.

She followed him, sorry to see a good man so misguided. "I bid thee good evening then. Please know that whatever I do, I do because I want to help, not hurt."

The man halted. "I have no doubt that your motives are the best. But even the best motives can't bring about what you wish. Thank you for the tea." He spoke as a friend, a deeply concerned one.

And she wondered why. Why did he sound as if he knew her?

He studied her face for another moment and then shook her offered hand and donned his hat. He was out the door, on his horse and gone quickly.

As Verity stared after him, Joseph walked inside. "I didn't expect us to start getting visitors so soon. Does that mean you're making progress?"

"I'm not exactly sure." Verity turned over in her mind all she had learned not from words, but from all the other unspoken language. She felt that she had now met all the major players in the drama of which she was a part, except for Orrin Dyke. And she'd set events in motion by speaking to the vicar at St. John's. *But I came to set those events in motion.* The people here might be reluctant, but God's work could not wait forever.

The next morning when Matt sat down at the kitchen table, his foul mood vanished instantly when Hannah set before him a bowl of pearly white grits with a small pond of yellow butter in the middle. Salivating, he helped himself generously and nearly smacked his lips. *Grits. Manna.* Matt savored their texture and taste on his tongue. He hadn't had grits since his mother had passed away. "Thank you, Hannah."

Hannah chuckled. "The boy been North too long."

"What's that?" Beth asked, looking at the bowl. At her mother's frown, she added, "Please, Aunt Hannah."

"That's grits and they're good. You'll like them." Hannah turned back to the stove. "Now you eat up, little girl. You won't have fun on an empty stomach."

"I'm going to get Barney to let me pet him again today," Beth announced as she helped herself to a small serving of grits.

"Who Barney?" Hannah asked, pouring more coffee around the table.

"It's the mongrel Mrs. Hardy let follow us home yesterday," Matt said, trying to sound disgruntled to tease the little girl.

"What's a mongrel?" Beth asked, eyeing Matt.

"It means we don't know who his ma and pa were," Joseph said. "I think he'll make a good watchdog after he gets used to us."

Matt tried to lose himself in the mundane conversation, but his plans for the day kept nudging him. The thought of them nearly took away his appetite—even for grits.

"Barney is going to be a good dog." Beth rocked in her

chair. "He was scared of that man last night, but after the man rode away, Barney let me pet him."

"I saw that Dace was here last evening," Matt said, trying to sound uninterested. "What did he want?

"Thy cousin came for a short visit," the widow said, glancing pointedly at her daughter.

Matt got the message. *I can wait.* He shoved all this aside and with great satisfaction took a second helping of grits. "So, young lady," he asked, "how do you like grits?"

"I haven't made up my mind yet, sir," Beth replied, stirring her spoon in her grits. "I like Aunt Hannah's scrambled eggs, though."

"Thank you, child." Hannah nodded toward Beth.

Matthew cleaned up his plate and rose. "Well, I've got a lot to do today." *A fool's errand and then probably a long ride.*

"Aunt Hannah, can I have the leftovers for Barney, please?" Beth asked. "And may I be excused, Mama?"

Hannah nodded. Verity smoothed her hand over the child's hair. "Yes. Stay in our yard."

Beth agreed and with pan of bacon ends and leftover eggs, she skipped out the door, calling, "Barney!"

"I think I'll sit on the front porch and whittle some and watch the leaves turning." Joseph thanked Hannah for breakfast.

Matt did the same, and the widow preceded him out the back door. They paused at the top of the steps to the yard. "What did my cousin come to see you for—if you don't mind my asking," Matt amended.

The morning sunlight glinted in her hair. He liked seeing her without her black bonnet. He imagined rubbing her springy curls between his thumb and forefinger. He clenched his hands, as if to ensure that they stayed put.

She rested one hand on the railing and blinked at the bright morning sunshine. "I don't mind telling thee, because it wasn't a personal visit. Thy cousin came to warn me away. He thinks the South isn't ready for change."

Anger burned in Matt's throat. He'd already told his cousin on no uncertain terms—

"Can thee think of any other reason he would come besides telling me not to expect the town to accept our school?"

"No, I can't." I *won't.*

She studied him as if trying to figure out if he were being frank.

That grated. But he'd been pretty unforthcoming when they'd met on the road home from the Ransford place. She knew there were things he wasn't telling her.

Should he tell her, now that she was staying? He kept noticing little things about her. Now it was her dainty ivory ears and he shifted his gaze past her to the mutt noisily lapping water that Beth had just pumped for him. "I've got an errand to do. It's time I get busy getting building supplies and hiring men."

"I'll wish thee good day, then. I still have some curtains to hang." She went back inside.

As he walked toward town, he tried to picture himself telling Verity about his childhood with Dace and Samuel. A wave of guilt hit him as he thought of Hannah and Elijah—were they wondering why he had not asked them about their son, whom he had loved like a brother as a child?

He hadn't found the right moment, or at least that's what he'd been telling himself. But the truth was, he wasn't sure he wanted to know what happened to Samuel. He wasn't sure he could stand to hear it.

Soon Matt stepped into Hanley's store. He'd been in town for well over a week now and it was time to launch his attack. Silence fell upon the crowded gathering place of the village. Matt went directly to Hanley as if they were the only two in the store.

Hanley greeted him from behind the counter with a wary nod. "What can I do for you today?"

"I was wondering if you'd like to order some lumber and building supplies for me so I won't have to ride to Richmond." Matt thought that giving the local storekeeper the chance to make some money might help with popular opinion about the school.

He heard footsteps behind him as someone entered the store, but he didn't look back. "I also want to know if there are any carpenters in the area."

"Is this for that school of yours?" The voice came from behind Matt.

It was funny how after all these years, Matt still knew Orrin Dyke's belligerent and mocking voice. He turned slowly, feeling every eye on him. Matt stared at the big beefy man, who was a head taller than him. "Yes."

"I'll tell you straight to your face, then. We ran your family out of town once and we can do it again." Everyone in the store and outside on the bench had frozen into place. A heavy feeling of expectation expanded in the silence.

"No doubt I am not wanted here," Matt countered, his blood simmering at the mention of his family being forced out of town. "But I am going to stay long enough to build the school and prepare the former slaves to vote—"

With only a few strides, Orrin covered the distance between them. "Get out of town or you'll wish you had."

"Try anything and you'll end up in jail." *Where you belong.* Matt stared at Orrin's cruel face and thought of how his mother had cried as they drove out of town. And the recent memory of Alec's battered body bumped Matt's hostility up another notch. *Bully. Go ahead and try something. Give me a reason to—*

Orrin raised his fists. Matt moved into fighting stance,

ready to defend himself, relishing the chance to release his anger on this very worthy target.

"Orrin," Hanley declared, "I have no quarrel with you. But I don't want any fighting in my store."

Orrin bristled. "I won't have any Yankee coming here and trying to give the coloreds uppity ideas. There will be no school for them in this town." He ended his statement with a crude epithet. The women and a few older men gasped at this public impropriety.

"There are ladies present," a very deep and completely unexpected voice chided from the doorway.

Just as Matt had instantly recognized Orrin's voice, he knew who'd spoken. He swung around to the entrance. "Samuel." And that was all he could say. It took all his strength not to hurry to Samuel and throw his arms around him. *Samuel. Friend.*

Wearing good clothes and a rifle on his shoulder, Samuel removed his hat and nodded. "Matt, it has been a long time."

Over fourteen years. Matt's throat constricted, but he forced out the words, "Samuel, glad to see you." It was a completely insufficient response to Samuel's homecoming. But with half the town gawking at them, Matt didn't trust himself to say anything further.

Orrin spat out a stream of nasty curses. "You ain't welcome in town, either," he yelled at Samuel, his face and neck now a bright ugly red.

Samuel merely stared into Orrin's eyes as if daring him to do more than curse. He looked as if planting a fist in Orrin's nose would be pure pleasure.

The outraged white man swung away from Matt and charged Samuel.

Samuel casually slid the rifle on his shoulder into his hands and aimed it at Orrin.

Matt couldn't believe it. He'd not thought it possible

for the tension in the room to increase, but it spiraled upward to a frightening pitch. A black man pointing a gun
at a white man. All the men surged to their feet, ready to
strike down this effrontery.

"There will be no pitched battle in my store!" Hanley
barked. "Do you hear me? I won't have it!"

Orrin ignored him and snarled at Samuel, "You get out
of town. If you come here for your ma and pa, get them and
leave. Quick." Orrin shouldered past Samuel and stormed
out the door.

Samuel lowered his rifle and completely ignored Orrin's
parting words. "I was on my way through town to Ransford's when I saw you through the window, Matt. How are
my mother and father? Have you seen them?" he asked, as
if nothing had happened.

Swallowing with difficulty, Matt could hardly keep hidden all the emotions dancing through him. "Your parents
are fine. You will find Hannah at my place, the Barnesworth house. She just started as our housekeeper."

Samuel nodded his thanks. "What has brought you back
to town, Matt?"

"I am here from the Freedman's Bureau to build a
school. I am hiring carpenters and others in the building trade."

"That is good news. I know how to swing a hammer. I
don't know how long I'll be in town—I have unfinished
business I need to take care of—but you can count on me
for some work."

Matt offered Samuel his hand, to the shock of those in
the store. Clearly they weren't ready to accept white and
black men shaking hands yet. Well, they might as well
start getting used to it.

"Are you headed home now?" Samuel asked.

"No, I have business here and perhaps in Richmond."

"I'll be off to visit my mother, then. I'll see you later, Matt." Samuel nodded politely and strolled out the door.

Matt acted as if he didn't notice the hostile glances sent his way. He turned back to the storekeeper. "Mr. Hanley, do you want my business or will I have to ride to Richmond?"

Chapter Six

That evening Matt found himself both eager and reluctant to go home. Riding home under the flaming red maples, he knew he'd have to face Samuel again. With Hannah at the Barnesworth house as housekeeper, Matt couldn't imagine the widow not opening wide the home to celebrate the return of Hannah's son. So he'd have to deal with Samuel's homecoming and in some way hold everything from the past deep inside. This predicament came, of course, as a result of coming back here. No wonder so many veterans were heading west. In one way, he wished he were halfway to Colorado right now.

In the hours since the confrontation at the store, Matt's memory had kept up a steady flow of memories of Samuel, only a year older than he. Matt recalled swimming in the creek on golden summer evenings, going rabbit hunting in crisp winter mornings with Sam—and Dace. Then a nervous deer peered out from the line of poplars along the road and darted in front of Matt, flaunting its white tail.

Holding his horse from shying, he had the same sensation of trying to hold back dozens of questions to ask Samuel. Where had he been? Why hadn't anyone spoken about him when Matt returned? These questions disturbed his already shaky equilibrium. They had been a threesome—

Matt, Samuel and Dace. Seeing Samuel only pointed up that Dace was still lost to him, probably for good, forever. Why did that twist his insides?

No matter—Matt couldn't avoid going home. He cantered down the lane, nearing the Barnesworth house. Long before he saw the crowd around his back porch, he heard the jubilation—snatches of song and loud voices. He slowed his horse to a walk and approached the back porch.

"Good evening, Mr. Ritter," silver-haired Elijah greeted him.

Matt smiled and lifted his hat in hello. "You must be happy tonight. You have your son again."

"Yes, sir, I am praising the Lord for it. Now Hannah and I can be easy about him."

Matt wondered if Elijah would feel easy when he heard that his son had pointed a gun at Orrin Dyke today. And publicly offered to work on building the Freedman's school. But it wasn't the place or time to address this. Matt turned his horse toward the barn.

"Good evening, Matthew," the widow greeted him as she stepped out the back door. She was carrying large pans of cornbread and a pot of butter toward the tables set up under the oaks. "You're just in time for Samuel's welcome-home meal."

What would she look like dressed in some color other than black? That bright copper hair clashed with the somber black. Pushing aside this nonsense, he touched the brim of his hat and headed toward the barn. He'd been right. The Quaker welcomed the celebration and insisted on hosting it.

This made him regret how unwelcoming he'd been the night she'd arrived. He took his time unsaddling and rubbing down his horse. He enjoyed the smell of horse and the routine, as well as the quiet of the barn, which contrasted with the jubilation so near.

But finally he had to go to the pump in the yard and wash his face and hands in the cold, bracing water. He headed for the long table under the oaks that had just begun to turn bronze. Verity had decimated their flock of chickens to provide for so many guests. The table was completely covered with bowls of sweet corn, greens, platters of cornbread and fried chicken.

He went to stand behind the empty chair at the head of the table. It gave him a funny feeling—he'd never taken this seat, the position his father had always occupied. But he was the man of this unusual household. Beaming, Verity stood to his right with Beth and Joseph and across from her were Samuel's family. Samuel was standing to Matt's left. Matt resisted the temptation to consider himself a part of these families. *I'm alone and I might as well accept it here and now.*

At Verity's quiet request, Elijah said a prayer of thanks for the return of his son and the food God had provided. And then Hannah sat down next to Samuel, taking her husband's hand as though drawing from him the power to do this—to sit at a table with white people.

This gave Matt the boost to begin asking the questions he'd wanted to ask. "Samuel, no one has told me how and when you left home."

"When I was fifteen, I ran away." Samuel helped himself to the bowl of sweet corn and passed it on. "I'd heard of an Underground Railroad stop that I thought I could get to before anyone discovered me missing. So I took off one spring night."

"Without telling his parents," Elijah added with a mix of pride and reproof.

"It must have been quite a shock for thee," the widow said.

Her soft voice reminded Matt of velvet. He looked down at his plate and wondered where his appetite had gone.

"It was a shock," Hannah said, and then pressed her lips together as if holding back tears.

Samuel looked sorry. "I know, it was hard of me. But I thought it best I just go, and I was young and heedless. All I wanted to do was get to freedom and I didn't care about anything else."

So Samuel had left two years after that awful night that had forced Matt's family to leave town. Matt noticed that the widow had stopped eating and was looking at Samuel as if trying to figure something out. Then it occurred to Matt—what had happened to make Samuel take the dangerous flight from slavery? What had happened to drive Samuel to care for nothing but freedom?

Matt listened as Samuel told about the Underground Railroad stop and traveling north by night with a "conductor." The table was quiet as everyone listened to Samuel, who now sounded more like a Northerner than a Virginian. And he had an aura of confidence, which Matt had noticed earlier as Samuel pointed his rifle at Orrin.

As if he'd read Matt's mind, Samuel said, "I've told my parents of our meeting at the store this morning, and about the school you're building."

Verity sat up straighter and sent Matt a questioning look. He avoided her gaze.

"Yes," Elijah joined in, "I think I can get you a few more hands. The Ransfords can't afford to pay their servants and field hands. The mas…" Elijah took a deep breath and corrected himself, "*Mr. Ransford* has tried to get everyone who hasn't left already or who has come back to sign work contracts. But he can't and won't pay until December after harvesting and selling the crop."

"How are times here, Matt?" Before Matt could reply, Samuel added, "I'll answer my own question. I have never seen this town look so bedraggled."

"Virginia bore a great deal of hardship throughout the war," Elijah said, nodding soberly.

"And don't I know it. So many battles were fought on this soil." Samuel cleared his throat and said with obvious pride, "I served in the Union Army."

Every slaveholder's worst fear had been realized when the Union Army had let free and runaway blacks enlist and fight. And Matt knew the black division had served bravely. Samuel should be proud. "So that's where you got your rifle."

Verity didn't look pleased at the mention of rifles.

"Yes, and I learned how to use it, too," Samuel said, a hint of iron in his voice.

Matt could not stop himself from adding, "Well, you'd better after you pointed it at Orrin Dyke." Hannah stopped eating and looked frightened, and Matt regretted what he'd said.

Samuel patted his mother's hand. "I was just letting people know not to tread on me. Or mine. I've grown fangs."

Matt knew that he and Samuel were the only armed men standing against Orrin and his ilk. He was fairly certain that Samuel would have to do more than just point his rifle before that school was built.

"It must have been very hard for thee not knowing where thy son was all those years," Verity said, her voice laced with sympathy.

Matt realized that whatever this woman said, it always came from deep in her heart. A precarious way to live.

Hannah nodded, brushing away a tear. Elijah said, "After the war, we stayed here because we didn't want to make any changes until we located Samuel. And we had hopes that we might hear something from or about Abby." Elijah looked at his son.

Abby? Matt hadn't thought of her for years. A pretty girl, she was the daughter of the Ransfords' blacksmith.

Samuel had already been sweet on Abby at thirteen. What had happened to Abby?

The widow looked inquiringly at Samuel, but Elijah answered, "Abby was the girl Samuel wanted to marry."

Hannah spoke up for the first time, as if forcing herself to say words she hated. "During the war, she was sold. A slaver came through buying slaves, we think, to take to Mississippi."

"But Abby might have been sold anywhere between here and Mississippi," Elijah added. The table had gone very quiet and Samuel's expression had hardened. To Virginia slaves, Mississippi had been synonymous with hell. The slaves had feared being "sold South" more than anything else because with no way to visit or send word, it tore apart their families forever.

"I'm sorry to hear that," Matt replied. But even though he knew right where Dace was, his family had been broken forever.

"Matt, I'll try to help you get the school built," Samuel said, "but I plan on going South to find Abby."

Hannah drew a deep breath. "Miss Verity, we thank you for sending the letter trying to find our son. We didn't know that he was already on his way here."

"I'm very happy that thy son has returned." Verity smiled. "And I will add Abby to my prayers. I'd like to make an announcement to all of you," she said, raising her voice. "I will be starting the school on my front porch on Second day morning next. I hope everyone will send their children seven to twelve years old to register and begin learning to read. Any adults who would like to learn can register when we've got our school built."

There was a moment of silence and then a burst of excited chatter. Matt frowned, but what could he say? The Quaker was in charge of teaching and he had a school to build. Then Matt recalled Orrin Dyke's red angry face. Well, what would come would come.

The sound of breaking glass woke Verity. She leaped out of bed, pulled on her wrapper and stood in the hallway, listening. She could hear Joseph's soft reassuring snores. She peeked into her daughter's bedroom—Beth was sleeping the slumber of the innocent. Had she imagined the glass breaking in a dream? What should she do if—

She heard the back door downstairs open and shut. Heart pounding, she hurried down the steps and into the kitchen. There in the moonlight stood Matthew, looking as if he'd just dragged on clothing and run here. She fought the pull to go to him. Again he had his rifle in hand.

"I heard glass breaking," she whispered, trying not to look at him.

"Me, too." As he moved to the window, his footsteps crunched on shards of glass. He pushed back the white curtain with the barrel of his gun and looked out.

She stood there, still trying to make sense of being awakened. "Was it a bird hitting the window?"

"No." He turned to her holding a rock in his hand. A large rock.

Verity gripped the back of the nearest kitchen chair. Rocks didn't fly through windows on their own. "I'll get the broom." At the sound of more breaking glass, she whirled around.

With the butt of his rifle, Matthew broke the remaining glass in the window and brushed all the glass to the floor.

Verity stifled a cry. "Would thee light the lamp or a candle? I don't want to miss any of the glass in the dark. And I'm barefoot."

"I don't know if that's wise," Matt said, his voice low. "A light will show our silhouettes and I don't want us to be targets."

"Targets?" She pressed a hand over her thumping heart.

"Yes, the rock thrower might still be out there." He laid his rifle down on the table and took the broom from her.

"Did thee see anyone on thy way in?"

He urged her into the closest chair and then began sweeping up the glass. "No, but that doesn't mean someone isn't still out there."

"I see." In the low light she watched him sweeping, her bare feet perched on the ladder-back chair rung.

"A rock's not such a big deal, you know," he said gruffly.

She curled her toes under. Oddly, being barefoot made her feel more vulnerable. "I know thee is trying to reassure me, but that only leads me to ask, what does thee consider a big deal?"

He didn't reply.

She couldn't see his eyes well enough to get a sense of what he was truly thinking, feeling, hiding from her. "I see thee has brought thy gun into the house," she said as he emptied the dustpan of shattered and clinking glass into the bin just inside the pantry door. "Perhaps we should discuss what thee truly thinks the town's response to our school will be and make plans in case violence is used against us." She tried to keep her voice even, but it trembled on the final syllable, giving her away.

Matt's jaw tightened. The Freedman's Bureau ought to have known better than to send a woman with a child into hostile territory. Just because Lee had surrendered didn't mean that Virginia had.

"I'll make us tea." The widow tried to rise.

He stopped her. "You should go back to bed." *I do not want to talk about what we may be heading into.*

"No, we need to discuss this. Thee has made thyself very clear that thee expects us to be on the receiving end of…" Her voice faltered.

"Receiving end of nastiness," he finished for her. He went to the stove and lit it, setting the kettle on the burner. Maybe a cup of tea would settle her nerves and he could get her to go upstairs more quickly.

"Didn't I warn you the night you arrived that you should turn around and go home?" he asked, feeling some savage pleasure at saying this. He sat down near her.

"It was a rock, not a cannonball. I will not be afraid. God's work cannot wait just because of a few—"

"How do you know it's just a few?" Maybe it was because she was a civilian that she couldn't conceive of someone wanting to harm her. He'd had four years of Confederates aiming gun and cannon at him to blow him away. And he'd seen the lethal hatred in Orrin Dyke's eyes.

In the moonlight she stared at him. "I know thee doesn't want me here."

"It's not that," he said, feeling heat rise in his face. He was getting too used to this woman's daily presence, to her direct way of speaking in her velvet voice and the way her face dimpled when she smiled. "I don't want you to get hurt." His words felt as if they'd come from deep inside. Silence. He hadn't meant to say that.

"And I don't want thee to get hurt, either, Matthew."

Her softly spoken words burst through him like a summer sun.

She went on, "Let's not waste any more words on this. I'm employed by the Freedman's Bureau, just like thee. I've been told to continue with my teaching and I'm going to. We must work together." She laid her hand over his.

His reaction was instant. Without meaning to, he turned his hand up and grasped her hand in his. Her palm was callused but her small hand was soft. It had been so long since he'd touched a woman's hand like this, alone in the shadows. More than just a gloved-hand clasp. More—

The kettle whistled and he rose, pulling his hand from hers. Soon he was setting a steaming cup before her.

She lifted her cup and inhaled. "I keep hoping that the people here will see that there's a better way."

He snorted and sat again. "They are blind. For some reason, they cling to slavery even when it has been abolished and even when it cost them countless lives and everything else. It makes no sense."

"It does in a way."

"I don't see it."

"The farther one lives away from the truth, the deeper the darkness one lives in. Jesus is the light of the world. If thee doesn't have Him, thee lives thy life stumbling around in the darkness of sin."

I know about darkness, Matt thought to himself.

"I like Samuel," Verity said.

He looked at her in the faint natural light. He smiled, her steadfast commitment to hope and compassion lifting his gloomy perspective. "I do, too."

"Thee and I have been put together and must work together. Please, Matthew, don't worry about me. That is not thy job here. God has provided angels to watch over us." She rested her hand on his again. "Now, what does thee think we will be facing in the weeks to come? Tell me honestly."

No matter what she said, protecting her was his job. No honorable man could do differently. He sipped his tea, but didn't move his other hand, not wanting to break their connection, even though he knew he should.

He watched the moving shadow of branches on the wall. "I think that we'll have to expect vandalism at the building site, at the very least. Once the school is begun, you should not go into town without me or Joseph with you. Or be here alone."

"Thee thinks then that I might be physically attacked."

The woman was cool, he'd give her that. She sounded as if they were merely discussing an interesting matter in the newspaper. "Yes, I think that is a very real possibility." He wanted to clasp her hand tighter, but worried she'd pull away if he did. What was happening? They shouldn't be sitting here, their hands touching. They were colleagues, but that was an odd situation, too. How often did a man and woman—not married to each other—work together?

She nodded. "I will do as thee says."

His eyes widened at this and he snorted again.

She chuckled softly. "I can listen to reason, Matthew. But still, I will be praying there will not be such opposition. I still hope that God may soften the hearts here and that His light will shine in this present darkness. I will keep thee apprised of my movements and try not to expose my child or myself to needless danger. But we must not make a rock into a cannonball in our minds. If God be for us, who can stand against us?"

Matt's mouth twisted down, but he hid it behind the cup. *Against us? Only most of Fiddlers Grove, including my own blood.* She drew away her hand and he was suddenly cold.

A week later, Verity prepared to greet her new pupils on her front porch. The day was cool—autumn was stealing over Virginia. She had set up a desk and had a stack of slates, a box of chalk and a fresh ledger to enroll her students. She smiled. "Good morning, students."

In the distance she heard the rumble of men's voices. Yesterday Matthew had hired several former slaves with carpentry experience. Today they were unloading the wood that had arrived from Richmond this morning. *Well, Lord, we're beginning our school today. Help me to start on the right foot. And please protect us.*

The children on the porch dressed in worn clothing

were very leery of her and her stomach fluttered. Would someone try to stop her today? She cleared her thick throat.

"I want the boys to move to the left side of the porch, and the girls to move to the right side." No child moved until Beth did, and then the children obeyed her instructions with a bit of mumbling and giggling.

"Every morning I expect you to come to school on time and sit on the correct side of the porch or room "

"But we ain't got any chairs," one little boy pointed out.

"Then thee will sit on the floor," Verity said, catching movement from the corner of her eye. She tried to see what or who had moved within her peripheral vision.

"Ain't a school supposed to have chairs?" the same little boy asked.

"Be quiet, you," one of the girls hissed. "Ma told us to be good and not sass the teacher. I'm tellin' if you don't stop—"

The boy stuck out his tongue at her. "Tattletale—"

"That's enough," Verity said in her most authoritative voice. Perhaps she had just imagined the movement—she gave up trying to find the source. "I am now going to enter thy names in the ledger." The children began telling her their names all at the same time. "No one is to speak unless I give them permission. Thee must raise thy hand and, if I give permission, then thee may speak." At the sight of a boy shoving another, she added, "And if anyone touches or hits someone else, they will be punished."

These words silenced and petrified the children. Verity walked to the desk and seated herself behind it, dipped her pen in ink and said, "We will begin with the boys. First boy, step up here please and state thy name." The first boy didn't move until he was shoved from behind and then he approached her with lowered eyes.

"Your name, please?"

"I'm Thaddeus." He set one bare foot on the other.

The same girl hissed, "You suppose to say, 'ma'am'."

"Ma'am," Thaddeus added.

Verity carefully wrote his name down. "What is thy surname?"

The little boy looked at her in some confusion. "I don't got one of those…ma'am."

"What is your father's name?" Again, something barely moved at the edge of her vision.

"Josiah, ma'am."

"Since he has been freed, has he added a second name to that?"

"I guess it's Ransford. He used to belong to Mr. Ransford. But my mama, she lived on the Ellington plantation."

"Then thee is Thaddeus Ellington Ransford." Verity finished writing his name while trying to glimpse who was moving in the surrounding oaks. The raised voices of the men who were now sawing wood floated over to the makeshift school.

When she looked up she found the little boy beaming at her. "Thank you, ma'am, I like that name. It's big."

"Then thee will have to live up to thy name, won't thee?" Verity smiled at Thaddeus. "Now please go and sit at the end of the line."

Thaddeus puffed up his chest and strutted to the rear of the line to sit down. After Thaddeus's example, each child presented himself and gave his name and who his parents had belonged to. They were thrilled when each of them was given a new "big" name.

Verity had nearly finished enrolling students when the talkative little girl, Sassy Ellington Ransford, hailed her. "Ma'am, ma'am, why is that white boy sittin' in the tree watchin' us? Can he do that?"

Verity looked where the girl was pointing and glimpsed fair hair amidst the oak leaves. So that's what she'd been seeing—Alec. Was he spying on her or the men building the school? Or did he just want to learn? Verity looked at Sassy. "There is no law against sitting in a tree. Now we will begin to learn the alphabet. At first I will teach you to say the sounds in order and then we will begin learning to write each one."

"What's an alphabet?" Thaddeus asked out of turn.

"What did I say about raising thy hand and waiting for permission to speak?" Verity was secretly enjoying the freshness of her eager students, but she had to instill the discipline that was so important to learning.

Thaddeus's hand shot into the air. After her nod, he asked, "What's an alphabet...ma'am?" He cast a triumphant look at his sister.

"The alphabet is the basis of written language. Each letter represents or stands for a sound. In order to read, one learns the letter for each sound."

Another boy raised his hand.

Verity nodded. "Yes?"

"Are you going to teach us Latin?"

"Latin? Why would thee need to learn Latin?" she asked in surprise.

"'Cause edjicated people knows Latin. I come to get edjicated."

Verity hid a smile. "One must learn English first. Latin comes later."

"Are you certain sure?" Sassy asked, and then covered her mouth with her hand. "Sorry, ma'am."

Verity nodded and then unfolded a large piece of heavy cardboard on which she'd printed the letters of the alphabet. She sensed movement in the oak tree again. A gust of wind shivered the oak leaves and she saw that it was indeed Alec, leaning forward to see her chart. How sad to have to sit in a tree to learn.

In the distance, she heard Matthew's voice giving directions and she paused to listen. For a brief moment, everything felt perfect. *Father, bless the building of this school and these students. Bring healing to Fiddlers Grove. Please.*

Then she recalled the sounds of breaking glass in the night. Would a rock through their kitchen window be the end of opposition?

Chapter Seven

During the quiet after supper, Verity walked outside in the twilight to Matthew's cabin. She needed to discuss something with him. In the still green yard, Beth was playing catch with Barney. As Verity passed her daughter, Beth announced with beaming pride, "Mama! Look! Barney brings the stick back to me every time!"

"Wonderful!" Verity waved, continuing on her way over the uneven ground. By now the grass would be turning brown in Pennsylvania and her father and brothers-in-law would have harvested the crops. Here there was just a nip of autumn in the air this evening. Rubbing her arms to warm them, she wished she'd donned her lamb's-wool shawl. She wouldn't be able to hold class on the porch much longer. Fall and winter came later in Virginia than Pennsylvania, but they were coming. Virginia was not so far south that they wouldn't get a hard freeze and perhaps some snow for Christmas.

The thought of Christmas pricked her heart. It would be her first Christmas away from her large family. Though they'd never celebrated the day with a tree, they'd always taken off from work and had a festive meal and small gifts. And Verity had enjoyed the pine boughs, wreaths, mistletoe and red ribbons her neighbors had decorated their houses with. She was knitting a special present for Beth this year, hoping it would ease the pain of being so far away from six doting aunts.

Another thought tugged at her heart. Matthew had family here but his remained a family divided. The wind was loosing her hair from its bun—as it always did. She shoved her hairpins in tighter. She wished she could help Matthew and free him from the dark shadows of the past he still carried. Like most men, Matthew did not even admit to emotions.

But she was not fooled. He must have come here to reconcile with his cousin. Maybe that's why he hadn't answered her questions about Dacian that day they'd walked home together from the Ransford plantation. This heavy thought weighed upon her, slowing her steps. It was odd how feelings could affect her physically. How could an emotion actually tug at her?

She arrived at the small cabin near the barn. The door was ajar, so she called, "Matthew, may I come in?"

He appeared at the door. "What's wrong?"

The assumption that she sought his aid had become his usual response. She gave him a half smile. "I need to discuss something with thee, something I didn't want Beth to hear. May I come in?"

His reluctance to allow her access to his sanctuary showed plainly on his face, but good manners dictated he must give way to a lady. He stepped back. "Of course."

She entered the cabin. His rifle stood at the ready next to the door. A rope bed covered with a worn army blanket was tucked against the wall. A candle burned on a small round table with two straight-back chairs. A soldier's room. An open journal lay upon the table with a steel-pointed pen and inkwell beside it. That interested her. Matthew kept a journal.

"What did you want to discuss?" he asked, sounding uncomfortable.

She pulled out the chair nearest her, unused to Matthew's private territory, and primly sat down. Matthew took his place beside the journal, which he moved aside. Evidently the ink was still wet, because he didn't close it. She wondered if her name appeared on its pages and then forced her mind back to the matter at hand.

She drank in the comfort of his nearness in this still strange place and then drew in a deep breath. "Alec sat in one of our oak trees all through school today."

"And?" he asked.

She pursed her lips. "I can't decide if he was there out of curiosity. Or out of a desire to learn. Or because his father sent him to spy on us."

Matthew studied her and then began to tap the table with the little finger of his left hand.

She studied him in turn. There was a deeper meaning in their unspoken exchange. Matthew had become important in her life here. His keep-away veneer remained persistent, but she was beginning to penetrate, glimpse the true soul that was Matthew Ritter.

"Does it matter why Alec was there?"

"It does. We've done nothing about his situation."

"I told my cousin about the beating." He sounded as if this were one of the hardest things he'd had to do since arriving in Fiddlers Grove.

Matthew, I know it's hard for thee to talk about thy cousin. I'm sorry. "And what did Dacian Ransford suggest?"

"He said that talking to Orrin might cause the boy more harm than good." His deep voice made his words even graver.

She sighed. "I wish the world were not such an evil

place. Sometimes it nearly weighs me down." She rested her forehead in her hand.

Unexpectedly he patted her arm in an unpracticed way that made it even more powerful. A knot formed in her throat.

"Verity, why do you care so much about Alec...about everyone?"

She looked into his solemn eyes and tilted her head. Was this the first time he'd called her by her given name? It felt so. Her stomach fluttered. "How can I not care that a young boy is suffering abuse at the hands of the father who should be loving and raising him to be a good man?"

"Orrin Dyke is not a good man."

The certainty in his tone did not lift her hopes. An unpleasant weight pressed on her lungs. *Poor Alec. Poor Mary.* "Thee doesn't think that Alec is spying for his father then?"

"I doubt it. He probably came just out of curiosity." Matthew withdrew his hand, but his touch lingered, startling Verity.

"I find it very odd that Virginians have no free schools. Didn't they see education as necessary for a knowledgeable electorate?"

He smiled in a way that twisted her heart. His smile mocked smiling. "The planters had the money and the power and they liked it that way."

"No doubt thee is right." She shook her head and rose, wishing she could help Matthew heal his wounds. *But it's not my place. Some pretty young maiden will do that.* "I will continue to pray about this. What we can do nothing about, our loving God will see to. Only He has the power to change hearts and minds. That is beyond us." *Thee is beyond me, Matthew. Whatever I have been feeling is not to be pursued. My heart is still with Roger. And thy heart is caught in the pain of the past.*

"Finally something we can agree on." Matthew had risen with her.

"I think, Matthew, that thee and I agree on many things." She said, smiling sadly. "I bid thee good night then, Matthew."

"Good night, ma'am."

She walked back to the house, burdened with the weight of all that had been unsaid.

"Fire! Fire!" The yells interrupted the Sunday-afternoon worship service at the Ransford plantation where Matt, Verity and her family were attending. Jolted, Matt spun around, trying to identify who was yelling. It sounded like the voice of a boy. Was it a prank?

The voice yelled again, "The Barnesworth barn is burning! Fire!"

That goaded Matt into action. He raced toward home. Behind him, he heard footsteps and shouting, but he didn't look back. He had over a mile to run.

Winded, he reached home first. Flames were devouring the stack of wood for the school and the frame they'd finished putting up yesterday, as well as the barn. For one second, he froze. Then he ran toward the pump halfway between the house and barn.

Verity and Samuel had arrived from the service. "We'll get buckets!" Verity called.

Matt began pumping. Samuel and Verity returned with fire buckets and wash buckets, handing them to those who'd followed.

Samuel took the place nearest the flaming barn and threw the first bucket of water on the fire, making it hiss. Verity, Beth and the others swarmed around the pump, letting the water from the pump fill their buckets. Then they formed a fire brigade line and began moving the buckets to Samuel and then back.

Soon a few of the nearest neighbors joined them. All was chaos—people shouting and coughing, the fire roaring like a giant beast. Their clothing and shoes became soaked with cold well water. Sparks and burning debris floated and swirled around their heads, stinging as they burned flesh. Matt pumped and pumped. His arms ached, threatening to cramp. Still, he pumped.

At last Joseph called, "I think it's out!"

Matt's arms hung at his sides, burning as if they'd caught fire. He emptied the bucket of water he'd been about to pass on over his sweaty head. His legs folded under him and he slid to the wet ground to sit. Panting, he looked around, exhausted.

It was a strange scene in the bright daylight. Over a dozen men, women, and children had helped fight the fire. They were either sitting on the ground as he was or they were leaning over with their hands propped against the tops of their knees. All were gasping. But farther in the distance, Matt was aware of people standing by, just watching.

This stunned him. Usually a whole town pitched in to help fight a fire. It could spread so easily that it endangered them all equally, no matter whose home it was. As he stared, a few of the figures moved away and disappeared. And as soon as they could stop gasping for breath, their nearest neighbors departed without a word of farewell or a backward glance.

Soon it was just Matt, Joseph, Verity, Elijah, Samuel, Hannah and the other former slaves who'd come to help. He gazed at the ruins of the barn and the charred remnants of the wood frame for the school. And then the stench hit him.

"I smell kerosene," Samuel said between gasps and coughs.

Matt nodded, rubbing his chest as if to loosen his constricted lungs. "It burned fast."

"What does thee mean?" Verity panted.

"I mean—" Matt turned his gaze on her "—someone poured kerosene on the barn, wood and school so the fire would destroy as much as possible before we got here."

Rage and sorrow warred in Matt's heart. It had started again.

Verity's face fell. Beth slumped against her mother on the ground, shivering and crying silently.

He stared at Verity. Her bonnet had slipped down to her shoulder. Her damp auburn curls had come undone, flowing over her slender shoulders. She looked paler than usual and her sodden clothing clung to her thin, wraith-like form. Just like his frail mother, all those years ago.

She shouldn't be here, facing this. It's too much for a woman. He'd have to protect her and her family. They were his responsibility. *I don't want to see her hurt.* He stopped there; going further would slice too close to the bone.

"Where are the horses?" Joseph asked, his face frighteningly red from the exertion. Matt had seen his father look like this before his death—it was a symptom of heart trouble. He worried that another event like this could be deadly for Joseph.

"The horses?" Matt looked around. Had their horses been stolen? Or had they perished in the fire?

"We'd have smelled the burning flesh if they'd been in the barn," Samuel said. "They should be safe."

"And we'd have heard them panic, too," Joseph added.

How about Beth's stray? Matt scanned the yard and saw the dog peering out from under the porch. Relief rolled through him like a tide.

"We thank all of thee for thy help," Verity said, looking around.

"Someone was bold enough to start this fire in broad daylight," Joseph said.

"And it probably wasn't just one person," Samuel added.

Elijah said with rich irony, "Do we need to discuss

why someone wanted to burn down the barn, school and wood?"

Verity noted the sarcasm in Elijah's voice. "I knew they didn't want a school here," she said, "but don't they understand freedom of opinion?"

"No," Matt snapped. They hadn't fourteen years ago. Seeing dismay in her eyes sharpened his pain. This honest woman deserved better.

Samuel snorted. "General Robert E. Lee himself said that slavery had evil effects on both the slaves and their masters. You are quite right, ma'am. Some people here know nothing of freedom of any kind. Though slavery is gone, they cling to its vestiges in a blind passion."

"This is about reenslaving black people," Elijah stated. "They know that education will make that impossible."

"I do enjoy a good philosophical and political discussion," Joseph commented dryly, "but my back aches too much right now. We should be discussing what to do about our barn."

"We will have to build a new one," Verity said, rising and helping Beth up.

He'd known she'd say that. "We will. And we'll build the school, too." Matt turned to Elijah, determination flaming through him. "How many of your people would come to a barn raising this Saturday?" *No one's running me out of town again or hurting this woman and her family. Samuel said he's grown fangs, and it's about time I showed this town I have, too.*

Yesterday's fire still smoldering in his gut, Matt rode into town and hitched his horse. He strode into the general store that had been in Fiddlers Grove since 1776. Ironic, Matt thought. He wondered if anyone in town understood what had been won in the American Revolution. If they didn't, he was going to teach them today.

By setting his barn afire, someone had commenced the next battle for freedom. Matt was going to make it clear to Fiddlers Grove that he and Verity would win this battle. The Freedman's School would be built here.

The old men sitting outside on the store's bench rose, and followed Matt inside. The store was full of people and they instantly fell silent at Matt's entrance—again. Of course, the burning of his barn had been the topic of discussion this time. The town gathered at the general store. That's why Matt had chosen it as the place to announce his declaration of war.

He halted in the middle of the crowded store. And as one, they all drew back from him. He looked around, fixing his glare on each and every one in turn. "You all know about yesterday's fire. You probably know who set it. Now I have something else you all need to know. I'm going to telegraph the Yankee commander in Richmond today and ask for Union soldiers be sent to Fiddlers Grove *if* there is any more violent opposition to the Freedman's School. Your town will be occupied like Richmond." *You've messed with the wrong person. I'm not getting run out of town a second time.*

"You've got nerve telling us Negroes got to have a school," one old codger barked.

Another joined in, "Telling us that Negroes are going to vote. Hogs'll fly in Virginia first. You think you can tell us what to do—"

"I *can* tell you what will be done here. I've been authorized by the War Department to do just that." Matt felt the words fly from his mouth. Anger surged inside him as if it were a living thing.

"We're not going to ratify the amendments they're pushing through Congress. We got rights," the first codger objected, nearly dropping his pipe. "We're going to stand up for those rights in the Constitution."

"Did you care about my parents' rights when you forced them out of town?" Matt demanded, his frustration sparking inside him like a thunderbolt. "You lost the war and you're going to lose this battle, too. The South will change or suffer another war. Or worse. Mrs. Hardy and I are federal employees. Messing with us could send you to federal prison. Think about it."

Shocked silence was his only answer. He stalked out to his horse and mounted, galloping toward the next town and the telegraph office. In his mind, he saw Verity's frightened, smoke-smudged face. The image prompted him to dig his heels in and ride faster.

On the cloudy Second Day morning, the day after the horrible fire, Verity set out on her errand. She had meant to discuss what she planned to do today with Matthew, but he had ridden away just as she was about to start out. So she'd left on her business, praying for courage all the way. Yesterday's fire showed her that she must do something radical to reach out to the people of Fiddlers Grove. She had to take action, to stop the cycle of violence. She must turn the other cheek.

Now she walked resolutely up to the Ransford door and knocked, using the tarnished brass knocker twice. She glanced around, trying to calm her quivering stomach.

The door opened and an obviously shocked Elijah stared at her.

"Good day, Elijah. Are the Ransfords at home to guests?" Speaking these words sent another cascade of tremors through her. Did she have the nerve to do this?

Elijah's Adam's apple bobbed a few times as if he were having trouble speaking. Finally he said, "I will inquire. Won't you step inside, ma'am?"

She smiled and stepped over the threshold. Elijah left her and she stared around the entry hall, noting that cobwebs hung from the candle lamp high above her. And dust collected in the corners of the room. Evidently the lady of this house did not dust.

"Why have you come here?"

Verity looked at Lirit Ransford, who was coming down the ornate curved staircase like a haughty princess in a fairy tale. "I bid thee good morning."

The pretty woman paused on the third step from the bottom. "I asked you why have you come here."

Verity refused to be daunted. After all, the worst that could happen was that Lirit Ransford would refuse the invitation.

When Matt arrived at the Barnesworth house, a sharp jab of hunger made him realize that he'd missed the noon meal. After unsaddling his horse, he bounded up the steps into the kitchen that had begun to feel like home, hoping Barney hadn't been given all the leftovers.

He found Verity sitting at the table, writing. He was immediately captivated by her small hand holding a pen. He recalled how tiny her hand had felt in his. Hannah stood by the stove, frowning. He stopped and waited for them to acknowledge him.

"I think Joseph will be able to bag us a wild turkey," Verity was saying. "And I brought pumpkins from Pennsylvania, so we'll have pumpkin pie." She looked up and welcomed Matt with a smile.

He'd never seen a smile more welcoming than Verity's. "Hello. I'm sorry I missed lunch," he began.

"Don't you worry yourself," Hannah said, reaching into the pie safe. "I kept something for you." She handed him a plate covered with a spotless kitchen cloth. "Wait till you hear the news."

He sat down, momentarily distracted by the sight of the plate heaped with ham, cornbread and jellied apple slices.

"I got dustin' to do if y'all excuse me." Hannah said, sounding disgruntled. She left them abruptly.

Matt looked to Verity. "Anything wrong?"

"Hannah doesn't approve of what I've done." Verity didn't give him any time to respond. "Where was thee off to this morning?"

Hunger and thirst came first. "Is that coffee?" He pointed to the pot on the stove.

"Yes." She made to rise.

"I'll get it." He went to the stove. "I'm used to waiting on myself."

"Thee is an unusual man, Matthew Ritter." She grinned.

Glad he'd made her smile for a change, Matt shrugged and sat down. "I sent a telegram to the commander in Richmond, telling him about the fire and alerting him that we might need troops if any more violent opposition occurs here."

Verity drew in breath, looking shocked. "Does thee think there will be more violent opposition?"

He paused to swallow the salty ham. "Yes, I think there's a good chance, especially since we're going to re-build. I went to the general store before I left and warned everyone there what I was doing. The former slaves and their children are going to have a place to learn to read and write." His words bolstered his feeling of strength. "I didn't fight four long years   " *watch good men die* "—for my cousin to keep everything as it was before the war."

Verity looked worried. He chewed more slowly, trying to figure out what was going on. He recalled that Hannah had been upset with Verity. "Now, what did you do that Hannah doesn't like?" he asked, almost grinning. *How bad could it be?*

"This Thursday is Thanksgiving."

Thanksgiving? His family hadn't really celebrated this

holiday. President Lincoln had it made a national observance in, what—'63? He nodded. "What about it?"

"Now that it's a national day devoted to giving thanks to God for the many blessings, I thought—"

Hannah walked into the room and asked in a huffy tone, "You tell him about that Thanksgiving dinner you planning?"

"Yes," Verity said, "I am."

"Did you tell Mr. Matt what you done this morning?" Hannah opened the oven and peered inside.

Hannah's words snatched away Matt's appetite. "What did you do?"

Verity looked him straight in the eye. "I invited thy cousin and his wife to share Thanksgiving dinner with us."

He felt his jaw drop. His fork clattered to the plate.

"And they accepted," Hannah pronounced, shaking her head with eyes heavenward.

Matt stared at Verity. Was the woman out of her mind?

Twilight was coming earlier now. Matthew had avoided Verity all day and had spoken to her in one-syllable words since her announcement. She walked toward his cabin, her soft shawl snug around her. They must discuss Thanksgiving. She must make him understand why she was doing this. But when she knocked on the closed cabin door, there was no answer. "Matthew, may I speak with thee?"

No reply.

She pulled her shawl even tighter around herself. The night would be a chilly one. She looked up and saw a trail of smoke coming out the chimney. "Matthew?" she tried once more.

No reply.

She stood there a few more moments and then walked back to the house. *I intended to discuss the invitation with thee, Matthew.*

Couldn't a family disagree on an issue yet remain friends? She'd married outside her parents' faith. Though they would have been happier if she'd wed another Friend, they had accepted Roger as a good man, as her choice of husband.

What had happened between the cousins? She sensed it must have something to do with the issue of slavery. Matthew's family had left when he was twelve. Samuel had run away at fifteen. What deep past wound had she opened up with this invitation?

The wind tugged her shawl, her hair. Pulling her shawl tighter, she bent her head into the wind and prayed for wisdom, blessing, love and healing to come to this town.

Chapter Eight

Thanksgiving morning

All morning Verity had helped Hannah in the kitchen with the Thanksgiving meal. She had just come up and changed into her best black dress before her guests arrived. Her guests, or her enemies?

Matthew had come in for breakfast before the rest of them and then vanished. Why, she wondered as she sat in front of the trifold mirror. She sighed at the wan reflection of her worried eyes. In the house that she'd grown up in, there had been no mirrors. As a child, the only time she had seen what her face looked like was when she glimpsed her reflection in the local creek on a sunny day.

This vanity had been her wedding gift from her husband. When she had objected that it was vanity indeed to look at oneself in a mirror, he had laughed and said that he wanted her to see how beautiful she was. And what a fortunate man he was.

She had been scandalized. It had taken a year before she could look into the mirror as she undid her hair every night and brushed it before braiding it again. She gazed at the daguerreotype of Roger on the vanity and pressed her fingers to his image. The sight of him gave her the confidence to face the situation she'd created. She knew a part of her would always love Roger, the father of her dear daughter. *But thee is gone, Roger. I will not see thee again till I see thee in eternity.*

She lifted the blue velvet box from one of the drawers. Opening it, she drew out and fastened the silver locket her husband had given her on their first anniversary. Maybe his giving her silver for the first anniversary had been an omen that they would never reach their silver anniversary. *No, I don't believe in omens. That's just foolish superstition.*

She needed armor today. The locket and the love it symbolized would protect her heart. *I must be bold like the apostle Paul. The Lord has not given me a spirit of fear.*

Fingering the cool oval locket, she heard the approach of a carriage. Would the Ransfords come in a carriage instead of walking? Recalling the haughty manner Lirit Ransford had displayed three days ago when Verity had invited her, she wouldn't be surprised.

The rag-doll feeling came over her again. It was as if she were being moved by outside forces. Was this because being a confronter was not what she wanted to be? Sighing, Verity rose and walked to the top of the stairs. The scents of sage, nutmeg and cinnamon hung tantalizingly in the air. Verity wished her appetite would come back and banish the panic roiling in her stomach. Beth stood next to her on tiptoe, looking over the railing on the landing. Verity offered Beth her hand. "Let's go welcome our guests."

Her daughter gave her a quizzical look. Verity took Beth's small hand and led her down. The girl had picked up on the undercurrent of tension that had run steadily in this house the past two days. As they walked hand in hand down the stairs, Verity wondered if Matthew would come or stay in his cabin. She and Beth stepped down into the entrance hall just as Hannah opened the door. An icy wave of apprehension washed through Verity.

She put on her brightest smile. "Good day! Welcome to our home."

Hannah said nothing as she stalked away toward the kitchen. Her stiff back announced to all her attitude toward this "nonsense." Beth hid behind Verity's skirt. Verity stroked her fine dark hair, trying to reassure her. "Dacian and Lirit, I'm so happy thee have come to share our Thanksgiving meal."

Dacian closed the door against the stiff breeze, took off his hat and hung it on the hall tree. "Good day, Mrs. Hardy." He bowed. "And I'm happy to meet your pretty little daughter."

"Yes, Beth, this is Dacian Ransford and his wife, Lirit." Verity offered him her trembling hand. Beth curtsied.

"I don't know why you think you may address me by my given name," Lirit Ransford snapped.

"I beg thy pardon," Verity said, controlling the quaver just beneath her words. "I was raised a Friend and we never use titles. Of course, if thee prefers, I will call thee Mrs. Ransford. I don't wish to cause—"

"You may do that, then," Lirit cut in. "And I shall call you—" the woman paused, giving her a taunting look "—Mrs. Foolhardy."

"Lirit," Dacian cautioned her in a low voice.

Mrs. Ransford lifted her chin, unrepentant.

Oddly the unmasking of the woman's hostility steadied Verity. "Thee may call me Verity or Mrs. Hardy or whatever thee thinks best, Mrs. Ransford," Verity said with dignity. "Won't thee please come into the parlor?"

"Ladies," Dacian said, and motioned for them to precede him. Soon they were all seated in the parlor—the Ransfords on the sagging sofa and Verity with Beth on the worn love seat across from them. The Barnesworth parlor was a mix of tattered upholstered furniture, Chippendale and primitive pieces obviously crafted by a local woodworker. A stiff silence settled over them. Beth didn't even fidget.

Help me, Lord. Verity cleared her throat. "Today may be a holiday new to thee."

"Yes, it is, ma'am," Dacian said.

"We've never celebrated Yankee holidays," Mrs. Ransford said, her low opinion of such things evident in her arrogant tone. She sneered when she looked around at the dilapidated parlor. The wallpaper was faded and peeling in places.

Verity had itched to do some upkeep on it, but she was here to teach and begin God's work of healing, not to strip wallpaper and paint walls. *Please, Matthew, come help me. Thee knows these people. I don't.* Verity tried again, saying, "We are one nation again and so Virginians can celebrate Thanksgiving also."

Mrs. Ransford sniffed.

"I believe that we can all agree that having the war ended at last is something to celebrate," Verity ventured, her misgivings over issuing this invitation expanding moment by moment.

"Yes, ma'am. I take it that you are a widow," Dacian said, obviously trying to make conversation.

Her throat convulsed, but she forced out, "Yes, my husband fell at the Second Battle of Bull Run."

"I believe we called that the Second Battle at Manassas," Dacian said.

Mrs. Ransford's face flushed. "I lost my only brother in that battle." She glared at Verity. "Maybe your husband killed Geoffrey."

The woman's bald words snapped Verity's composure, her hand itching to slap Lirit's sneering face.

"Who can tell who shot whom in the midst of a battle,"

Dacian said solemnly. "I try not to think of all the men I killed."

His grave words sluiced over Verity like a bucket of icy water. Pain spiraled through her, bringing tears. The four years of the war had been the worst of her life. She pulled out her handkerchief and dabbed at her eyes. "The war was horrible. That's why I invited thee here today. The war must end. Healing must begin."

"Yes," the man agreed.

Beth looked back and forth between the two women. "Who did my papa kill? Who's Geoffrey?"

Not looking at Lirit, Verity wiped her eyes and patted Beth's hand. "Thee must not take all we say at face value. No one knows how or why Mrs. Ransford's brother fell in battle but God."

Mrs. Ransford had conscience enough to look abashed. "I didn't mean anything bad about your father, little girl."

Verity took advantage of the shift in this proud woman's tone. "I've been wanting to get to know the women of this town. Are there any ladies' sewing groups or mission societies here?"

Mrs. Ransford's face lifted in an unhappy mix of smugness and derision. "I'm hosting the next meeting of the Daughters of the Confederacy Monday next at three in the afternoon. I'm sure you would be welcomed with open arms." Thick sarcasm oozed from every word, her face smug and condescending.

Verity swallowed a hasty retort, holding on to her patience. She knew this wouldn't be easy. But love always triumphed over evil if one held on. Christ had won the victory over sin and death by holding on in the face of cruel mocking, torture and the cross.

The memory of the fire just days ago had finally convinced Verity that some in Fiddlers Grove would not hesitate to hurt her if they could get away with it. Still, she must do what she thought God had called her to do. It was possible that Lirit Ransford could help her with her personal mission—the meeting she was hosting could prove the perfect opportunity, as strange as that might seem. "Thank you, Mrs. Ransford, for the kind invitation."

The woman opened her mouth, but Matthew appeared in the entrance to the parlor, sparing Verity from further insult. Both Ransfords stared at him. He was dressed in his Sunday clothes and looked very handsome. Joy and uncertainty clashed within Verity as she rose to greet him.

"Matthew, I'm so glad thee has come."

"I wouldn't miss dinner." Matthew strode into the room and halted in front of his cousin. "I see you came to celebrate Thanksgiving with us." Matthew's wry tone nearly matched Mrs. Ransford's mocking words.

Oh, dear. What have I done? Verity realized her fingernails were digging into her own flesh.

Dacian met Matthew's gaze but gave no indication of sentiment for or against his cousin.

Hannah stomped down the hall to the parlor entrance. "Dinner's ready."

Verity wished Hannah wouldn't make her negative opinion quite so evident. Completely devoid of appetite, she rose. "Won't thee please come to the dining room?"

Joseph appeared in the hall, carrying the platter with the golden-brown roast turkey. "Hello, hello," he greeted the guests, nodding them into the dining room across the hall. Joseph set the platter in the middle of the table, laid with the Barnesworth chipped china and a centerpiece of fall leaves and acorns that Beth had gathered. Then Joseph shook hands with Dacian and bowed to his wife.

Soon Joseph had everyone seated and he offered grace. Verity could only be grateful for Joseph's imperturbable cheerfulness. The delicious aromas seemed to affect everyone. Mrs. Ransford almost smiled while Joseph carved.

The dishes passed from hand to hand while Joseph entertained them with the story of the merry chase the flock of wild turkeys had led him on.

As she listened to the story, Verity kept one eye on Matthew. He said not a word but twice looked at his pocket watch. Why? She took her first mouthful of creamy mashed potatoes. And then a knock came at the door.

Matthew rose. "I'll get it, Hannah!" he called, and went to the door.

Verity froze, her fork in midair, as she recognized the voice of the person Matthew had just ushered inside. *Oh, no.*

Then Matthew returned. "Since you invited guests to join us for Thanksgiving dinner, Mrs. Hardy, I felt free to do so, as well." He stepped aside and there was Samuel, standing in her dining room.

The reaction was instant. Mrs. Ransford leaped to her feet. "I won't tolerate an insult like this. I'm leaving." She threw down her linen napkin. "Dacian, take me home."

Dacian remained motionless. A raw, dangerous silence hovered over the holiday table. Verity's heart pounded. Then Dacian said to Verity, "Ma'am, did you do this to insult us?"

Verity didn't like his equating sitting with Samuel, a good man, with an insult. Maybe she had been foolish. What good could one meal do in face of such prejudice? She looked Dacian Ransford directly in the eye. "I invited thee because after our barn was burned, I felt I had to do something positive to end the violence. I was hoping that somehow at this meal I could start to reach out to this community, to soften not harden hearts. We've already discussed frankly why I came here, Dacian."

The ugly silence in the room continued. Then Matthew broke it and said, sounding disgusted, "She's an idealist, Dace. She can't help herself—"

His voice was drowned out by Barney's frantic barking just outside the dining-room window. Verity stiffened. What now?

Beth leaped up. "That's Barney! Maybe those bad men who burned our barn came back!" The little girl raced from the room. "They might hurt Barney!"

"Beth! Wait!" Shock and caution pulsing through her veins, Verity jumped up, racing after her daughter. "Beth!"

Outside the back door, Verity paused. Ahead still barking wildly, Barney was now running with Beth toward the cabin. Verity chased after Beth, aware that Matthew was right behind her, followed by Samuel and Dacian.

The cabin door was open. Verity burst inside to see Barney panting and whining near the bed. Beth stood beside him. "Mama, somebody hurt that boy Alec." Beth's voice was high and thin. "Mama, he's bleeding."

Verity's hands flew to her mouth, stifling a gasp. Alec lay halfway on Matthew's narrow bed. Blood dripped from his mouth onto the floor and both his eyes were swollen nearly shut.

"Mama, is the boy going to die?" Beth's voice was shrill. "Mama?"

Verity went to her and pulled her close, her pulse leaping and stuttering. *Dear Father, this poor boy.* "No, we will make him better." She turned to Matthew standing in the doorway. "Please, will you carry him to the house?" She could not hide the strain in her voice. She sounded as if she were tightening a stubborn screw. She felt like it. *Oh, Lord, this cruelty is so hard to witness. What can I do to stop this suffering?*

Verity pressed Beth's back against her to make room for Matthew. He scooped the boy into his arms and headed for the main house. Within minutes, Verity was breathing hard and fighting back tears as she followed Matthew up the stairs. She looked back at Samuel, Dacian, Joseph and Beth standing in the hall at the foot of the stairs. She held back tears and tried to look calm. "Please go back in and eat. Beth, stay with your grandfather and entertain our guests." She didn't wait for a response.

Matt took Alec directly to Beth's room. He waited for Verity to turn down the bedding, then he gently laid the boy on the canopied bed, wishing he could do more. He stood back as she examined the boy yet again, touching her hand to his forehead, pressing her ear against his thin chest to listen to his heart, and then moving his limbs. When she tried to move Alec's right arm, he moaned. She very carefully moved her fingers around the elbow joint and then probed up and down the length of the arm. "He may have a break in his arm."

Matt felt sickened at the sight of the boy's battered face.

Hannah hustled into the room with a wash basin, rolled bandages and some small brown corked bottles of medicine. Samuel followed her with a kettle of hot water, steam still puffing from its spout. "How is that boy?" Hannah's voice was soft, muted.

Verity turned. "Thank thee, Hannah and Samuel. That's just what I need. I can handle this with Matthew's assistance. Please go down and make sure our guests have everything they need. And please watch over Beth. Seeing this has upset her. She has bad memories—we nursed soldiers after Gettysburg. She has a soft heart."

"Just like her mother," Samuel said, and Matt silently echoed the sentiment. Matt's chest tightened into a painful knot. He tried to imagine what a very little girl would recall of the noise of battle and bloodied wounded. The thought of Beth having to witness the horror of war was almost more than he could bear.

Verity smiled. "Thank thee both."

Samuel and his mother left them. Matt hovered near

Verity, ready to do whatever she needed. He watched her bathe the boy's face and dab tincture of iodine on the many cuts. Alec seemed to be awake but unresponsive. He winced at the iodine but made no outcry. Matt's thoughts turned to Mary. Was she safe or lying somewhere bruised and bleeding, too?

"Matthew, would thee undress Alec while I go get a nightshirt from Joseph's room?"

"I got…to go home," Alec finally whispered, wincing with pain at each word. "I just…came to get away. And you helped…me last time."

Matt moved closer to the bed. Anger was replacing shock and gathering tight and hot in his gut.

"Thee will go home when thee is better," Verity said in a no-nonsense tone.

"My ma," the boy moaned. "She needs me."

Verity gave Matt a significant look and left the room.

Matt reached to unbutton Alec's threadbare, blood-spattered shirt. No one should have let sweet Mary McKay wed Orrin Dyke.

"Sir, please—"

Matt made his voice strong and sure. "Mr. Ransford is downstairs, Alec. He will make sure your ma is protected. Now lie still and don't argue. You did right coming here."

The boy passed out. Matt quickly undressed him and pulled the blanket over his bruised body. Verity entered with the nightshirt. "Will thee help me put it on him?"

Matt supported the boy's neck and shoulders while Verity pulled the nightshirt over his head and arms. Her motions were efficient yet gentle and motherly. Watching her tend to Alec attracted him in a new, more powerful way. She might be an idealist, but when faced with dreadful reality, she knew how to handle it.

As he watched her hands move, he could almost feel her gentle touch soothing him also. After the nightshirt was on, she took a linen towel and fashioned a sling, which she tied around the boy's right arm. Then she stepped back and looked up at Matt. "Something must be done for this child."

He nodded, unable to speak because of the anger surging up like hot air from a bellows.

There was a knock at the door and Samuel stepped inside. "I'm going to sit with the boy while you two go down and eat." He held up a hand. "My mother's orders. Don't think you can go against her. She wants you downstairs and me upstairs."

Matt hesitated. He'd done right by inviting Samuel— and he'd done wrong. His reactions tangled inside him like a kite's string caught in the branches of a tree.

Verity nodded and walked to the door. As she passed Samuel, she patted his arm. Matt followed her down to the dining room. She paused at the doorway. Looking over her shoulder, Matt glimpsed Joseph at the head of the table with the Ransfords to his right and Beth to his left. They were eating pumpkin pie and whipped cream. Matt's mouth watered at the scent of nutmeg and cinnamon, but his stomach clenched at facing Dace and Lirit again.

"How is Alec, Mama?" Beth asked, her face drawn and worried.

Matt seated Verity at her place and then sat by her side, across from his cousin. Hannah bustled in and put down plates of food in front of Verity and him. "I put your plates in the oven so they kept warm."

"Thank you, Hannah," Verity said with a sigh.

Matt didn't like how tired and worn down she sounded. But what could he do about that? What could he do for Alec? He picked up his fork and began eating, hardly tasting his food.

"How's the boy, Mama?" Beth asked again.

Matt chewed slowly, waiting for Verity to answer.

"He's resting," Verity replied, her fork motionless in her hand. "Has thee finished eating?"

"Yes. Thank you. May I please be excused to go see Alec?" Beth asked, sitting on the edge of her chair.

"I think thee had better go out and play with Barney. He is moping around the back porch for thee. And after all, he must be rewarded for letting us know Alec needed our help."

"You want me to go and play with Barney?" Beth asked, rising.

Verity nodded. Beth curtsied to the Ransfords and left the room.

Matt touched Verity's arm. "Eat. Don't let your food go cold. Hannah will have a fit." Verity nodded, her lower lip trembling.

"Will someone please tell me what is going on in this crazy house?" Lirit demanded.

Matt waited for Verity to reply, but she merely began eating. He found he could contain himself no longer. "Orrin Dyke is abusing his son. We found Alec beaten in my cabin back by the barn. We brought him inside and Verity—Mrs. Hardy has treated his wounds."

"Well, what can you expect from trash like Orrin Dyke," Lirit said dismissively.

"Calling names doesn't help the boy," Dace said.

"The boy isn't our responsibility," Lirit snapped back.

Verity looked up and fixed Lirit with an unwavering stare. Lirit blushed finally and looked down at her plate. "Dace, I think it's time you took me home. It appears that Mrs. Hardy has other matters to attend to," she said.

Dace gazed at his wife. "Very well. I'll take you home, Lirit, but then I will return here."

"Why?" Lirit pouted.

"Because I am still Dacian Ransford, and the welfare of Mary Dyke's son is my concern. The Ransfords have always taken care of the people in this county. And may I remind you, you are a Ransford, too."

The Ransfords had always taken care of the *white* people in this county, Matt silently amended.

Lirit rose in a huff. Matt had never liked Lirit much, and he liked her even less now. He recalled all the times when they were children and she'd ruined their fun with tears and tattling. Some people never changed.

Joseph said with gallantry, "If you will trust me with your lovely wife and team, Mr. Ransford, I'll drive your lady home and then return with the carriage."

"Thank you," Dace said. "Lirit, I will be home as soon as matters here are concluded." Face averted, Lirit swept from the room without thanking Verity for the meal. Joseph hurried to help her into her cape in the hall. Dace stared down at the remains of his pumpkin pie and cup of coffee.

Matt pitied his cousin, married to such a woman. Why had Dace married Lirit anyway? *When I marry, I...* He found he could not finish the thought, it startled him so.

When Joseph and Lirit had gone, Dace looked up. "What do you think we should do about this, Matt? I can confront Orrin, but—" Dace paused and then continued, sounding bitter. "I don't have the clout I once had in this town. Money is power and I don't have the money I once had."

Caught up short, Matt could hardly believe his cousin had just admitted this.

"I think that thee still has thy position in the community. Thee still owns thy land," Verity said.

"She's right." Matt added. "You're still the Ransford. Your father's family has been the most prominent in this county for over a hundred years." The memory of Dace's father fanned the flame smoldering inside Matt. Why hadn't he weighed in on the side of Matt's family? Then

Matt chided himself. *What has that got to do with the present, with Alec and Mary? This is about their horrible situation, not ancient history.*

Dace looked from Matt to Verity. "I'll go talk to Orrin. But what if it just spurs him to more cruelty? What if he turns violence onto Mary, too?"

"What makes you think he hasn't already?" Matt asked, thinking of how Alec was always concerned about his mother.

"Yes, I'm afraid that a man who beats his son usually mistreats his wife, too," Verity said. "I'm pleased that both of you want to do something for Alec and Mary. My family has tried to help women in this type of home situation in the past. And unfortunately they have been actively opposed and criticized for interfering with a husband's right to rule his home."

Dace lifted his chin. "A man who strikes a woman or beats a child in this manner is a cad, and every right-thinking man should agree."

So his cousin had learned some compassion over the years. Matt finished his meal and then accepted pumpkin pie from a sober-looking Hannah. Dace stirred his coffee and stared into it moodily. Verity spoke of her family in Pennsylvania, evidently trying to salvage the ruined holiday. Her soft voice soothed him. When she finished eating and excused herself to go up and check on the boy, Dace and Matt sat across from each other alone in the quiet room.

Dace broke the silence. "You invited Samuel to insult me, didn't you?"

"Interestingly, my main intention was to demonstrate to Mrs. Hardy how impossible it is to do what she wants to do here. She wants to bring peace and reconciliation, and make people accept the changes that are coming. Mrs. Hardy is an idealist, not a realist."

"She told me that, too." Dace stirred his coffee, watching the spoon swirl the dark brew.

"And we both know it's impossible, don't we?" Matt pressed his cousin.

Dace didn't respond, but his expression said Matt was right. The sound of the returning carriage gave Dace a reason to leave. "I'll go have a word with Dyke. Please thank Mrs. Hardy for the best meal I've eaten in a very long time. And my compliments to your cook."

Matt rose and nodded.

After Dace had left, Matt stood in the hallway, listening to the quiet. Then he mounted the steps one by one, drawn against his will to the gracious woman of the house.

Chapter Nine

Matt found Verity alone—Samuel must have gone down to the kitchen. Matt stood for a moment in the open doorway, wanting to say something comforting but not knowing what. Then he noticed her shoulders were shaking. It rent his heart in twain.

With two long strides, he was at her side and she was in his arms. "Don't cry. Don't cry," he murmured, breathing in her familiar lavender fragrance.

The top of her head just brushed his chin. The sensation of her springy hair against that sensitive area made it hard for him to draw breath. He stroked her hair and felt its fullness and life. She was so small, so slight that he felt he must be careful not to hold her too close, to crush her. How could a woman so small have such big ideas, such passion to help others? How did she bear all that compassion and all the pain caring brought?

Her weeping slowed, and then she was looking up at him. The tears glistening in her eyes only added to her beauty. He could see each tear in her lashes and her eyes were the perfect shade of brown, so warm and confiding. He pressed her closer, gently, as if holding a living bird in his hands. Her forehead was right next to his lips now.

If he moved only a fraction of an inch, they would touch her, kiss her.

Sanity hit him. He released her slowly, reluctantly. If he gave in to temptation and kissed her, their whole relationship would change. *We have to work together. And I won't lead her to believe there might be something more for us.*

She stepped back and looked down, wiping her eyes with a handkerchief. "I'm sorry for breaking down like that. It's just hard to see a child suffer so."

Matt tried to speak, but his throat was too thick. He cleared it and tried again. "Dace has gone to confront Dyke."

She looked up at him quickly, her face full of worry. "I must pray about that." And right before his eyes, she dropped to her knees, put her hand on Alec's shoulder and bowed her head.

He watched her, hoping God was hearing her and would not let more harm come to Alec and Mary. He bowed his head, too. *God, this woman has enough to worry about without this. Let Dace succeed in putting the fear of You in Orrin.* He looked up. It had been a long time since he'd prayed.

Verity rose and turned to him. "I'm sorry I didn't discuss inviting thy cousin and his wife to dinner today. On First Day, I truly intended to, but thee went off and I didn't want to wait to issue the invitation. I felt the Spirit moving me to go to them."

"And I'm sorry I invited Samuel only to upset Dace and Lirit." And honesty forced him to add, "And you."

She rested one of her delicate hands on his arm. "Thee is a good man, Matthew Ritter. But thee spent four years learning to kill, suffering overwhelming horror and grief day by day. Does thee think I know nothing of war? Our farm was only a short distance from the battleground of Gettysburg. Beautiful green farmland turned into a killing field." A tremor visibly shuddered through her. "I can think of nothing worse than war." She gripped his arm. "I want to bind up our nation's wounds as President Lincoln bade us. And I think, Matthew, that thee came to Fiddlers Grove to do the same."

"There can be no binding up here," Matt said, his voice hoarse. He hated showing evidence of emotion. But her hand was warm upon his flesh and he seemed to lose himself in the sensation.

She squeezed his arm and then turned back to Alec. "We shall see, Matthew Ritter. We shall see."

Matt sat at his table and wrote in his journal, a habit his parents had started him on when he learned to write. He found that writing down his thoughts often helped him see what he should do next, and he was hoping for some clarity about the boy. The journal didn't help this time, unfortunately. He heard the sound of the carriage and walked to the door to see Dace. Dace didn't get down, so Matt went to meet him. The wind chilled him in his shirtsleeves.

"I talked to Dyke."

Matt read grimness in his cousin's face. It chilled him more than the wind. "How did he take it?"

"Not good. He told me Alec was his business. And reminded me I wasn't his boss." Dace slapped the reins and began to turn his carriage toward home. "He'll want revenge on someone. Watch your back."

On the sunny but chilly Seventh Day morning, Verity stood on her back porch and gazed at a stack of new lumber, which stood beside the charred, acrid-smelling remains of the burned barn. Her outward calm was thinner than eggshell.

The wood had been delivered yesterday. Today, many men had come with shovels, saws and hammers. Along with Matthew and Samuel, they milled around her yard, laughing and joking amidst the ruins. Today, they would raise the new barn. In the coming week, the school would rise. And just in time since the chill of the west wind would soon make school on the porch impossible.

Verity couldn't help but notice that Matthew's was the only white face in the yard. She looked up the road once more. If only one white man from the town came to help today, she wouldn't have this deep worry gnawing at her. She still hoped that Dacian would make an appearance today.

"Good day, Elijah, Hannah," she greeted the couple as she walked down the few steps. She tried to smile, but it was a poor, wobbly attempt. She'd spent most of the night praying for God's protection for Matthew, her family and the people who'd come out today to rebuild their barn. But she'd experienced that awful feeling that her prayers had hit the ceiling and fallen back onto her head.

"Good morning, ma'am," Elijah replied. "I've come though I've never built anything in my life. I hope I'll be a help rather than a hindrance."

Hannah must have sensed Verity's low spirits, because she came alongside her and gave her a hearty hug. "You be all right. Everything be all right. God is here today."

Verity smiled, but could not shake the image of the barn burning. The memory left her sapped and shaken as if she were just recovering from a fever.

Though Matthew had said little, Verity knew Orrin Dyke would strike back at them. Alec was still asking to go home, but Verity had insisted he stay. And with a badly sprained ankle and a broken arm, he couldn't get home by himself.

She'd not overheard Matthew and his cousin, but she'd seen the two of them talking late on Thanksgiving evening from the window. Dacian Ransford had gone to confront Orrin Dyke, and he had not looked encouraged as he'd driven away.

Lord, please, if there's more trouble, Matthew will tele-graph for troops and Fiddlers Grove will become a battle-field. The animosity will grow and fester. Please foil any attempts to stop us from building the barn and then the school. No feeling of peace came.

Elijah, Hannah and Verity obeyed Joseph's beckoning wave and joined the circle of men and women around the burned remnants. "Brother Elijah, would you offer a prayer for our work today?" Joseph asked, doffing his hat. Matthew stood beside Verity, looking dour.

Verity noticed his rifle propped against a nearby tree and a pistol on his belt. The sight of the guns upset her, but when she looked at Matthew, she was overcome by the memory of him at Alec's bedside on Thanksgiving afternoon. She hoped no one noticed her warm blush as she remembered the feel of Matthew's arms around her.

Elijah prayed for strength and safety. At the end, every-one said, "Amen." Then she and Hannah went inside. Jo-seph had bought her another dozen chickens. It would take all morning to dress, fry and get them on the table, along with cornbread, turnips and apple pies to feed the workers.

On her way inside, she glimpsed movement beyond the trees around her property. A few white men were just standing there, watching. Were they gathering for an at-tack? Or was this just intimidation? She recalled the ter-rible scene the day before she'd left Pennsylvania when Roger's cousin had spewed such hateful words about what they'd do to her here in Dixie. She met Hannah's troubled eyes, which probably bore a resemblance to her own.

"Think they'll do anything today?" Hannah muttered.

Verity shrugged, unable to say a word, her throat tight. Who knew? Just in case, someone came to cause trouble, she'd ordered Beth to stay inside with Barney and keep

Alec company upstairs. The boy was still in too much pain to go home, and Verity worried Orrin Dyke would lash out at the boy because of Dacian's interference.

"Well, Hannah, we have food to prepare," Verity said, and turned toward the kitchen. A few of Hannah's friends were waiting there, having come to help with the cooking while their husbands worked on the barn.

The sounds of saws and hammers continued all morning. Verity filled the pie crusts with apples and sugar, chatting with the women as they fried the chickens and peeled the turnips. But through the windows, she kept track of the white men gathering in the shelter of the trees around her property.

Their number had been steadily increasing all morning. And now a few had begun taunting the men working outside. Verity's stomach knotted. She could practically see the flames and smell the kerosene. *But what choice do we have, Lord, but to rebuild? The horses must have shelter in the winter. And we must build the school. We can't give in and run away.*

To distract herself, Verity asked, "Have any of thee women ever heard about the movement for women's suffrage?"

More taunts outside. Verity tasted blood and realized that she'd bitten her lower lip.

"What suffrage?" one of the women asked. "Don't sound good."

"Suffrage means the right to vote," Verity answered. "Women deserve the right to vote just as much as men. We're just as smart as they are."

"Smarter," Hannah said with a grin. "We have to be." All the women chuckled.

The volume of the taunts suddenly escalated and Verity could hear threats, racial epithets and foul words. The women in the kitchen fell silent. Then Verity realized that she wasn't the only one who was worried. Each face around her looked strained. The chatter had been their attempt to deny what was happening. And what might happen.

"What we going to do if someone try to stop our men-folk?" Hannah put the overwhelming question into words.

Verity gave up the pretense of working on the pies, wiping her hands on a dish cloth. Alarm coursed through her. She braced herself, drawing up her strength. "Nothing is going to happen. Matthew made it quite clear that he'd telegraph for Union troops if "

A rock crashed through the kitchen window. The women screamed as one. *Dear Father,* Verity prayed silently. A rifle shot sounded. And then another. Beth screamed upstairs. And Barney was barking wildly again. Heart pounding, Verity ran into the hall and up the stairs to her daughter.

Matt had expected trouble. Counting the white men gathering around them had been like watching storm clouds roll in. And now the thunder and lightning had started. Firing his pistol at the first man to shoot, Matt ran for cover and grabbed his rifle. He hefted it to his shoulder. A shot thudded into the tree above his head. Had he survived four years of war just to die here? The familiar crosscurrents of wanting to fly to cover and forcing himself to face enemy fire twisted inside him.

Matt aimed and fired. All around him a free-for-all had broken out. White men were struggling with black men, who were fighting back with bare fists, hammers and shovels. He aimed for the few snipers who sheltered behind the big oaks and were trying to pick off as many black men as they could. He glimpsed the red of a shirt near one trunk, fired and heard a yell. He kept firing toward the trees that concealed the snipers. Finally, the shooting stopped. He reloaded his rifle, watching for more sniper fire.

He was glad Verity, Beth, Hannah and the rest of the women were safe in the house. Then, out of the corner of his eye, Matt glimpsed Orrin running toward the front of the house.

No, you don't. Matt raced after him, stopping twice to shoot as sniper fire started again. Finally he bounded inside the widow's front door and saw Orrin crouched on the floor, starting a fire on the parlor rug.

Matt lifted his rifle. "Stop. Smother that. And step away, Dyke."

The bigger man roared and charged at Matt. Matt hit Orrin's jaw with his rifle butt. Orrin jerked, but it didn't stop him. He slammed Matt back against the wall, his hands around Matt's neck.

Matt gasped for air, jamming his rifle butt into Orrin's belly and shoving forward. *I have to put out the fire.*

Orrin wrenched Matt's rifle from him. Matt landed another blow on Orrin's jaw and knocked the rifle out of Orrin's hand. Then it was fist to fist. Matt kept punching. Orrin pounded him, his fists like flat irons—it was like fighting a bear.

Verity ran down the steps. "Stop!" she shouted. "Fire!"

Neither man paid any attention to her. Matt kept maneuvering for more room. Finally, he was able to grab his rifle off the floor. "Put your hands over your head or I shoot!" The fire had now engulfed the rug.

Orrin shouted and lunged toward Verity. Matt shot but missed. Orrin grabbed Verity and held her in front of him. "Get back! Or I'll snap her neck!"

Matt blazed with anger. The sofa near him was catching fire. "Get your filthy hands off her!"

"No! You drop your rifle! Or I snap her neck!" Orrin pressed Verity back against him with one arm around her neck.

Samuel burst through the door.

Orrin bellowed with rage, threw Verity at Matt and lunged for Samuel.

By the time Matt got to his feet and helped Verity up, Orrin had run outside. Samuel was unconscious in the entry hall. Smoke billowed up from the hungry flames devouring the carpet. Grabbing up the rag rug in front of the open door, Matt began beating out the rug and sofa fire.

Verity knelt beside Samuel's body. "Wake up!" she shouted, shaking him. "Fire!" Then, hearing Barney barking, she called up the stairs. "Beth! Alec! The house is afire! Run outside!"

Finally Samuel blinked, moaned and sat up.

Verity left him, got a small rug from the dining room and ran to Matt. Side by side, they beat out the sofa fire. Coughing, choking, Matt tried to speak to Verity but couldn't. She leaned over, rubbing her neck where Orrin had held her tightly. Samuel helped Matthew drag the smoking sofa outside. Verity joined them in the welcome fresh air.

Verity looked toward Matt and gasped—one of his eyes was swollen shut and his lips were split and bleeding. But he was breathing and standing. She looked beyond the porch and was crushed by what she saw. Many had fallen in the gun battle. Fear pierced her like an ice pick. Beyond the porch, Hannah was kneeling beside Elijah on the ground. "Did any die?" Verity called to her.

Hannah stood. "I don't think so, but we got a few shot and the rest are beaten up pretty bad." Samuel started toward his mother.

Matthew went back in the house and then tossed what was left of the parlor rug into the yard. "Samuel," he called, "go and see who needs help most. Then bring them inside. We'll use the dining room and parlor as a field hospital. The fire burned the rug and scorched the sofa, but it didn't get to the walls. We can be glad that Orrin doesn't know much about setting fires without kerosene."

Verity hurried to help Samuel. As she examined each man lying or slumped on the grass around their yard, visions of Gettysburg flashed in her mind. All this over a barn raising. Those who were able to walk headed home on foot in groups. Verity could see white men carrying their wounded away through the trees. Matt and Samuel were bringing the injured inside where Hannah quickly began treating wounds. Verity hoped her nursing supplies would hold out.

After Joseph, Beth, with Barney beside her, and Alec had been in bed for many hours, Matt, Verity and Samuel sat around the kitchen table, too exhausted to move. Hannah was sleeping in the parlor on a rocking chair and footstool, keeping watch over the few men who didn't have family to nurse them. With a bandaged head, Elijah had gone back to their cabin without her.

Matt tried not to stare at Verity. Everything in him wanted desperately to hold her tight. His determination to protect her had only grown more fierce as the danger increased. "In the morning, I'm going to telegraph the commander in Richmond that we need troops here so we can build the barn and school," Matthew said harshly.

"Be sure you're armed," Samuel warned. "Orrin might try to ambush you if you give him half a chance."

"Don't worry. I'll be ready for anything." Matt was assaulted by the image of Orrin Dyke holding Verity, ready to kill her. He gripped the cup so tightly that his knuckles turned white.

A soft hand touched his. "Is thee all right? I can put a cold compress on thy eye again."

His gaze connected with Verity's and the tender concern in her eyes nearly unmanned him; tears he wouldn't shed collected behind his eyes. "I'll be all right," he said, sounding gruff and unfriendly to his own ears.

She squeezed his hand and then let go. "It seems people here haven't had enough of violence."

"Evidently not," Samuel said, lifting his coffee to his bettered mouth. His arms were so tired, his hands shook.

Matt was so glad Samuel had been at the barn raising. He was still a friend and had stood by them. *I should probably be glad that Dace stayed away. At least he didn't join in the attack.*

Verity leaned her head into her hand. "We should go to bed." But neither she nor Samuel nor Matt moved.

In the lamplight, Matt gazed at Verity. Her copper hair had come down completely and the long waves made a curtain that hid her face. *Orrin Dyke, you will never touch another hair on her head.*

Samuel rotated his neck as if it hurt. "I'll stay here tomorrow, Matt, while you head to the telegraph office. And you should ask for an army doctor. A couple of the wounded need professional care."

Matt nodded.

"Where will this all end?" Verity whispered, her brown eyes lifted to him.

Matt had no answer for her. He knew Fiddlers Grove would lose this battle in the end, but at what cost to the town and to the three of them around the table?

"I don't know the final outcome, but I do know you are doing what is right," Samuel said. "Good people cannot give in to evil. Where would I be if Matt's family hadn't spoke out against slavery and its injustice, or if your family hadn't joined the Underground Railroad? Hadn't helped me to freedom? Hadn't been willing to fight a war?"

Matt nodded, gripping his cup so he wouldn't reach for Verity's hand. They were colleagues and should remain so. "We can't give up."

Verity nodded. "I'm going to see if I can get a few hours of rest." She staggered to her feet.

Matt rose and grasped her arm to steady her. "I'll help you."

"No," she said, touching his arm, "I can make it. I want to check on our patients first anyway."

Matt knew that if they had been alone, he would have pulled her close and held her. *Not a good idea.* She left the room, her light footsteps quiet in the hallway.

Samuel rose, too. "I'm going to sleep on the floor next to my mother."

Matt nodded and headed toward the back door, picking up his rifle standing there.

"She's a good woman, Matt. You should marry her."

Startled, Matt swung around, but Samuel was already out of the room.

Chapter Ten

Two days later, on Second Day morning, Verity stood beside her father-in-law in the bright but chilly sunlight. Joseph was positioning old cans in a line on the fence around the small empty paddock beside their barn. The horses that had been tethered to trees nearby nickered loudly. Verity stood, wringing her hands. She was already keyed up.

Union troops would arrive in Fiddlers Grove today, the same day that she had planned to attend the meeting at Lirit Ransford's house. And now Joseph was trying to get her to use a gun. "Joseph, I didn't approve of thee bringing guns with thee." *How can I stop the violence? Where has Matthew gone this morning? Why isn't he here to meet the troops?*

"You've said that about ten times already," Joseph replied mildly. "It's good I did bring a few firearms. And I'm going to make sure that I still can hit what I aim for. And you should, too." He walked backward, putting distance between him and the target.

He motioned for Verity to follow him. "During target practice, everyone must stay in back of the person who is firing. When I taught my boys how to handle a rifle, I was always careful about gun safety."

"Joseph, thee knows that I cannot do this. I cannot fire a weapon."

Joseph fixed her with a dark stare. "When we were attacked while raising the barn, what if Matt and Samuel hadn't had their guns? I should have had mine with me. It won't happen again. I'm not young enough to defend us with my fists. Cold steel and lead will have to make the difference."

Verity didn't know how to persuade him. "I can't do this."

"What if I'd been shot and they had tried to kill or hurt you and Beth? And I mean more than just beating her."

Verity couldn't meet his fierce eyes. She knew he was referring to rape. The idea that any man would use that kind of low, vicious violence against her, much less her sweet little daughter, made her mind go blank.

So she stood there wringing her hands. "I'm sorry, Joseph, I can't. I can't, no matter what. It is against all of my beliefs. I will have to depend on God's mercy." She hurried away, her heart still pounding at the thought of holding a gun, much less firing it.

Faithful Barney beside her, Beth awaited her on the back porch. Not surprisingly, she had been clingy and weepy ever since the attack the other day. When Verity reached her daughter, Beth put her arms around Verity's waist and hugged her as if she'd been gone for days to a foreign shore, not just a few yards away in plain sight. "Mama, I'm glad Grandpa has a gun. Is that bad?"

Verity smoothed back stray tendrils of her daughter's hair. Guilt had stalked Verity relentlessly since the attack. Did she have the right to put her father-in-law or her daughter through this? "No, it isn't bad."

"If the bad men come back, Grandpa will shoot them before they can hurt us. Won't he?"

Each question was a razor slicing into Verity's sore

heart and raw conscience. *My daughter shouldn't have to ask these questions, Lord. No child should.*

Verity stroked her daughter's hair. "Beth, thy grandfather came along to protect us. He is doing what he thinks is best in order to keep us safe. But in the end, God is our shield and defender, the Ancient of Days. We must trust in God."

Beth did not look comforted by this response. *Oh, Lord, teach my child to lean upon Thee and not her own understanding.*

Verity went inside to check on her remaining two patients on pallets in the parlor. A low fire burned, warming the room. The army doctor was to come today and remove the bullets lodged too deeply for Verity to access. Verity had cleaned and rebandaged the wounds several times to keep down the infection. But the two men were weak and listless.

Hannah was helping one patient drink water. The mantel clock chimed eleven times. How would she stand the tension four more hours until she ventured out into this town that hated her? Would she be able to enlist the help of Lirit and her friends for her personal mission or would the arrival of troops put an end to that? Would the festering evil in the South kill her heartfelt hopes and prayers?

Three o'clock loomed. With feet like blocks of lead, Verity set out. She carried the precious box in her oak basket. Feeling unprepared, she arrived at Ransford Manor. Passing between the imposing Doric columns, she knocked on the broad double doors. In spite of the fact that the shiny black doors and white columns were peeling, the setting was quite impressive—and quite daunting.

Elijah answered her knock. "Good day, Miss Verity." He looked as if he wanted to ask why she'd come here today.

He no longer wore a bandage but he still had a swollen eye from the skirmish over the barn raising.

She gave him a brave smile. "Good day to thee, Elijah. Mrs. Ransford has invited me to the tea."

His eyebrows rose. Finally he stepped back and she entered. The house smelled of old polished wood and candle wax. The hall had been swept and polished since her last visit. The chatter of women came from the room to the right of the staircase. Verity was certain that they couldn't be talking as loud as it sounded to her now.

"I'll tell the mistress of the house that you are here," he said in a hollow voice.

Verity's heart fluttered like a captured bird.

"That's all right, Elijah." Mrs. Ransford stood in the doorway to her parlor in a faded pink dress in the antebellum style, and wearing a gold locket at her throat. "Mrs. Hardy," the lady greeted her with a mix of hostility and mockery, "you decided to come today after all."

"Yes, I have come." Verity hoped her trembling wasn't visible.

Lirit's gaze swept over her with scorn. "Then come in and meet the Daughters of the Confederacy. They will be overcome with joy to meet you in person at last."

Ignoring the heavy sarcasm, Verity entered the parlor. Numbness started spreading through her limbs, fear freezing her. She looked from face to face. The hostile expressions on each told her that they had not expected or desired the Yankee schoolmarm to show up for tea. Verity took a deep breath and said, "Good afternoon, ladies. I have something I'd like to share with you."

A large woman with a blotchy complexion rose and snapped, "You are not welcome here. Please have the courtesy to leave."

Verity knew the moment had come. It was now or never.

"I am here at Mrs. Ransford's invitation and I have something to share with all of thee—"

"Of all the nerve!" A second woman in a worn lavender dress rose and faced Verity. "We don't want to hear anymore about that Negro school you want to build here. Please leave."

"Thy hostess invited me here and I am going to stay until I've said what I came to say." Verity cast a glance at her hostess, who gloated in the parlor doorway, plainly enjoying Verity's hostile reception. Verity straightened. The time for truth-telling had come. "I'm sure that Lirit Ransford invited me here this afternoon for tea so that I would suffer public insult. But I have something of importance to tell thee—" Verity's voice gathered strength "—which has nothing to do with my Freedman's school. I'm not leaving until I have spoken to all of thee."

"Personally I cannot wait to hear what y'all have to tell us," Mrs. Ransford taunted.

Verity ignored her, though her heart skipped and thumped against her breastbone. "I do not think any of thee know that I come from Gettysburg, Pennsylvania."

Their reaction was instantaneous. The mere mention of her hometown and the horrific battle that had cost thousands of Union and Confederate lives cast a grievous pall over the room. The large woman with the blotchy complexion slumped back into her chair.

The other woman in the lavender dress also sank down. "How can you bring that up? So many of us… How could she?" she whispered.

Verity tried to catch her breath and soften her voice. "I do not mention this to hurt anyone. But my sisters and I, along with our congregation of Friends, worked to save the lives of soldiers during that terrible battle. In the midst of all the killing, our men went out onto the battlefield and carried wounded off to our meeting house, which we set up as a hospital. My sisters, the other women of our meeting and I worked tirelessly for over two weeks trying to save lives on both sides."

Suddenly Verity couldn't go on. The appalling memories of Gettysburg made it impossible to speak for a moment. Cannon blasting, drums pounding, rifles firing; men screaming, cursing, the earth shaking under her. And blood, blood, blood everywhere. Before she disgraced herself by fainting, Verity collapsed onto the empty chair nearest her. She couldn't feel her feet, but her heart danced wildly.

The only sound was of two women weeping quietly.

"Why did you bring this up?" a woman who wore spectacles whispered. "Do you think that your nursing should impress us?"

Shaken to her core by memories, Verity was beyond being insulted. She had begun; she would finish the course. "As my sisters and I cared for the soldiers both Union and Confederate, we tried to gather their names, their hometowns and any other information we could about them. We gathered their mementos, insignia from their uniforms and pieces of identification or personal possessions. We wanted to be able to let their families know what had happened to them." Verity's throat constricted again and she tried to swallow the horrible memories of the overwhelming smell of blood and dirt and sweat. "But some of the soldiers—" she forced herself to go on "—were never able to give us their names and some no one recognized. So we put their belongings into envelopes and marked on them anything, any clues that we might have about their names and where they came from."

With numb fingers Verity fumbled open the covered oak basket that sat on her lap. She lifted out the topmost bulging envelope. "This soldier died without regaining consciousness. We found this watch." Fighting to draw breath, she held it up. "Inside the inscription reads, 'To Jesse from his loving parents.' And we found this picture in his pocket." She held up a daguerreotype of a young woman. "He wore the insignia of the South Carolina militia. And we heard him speak the name 'Louisa' several times."

"I don't understand why you are putting us through this," said the woman in the lavender dress, who was weeping.

"I know what it feels like to lose a husband in battle. But I was fortunate enough to receive a letter from my husband's commander telling me about Roger's final days of life and how he died. The commander sent me his watch, and other personal effects. But not all women—wives, mothers, sisters, daughters—were as fortunate as I was. My sisters and I saved these precious envelopes for after the war. We did this in hopes that we would be able to find the women, the families to whom these keepsakes would mean so much. But we are at a loss with regards to finding these people." Verity felt a headache begin behind her eyes.

"What you expect us to do?" the large woman asked, no longer sounding hostile but now only quietly distressed.

"I am hoping that thee, all of thee, will take on the task of finding the families of these men as a work of charity. I know that thee all have relatives and friends all over the South and can also contact people who fought with thy husbands. I'm hoping—my sisters and I are hoping—that thee will be able to return these mementos to the rightful heirs."

There was again silence, except for the weeping. Then Verity felt tears dripping down her face. She hadn't even realized she'd been crying. She found her handkerchief and wiped her face. "Will thee accept this work of charity?"

From outside came the sound of horses. Lirit moved to the window. "Yankee troops have come," she said in a flat tone. "Matt Ritter's riding with them. We should have known that he'd come back and take revenge on us."

Verity tensed, feeling the progress she'd made with the women slipping away. *Dear Father, please, no.*

Late that afternoon in the chill early darkness, Verity walked the last few steps to her house. Feeling a hundred years older than she had this morning, she saw that their paddock was occupied by several strange horses. She trudged up the steps and inside, hearing male voices in the parlor where the last few wounded lay. She took off her bonnet and hung it on the hall tree. After the emotional scene at the tea, Verity felt worn out. And now she must face Union troops, an army doctor and Matthew. She clearly understood why Matthew had to summon these troops. But was there any way she could avoid a local backlash?

She moved into the parlor, her head aching. The army doctor was kneeling beside one of the patients, examining an open wound on the patient's shoulder. Unfortunately, this sight no longer had the power to shock her.

Matthew was standing nearby. At sight of him—his dark good looks—her heart sped up. She tried to temper this reaction, but it was in vain. "You went to meet the troops?" she asked, trying to ignore the unseen pull toward him.

"No, I went to Richmond to swear out a warrant for Orrin Dyke's arrest," Matthew said, not meeting her eyes.

"His arrest?" She folded her arms around herself and tried to smooth back her unruly hair.

"Yes. Isn't that what you'd expect? He attacked me, set fire to the house and threatened to kill you. All of those are punishable felonies."

Her hair was straying from her sagging bun, and she was pushing in her loose hairpins. When she realized she was doing this for Matthew, she lowered her arms and cleared her throat. "Thee is right, of course. Orrin Dyke broke the law." It was odd how her mind had become muddled here, as if the normal rules of crime and punishment were still suspended by the war.

"A few of the soldiers came back with me and they've gone on to arrest Dyke at his house," Matthew said.

Fighting her desire to gaze at Matthew, she nodded. It would be a relief to have Orrin Dyke behind bars. She wanted to tell Matthew what she'd done today, but she suspected that he wouldn't be pleased. It was strange how they always seemed to be at odds, even though they were on the same side.

Now she knew from what Samuel had said the other night that Matthew's family had been driven out of Fiddlers Grove because they had been abolitionists. This must have been what had caused the bad feelings between Dace and Matthew, and it was understandable. Terribly sad, but understandable.

The army doctor rose and bowed to her. "You are a fine nurse, ma'am. I only need extract the balls from these men and they will be on the mend."

"Thank thee," Verity replied. "My sister Mercy worked with Clara Barton throughout the war. On her few furloughs, she taught us to treat war wounds."

"Women like your sister did so much for us doctors." He moved to shake her hand. "Please offer my compliments to her."

Verity shook his hand and smiled.

"Ritter, why don't you take Mrs. Hardy outside?" the doctor said. "I'm sure that this woman here is capable of assisting me." He nodded toward Hannah.

The doctor had just complimented her on her nursing skills, but he still thought a "lady" shouldn't be present at surgery. She hid a wry smile, allowing Matthew to lead her into the kitchen, a hazardous venture. She steeled herself, knowing she must not let his effect on her show. It would be embarrassing for both of them.

This was the first time they'd been alone for days. She waved him to take a seat. The kitchen smelled of roast beef and onions—Hannah must have their supper in the oven. She went to the stove to see if there was any coffee left to put off sitting across from him. There wasn't any so she prepared the percolator for more and stoked the fire under the pot. She found her traitorous eyes gazing at his profile, admiring his straight nose and firm chin.

"I thought I asked you not to go off alone," Matthew scolded.

"I don't remember thee saying that." She clutched two faded blue potholders in her hands.

"I did. Where did you go?" He looked her in the eye.

She avoided his gaze and moved to the dry sink, refolding a couple of kitchen towels there. Again, the time had come for honesty. She took a deep steadying breath. "I went to Ransford Manor to attend the Daughters of the Confederacy meeting that Lirit invited me to on Thanksgiving."

"You what?" He stood up, scraping the wood floor with the chair legs.

She lifted her chin and held her ground. "Thee heard me, Matthew."

"Are you a glutton for punishment?" He looked at her as if she were completely deranged. "Wasn't the Thanksgiving debacle enough for you?"

"I had something I had to do." She went to the table and sat down, her knees weak with the memory of walking into that den of lionesses with Lirit Ransford sneering at her.

Not taking his eyes from hers, he sat back down across from her.

She tried not to stare into his dark eyes, nor at the cleft in his chin that beckoned her to press her finger to it.

"What was so important that you went out alone and unprotected when Orrin Dyke was still at large?"

"I had to try to reach them, to appeal to them. I came here to teach school, but I have another mission to carry out, Matthew." The coffeepot was beginning to rumble, simmering.

"What mission?" His arm was on the red-and-white-checked oilcloth, his hand just inches from hers.

Its nearness made her own hand unnaturally sensitive, as if already feeling his skin against hers. "My family's Friends Meeting House was used as a field hospital and my sisters and I nursed wounded during and after the battle of Gettysburg." She passed a hand over her forehead. "You know how dreadful that was," she appealed to him, a shiver coursing through her. "So many died without telling us who they were and where they were from. My sisters and I gathered mementoes from their uniforms and pockets, keeping them in separate envelopes. I brought them with me to Virginia."

His hand clasped hers, sending warmth through her. His voice was low and rough. "I don't understand what you thought the women in Fiddlers Grove could do with them."

Despite his words, she glimpsed understanding in his eyes. "They have relatives and friends all over the South." Her voice lifted, filled with passion and the hope of comforting others who had lost beloved men just as she had. "They can begin the work of getting the mementoes to the loved ones who would so long for them. It may take years but... I hope they will take on this work of charity. It would mean so much to those left behind."

He stared at her and said nothing. His thumb gently stroked her palm. They listened to the coffeepot bubbling on the cast-iron burner.

She finally broke the silence. "I had to try, Matthew. Thee sees that, doesn't thee?"

"Did they stone you or just tell you to get out?"

The bitterness in his voice stabbed her. She tightened her hold on his hand as if it were a lifeline. *Oh, Matthew, when will thy hurt be healed?* "The ladies looked stunned at first. Just the mention of Gettysburg shook them. I left the box of mementos with them and I hope they will take on this task. It has been a burden on my heart."

He wouldn't look at her, but he didn't withdraw his hand. "You're too good for this time, this place."

"I am not good, Matthew. Only God is good."

"No, you are good." He drew her hand to his lips and placed one brief, tender kiss there.

Verity closed her eyes, her every sense focused on the spot his lips had touched. *Please, Matthew, tread lightly. Caring for each other is not to be. Not here. Not now.* But she had to fight herself to keep from pressing her hand to her cheek. The percolator was nearly boiling over. She leaped up to take it from the burner. *Oh, Matthew, I can't care for you.*

The next day Matt stood in the yard where the new barn would rise in a matter of hours. His spine was straight and his jaw was like iron. The local men who were able to work stood around the barn site with a dozen soldiers who were meant to stay until both the barn and school were built. The soldiers had decided to help, since sitting around in the chilly wind didn't agree with them. Plus the sooner the buildings were up, the sooner they could get back to Richmond.

So let trouble come, Matt thought as he walked toward them. If anyone tried to stop them today, they'd end up in the Richmond Union stockade for a very long time.

This wouldn't be a normal, festive barn raising. Verity

and Hannah were still tending the wounded in the parlor. The food prepared on Friday had been given away, so the men had brought their own food with them in pails. And they'd left their women at home.

The men still bore swollen bruises and half-healed cuts from the last skirmish in this yard. Matt still ached from Orrin's fists. And they all kept looking over their shoulders as if expecting those against them to come and start fighting all over again—in spite of the presence of Union troops.

Matt was pleased that for once, Verity had listened to him and agreed to stay inside along with Hannah and Beth. Alec was still laid up, but soon he'd be able to go home on his own. Orrin Dyke had run for it and was still at large, but now with a price on his head. Perhaps luck would be on their side this time. Matt looked around and shouted, "Let's get started!"

"Let's pray," Joseph suggested.

Matt prickled with irritation, but the men around him looked relieved. He bowed his head with them but looked up instantly at the sound of a horse approaching. His cousin was riding toward the back door as cool as can be. *I'm ready for you, Dace.* Matt's hands balled into fists.

But Dace merely halted and tethered his horse to the back porch railing. He waved at Matt and then sat down on the top porch step.

Matt stared hard, not knowing what to make of Dace's appearance. Then he turned, calling, "Let's get this barn up!" Hammers and saws sounded in the quiet morning. The men began singing "Down by the Riverside."

When Matt looked up again, he saw that the vicar of St. John's had come, too, and was leaning against the railing, talking to Dace. And then the preacher from the community church—the one who'd ordered them to leave— sauntered up and joined them. The men around him kept working, but they stopped singing. Matt felt their keen watchfulness, matched by his own heightened sense of perception.

Then Jed McKay, Mary Dyke's father, rode up on an old nag, followed closely by Mary in a buckboard. "I can't believe my eyes! Have you three gone plumb crazy?"

"Pa—" she said.

"Be silent, girl! Women are not to speak in public. Says so in the Good Book. Preacher," McKay said, glaring at his pastor, "why are you here? You ain't got anything better to do?"

"I'm here to make sure no violence is done today. We may not like this school, but I don't want Union troops in Fiddlers Grove any longer than necessary."

"Yes," the vicar agreed, "the school is going to happen with or without us. Why fight it?"

"Fight it? I'll fight it with my last breath!" McKay bellowed.

Matt saw Verity just outside the back door. The two clergymen and Dace rose and tipped their hats at her. *Stay there, Verity.* Matt didn't want her drawing fire. Readiness for battle set his nerves on edge.

McKay shook his fist. "The U.S. Congress rammed the Thirteenth Amendment through before the South could do anything about it. So the slaves are free. But are y'all in favor of the Fourteenth Amendment? Do you really want blacks to be full citizens? Like white people?" McKay demanded.

"Thee cannot hold back the future," Verity insisted. "And what is wrong with letting children in this town learn to read?"

McKay pointed a finger at her without looking her way. "Orrin Dyke was the only one in town that was willing to stand up to this Yankee schoolmarm. And y'all let her run him out of town! Can't you people see that she's just not like us?"

"Orrin started a fire in the house," Matt yelled. "Attacked Mrs. Hardy and me, Jed McKay." He closed the distance between them. "He's a wanted man. That's why he's run away! He's a coward. Is that what you call a *good* man?" Matt let all his disdain flow in each word.

To Matt's surprise, Dace said, "The barn and the school are going up. Go home, McKay."

Jed turned on Dace. "What I want to know, Ransford, is why you've been in her pocket since she came to town. If you'd just taken a strong stand against this woman, the men in this town would have rallied behind you like they did when you got up our company to fight. Why have you tolerated this? In fact, you've encouraged her. You even sat at table with her!"

"The answer is quite simple," Dace replied. "She saved my life."

Jed McKay stared at him, openmouthed. The men in the yard turned toward Dace and then gawked at Mrs. Hardy.

"What does thee mean?" Verity asked, sounding shocked.

Matt tried to make sense of Dace's words. Dace couldn't be serious.

"Mrs. Hardy," Dace said, holding out his hand, "I have not wanted to tell you because I thought it might make you feel uncomfortable. But I was one of those sad men you nursed in your Quaker meeting house during the Battle of Gettysburg."

Verity gasped and her hand went to her throat in surprise. "Thee?" Tears welled up in her eyes.

Matt tried to grasp this—Verity nursed Dace?

"Yes. At first I wasn't sure that it had been you, but after my first visit, I knew. I could not mistake your lovely caring voice. It was life to me one very long, pain-filled night." Dace's voice sank and became rougher.

"I—I'm sorry I didn't recognize thee," Verity stammered, taking Dace's hand.

"How could you? I was one of hundreds. But I remember lying there and hearing the doctor tell you that I needed very careful nursing through the night or I'd die. And you stayed with me, bathing my face and cleaning my wound over and over. I'm sure if you hadn't, I would have died that night. I was too weak even to ask your name or to thank you."

"I'm glad I could help you," she said.

Dace's words brought back harsh memories forever etched on Matt's mind and heart. He wiped his eyes with the heels of his hands.

Jed McKay cursed loud and long. "What does it matter? She is bringing wrong ideas into this town! You give blacks school-learning and the next they'll want is the vote. Haven't you read about the riots in Louisiana and Tennessee? The Negroes there demanded the vote! You mark my words—you'll have blacks voting and running for Congress in Virginia if we don't put a stop to this right now!"

Matt stood straighter. "You're right, McKay. And the sooner the better."

A stunned silence filled the yard. McKay glared, red-faced and white-lipped. "We don't want or need Yankee schoolmarms teaching blacks to be 'colored gentlemen.'" He made the terms sound like vile insults as he dismounted. "We can keep blacks in their place in this town if you stand with me today and run this Quaker and Matthew Ritter out of town! Who stands with me? Who stands for what is right?"

The troops almost casually reached for their rifles and turned them on McKay and the other two whites. The black men brandished their tools as weapons, ready for anything.

Then Samuel stepped forward. "Any man that can be happy to have his daughter married to a brute like Orrin Dyke is a man I can disagree with—cheerfully."

"You've got that right," Matt seconded.

"No one asked you to open your mouth, boy!" McKay roared. He charged Samuel. Dace leaped forward and grabbed Jed's arms. The old man struggled against him.

"Orrin *is* a brute." Mary Dyke's thin, frightened voice shocked everyone into silence. "I told my father that Orrin beat me and he told me to mind my man and I wouldn't be ill-treated. He was wrong. Orrin didn't need a reason to hurt me and my son." Mary's voice shook with feeling. "I'm glad Orrin's gone. I hope he stays gone."

"You dare to speak against your husband in public?" McKay demanded.

"I dare because of this woman." Mary nodded toward Verity. "I didn't think women could make a difference, or could stand up to men. But she did. She stood up to the women, too, and showed them what she was about. I didn't know a woman could do that. If Mrs. Hardy can stand up to all of you, so can I."

Then Jed yanked himself free of Dace's grasp, mounted his horse and rode away without a backward glance. All eyes watched him until he disappeared from sight.

Mary approached Verity, the men giving way to her. "I've come to take my boy home, ma'am. Thank you for giving him shelter. I knew he was safe with you. May I see him please?"

"Of course." Verity motioned Mary up the steps and took her inside.

McKay should be horsewhipped for letting Orrin abuse his daughter and grandson. After a quick glance at his cousin, Matt turned away, choked up. "Show's over! Let's get moving! The sun goes down early these days."

Matt felt good, really good. If nothing else, he'd come home and had run Orrin out of Mary's life. With Verity's help.

The long, eventful day was finally finished. Matt thought it might take him a long time to sort through his reactions to all that had happened today. He ached, but in a good way and for a good reason. The barn was up and only needed some finishing work, which Joseph had offered to do so the men could move right on to the school tomorrow. The workers had all gone home with pay vouchers and smiles. Now sitting at the kitchen table, Matt wrote out the last voucher to Samuel.

Samuel looked at it and smiled. "Matt, when we were boys, did you ever think that you'd be paying me—a free man—for building a school for black children and former slaves in Fiddlers Grove?"

Matt was caught up short. He hadn't thought of it in that way. "My parents hoped for, worked for something like that."

Samuel's face sobered. "They were good folk. I'm sorry they didn't live to see this day. To witness this miracle."

"This was a day of miracles," Verity said, walking into the kitchen.

Samuel rose. "Time I left for home. Good evening, Mrs. Hardy."

Matt had also risen at her entry. As Samuel passed through the back door, he winked at Matt.

Matt felt himself warm under the collar.

"Would thee like to take a walk, Matthew?" Verity asked. "I feel the need of some fresh air to clear my head. So much has happened this day."

He nodded. "Good idea." The truth was, he wanted Verity to himself. The house was crowded with soldiers bedding down in the parlor, the dining room and the entry hall. Verity had insisted they sleep inside because of the cold.

She tied her bonnet ribbons and Matt helped her on with her cape. He was careful not to touch her shoulders. Touching her might unleash all he fought to conceal. He shrugged on his wool jacket and they stepped outside into the cloaking darkness of early December.

The moon was high and bright as Matt walked beside Verity. He listened to everything with new ears, it seemed. Their footsteps sounded loud in the quiet. Matt was very aware of the woman who walked beside him, the rustling of her starched skirt. Though he longed to claim her hands, he kept his arms at his sides.

Finally she broke their silence. She did not turn toward him. "Thee doesn't believe in miracles then?"

He was about to say he didn't—then he recalled all he'd witnessed today. "I haven't for a long time," he said finally. "Is it a miracle or coincidence that Dace was one of the many you nursed at Gettysburg?"

"I call it Providence."

"Providence?" Matt asked, and shoved his chilled hands into his pockets.

"Yes. Surely my reunion with thy cousin is no mere co-incidence. I don't believe in coincidence. Far in advance, God knew that I would come to Fiddlers Grove to open this school for freed slaves."

Leaves were falling in cascades from tree branches, sounding like sighs and whispers. Once again Matt wished Verity wouldn't wear such a deep-brimmed bonnet. He wanted to watch her vivid expressions. For a woman who radiated peace, she felt and showed everything vibrantly. "You believe that God had this all planned?" he asked, knowing what her reply would be.

An owl hooted in the moonlit darkness. "I do. God saved Dacian's life that awful night, not my poor nursing. He saved thy cousin for this purpose. And God preserved thy life, too. Thee is a part of this, a part of God's fore-knowledge and providence."

Her voice grew stronger, with the passion that he loved in her. And hated. *Don't care so much, Verity. That's the way to pain. I'm afraid for you.* He turned his collar up against the cold.

"I don't know," he hedged. "It all sounds wonderful when you say it like that. As if God has a grand plan with parts for each of us to play—"

"It's the war, isn't it?" she interrupted. "The war cost thee much."

"I don't want to talk about it," Matt insisted, suddenly flushed. He didn't want to go back to those years, a collection of days no living soul should have had to face. "I won't."

"As thee wishes. I'm sorry. I remember..." Her voice trailed off.

She sparked his anger. He stopped her and gripped her slender shoulders. Her face shone pale in the moonlight. "You only survived one battle," Matt growled, "and you weren't in the midst of it all..." How could she know what it had been like, having to face over and over the possibility of pain, dismemberment and perhaps anonymous death.

He thought of the prebattle ritual of writing his name and town on a slip of paper and having a friend pin it to his collar. That way, if he fell, he wouldn't die nameless. The men from whom Verity had collected belongings must not have done this. Or their slips of paper had gotten torn off or lost. *God, no one should ever have to do that. No one.*

A gust of wind billowed her dark skirt. "I know. I don't know how thee did what thee did, survived what thee survived. But I know enough to know that it cost thee much, too much. And through it all, thee remained a good man, a kind man. How did thee manage that?"

He heard the sorrow and compassion in her voice, and

he could hold off no longer. He pulled her into his arms. "Just put it behind you. Just say it's over."

"But it isn't over."

He didn't ask her what she meant. He drank in the sensation of her breathing against him, of her bonnet touching his face. He pressed his cheek to her forehead, wishing she were wrong. But she was right—it wasn't over. The school wasn't built and Orrin Dyke was on the loose. The hate just went on.

Chapter Eleven

It was a week later on the morning of Second Day. This would be the very first day that class would be held in the new school. Verity couldn't recall ever feeling quite this happy or uplifted. Halfway between their house and the school, she and Beth walked hand in hand through the windbreak of poplars. The morning air was crisp and clear. Behind them, smoke from the chimney puffed high and white in the blue sky, following them. For the first time in her life, Verity felt like singing out loud, hearing her own voice. Then she laughed at the silly thought. *I don't even know if I can carry a tune.*

Beth, who had finally conceded and left her dog at home with Hannah, looked up. "Mama, is this going to be a good day?"

The worry in her daughter's strained eyes pierced Verity. She halted and pulled Beth into a tight hug. "Dearest daughter, today will be a very good day. We open the school today. The children in Fiddlers Grove will be able to learn to read and write."

"But only the black children, right? Alec won't get to learn." Beth's dismay over this darkened her deep brown eyes. Even Beth's voice drooped.

Her happiness dimming, Verity looked over the top of

Beth's bonnet. *Father, I thank Thee that my daughter has a tender heart.* "Beth, whether Alec learns or not isn't up to me. But I wouldn't stop any child from coming to school—ever." *Maybe, Lord, Mary would let him come over to the house and I could teach him his letters at the kitchen table.*

Beth tugged at Verity's arm. "So if Alec came to school today, you'd let him stay?"

Verity bent, kissed Beth's forehead and cupped her chin. "Of course." But Alec wouldn't be coming to school today. The whites here had made it clear they would have nothing to do with the Freedman's school—even though that meant their own children would remain illiterate. Verity drew Beth along with her. *There are none so blind as those who will not see.*

The new white one-room school loomed ahead of them. The frozen grass under their feet crunched. On Seventh Day, the desks and blackboard had arrived and had been installed the same day. It had taken only four days for the willing workers, with the soldiers' help, to put up the school, paint it and then outfit it.

At twilight yesterday, Verity had walked down the center aisle and placed a large, leather-bound dictionary on her desk. Then she'd laid her hands on the two stacks of textbooks there—one a reader and one a math book. *It will be so good to be in the classroom once more.*

The bubbly feeling came again. Then ahead she saw the children and their mothers, bundled up against the cold and waiting outside the school door. Thaddeus Ellington Ransford ran toward them. "Schoolteacher! Schoolteacher! Now we got us a real school. Does it got chairs?"

Verity couldn't help herself. She chuckled. "Yes, yes! We have desks with chairs."

"Mama!" Beth shouted, pointing ahead. "It's Alec! Alec, did you come to school today?" Beth broke away from Verity and ran to her friend.

Alec still wore the sling, but he was walking now. His mother was standing behind him, looking uncomfortable but determined. "Good morning, Mrs. Hardy."

"Good morning, Mary." Verity looked around. There seemed to be two camps—one on each side of the door. The black mothers and children stood to the left, and a few white mothers and children to the right. Verity's spirits dropped to her toes. Would there be a confrontation on this bright, promising day? *Father, help.*

"Mrs. Hardy, I know this school is just for freed slaves and their children, but Alec wanted to come. He wants to learn…" Mary said, her frail voice fading away.

"Don't worry, ma'am." Beth spoke up with palpable confidence. "My mama won't turn away anyone who wants to learn. She told me so." Beth gave Alec a look of delight and danced on her toes. "You can learn, too, Alec. Reading is fun!"

Verity glanced at the black mothers, who looked skeptical. *This must come from thee, Lord. I couldn't have caused it.* She decided the best course of action was just to go on as if this unexpected turn hadn't occurred. *Please, Lord, keep care of this. It's beyond me.*

She walked to the door and unlocked it. Earlier this morning, Joseph had come over and started a fire in the Franklin stove in the center of the school, so the school was pristine, welcoming and warm. "Come in! Come in! Hang your coats on the hooks on the back wall. Those children who have already been registered and attending school, take your seats according to your age as you did on the porch."

The black children scrambled to take their seats, all the while exclaiming over the brand-new desks. Alec hung back, but Beth dragged him forward by the hand. "Alec, you're a boy so you sit on this side. And you're bigger, so you sit back here."

The black mothers had gone forward to examine Verity's desk. The white mothers—Mary and, to Verity's surprise, two women whom Verity had seen at the Daughters of the Confederacy meeting—walked in hesitantly, looking all around. They motioned their children to sit in the back behind the black children.

Before Verity could say anything, Sassy Ellington Ransford stood up and waved to them. "You white chil'run got to come up to the teacher and tell her your name—all your names. If you ain't got three, she'll give you what you need." Sassy waved again, summoning them forward. "Come on. She got to write your names in the book so she can mark down when you come every day. It's called taking roll."

The white children followed their mothers and moved forward, looking as if they'd been transported to China and couldn't believe their eyes or ears. Trying not to laugh at Sassy's instructions, Verity took off her cape and bonnet, and hung them on a hook on the wall nearby. Then she sat at her desk and opened her roll book and inkwell. With her pen in hand, she said, "Tell me your full names, please, one at a time."

She enrolled three white boys including Alec, and one white girl—Annie, the granddaughter of the large woman with the blotchy complexion who'd ordered her out of Lirit's parlor. The woman, Mrs. Augusta Colbert, gave Verity an intense look. "We're trusting you to know how to do this."

Do what? Teach? Integrate a school? Verity tried not to appear as baffled as she felt and merely nodded, trying to look confident.

With that, the mothers departed, leaving Verity facing the children. The black children sat in the front rows and the new white students sat behind them. Beth had taken her accustomed seat near Sassy. All the children looked eager and uncertain. The mixing of the two races—something that Verity had never expected—seemed to put everyone on edge. Except for Sassy.

Verity took a deep breath and began calling roll, name by name. Each of the experienced students stood and replied to her, and then sat back down. Sassy turned and alerted the white children in a stage whisper that they should do that, too. So when Verity called, "Alec Jedediah Dyke," Alec rose and replied, "Present, ma'am." Then, as if he couldn't help it, Alec grinned—it was the first smile she'd ever seen on his face. Verity blinked away the moisture gathering in her eyes. *I thank Thee, Father, for this moment. It gives me hope.*

After roll, Verity began the daily alphabet instruction. The experienced students recited with enthusiasm while the new ones only observed. It would probably take some time for them to become comfortable enough to join in.

As Verity was about to finish the first math lesson, Matthew and Samuel came through the door. Her heart skittered in her chest. *Oh, no, what's wrong now?*

"Good morning, Mrs. Hardy!" Samuel called out with a smile. "Good morning, students!" He stopped short when he caught sight of the white students. Matthew halted beside him, looking uncomfortable.

Oh, dear. She'd surprised him again. And he didn't look pleased. Verity drew in a breath and forced a smile.

"Hello, Mr. Ritter," Alec said. "And you, too, Samuel."

Recovering quickly, Samuel waved to Alec and the other children. Matthew nodded at them, still looking perplexed by the white children at the back.

"What may we do for thee today, gentlemen?" Verity asked, hoping to forestall any questions about the additions to her classroom.

"Well… I…" Samuel said. "We thought that this new school needed some decorating." He looked around, grinning. "I mean, it's almost Christmas! When I went to school in the North, we always had a tree and pine branches on the windowsills. And I thought that Fiddlers Grove's first school needed them, too." Samuel put an arm around Matthew's shoulders. "And Matt here agreed with me."

A sudden lightness rose inside her. She smothered a chuckle. She could just imagine how enthusiastic Matthew had been about this idea. "Well, what do you think, children? Should our new school be decorated for Christmas?"

Beth jumped up, waving her hand. "Yes, Mama—I mean, yes, ma'am!"

Bouncing on her toes, Sassy had joined Beth and actually had to put both hands over her mouth to keep from speaking without waiting for permission.

"Sassy?" Verity said.

The little girl waved her hand like a flag. "Please, ma'am, we want to decorate our school! We never had a Christmas tree like they did in the big house!"

"Then I think that first the girls and then the boys should line up and put on thy coats and scarves. Then form a line and wait for permission to go outside. Thee will not run and thee will stay close to me." Verity pointed toward the aisle and the coatrack. The girls lined up and soon all the children stood in two lines, waiting to head outside.

Matthew found his voice. "We left the hatchets outside and we have a wooded section at the back of this property with pines and holly trees on it. I thought we'd cut one for the school and one for the house," Matt said.

"Wonderful." Verity beamed at him, tugging on her gloves.

A warmth glowed inside him to see her so happy after all she'd gone through over the past weeks. He smiled as he helped her with her cape.

"Will thee two gentlemen lead us then?" At his nod, she said, "Children, please follow Matthew and Samuel."

Samuel stayed at the head of the party, encouraging the children with teasing. The children's zest was contagious—Matt felt his mood lifting. As they tromped over the frozen grass, he drifted back to Verity's side, bringing up the rear.

The clear, cold air was invigorating and he breathed it in deeply, trying to shake off his powerful attraction to this woman. He leaned close to her, wishing her bonnet away. Its brim hid her face from him. He whispered, "How did the white children come to be in the school? Did you do something?" *And not tell me as usual?*

She tilted her head so he could see her face, framed by the brim. "I arrived at school and there they were with their mothers. I was taken completely by surprise. But I'm not sorry. I hope more white children will come."

What would the Freedman's Bureau have to say about white children in this school? Well, that would have to take care of itself. He wasn't going to tell Verity Hardy that she couldn't let white children into her classroom. He wasn't crazy.

"What kind of tree do you children think we should have in your school?" Samuel called out.

"A big one!" Thaddeus shouted.

"The biggest one!" Sassy seconded.

Verity chuckled and Matthew felt laughter rolling around in him. He finally let it come up his throat. He laughed out loud. "The biggest one?" he called out. "We'd better not get one so tall that we have to cut a hole in the roof."

The children giggled at this. And Verity touched his arm. He looked down and she was beaming at him again. Making him forget they were colleagues. Making him want more, much more from her.

Soon they reached the wooded area. There were white pines, yellow pines, spruce trees, cedar trees. The children scrambled around, shouting about each tree they deemed a possible choice.

Matthew now realized how much all the opposition from the town had affected him. Each moment of listening to the children, listening to Samuel teasing them, lifted him and seemed to chip away at the burden he'd carried not for weeks but for years. He found himself keeping close to Verity, as if she were his North Star, glowing and leading him away from...what?

He couldn't put it into words. It just felt good. Just being near her, hearing her soft voice and her chuckling. Over and over, she turned her face up to him, beaming, shining, happy. Her enjoyment infused him, too.

Right here, right now it was hard to recall that Orrin Dyke was still at large. And that many in Fiddlers Grove would be outraged that white children had attended school with black children, and that together they were running around in the woods, choosing a Christmas tree.

Then he felt it—an icy dot melting on his face. He looked up. Snowflakes were drifting down. The children squealed with delight. "Snow! Snow!" they called out. "It's snowing!"

"God is blessing us," Verity murmured, her face skyward, her eyes shut.

And Matt leaned down and brushed her lips with his. Verity's eyes opened wide. Heart racing, Matt turned from her, calling, "Who's found the tallest tree?"

Over the next few weeks, Verity wondered if she'd imagined Matthew's lips brushing hers. But every time she looked around her classroom, she was reminded of the day they'd gone together to cut the Christmas tree for the school, and she knew it wasn't her imagination.

Christmas Eve had finally come. And she would be taking another chance, making another attempt to break down the barriers in the town.

At the front of the dimly lit classroom, the yellow pine tree they'd cut stood, lovingly decorated with strings of popcorn, sprigs of holly with red berries, pinecones painted white and white candles clipped to a few branches. And adorning each windowsill was a single candle in a glass globe set on pine boughs with bright red holly berries and shiny green holly leaves. Matthew's kiss remained as real as these solid reminders of the day he'd kissed her.

His kiss had been like the touch of an angel's wing or what she imagined an angel's wing would feel like—light and fleeting, just like the snowflakes that had been falling that day. *Matthew Ritter did kiss me.*

And he will be vexed with me again. Matthew had been called to Richmond four days ago for meetings about starting the Union League of America the day after Christmas. And while he was gone, she'd made another decision that he probably wouldn't like.

"Schoolteacher, we done making the school look like a barn," Sassy announced to Verity, bringing her back to the hubbub of her classroom. Outside the windows the sky was dark. Only the moonlight through the windows, the candles and one oil lamp at the front illuminated the shadowy classroom. The Franklin stove warmed the room. Verity's heart was skipping, worry and anticipation making themselves felt.

Verity glanced down at Sassy's bright eyes and full smile, cupping the little girl's cheek. She then checked the room to see that everything was in place. Her desk had been moved to the rear beside the door. And where it usually stood was a manger with hay and various tackle that one would find in a barn—hay bales, rakes, harnesses, a sawhorse. They brought with them the earthy scent of livestock and wood.

"School look different at night," Sassy said in a lower and softer voice than usual, with a note of wonder in it.

"Yes, it does. It looked like this the night Jesus was born in Bethlehem." Each boy had a dish cloth tied around his head as the only costume. The girls wore white ribbons around their heads as halos. Verity had tried to enlist a few boy angels, but the universal sentiment from Fiddlers Grove boys—regardless of color—was that angels could be played only by girls. She had bowed to their preference.

"Did He have a Christmas tree?" Thaddeus asked, sidling up to her. Like most children, he had an insatiable urge to be touched, to be loved. Verity squeezed his shoulder.

"No, Jesus didn't have a tree," Alec said, standing in the center aisle, his voice kind to the younger boy. "It was in olden times. They didn't do Christmas trees, remember? Teacher told us about it."

Verity couldn't believe the change in Alec. A few weeks of coming to school and being recognized as an excellent student had made such a change to him. The image of the first time she'd seen Alec battered and bruised flashed in her mind. She swallowed down the harsh memory, nerves clenching inside.

"Oh, I forgot Jesus didn't have a Christmas tree," Thaddeus admitted, hanging his head.

Verity squeezed the boy's shoulder again. "Thee will remember next time."

Thaddeus beamed at her.

"Mama," Beth said with a smile that spread over her face, "I hear people coming!"

Verity was certain that she'd heard voices outside for the past few minutes. She looked at her students. "Now, we've all practiced this a good long time." *The past three days.* "The only thing that will be different is that Mr. Ransford will be doing the reading, not me." Another decision Matthew probably wouldn't like.

The thought of having Fiddlers Grove's most important citizen come to take part in this production with them seemed to ignite a special excitement that raced through the children. Sassy and Beth weren't the only girls dancing and clapping.

"Now get back behind the curtain and I'll let everyone in," Verity said, herding them all behind a large white bedsheet that she and Hannah had hung right after school today. Joseph was already there to help keep peace.

Then she took a deep breath and opened wide the school door. "Come in!" she invited, alive in the moment. "Welcome! Merry Christmas!"

Dacian Ransford was first at the doorway. He let his obviously truculent wife precede him. He bowed over Verity's hand and she showed him to the front of the classroom, where a Bible and a lamp sat on a desk to the right. Lirit sat down in the rear, as far as possible from her husband. Then the black parents streamed in, followed by Joseph.

Verity noticed that everyone had dressed up for the occasion and she was glad she'd worn her best black. A few white parents sifted in and arranged themselves near the back of the room as if they didn't want to be noticed.

The little school was soon packed. Mothers and teenagers sat in the desks while the men stood around the perimeter of the room, holding their hats in front of them. Verity noticed that in the rear the curtain was billowing and she detected the telltale movement of pushing and shoving. But before she could get there, Hannah had gone behind the curtain to help Joseph and was giving the children a stiff lecture in a low but stern voice.

Verity had planned this event for six in the evening as most of the children were little and needed to get home for early bedtimes. Noting that it was time to get started, she walked up the center aisle. When she turned to look out over the assembly, everyone fell silent.

Speaking in front of so many strangers gave Verity the jitters. Their faces flickered in front of her eyes, but she persevered. "I'm so happy that thee were able to come this evening to our first Christmas play. I hope it will be the first of many. Elijah, would thee please offer a prayer for us?"

Standing, Elijah cleared his throat and asked for God's blessing, thanking him for Jesus's birth. When everyone lifted their heads again, Verity said, "Now the children of Fiddlers Grove's first school will enact the Christmas story for thy enjoyment and blessing. Dacian, will thee begin reading, please?"

Verity walked swiftly to the rear, where the oldest students in the class, Alec and Beth, waited to start. *Lord, bless this hour to Thy glory.*

Lifting the open Bible beside the oil lamp, Dacian began, "I am reading from the Gospel of Luke, chapter two.

"And it came to pass in those days, that there went out a decree from Caesar Augustus that all the world should be taxed. (And this taxing was first made when Cyrenius was governor of Syria.) And all went to be taxed, every one into his own city."

Verity motioned Alec and Beth to begin slowly walking down the center aisle, Alec supporting Beth on his arm. A rustle of excitement rippled through the crowd as every head turned to watch. Verity had let the students vote who would make the best Mary and Joseph, and these two had been the unanimous choice.

"And Joseph also went up from Galilee, out of the city of Nazareth, into Judaea, unto the city of David, which is called Bethlehem; (because he was of the house and lineage of David:) To be taxed with Mary his espoused wife, being great with child. And so it was, that, while they were there, the days were accomplished that she should be delivered. And she brought forth her firstborn son, and wrapped him in swaddling clothes, and laid him in a manger; because there was no room for them in the inn."

At this point Alec lifted a sheet in front of Beth. When he lowered it, Beth was holding a rag doll swaddled in a white blanket. Quickly, Verity sent Sassy and Annie up the aisle, leading all the other girls with their white-ribbon halos.

When they were halfway up the aisle, Verity sent five boys with canes held like shepherds' staffs after them. She wished Matthew were here to see the joy on the children's faces. Then he might not disapprove of this quite as much. She drew in more air, holding down her churning tension.

"And there were in the same country shepherds abiding in the field, keeping watch over their flock by night. And, lo, the angel of the Lord came upon them, and the glory of the Lord shone round about them: and they were sore afraid."

Halfway up the aisle, the shepherds dropped to their knees, the canes clattering to the wood floor. Sassy, the angel, motioned broadly with her hand.

"And the angel said unto them…"

Sassy and Annie shouted, "Fear not!" Verity had been certain that Sassy couldn't keep quiet the whole time and had taken the precaution of giving her a line. She was so proud of her students she didn't notice the classroom door open.

Matt and Samuel slipped inside the warm and darkened classroom, closing the door silently behind them. Verity did not look up. She appeared to be concentrating intensely as Dace read from the Bible.

Matt wasn't prepared for his reaction to seeing Verity after several days away from her. Awareness of her flashed through him like a summer wind. Without Verity's presence, Richmond had felt sterile and lacking.

Dace glanced toward the little angels and, grinning, continued.

"For, behold, I bring you good tidings of great joy, which shall be to all people. For unto you is born this day in the city of David a Saviour, which is Christ the Lord. And this shall be a sign unto you; Ye shall find the babe wrapped in swaddling clothes, lying in a manger. And suddenly there was with the angel a multitude of the heavenly host praising God, and saying, Glory to God in the highest, and on earth peace, good will toward men."

Verity's bright hair gleamed in the low light. Her intent profile was visible against the glow of the lamp near Dace. Matt watched as she motioned all the girls to stand behind Dacian. They nodded, and the one who'd shouted loudest dragged the lone white girl with her, leading the rest of the girls to the front.

Matt was struck by the simple beauty of the setting. The white candle in each window and on the Christmas tree. The bright faces of the children all sporting the ridiculous head cloths or ribbons. The way the parents leaned forward watching their children. A feeling he couldn't name filled him up.

Dacian's voice quavered with amusement, and then he went on in a serious tone.

"And it came to pass, as the angels were gone away from them into heaven, the shepherds said one to another, Let us now go even unto Bethlehem, and see this thing which is come to pass, which the Lord hath made known unto us."

The five shepherds picked up their canes and walked toward Beth and Alec.

"And they came with haste, and found Mary, and Joseph, and the babe lying in a manger. And when they had seen it, they made known abroad the saying which was told them concerning this child. And all they that heard it wondered at those things which were told them by the shepherds. But Mary kept all these things, and pondered them in her heart. And the shepherds returned, glorifying and praising God for all the things that they had heard and seen, as it was told unto them."

Then the shepherds walked back up the aisle and, passing Matt, disappeared behind the white curtain.

"Now I will read from the Gospel of Matthew, chapter two," Dacian continued.

"Now when Jesus was born in Bethlehem of Judaea in the days of Herod the king, behold, there came wise men from the east to Jerusalem, Saying, Where is he that is born King of the Jews? for we have seen his star in the east, and are come to worship him."

Verity waved on three boys carrying small boxes in their hands.

And as Matt watched them, it occurred to him that the three of them—Samuel, Dace and himself—had been like these boys until they'd been torn apart by slavery. Now years later, they stood together in the same room, something he'd never expected to live to see. The hope for real togetherness rose in him unbidden. He tried to keep it down, but still it rose.

Then Dace's voice, so reminiscent of Dace's late father, came again in the near darkness, sounding so solemn and reverent.

"When Herod the king had heard these things, he was troubled, and all Jerusalem with him. And when he had gathered all the chief priests and scribes of the people together, he demanded of them where Christ should be born. And they said unto him, In Bethlehem of Judaea: for thus it is written by the prophet, And thou Bethlehem, in the land of Juda, art not the least among the princes of Juda: for out of thee shall come a Governor, that shall rule my people Israel. Then Herod, when he had privily called the wise men, inquired of them diligently what time the star appeared. And he sent them to Bethlehem, and said, Go and search diligently for the young child; and when ye have found him, bring me word again, that I may come and worship him also. When they had heard the king, they departed; and, lo, the star, which they saw in the east, went before them, till it came and stood over where the young child was."

The three kings arrived at the barn and greeted Mary and Joseph with a lot of hand-waving, and then they dropped to their knees before the baby.

"When they saw the star, they rejoiced with exceeding great joy. And when they were come into the house, they saw the young child with Mary his mother, and fell down, and worshipped him: and when they had opened their treasures, they presented unto him gifts; gold and frankincense and myrrh. And being warned of God in a dream that they should not return to Herod, they departed into their own country another way."

The three kings rose and walked back up the aisle to the white curtain, striding regally, not little boys in ragged clothes with torn dish cloths tied on their heads.

Matt watched Verity as she gazed forward. When he had arrived home a few minutes ago, he had immediately looked for her at the house as if he weren't really home until he spoke to her. He'd found Samuel, who had been on his way to the school.

When Samuel had told Matt about Verity's Christmas play with both white and black children, Matt marveled at her audacity. Was there anything this woman wouldn't do?

Then, interrupting Matt's concentration, Samuel tapped him on the shoulder before slipping outside.

Dace finished the story.

"And when they were departed, behold, the angel of the Lord appeareth to Joseph in a dream, saying, Arise, and take the young child and his mother, and flee into Egypt, and be thou there until I bring thee word: for Herod will seek the young child to destroy him. When he arose, he took the young child and his mother by night, and departed into Egypt."

Then Dacian looked up and said, as if he were in St. John's on a Sunday morning reading the epistle, "Here endeth the lesson."

"Come out, children, and take your bows!" Hannah called, hurrying the children out from behind the screen. The whole class of children met at the front, bowing and curtsying to loud applause and whistling from all around the room.

In this enthusiastic clamor, Matt heard Verity's triumph. How did she do it? How did she get whites to bring their children here? True, it was only the children of three white families, but they were here. It had to have been Verity's visit to the Daughters of the Confederacy meeting and the precious box she'd entrusted to them that had made the difference.

Listening for Samuel, Matt looked around and found his cousin looking back at him. The tug of family still plagued Matt. But maybe *plagued* wasn't the right word. Dace had come around a lot. Matt felt as if his heart were being drawn toward his cousin. *What do you remember, Dace, of what happened all those years ago?*

Dace cleared his throat and the room fell silent. "Now I'm told the children will entertain us with a Christmas song to end this lovely presentation." He nodded and strode to the rear to stand behind his wife, who was already waiting by the door, evidently ready to depart.

Head cocked to one side, Matt listened carefully for sounds from outside. What was taking Samuel so long?

Grinning, the children paraded up the aisle together and with loud whispered reminders from one of the girls, arranged themselves into a choir. Verity nodded and they began singing:

"Children, go where I send thee
How shall I send thee?
I will send thee one by one
One was the little bitty baby
Wrapped in the swaddling clothes

Lying in a manger
Born, born, born in Bethlehem"

Then over the children's singing came a loud thumping
on the roof. Matt folded his arms. He shielded his mouth
with his cupped hand so no one could glimpse his broad-
ening smile. The children kept singing, but stared at the
ceiling above them. Matt stifled a chuckle. He'd enjoy
watching this, watching Verity be taken by surprise. And
he'd savor her delight.

Chapter Twelve

When Verity heard the sound of a cow bell clanging, she didn't know what to think. Then the door burst open and Samuel stepped inside, carrying a wooden crate. Verity stared at him. The children stopped singing.

"Children!" Samuel shouted. "What do you think just happened?"

"What?" Annie asked breathlessly, her hands pressed together in front of her chin.

The same anticipation made Verity hold her breath.

"Santa heard you singing and stopped by."

Almost all the children began dancing and jumping with excitement. Even Alec looked excited.

Watching the children's eagerness sped Verity's own pulse. She peered ahead, trying to see what was in the crate.

"And do you know what he said?" Samuel asked.

"What?" the children replied.

"Santa said he couldn't stay, but he said you all deserved something special for such good singing. Now you all line up." Samuel turned toward the door, where Verity noticed Matthew lurking in the shadows. "Mr. Ritter is going to hand out Santa's gifts to each of you good boys and girls."

Verity pressed her hands together.

Matthew looked chagrined, but the children lined up, still bouncing on their toes. He took the box Samuel was pushing toward him and sighed loudly.

Verity studied Matthew's stoic expression. How would he handle this?

"What did Santa bring us, mister?" Thaddeus asked, neck craning to see the contents.

A frown creasing his forehead, Matthew hesitated and then gave in. He stooped and lifted the lid of the crate. "Whoa. Look here. Oranges." He pulled out one and handed it to the first girl in line. Not surprisingly, it was Sassy.

The children all squealed, "Oranges! We never got oranges before!" Sassy yelled.

Verity stood to the side of the classroom, watching Matthew handing out the fruit to each thrilled child. Happiness radiated within her. Samuel slipped to her side. "I thought Matthew should hand out the fruit. He bought it in Richmond for your schoolchildren."

"He did?" Verity was surprised and touched. She couldn't imagine how much these oranges had cost him in Richmond in December. *Oh, Matthew, how dear of thee.* "How did he find out we were having the play?"

"He didn't know until he arrived at the house tonight and I told him about it. He'd planned for you and Beth to deliver them to your students tomorrow on Christmas. I decided it would be more exciting if they were handed out here, tonight. From Santa, of course." Samuel grinned.

This would be a Christmas to remember for these children born into the privations of the war. And Samuel had done right to urge Matthew to hand out the gifts he brought.

The war had left them all trying to catch up on simple pleasures, the delights of everyday life that had been taken for granted before four years of vast suffering and horrible carnage. Before tonight, Matthew probably hadn't ever had the chance to experience the joy of giving to children. Did anything match the joy of watching children excited over Santa?

"You're still coming for dinner tomorrow with your parents?" she asked Samuel.

"Wouldn't miss it—especially since I'm leaving the next day to find Abby."

Verity touched his arm, worried that he might find only pain and loss. *God, be with this good man.*

"Wonderful play." Samuel gripped her hand briefly and then went to stand by his mother and father.

It didn't take Matthew long to hand out all the fruit. Verity enjoyed watching Matthew's smile broaden until it lit up his whole face. Children were good at that—good at reminding adults of what really mattered in life.

The winter wind rattled the windows, reminding the parents to gather their children and head home. At the door, each thanked her as they left. Dacian came over and wished her a merry Christmas.

Verity offered him her hand and said, "I don't know if you'd be able to, but you and Mrs. Ransford would be very welcome to stop over on Christmas Day."

"And will Samuel be coming, too?" Mrs. Ransford snapped.

"Yes, he will be there with his mother and father," Verity replied, not the least bit surprised that Lirit brought this up again.

"Thank you for the invitation," Dacian said. "We may drop by for a cup of cheer."

"Please do," Matthew said, moving to stand by Verity. His nearness topped off her happy glow. She had to stop herself from claiming his arm.

Dacian looked up at his cousin. "Merry Christmas, Matt."

"Same to you."

Verity heard the emotion that Matthew was trying to hide behind his gruff reply. She inched closer to him. He smelled pleasantly of leather and fresh air, an enticing blend.

Dacian shook Matthew's hand. With lifted nose, Lirit led her husband out. And soon the school was empty except for Verity, Joseph, Beth and Matthew, who'd stayed to sweep up the stray straw. Verity listened as Joseph talked to Matthew, drawing out all he'd learned in Richmond about starting the Union League.

Beth yawned and Verity realized it was time to get her to bed. Then Verity would get to play Santa. Her own parents had shocked some of the other Friends by including Santa in their celebration of Christ's birth. But her father had loved the story of the jolly old elf and had scoffed at the naysayers.

Her father would have heartily approved of the gift Samuel and Matthew had given these children this night. Who could disapprove of such innocent joy?

The house was silent as Verity crept down the creaky stairs to slip Beth's Christmas presents into her stocking on the mantel. When she stepped into the moonlit parlor, with its Christmas tree, she was caught up short. Matthew was there also, putting something into Beth's stocking.

He turned to her and whispered, "I got her some new red hair ribbons."

The wonder that Matthew had thought to buy hair ribbons for her little girl caught Verity around the heart and made it impossible for her to speak. Tears came to her eyes and she turned away.

"What's wrong?" he whispered as he came up behind her. "Shouldn't I have bought ribbons?"

She pressed her hand to her mouth, trying to hide the

fact that she was fighting tears. "She'll love the ribbons," Verity whispered.

"You're crying." Matthew laid his hands on her shoulders and turned her toward him. "Why?"

Verity shook her head, unable to put into words how his gift had touched her.

Matt tried to think why his putting ribbons in Beth's stocking should make Verity cry, but came up blank. It was just one of those inexplicable things women did. Then he caught her lavender fragrance and his mind went back to the day they'd cut the two Christmas trees. The memory of her lips went through him like a warm west wind.

Then she did something unexpected. Her hand grazed his cheek and slid into the hair over his right ear. In that exquisite moment he thought he might die of the glory of it. It had been so long since any woman had touched him. He savored the sensation like a starving man letting sugar dissolve on his tongue.

In the moonlight she lifted her fair face to his. For the first time he saw the invitation he hadn't known he was waiting for until this moment. Slowly, as if they were puppets on strings, their faces drew toward one another. Their lips met and it was a tender meeting. Matt closed his eyes and leaned into the kiss. Warmth flooded him. He had yearned for this moment—without even realizing it.

He let his lips roam over hers. They were sweeter and softer than he'd remembered. His thumbs made circles on the collar of her cotton flannel wrapper. Her underlying softness worked on him, melting his final resistance to this woman.

At last he drew back, his hand cupping the back of her head. He looked down into her caramel-brown eyes glistening in the low light. "We're colleagues here and now. But we won't be forever."

She nodded.

Did that mean she agreed that they might be more than colleagues sometime in the future? He couldn't go on without revealing more of his tangled, unexamined feelings than he was prepared for at this time. But this woman had brought healing to Fiddlers Grove—and at least some measure to him.

Because of her, he was speaking to his cousin and had even worked with him to deal with Orrin. He'd thought he'd come here because of his mother's deathbed request. But he had come here to fill in the hole that being forced to leave his home in 1852 had left in his life. He'd come to find his family, his friend Samuel.

And did he indeed love this woman? Was she the right one? *She must be. I've never felt this way about any woman before.*

"Good night," he whispered, making himself end their sweet interlude. Hesitating, hating to leave her, he traced her soft lips with his index finger once and then turned and left.

Verity stood still for a very long time after he'd closed the back door. Then she went and tucked into Beth's stocking the new red mittens and scarf she'd secretly knitted, and a peppermint stick. Verity had already received her own Christmas gift—Matthew's kiss and half-spoken promise.

They had come to an agreement tonight. Both of them were committed to their work here, and that took precedence over their personal feelings. If they went forward as a couple now, she would not be able to focus on her mission as teacher and peacemaker here in Fiddlers Grove. The Freedman's Bureau did not employ married women as teachers.

But if she'd understood Matthew right, a time was coming when she could put widow's black behind her. She leaned her head against the smooth wooden mantel and let lush wonder flow through her every nerve. *Thank Thee, Father, for this very special Christmas gift.*

In the thin wintry sunlight of early January, Verity walked up and down the rows of desks, her skirts swishing over the wooden floor. Friendly voices hummed in the room. Children were quizzing each other, preparing for a spelling test that would start in just a few moments. Then the school door opened and Annie's grandmother burst inside, ushering cold wind into the warm schoolroom.

Matt stared out the kitchen window toward the school through the windbreak of leafless poplars. He wondered how the latest news from Washington would affect their work here. The Richmond newspaper lay on the table. He'd read the headline countless times in the past few minutes. Every newspaper had brought troubling news from Washington, D.C., but this was the worst. It couldn't bode well for them.

President Johnson had been fighting the Radical Republicans in Congress over the South's refusal to ratify the Fourteenth Amendment, which would make former male slaves voting citizens. When Matt thought how the latest development in this conflict might affect the tenuous peace here, his stomach churned. He knew Verity, who'd always had higher hopes than he had, would be devastated.

Matt saw Dace galloping up to the back door. He knocked and entered without invitation. Then Dace pulled the same Richmond paper from inside his coat and shook it at Matt. "Have you seen this?"

Startled, Verity looked up at the woman. "What is it? What's happened?"

"We've found Jesse!"

For a moment Verity could not figure out who Jesse was. And then it came back to her. The day she'd visited the Daughters of the Confederacy meeting, Jesse had been the first lost soldier she'd revealed to the ladies. "Thee did!" Verity shouted in joy.

"Yes." Annie's grandmother swept up the center aisle. She held out a letter in both gloved hands. "I just received a letter from his wife, Louisa. We had contacted the South Carolina militia adjutant and he fowarded our request to the family of the man he believed to be our Jesse. She begs us to send his effects to her."

Thinking of Louisa and the comfort that word of her late husband would give her, Verity could not stop her tears. "Oh, I am so happy, and my sisters will be, too. Oh, praise God." Verity opened her arms and the two women embraced.

Dace halted in front of Matt and looked at the paper on the table. Dace threw his copy on top of Matt's. "You've read it, then?"

"Yes." Matt glanced down again at the headline: Congress Divides South into Five Military Districts.

"It's monstrous," Dace exclaimed. "According to this, Virginia isn't even a sovereign commonwealth anymore. The Union military will rule us. Are you Yankees trying to get us to secede again?"

You Yankees. He and Dace were enemies again. The past few weeks had just been a lull in the long war. Matt rubbed his taut forehead, his gut tightening.

"When my slaves were freed, I lost most of my wealth. Then after the surrender, the Union government confiscated my harvested tobacco and cotton. I'd stored four years of harvests on *my* land that I hadn't been able to sell due to the Union blockade. Then they stole everything but the house, leaving me nearly penniless.

"Now, because before the war I owned too much land to suit the abolitionists in Congress, I was barred from taking the oath of loyalty to the U.S. or holding office. Virginia was in the process of writing a new state constitution. I had hopes of at least regaining the vote. Now this." Dace looked at the paper with loathing.

Dace felt that his right to vote was more important than Samuel's? Matt's ire fired up. "What did you think was going to happen, Dace? The war supposedly settled once and for all the issue of slavery—"

"I can accept the end of slavery," Dace cut in. "I must."

"But you don't accept that Samuel is free now and will vote just like any other man," Matt said. "And people like Orrin Dyke are still actively fighting the changes that freeing the slaves must bring. In other Southern states there have been race riots and lynchings. The slaves can be free as long as they don't act free. Isn't that what you mean, Dace?"

With his clenched fist, Dace hit the table, turned and stalked out.

Annie's grandmother had left to spread the good news. Now Verity stood in front of the row of first-graders and began dictating their spelling words. The children had their chalks poised over their slates and were listening so hard that it made her smile. "Spell *rob*." Squeaky chalk scribbled on the slates.

The joy of locating the first family of a lost soldier still bubbled inside her. Verity couldn't wait to write her sisters this evening. This was cause for celebration. *Wait until Matthew hears. Maybe now he will believe in the power of love to reach hearts and change minds.* Then she made herself concentrate on the spelling test. "Spell *mob*," she said.

After school on that happy day, Verity strolled home, lighthearted, through the early twilight. She'd stayed late, tidying up the schoolroom and correcting papers written by the older students. As she approached her home, she noted that there was a strange carriage parked in front of her house. Who could be visiting? Verity hurried up her back steps and into the warm kitchen, where Hannah was standing at the stove. Verity bent to pat Barney as he greeted her. The room was fragrant with the scent of ham roasting. Beth was at the table, doing her homework.

Hannah swung around to face Verity. "I'm glad you come home, Miss Verity," Hannah whispered. "Joseph and Matthew are in the parlor, entertaining two gentlemen. I didn't like the look of them."

Verity took off her gloves, cape and bonnet and hung them on a peg by the door, smoothing back her hair. "Who are they?"

"I don't remember their names, but one is black and one's skinny and white. Looks like he never had a square meal."

Verity grinned. "Do we have enough to invite them to eat supper with us?" Hannah nodded. "Then I'd best go in." Patting Beth on the back, Verity headed to the parlor. She paused at the entrance to the room, a smile of welcome on her face.

Joseph jumped up from his chair, but Matthew made the introductions. "Verity, these two gentlemen, Mr. Alfred Wolford and Mr. Jeremiah Cates, are from the Freedman's Bureau. Gentlemen, this is Mrs. Verity Hardy."

She walked forward, holding out her hand.

The two men who'd stood up were staring at her in a funny way. It turned out that Mr. Wolford was the tall, thin white man and Jeremiah Cates was the large, robust-looking black man. After they had shaken hands, she said, "Please be seated again, Friends. I'm so happy to entertain thee in my home."

"Don't you mean the Freedman's Bureau's home, young woman?" Mr. Wolford glowered at her.

This caught Verity just as she was about to lower herself into one of the chairs. "I beg thy pardon?"

"This home, in fact, belongs to the Freedman's Bureau, doesn't it?" Mr. Wolford insisted in a scratchy voice that was higher than expected. His Adam's apple bobbed in his scrawny throat.

"Thee knows that is true." Verity sat down. "But why does thee bring it up?"

"We bring it up," Mr. Cates said in his full deep voice, "because rumor has it that you have overstepped your bounds, ma'am." He sat down again, while Mr. Wolford remained standing.

"Indeed?" She widened her eyes in surprise. "And thee listens to rumors? I never do." Of course she shouldn't have included those final three words. *But it's the truth.*

She glanced at Matthew to see if he could offer her any enlightenment as to what was going on here. He merely stared at her in stony silence. Smothering fear pressed on her lungs. *What do these men want?*

From his stance at the fireplace, Mr. Wolford glared at her. "Young woman, we've heard rumors that the Freedman's school here has openly included white children. And your father-in-law has admitted that this is true." Mr. Wolford sounded as disgruntled as if he were at table and someone had pulled away his plate of food.

"So, ma'am, you see it's good we listen to rumors," Mr. Cates said with a sly, smooth smile.

Her gaze on Matthew, Verity replied, "That is true. We have four white students attending here." As she thought of this triumph, sparkling happiness filled her as usual. "Why shouldn't white children attend public school? They would in the North." Matthew's face was clenched and rigid.

"Now, ma'am, is it fair for children whose parents

owned slaves and fought against the Union to receive a free education at the government's expense?" Mr. Cates asked in his rolling baritone. "You are forgetting who the enemy is."

Verity tried to stifle her increasing apprehension, a stiffening at the back of her neck. "Do we still have enemies a year after the war ended? The war is over, Friends. I didn't come here to prolong it. I came to do what President Lincoln wanted us to do. I wanted to bind up the nation's wounds, to bring help and healing here. White children should not be punished for the actions of their parents. And I would think that having white children and black children attending the local school together would advance this—"

"Young woman, this isn't a Christian mission," Mr. Wolford snapped. "The Freedman's Bureau is a government body with very specific purposes paid for by taxes."

She again looked to Matthew, appealing for his backing. He said nothing, but looked back at her with a pained expression. She tried reason again, saying, "I don't understand why four white children in school is objectionable. I assure thee that the black children don't complain. Perhaps thee doesn't understand the situation Mr. Ritter and I faced when we arrived here."

"Mr. Ritter gave us some indication of this, ma'am. But we would be glad to hear what you have to say." Mr. Cates motioned to her to speak.

Some indication? An odd sensation came over her, like ants crawling up her spine. What had Matthew told these men about her? "When we came to Fiddlers Grove, the white people here were set against having a Freedman's school in their town," Verity began.

"And they didn't hesitate to make this known." Joseph spoke for the first time. "They attacked Matt, attacked my daughter-in-law, burned our barn and tried to burn our house down. Or should I say the *Freedman's Bureau's* house down?" Joseph looked flushed and angry. "Why wasn't the Bureau here then to try to protect *its* house and my daughter-in-law?"

Seeing the men's expressions hardening into anger, Verity spoke up, her words stumbling over each other in her haste. "I think that my father-in-law is trying to tell thee that we had a very difficult time at first. But with God's favor, I won some of the people over by appealing to their better selves."

"Young woman, where in your instructions did it say anything about including white children in a Freedman's school?" Mr. Wolford demanded, ignoring what she'd said. "A Freedman's school is to educate black children and adult Negroes—freed slaves—who must learn how to read and write in order to become informed voting citizens."

"Aren't white children supposed to become informed voting citizens, too?" Verity asked in what she hoped was a reasonable tone, fire beginning to burn in her stomach.

"That is not the point in question," Mr. Cates replied, rising to stare down at her. "Are you aware that the former Southern states have been dissolved and the South is now under military jurisdiction? The South is unregenerate. They will not ratify the Fourteenth Amendment, giving former slaves citizenship."

Each word hit her like a well-aimed missile.

"The Freedman's Bureau is a bureau in the War Department," Mr. Wolford added. "You and Mr. Ritter were given very generous funds in order to carry out a specific program to benefit black children and freed slaves, just as Mr. Cates has said. Not to open a school for all the children of Fiddlers Grove, Virginia."

Mr. Cates nodded his agreement.

Verity stared at them in dawning disbelief. *No, no, please, no.* Were they listening to themselves? "White children sitting in the same building as black children costs the U.S. nothing."

Frowning, Mr. Cates said, "I don't like repeating myself, but you have overstepped your bounds, ma'am. No doubt from the best of motives. But as usual, a woman doesn't easily grasp legal distinctions."

The man's casual insult of her intelligence just because she was female left Verity openmouthed, gasping, speechless. *When someone deems thee inferior because of thy dark skin, does thee like it?* She bit her lower lip to stop herself from tossing this question into his condescending face.

Mr. Wolford moved toward the parlor door. "Mr. Cates and I will be staying in the area. We expect that you will dismiss the white children from the school. Otherwise we will have to inform the Bureau that *you* should be dismissed."

One last time, Verity tried to catch Matthew's eye, but he wouldn't meet her gaze. Her face burned from their scorn.

"Mr. Ritter, we'd like to meet the men you mentioned earlier, the ones you think will carry on the Union League after you leave Fiddlers Grove." Mr. Cates's rich voice boomed in the strained silence in the room.

Matthew was leaving Fiddlers Grove? Verity felt as if she'd been hit with a second hammer.

"Good evening, ma'am." Mr. Cates gave a perfunctory bow and left, followed by Mr. Wolford who gave her only a parting glare. Matthew departed without even a backward glance.

When Joseph returned from seeing the men to the door, he and Verity just looked at one another.

"Does that mean they are going to put Alec and Annie and the other white students out of our school?" Beth stood in the doorway into the parlor, Barney whining at her feet.

Seeing Beth's troubled expression made Verity feel nauseated. She sat back down. "I can't believe... I just can't believe it."

Beth hurried to her, her dark braids bouncing. "You're not going to let them do that to Alec, are you, Mama?"

Verity rested her head on her hand. She tried to understand why Matthew had remained silent while these two bureaucrats had scolded her for doing what God had sent her here to do. Surely there was something she and Matthew could do to avert this. Sending Alec and Annie and the other white children away was too awful to imagine. There must be a way to stop these men from ruining everything.

Then an awful realization trickled through her like icy water. Why did she think Matthew would help her?

Matthew had sat here in the same room and had said nothing to defend her. He'd remained as remote as a disapproving stranger. But then, Matthew didn't support what she'd done here. He'd only tolerated it. At this thought, she pressed a hand to her pained heart. How did that mesh with the promise she thought he'd made to her in this very room on Christmas Eve?

Matthew stepped inside the back door and hung up his jacket and muffler. In the warm, shadowy kitchen, he turned and saw Verity, obviously upset. He'd almost gone to his cabin for the night—he hadn't wanted to face this. But he wasn't a coward. He'd seen the light in the kitchen window and knew that she was up and worried.

I can't do anything about Wolford and Cates. I can't change anything here for her. He felt like a failure. Was this how his father had felt all those years ago when he'd done right but was helpless to change Virginia or to protect his family from injustice?

Verity stared up at him, hurt visible in her warm brown

eyes. He folded his arms across his chest to keep from reaching for her.

He searched for something to say, something to keep from discussing what she would want to discuss. What he could do nothing about. What he was helpless to alter. "Hannah's gone home for the night?"

Verity looked confused. "Of course. Did thee eat?"

Food? Had he eaten? "No." His stomach growled as if upon command. He looked past Verity, not wanting to meet her gaze. Facing enemy fire had been less taxing than remaining silent while Cates and Wolford had berated her. But how could he disagree with them? Everything they'd said was absolutely, point-by-point true.

"Hannah left thee a plate in the warming oven." Verity went to the stove and with the quilted potholders drew out a plate covered with a pie tin. "Will thee sit, please?"

He moved to the dry sink first and washed his hands, wiped them over his face, washing away the dust of the day. He felt as if he'd lived a hundred years since morning. *First Dace and then Wolford and Cates—what a great day.*

When Matt turned, Verity was pouring him a steaming cup of coffee. He sat down at the table and stared at the plate of ham, turnips, biscuits and gravy. Why was she still doing this for him? Didn't she hate him for his unavoidable silence?

She sat across from him and clasped her hands in her lap, leaning forward. "I have some good news."

Watching her try to smile for him sliced him to the quick. "Oh?"

"Yes. Annie's grandmother heard from the family of the first of the lost soldiers. That's good news, isn't it?"

Even this didn't lift his mood. He picked up his fork and began trying to eat, though he had no appetite. He stared at her, mute. *I have no good news for you, Verity.*

"Where has thee been, Matthew?" She betrayed her nervousness by starting to pleat the red-and-white-checked tablecloth.

He closed his eyes. The weight of powerlessness was nearly crushing the breath from him. After four years of blood and horror, the active war had ended, replaced by a guerrilla war of hard-eyed resistance. That's what Cates and Wolford were fighting.

He'd tried to hold back the sadness that had begun earlier when he'd spoken with Dace. Despair from their brief, harsh exchange had washed over him in wave after relentless wave. They were set on opposite sides just as they had been since the day the good people of Fiddlers Grove had thrown rocks through the windows of his parents' house. In his mind, he heard again the shattering glass, flying, crashing.

"Matthew," Verity said, touching his sleeve, "those two men said I must not let the white children come to school. But I don't know how to do that. If I send the white children away, it will be a betrayal of everything I believe to be right and just."

Her words didn't surprise him. He chewed mechanically. She wasn't the kind of woman to give up, even if peace were something she could never achieve in Virginia. He looked past her, out the dark window.

She tilted her head so she could keep eye contact with him. "In the letter of the law, Mr. Wolford and Mr. Cates are probably right. I was sent here to educate freed slaves and their children. But what happened here was different and special. All over the South, there are lynchings, riots, terrible things happening." Her voice became impassioned. "Here in Fiddlers Grove, we have relative calm. And black children and white children are attending the same school, the school thy cousin told me would be burned down. What we have done here is what should be done all over the South. And they want me to end it. I can't do that. I won't."

He swallowed and looked her in the eye. "If you refuse to do what they say, they will fire you. And then they'll dismiss the white children themselves." He heard his words, stark and harsh. *But it's the truth. We can't avoid the truth, Verity.*

She twisted his sleeve. "Can't thee think of anything I can do to stop those two men from doing this?"

His fork stopped in midair. "No. There is nothing you can do. Sometimes problems are too big to do anything about." *You're a grown woman. Didn't you see this coming?*

"How can you say such a thing, Matthew?" she pleaded.

And then the words that he'd held back for years came pouring out. "When I was twelve, the issue of slave states versus free states spilled over into local politics. A free black man had been captured by roaming slave-catchers. And even though there were witnesses who knew he was free, he'd been forced back into slavery in this county. My father was a lawyer and he gathered the evidence, took the local planter who held this free man as a slave to court and the man was set free.

"Two days later, a mob came at night. They were wearing cloth bags with eyeholes over their heads. They broke all the windows in my parents' house, set the barn on fire and shouted death threats." He looked into Verity's eyes, now shining with tears.

"We packed and left the next day." He put down his fork. The old outrage pushed him up out of the chair. He snatched up his things and walked out into the cold night. *Some things just can't be fixed, and this place will never be home again.*

Chapter Thirteen

The next day, Verity answered a polite knock at her back door. There she greeted Elijah and asked him inside. Before she closed the door, she glanced outside toward Matthew's cabin, wondering if he was coming back to the house today. The only sign of life around the cabin was the white trail of smoke from the chimney. Her longing to see Matthew added to the dull ache within her, an emptiness.

With a knowing eye, Hannah had informed Verity when she'd come down that Matt had come in for an early breakfast and gone directly back to his cabin. Verity smarted over the way they'd parted last night. He'd been so closed off to her. *What can I do about this?* The answer came swiftly. *Nothing.*

Elijah hung his hat on the peg by the door. "Hannah told me about the Yankees telling you to send the white children away. I feel very bad about Alec and the others. Those poor children are only pawns."

"And don't Miss Verity look frazzled?" Hannah went to the stove, warmed Verity's cup and poured Elijah and herself coffee. Then the three sat down at the table together and Verity felt the comfort of their friendship. No longer did Hannah feel unnatural sitting down with her. How much longer would she be here with these dear friends?

"I met Mr. Cates and Mr. Wolford last night. Matthew brought them to my cabin," Elijah said, gazing at her with obvious concern. "They want me to take a leadership role in the new Union League here. But I might not be around much longer."

Hannah halted and stared at her husband. Verity lifted both eyebrows in silent question and looked from Elijah to Hannah and back.

"I received a letter this morning after you left, Hannah. Mr. Dacian read it for me. Our Samuel is on his way here with his intended wife, Abby, and her two children," Elijah announced with evident pride, a sudden rise in his voice, a smile lighting up his whole face.

Hannah threw both hands high. "Thank you, Jesus!"

"Samuel found her, then?" Verity asked. Finally, some good news. She smiled, though the persistent hurt dug its claws into her. "I'm so glad."

Hannah rose and the two embraced.

Choking back tears, Elijah continued, "Samuel tracked down the slaver who bought her. And for a price, he told Samuel the name and town of each of the planters who had bought slaves from him that year. Luckily, the man had kept very precise records."

"So that means I'm already a grandma," Hannah exclaimed, beaming as she wiped away tears with her full white apron. "I can't wait to see them. Oh, praise the Lord. He hath done great things!"

Verity pressed her lips together. Seeing such joy made her burden weigh more heavily upon her. *I am happy for Samuel's family. I am, Lord.*

Elijah's smile was broad and full. "We will make plans for a wedding when they get here." He paused. "I'm so sorry you're having difficulties with those two Yankees."

Like a harsh broom, the mention of Cates and Wolford

whisked away Verity's gladness for Samuel and his family. She looked down at the tablecloth.

"I know the men are against what you've done here," Elijah said, "but I think that the League will do a lot of good here." He paused and looked troubled. "We've heard rumors that Orrin Dyke is back in town."

Orrin Dyke. Better and better.

"Well, I sometimes had a hard time believin' that you had white children and black children *together* in a school in Fiddlers Grove," Hannah said matter-of-factly, letting herself down on the chair and making it creak.

"It was a miracle." Suddenly sober, Elijah sipped his coffee.

Verity thought of all God had done here in Fiddlers Grove. It should be happening all over the South, instead of the race riots and lynchings. Every awful and cruel thing that Mr. Cates and Mr. Wolford had said was taking place all over the South. They were only reacting to what, in their opinion, had to be stamped out and stopped, not what should be started. She couldn't blame them. Race hate and resentment and murder were devouring the South. Just as the war had. Hate begot violence and violence begot hate and on and on. Verity's neck hurt and she rested her head on her hand.

Hannah spoke up, "You were doing just fine, Miss Verity. You had the school going and the children were learning and things were looking good here. Elijah and I even thought we might stay."

"I hated to leave my little flock, you see," Elijah added.

"But now when Samuel come, we'll leave with him and Abby and the children to go to New York, where he owns a house and land. It seems what's best." Hannah patted Verity's hand.

"I don't blame you," Verity said. And she didn't. How soon would she be asked to leave?

"What are you going to do about the school?" Elijah asked cautiously.

She pressed a hand to her throbbing temple, trying to overcome the helpless worry that not even prayer had shaken. "I don't see my way clear yet. I keep hoping way will open." How many times had she heard her mother say this phrase—*Way will open.* It meant God would open a way for them to accomplish what He wanted.

God could show Verity a way to keep Alec in school—if that was His will. But how could that not be His will? Verity whispered, "Everything was going so well." But God's Spirit didn't stir within her. She looked around at the kitchen she'd used for less than a year and felt just how hard it would be to leave this place. Leave Matthew.

The very next school day what Verity dreaded happened. Mr. Wolford and Mr. Cates entered her school and walked up to her. "It is plain to see that you are not complying with the dictates of the Freedman's Bureau." Mr. Wolford turned and faced the children. "This school is not for you white children. Leave the books and everything on the desks and go home."

The children had fallen silent and were looking at the two men in utter shock. Alec stood up. "Miss Verity, ma'am, what do you want us to do?"

Before Verity could reply, Mr. Wolford spoke up again, "Mrs. Hardy is no longer the teacher here. This is a school for black children only. You white children must leave right now. Put on your wraps and go home."

Alec looked stubborn. "We don't know who you are. And you're not telling us what to do. This is our school."

Mr. Cates started up the aisle toward Alec.

"Alec!" Verity called out in fear. "Please do as these men say."

Mr. Cates stopped and turned back to Verity. "It's too

bad that you did not cooperate with us earlier. Your allowing these white children to attend school just let a few Rebs here get the U.S. government to pay for educating their children and they took advantage of it. But they don't want black children to read or write, or black men to have the vote. You may have thought you were doing right, but you weren't."

She clasped her hands together, holding on for the children's sake.

As if not quite believing this was happening, the white children silently rose from their desks, went to the pegs at the rear of the classroom and put on their coats. Alec looked flushed and angry.

Beth rose and stood in the aisle. "Do I have to go too, Mama?"

Verity didn't know what to tell her own child.

Wolford glared at Beth. "Is this child yours, young woman?"

"Yes."

The two men exchanged glances and Wolford began, "The rules are quite—"

"Beth," Verity interrupted him, "go home to Hannah."

"Miss Verity, ma'am," Annie whimpered at the door, "I don't want to leave school. I like school." Beth stood beside Annie, tears trickling down their cheeks.

Verity blinked her eyes, suppressing her own tears. "I'm sorry, children. I'll think of something."

The white children walked out the door and closed it behind them as the black children sat at their desks, stunned. The two men left without another word. Verity stared down at her desk. *I must not upset the children more than they are already.*

"Ma'am," Sassy said, waving her hand, "I didn't want Annie and Beth to go. They nice white girls. I like them."

Verity looked up. "Yes, they are nice girls. And I know

they like you, too, Sassy." Verity's voice trembled. "I hope that I'll be able to find a way to make sure that Annie and the other white children can continue learning." Verity rose and took a deep breath.

"This is what happens after a war, children. I hope thee will remember that. The war will never be over until the hearts of men change. And only God can do that."

She recalled how Matthew had looked last night. Something inside him had shut down. She could see the same look now on the faces of the children. She tried to summon up as much strength as she could, smiling at her students. *I couldn't reach him, Lord. What do I do for Matthew, for the children?* "Now let's get back to our lessons. But I hope thee will never forget what war and hatred can do."

Matt jerked awake. He opened his eyes, feeling groggy. Then he heard gunshots in the distance and shouting—jubilant hooting. *The house! The school!* Heart pounding, he scrambled into his trousers and boots. He grabbed his rifle and charged outside into the cold night.

No light shone in the house, but he saw flickering near the school. He ran over the frozen grass. His breath puffed white in the cool night air. Ahead he saw something burning in front of the school at the far side of the property.

He halted behind the windbreak of poplars and tried to make sense of the scene. A crowd of men yelling the Rebel battle cry with glee and shooting their rifles in the air surrounded the school while a cross burned in front of it. Then it all clicked in place. He'd read about the new Ku Klux Klan, Southerners wearing sheets and masks and burning crosses in front of the houses of anyone who opposed them.

And then the significance of the symbol of their hatred hit him. They were perverting the symbol of Christ, mocking His selfless sacrifice. It didn't matter that Matt had felt far from God through the awful bloody war. No one—no one—had the right to show such scorn to Christ.

Flames of outrage roared inside Matt. He champed at the bit to charge forward and extinguish this insult to all that was holy. But he was outnumbered. He stood still, his rifle ready. If anyone moved to torch the school, he'd shoot them where they stood. Minutes passed. He gripped his rifle. Ready to aim. Ready to fire.

Then in the darkness, a horse with two riders galloped close to Matt, heading toward his cabin. Matt was torn, but he recognized one of the riders—Dace. Matt raced after them. *Why would Dace be coming for me?*

As Matt ran after them, the second rider—Samuel— looked back. And then Dace pulled up on his reins. Samuel sat behind him. Matt bounded up to him. "What is it?" Matt asked, breathless.

"The cross burning's just a diversion!" Dace shouted over the gunshots and yelling. "Dyke's attacking your Quaker!" Samuel slid from the saddle and motioned toward Matt. He leaped up behind Dace. He threw his free arm around his cousin, holding his rifle high.

The two of them galloped on toward the house. The commotion around the schoolhouse filled the air with noise. As they approached the house, Matt could see, by the scant moonlight, Orrin on the front porch, striking Verity.

The big man was backhanding and forehanding her. Matt jumped from the saddle. As he ran forward, he caught a flicker of motion to his left. With instincts forged in battle, he turned and squeezed off a shot. An unseen man yelled. And then Matt was charging up the steps.

Matt raised his rifle to aim at Orrin, the sound of Verity's screams sending rage coursing through him. Before he could shout for Orrin to stop, someone collided with him, knocking the rifle from his hand. In the darkness, hands grabbed Matt by the throat, strangling him. "Hey! Orrin! It's the Yankee Ritter! Can I kill him?"

Matt struggled to break the man's grip around his throat.

"No! That Yankee is mine!" Orrin rammed Matt. His meaty fists once again pounded Matt's face, rattling his head. Matt fought back, but Orrin was a bigger man. Matt drew up every bit of his stamina and strength. *Where's Verity? I have to get to my rifle.* Suddenly another gunshot sounded. Orrin jerked and flew backward. Matt staggered. Gasping, he lunged for his rifle. He fell to his knees feeling for his gun.

Another shot. Matt lifted his rifle and rolled to shoot Orrin, but the brute was down.

"Matt!" Dace called from the shadows below the porch. "Are you all right?"

Matt tried to catch his breath, but couldn't.

Then Dace was there helping him to his feet. "Are you shot?"

Matt shook his head. Then he rushed the few steps to Verity. Sweeping her up, he carried her inside the parlor and laid her on the love seat. "Verity? Verity?" He ran his hands lightly over her, feeling for blood soaking her clothing and for limbs twisted in awkward angles. No blood. No broken bones. He gasped with relief.

But she'd fainted. Or had Orrin knocked her unconscious—or worse? He pressed his head against her chest, listening for her heartbeat. It was rapid but strong. He looked around for the rest. "Joseph? Beth?"

"Here. I'm here." Joseph staggered into the room, supported by Dace. "When they broke down the door, they knocked me out." Dace helped Joseph onto the rocker by the fireplace. "Beth's sleeping."

Then Samuel came in, his rifle in hand. "Why don't you build up the fire, Matt? So we can see what needs tending here." Samuel walked over and lit the oil lamp on the mantel. Though he didn't want to leave Verity's side, Matt started a fire in the hearth.

Then Dace and Samuel stood around the love seat where Matt again knelt, all of them gazing down at Verity, unconscious. Her lip had been split and her eye was swollen. Matt wanted to kill Orrin Dyke with his bare hands. Dace handed him a handkerchief and Matt dabbed her lip with it. Rage still tore through him.

He looked up at Dace. "Is Dyke dead?"

"Yes, I shot him," Samuel answered.

Dace glanced at Samuel, shocked.

Matt could feel only satisfaction. The bully would never strike a woman or child again. "Dyke must have set up the cross-burning to cover attacking Verity."

"Probably." Samuel still looked angry and ready to shoot more Klansmen.

"I shot one of his lowlife cousins," Dace said. "Matt, you must have winged another one, who hightailed it away. I'm sorry we didn't get here sooner, but Alec had to run the whole way from his place to mine. He'd overheard what his dad was going to do and he came for me to stop it."

Matt heard the bitterness, anger and irony in his cousin's voice. "You didn't know, then, that the Klan has popped up here?" Matt asked his cousin.

Dace gave him a dark look. "I thought it was just a matter of time. But burning a cross is one thing. Attacking this good lady is quite another. I wouldn't permit *any* woman to be attacked, even if she hadn't saved my life."

Dace's words ignited the flash and flame of Matt's old anger. "Well, at least you did more for this lady and her family than your father did for my family all those years ago. When they broke out all the windows and rode around our house shooting guns, my mother was terrified. She trembled and wept for days."

"At least she survived," Dace snapped. "If my father

hadn't stepped in, all three of you would have been lynched that night."

Matt gawked at his cousin.

"I'm not saying it was right. But your father knew the temper of the county at that time—"

"He did what he knew was right," Matt declared, rising. "That man was a free black and he didn't deserve what had been done to him. The judge would have been happy to rule against the man, but the facts and documents were crystal clear." He glanced down at Verity, still lying silent and motionless.

Dace frowned. "I didn't know that. All I know is my father let it be known that if any harm came to your family, he would make the ones involved pay for it with their lives. He was prepared to call out anyone who harmed them."

"Dace." Samuel spoke up in his steady, cool voice. "From your way of thinking that was what your father should have done in the situation. But to my way of thinking, Matt's father shouldn't have been in danger for seeking justice for a black man. Just for doing what was right. If you'd been that free black, how would you have felt being pressed back into slavery?"

The three friends stared at each other.

Samuel continued in that calm, clear voice, "I know what it felt like to be a slave. And the fact that I ran away should have told you what I thought of it."

"Why did you run away?" Dace sounded as if he'd long wondered about this.

A brand-new thought pierced Matt. Had Dace missed him and Samuel? *I never thought of that.*

Samuel sucked in breath. "I fell in love with Abby— you all knew that. But by the time I was fifteen, I realized that I could never protect her. I could marry her but still not keep her safe from any white man who would want her." Samuel's voice was tinged with anger. "Falling in love made me feel powerless in a way I had not before. And I realized that no matter how long I stayed here or how hard I worked, I would never be more than a *boy*. I would never be a man. I couldn't stand that, so I made my plans and my connections and I got on the Underground Railroad, headed north."

"No one would have harmed Abby on our plantation," Dace said, sounding defensive.

"Are you sure about that?" Samuel challenged with keen sarcasm.

"My father and I—"

"What about your overseer, Dace?" Samuel asked. "What about the fact that though Abby's family had been slaves on the Ransford plantation for over a hundred years, your wife sold Abby South—away from her people—just so she could buy a new dress?"

Silence. Matt watched Dace chew the inside of his cheek, an old childhood sign of stress. Dace clearly didn't like what he was hearing, but it was the truth.

"Samuel, your leaving didn't help Abby any." Joseph spoke up, reminding Matt he was in the room.

Samuel looked stung. He gave a dry, mirthless chuckle. "I was only fifteen. I wasn't very wise at that age." He paused. "Dace, slavery is still tearing you all apart. How many people have to die before the South admits it was wrong? Before you admit that my dark skin doesn't make me less of a man?"

Matthew waited for Dace to reply to Samuel's question. But Dace gave no answer. Evidently Dace would not willingly accept a future that included free black men voting. Dace sat down on the love seat and put his head in his hands. "Lirit ran off today. She left me a note and took off with some stranger."

Matt looked at Samuel. This news shocked neither of

them. Matt leaned over to listen to Verity's heartbeat again. Her soft hair tickled his face. *Please wake up. Soon.*

"You're well rid of that woman." Joseph spoke up. "Find yourself a sweet woman this time. Pretty lasts only so long. True beauty that shines from a woman's heart lasts for eternity. And it helps if she's a good cook." Joseph smiled and then rose from the rocker. "Will one of you help me up to my bed? I'm an old man and I'm feeling it tonight. Thank God little Beth slept through all this. The sleep of the innocent."

Samuel went to help Joseph. Dace said, "I'll go get help to remove Orrin and his cousin's bodies. And I'll put out the word that I killed them."

Matt knew why Dace was telling this lie—it was to protect Samuel and his family. Otherwise, the Klan would come after them.

Samuel paused at the door and looked back at Dace. "Thank you, Dace. And how would you like to host my wedding to Abby in a couple of days?"

"I'd like that fine," Dace said, then exhaled deeply. "I'd like to see you and Abby happy. And you, too, Matt. If you let Mrs. Hardy slip through your fingers, you're a blockhead."

Matt felt a soft hand squeeze his and looked down. "Verity." He took her hand and kissed it.

"Matthew," she whispered, her eyes worried. "Where—"

"I'm here. Don't be frightened. Orrin's gone and we're all safe." He gently stroked the hair that had come loose from her hairpins. The past now made some sort of sense.

Dace, just like his father, had been caught up in the blindness of slavery but had not abandoned Matt's parents then. Or Matt now. Now he knew why Samuel had run away. And now Samuel had found Abby and was going to marry her. Even Dace had been given a second chance. He was well rid of Lirit. Matt heard his cousin's words again: *If you let Mrs. Hardy slip through your fingers, you're a blockhead.*

Verity whispered, "I was frightened. Beth, is she—"

"Beth slept through it all somehow. Don't worry." He kissed her forehead without thinking.

"Matthew, thee is kissing me again. What does that mean?"

"It means you're going to marry me, Verity Hardy. As soon as Cates and Wolford get another teacher here, you'll quit teaching. I'm going to take good care of you and Beth. And nothing is ever going to separate us again."

Verity drew in a deep breath. "Yes. Nothing is going to separate us again. But, Matthew, the children—"

He bent down and kissed her bruised lips gently. *She will be mine and I will be hers.* Then he swept her up and carried her toward the stairs. "I'll put you to bed, but I'm sleeping here in the parlor. I'm not taking any chances with your safety tonight."

"Whatever thee thinks is best, Matthew."

Matt grinned. He wondered how often his headstrong wife would repeat those words in the years to come. The corners of his mouth tried to crinkle up. *Thank you, Father, for this woman. I probably don't deserve her, but I'll do my best for her and Beth. With Thy help.*

Three days later Matt, Verity, Joseph and Beth, with Barney jogging happily by their side, walked to the Ransford plantation. A January thaw had blown in the day before. Today was balmy, sunny with beautiful white clouds floating in a true blue sky. When they reached the manor, they saw a large crowd of former slaves gathered on the sunny south lawn, dressed festively. Many happy voices were already singing. Matt led his family to join them. His family. A feeling of joy expanded inside him as he pondered those words.

As they approached the group, Matt was somewhat surprised to see Pastor Savage there. In the past Dacian Ransford, and his father before him, had performed slave marriages. But of course Samuel and Abby were not slaves anymore. Matt easily recognized Abby, whom he had not seen since he left in 1852. She was a very handsome young woman, despite the harsh blows life had dealt her. A boy who looked a bit older than Beth stood on one side of her and a little girl on the other side. During the marriage ceremony, the boy shyly moved to stand beside Samuel, and Samuel took his hand.

Matt felt good seeing Samuel, Abby, her children, and Hannah and Elijah so happy. The outdoor wedding proceeded, with solemn ceremony. Hannah and Elijah stayed at the front of the gathering, beaming.

Matt looked at Verity, who still showed signs of Orrin's attack. She had one blackened eye and a bruised face, and she moved slowly. He thought she might have a cracked rib. Would he ever forget seeing her struggling with Orrin? *No one will ever hurt her again,* he swore to himself. *No one.*

Gritting his teeth, Matt dragged his focus back to Samuel and Abby in time to hear Pastor Savage announce, "I now pronounce you man and wife. I present to you all today Mr. and Mrs. Samuel Freeman."

The gathering shouted and clapped with approval. Beth stood up and cheered. "Samuel got married, Mama!"

Verity smiled and nodded. Then her eyes met Matt's. She blushed and he smiled, tucking her closer. They would tell Beth tonight of their intentions to wed.

Before long, the gathering was dancing and singing. Samuel drew Abby's arm through his and led her and her two children toward Matt.

"Mr. Matt," Abby greeted him. "I'm happy to see you again. And this is your lady?"

"Yes," he said, drawing Verity's hand over his arm and wrapping his other arm around Beth.

Verity smiled. "Who are these lovely children?"

"This is my son, Ezra, and my daughter, Delia. Make your bows, children," Abby said. Both children obeyed, grinning shyly.

"How soon is thee taking thy family to Albany, Samuel?" Verity asked.

"We will be leaving tomorrow," Samuel said. "My father and my mother will be traveling to New York with us by train. I own a house near Albany with six acres."

Verity squeezed Matt's hand in hers. "We will miss thee. But perhaps after Matthew finishes his work for the Freedman's Bureau, we can visit thee."

"Both Abby and I would like that." Samuel stroked Delia's tightly braided hair and put a hand on Ezra's shoulder.

Matt drew in the hint of lavender that would always mean Verity to him. He wished she wouldn't wear that bonnet. Perhaps after they were married, he would suggest she stop wearing it so he could see her lovely face. He smiled at the thought of her reaction to this suggestion.

Beth was wearing the red ribbons Matthew had given her for Christmas. She glanced up at him and smiled, her innocent affection cutting through any remnant of his hard soldier's heart.

Dace approached them with Alec. "May I wish you every joy, Samuel and Abby."

Abby curtsied and looked down.

"Thanks, Dace." Samuel held out his hand. "And thanks for allowing us to hold our wedding here."

Dace hesitated and then gripped Samuel's hand. "Don't mention it."

Alec moved to Verity's side. "I'm going to miss coming to school, ma'am," he said.

Matt was pleased to see the boy here. Orrin had been

buried and mourned by very few, least of all by his wife and son. Orrin had been given a sweet wife and a good son and he'd treated them like trash. Why?

Verity patted Alec's shoulder. "It will only be for a little while."

"What do you mean?" Alec asked, hope in his voice.

"After I'm replaced at the Freedman's school, I'm going to invite any child who wishes to learn to come to my house every morning at eight. I can hold school around the kitchen table."

Shaking his head, Matt gently pulled Verity closer. "And when, dearest, were you going to tell me about this plan?" he asked, trying to suppress a grin.

Verity chuckled. "About now."

Matt let out a joyous, boisterous laugh. Life would be good with Verity and his new family by his side. He was finally home.

Epilogue

Verity sat in the kitchen in Fiddlers Grove, holding a letter. She'd written her family about her coming marriage to Matthew, and her sister Felicity had written right back.

Dearest Verity,

I'm so happy to hear about thy finding someone to love again. Matthew must be a very special man. Mercy and I still plan to remain spinsters. But we will take the train to Richmond and then hire a wagon to drive to Fiddlers Grove. We wouldn't miss thy wedding.

I have news, too. Does thee remember my friend Mildred? She passed away a month ago in Illinois. And I never expected it, but she has left me a bequest—her house! I had been praying for a way to help all the orphans left by the terrible war. Now I will be able to start a home for them! And the location couldn't be better, since her town is right on the Illinois side of the Mississippi River just north

of St. Louis. It will make it so much easier for or-
phans to reach us. I am so excited.
We will see thee soon.
Love,
Felicity

* * * * *

SPECIAL EXCERPT FROM

Love Inspired **HISTORICAL**

*When Bethany Zook's childhood friend returns to Amish
country a widower, with an adorable little girl in tow,
she'll help him any way she can. But there's just one
thing Andrew Yoder needs—a mother for little Mari.
And he's convinced a marriage of convenience to
Bethany is the perfect solution.*

Read on for a sneak preview of
Convenient Amish Proposal *by Jan Drexler
available February 2019 from Love Inspired Historical!*

Andrew shifted Mari in his arms. She had laid her head on his
shoulder and her eyes were nearly closed. "I hope you weren't
embarrassed by the man thinking that the three of us are a
family."

Bethany felt her face heat, but with her bonnet on it was
easy to avoid Andrew's gaze. *Ja*, the man's comment had been
embarrassing, but only because she felt like they had misled
him. Being mistaken for Andrew's wife and Mari's mother
made her feel like she was finally where she belonged.

"Not embarrassed as much as ashamed that he thought
something that was untrue."

Andrew stepped closer to her. "It doesn't have to be untrue.
Have you thought about what I asked you?"

Bethany nodded. She had thought of nothing else since
yesterday afternoon. "Do you think we could have a good
marriage, even in these circumstances?" She looked into
Andrew's eyes. They were open and frank, with no shadows
in the depths.

"You and I have always made a good team." Andrew
glanced at the people walking past them, but no one was paying

attention to their conversation. "I'm asking you to give up a lot, though. If there's someone you've been wanting to marry, you'll lose your chance if you marry me."

"What makes you say that?"

"Dave Zimmer said that he had proposed to you, and so had a couple other fellows, but you turned them down. He thought you were waiting for someone else."

Bethany tilted her head down so that Andrew couldn't see her face. She couldn't explain what kept her from accepting Dave's proposal a few years ago, other than it just hadn't felt right. Being with any man other than Andrew hadn't felt right. No one else offered the easy camaraderie he did, and she had never felt any love for any other man.

She shook her head. "There is no one else."

"Then you'll do it?"

Bethany pressed her lips together to keep back the retort she wanted to make. He made their marriage sound like a business arrangement. She couldn't tie herself to a man who would never love her, could she?

Just then, Mari lifted her head, roused by her uncomfortable position and the noise around them. She turned in Andrew's arms and reached for Bethany. When Bethany took her, the little girl settled in her arms with a sigh and went back to sleep.

If Bethany didn't accept Andrew's proposal, Mari's grandmother would take her back to Iowa, and she would never see her again. She swallowed, her throat tight. And if she didn't accept Andrew's proposal, she would never know the joys of being a mother. Because if she didn't marry Andrew, she would never marry anyone.

"*Ja*, Andrew. I'll do it. I'll marry you."

Don't miss
Convenient Amish Proposal *by Jan Drexler,*
available February 2019 wherever
Love Inspired® *Historical books and ebooks are sold.*

Looking for inspiration in tales
of hope, faith and heartfelt romance?

Check out **Love Inspired**® and
Love Inspired® **Suspense** books!

New books available every month!

CONNECT WITH US AT:

Facebook.com/groups/HarlequinConnection

 Facebook.com/HarlequinBooks

 Twitter.com/HarlequinBooks

 Instagram.com/HarlequinBooks

 Pinterest.com/HarlequinBooks

ReaderService.com

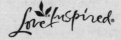

LIGENRE2018R2

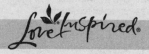
Rainbow Girl stepped into his field of vision from the kitchen area. *"Hallo."*

Eli's insides did funny things at the sight of her.

"Did you need something?"

He cleared his throat. "I came for a drink of water."

"Come on in." She pulled a glass out of the cupboard, filled it at the sink and handed it to him.

"Danki."

She gifted him with a smile. *"Bitte.* How's it going out there?"

He smiled back. "Fine." He gulped half the glass, then slowed down to sips. No sense rushing.

After a minute, she folded her arms. "Go ahead. Ask your question."

"What?"

"You obviously want to ask me something. What is it? Why do I color my hair all different colors? Why do I dress like this? Why did I leave? What is it?"

She posed all *gut* questions, but not the one he needed an answer to. A question that was no business of his to ask.

"Go ahead. Ask. I don't mind." Very un-Amish, but she'd offered. *Ne,* insisted.

He cleared his throat. "Are you going to stay?"

She stared for a moment, then looked away. Obviously not the question she'd expected, nor one she wanted to answer.

LIEXP1218

He'd made her uncomfortable. He never should have asked. What if she said *ne*? Did he want her to say *ja*? "You don't have to tell me." He didn't want to know anymore.

She pinned him with her steady brown gaze. "I don't know. I don't want to, but I'm sort of in a bind at the moment."

Maybe for the reason she'd been so sad the other day, which had made him feel sympathy for her.

He appreciated her honesty. "Then why does our bishop think you are?"

"He's hoping I do."

His heart tightened. "Why are you giving him false hope?" Why was she giving Eli false hope?

"I'm not. I've told him this is temporary. He won't listen. Maybe you could convince him to stop this foolishness—" she waved her hand toward where the building activity was going on "—before it's too late."

He chuckled. "You don't tell the bishop what to do. *He* tells you."

He really should head back outside to help the others. Instead, he filled his glass again and leaned against the counter. He studied her over the rim of his glass. Did he want Rainbow Girl to stay? She'd certainly turned things upside down around here. Turned him upside down. Instead of working in his forge—where he most enjoyed spending time—he was here, and gladly so. He preferred working with iron rather than wood, but today, carpentry strangely held more appeal.

Time to get back to work. He guzzled the rest of his water and set the glass in the sink. *"Danki."* As he turned to leave, something on the table caught his attention. The door knocker he'd made years ago for Dorcas—Rainbow Girl—ne, Dorcas, but now Rainbow Girl had it. They were the same person, but not the same. He crossed to the table and picked up his handiwork. "You kept this?"

She came up next to him. *"Ja.* I liked having a reminder of…"

"Of what?" Dare he hope him?

She stared at him. "Of…my life growing up here."

That was probably a better answer. He didn't need to be thinking of her as anything more than a lost *Englisher*.

Don't miss Courting Her Prodigal Heart *by Mary Davis, available January 2019 wherever Love Inspired® books and ebooks are sold.*

www.LoveInspired.com

Love Inspired®

Inspirational Romance to Warm Your Heart and Soul

Join our social communities to connect with other readers who share your love!

Sign up for the Love Inspired newsletter at **www.LoveInspired.com** to be the first to find out about upcoming titles, special promotions and exclusive content.

CONNECT WITH US AT:

Facebook.com/groups/HarlequinConnection

 Facebook.com/LoveInspiredBooks

 Twitter.com/LoveInspiredBks

LISOCIAL2018

Earn points on your purchase of new Harlequin
books from participating retailers.

Turn your points into **FREE BOOKS**
of your choice!

Join for FREE today at
www.HarlequinMyRewards.com.

Harlequin My Rewards is a free program (no fees)
without any commitments or obligations.